Ad Infinitus Creations

Sapling

The Blade of Ahtol

I0674150

Dan
Gillis

ISBN **978-0994842817 (First Edition)**

This is a work of fiction. Names, characters, places, events and
incidents are either the products of the author's imagination or
used in a fictitious manner.

All graphics and layout by Dan Gillis
Editing by Shawn Urban

Special commendation to Tammy Khoong:
Writing cohort and digital media genius

*To my dearest Trinell
for bringing the sunshine
needed for this first seed*

BLADE OF AHTOL MAP

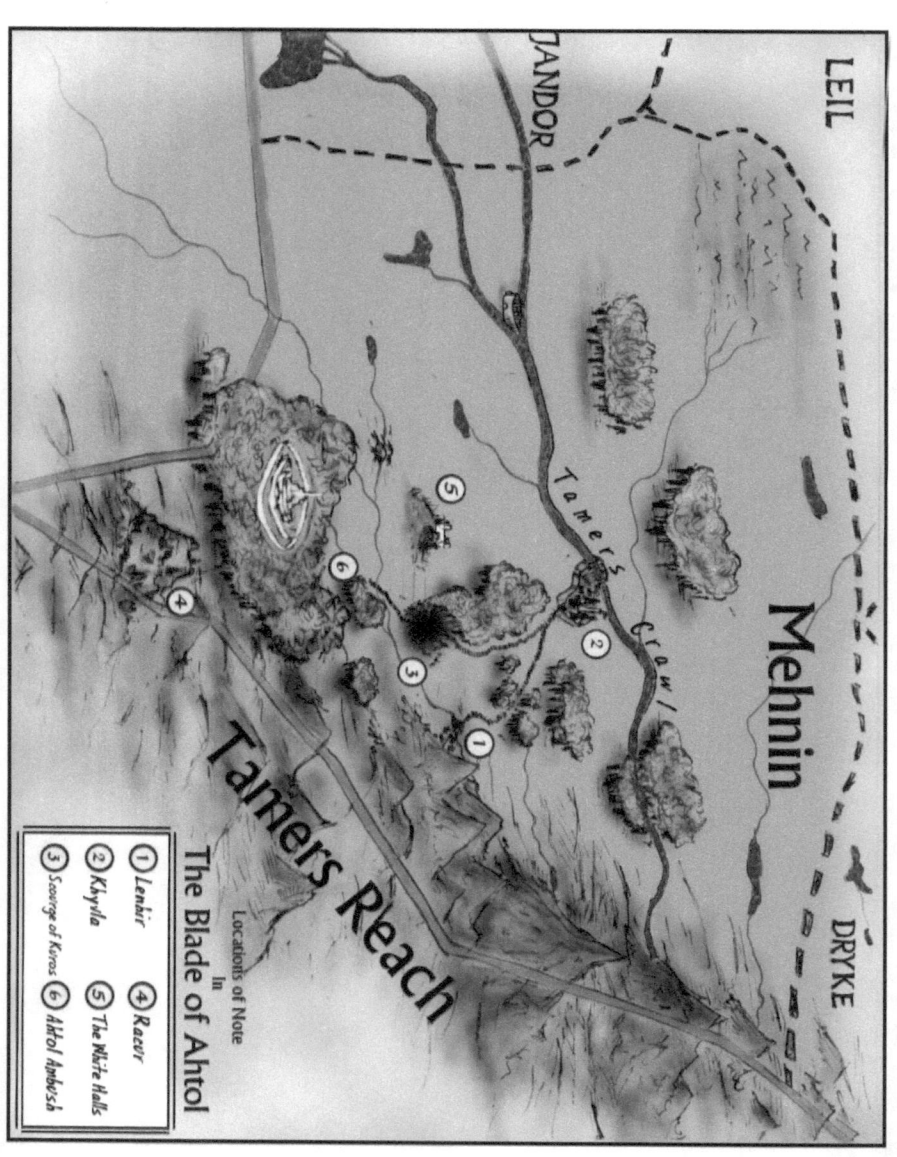

LEIL

JANDOR

DRYKE

Mehnin

Tamers Crawl

Tamers Reach

Locations of Note
in
The Blade of Ahtol

① Lenhir   ④ Raevir
② Khyila   ⑤ The White Halls
③ Scourge of Kyros   ⑥ Ahtol Ambush

Table of Contents

Supplements

Glossary

Aeredian Calendar

Map of Kenhar

PROLOGUE

THE AERLUIN WEAVE

THE YOUNG GIRL'S HAND stretched gingerly toward the worn door handle. Clicking and whirring sounds escaped through the cracks around the door frame. Mixed with the voice of industry was a warm and welcoming melody. The girl's young heart swelled as the music struck a familial bond. As her fingers touched upon the cool wood handle, the singing stopped.

"Come in, young one. I have waited for you."

The young girl smiled brightly at the sound of the voice and twisted the knob. The door creaked in resistance to her gentle push. As it opened, a vast array of colour and light greeted the girl's eyes. Flecks of dust waltzed and mingled in a dance of colour through the warm rays cast about the room, giving the room a musical quality. The ornate glass above was decorative and styled in patterns which depicted scenes and characters of stories unknown to the young girl, for she had not obtained the years of knowledge. All the shapes and colours were bound into a large circle which was the frame for the window. Strange motions suddenly caught her eye and caused her to bend down to inspect the source. She stared in awe as the refracted images shimmered upon the worn wooden floor.

She followed the vibrant shapes from one gem to the next. Soon her focus was drawn to another treasure. Rolls and rolls of bundled thread of every imaginable colour, gathered here and there, were stored upon numerous shelves and bound for use when needed. The shelves were built quite high as the ceiling of the room was vaulted far above.

As the girl took her few first tentative steps into the room, the greatest spectacle revealed itself. A massive loom stood majestically in the centre of the room. The girl marveled as the loom dwarfed any other that she had seen in the village.

Seated at the head of the loom was her grandmother. The old woman, bent with age, remained fixed upon the weave before her. The girl stared in wonder at the pattern forming upon the loom as she drew near. The warp lines stretching into the loom revealed harmonies of colours and yet within the centre of the pattern was a myriad of green shades.

The girl spoke after a few quiet moments of awe, "What is it grandmother ... this pattern in the cloth you are

2

making?" The aged woman slipped the shuttle through the shed with a simple flick and, with a firm press upon a loom pedal, the beater joined the thread with the pattern.

She spoke as she moved her hands lithely and quickly - the hands of a master artisan. "This weaving is to honour one of our most cherished beliefs and traditions. That of the Sapling."

The young girl reached up and pressed her finger to the formed fabric and ran it across a part of the pattern which depicted the Sapling tree.

"As you can see, this material is much like Aerluin's weave. Individually, each thread is vulnerable and limited in its use. When the threads mingle together they are strong, vibrant and lovely. This pattern can only be made by all these threads working as one. And so it shall be with the Sapling."

The girl looked up to her grandmother with wonder and curiosity. The weaver set the shuttle down and moved her foot slowly to the floor. The loom's voice was quieted without the master to guide its song. The old woman turned herself upon her seat to face the girl. Young hands and chin rested lightly upon the artisan's knee and silent eyes were cast upward. Kind eyes looked down in turn upon the child and the woman changed her craft from weaving thread upon the loom to words of song.

"To understand the advent of the Sapling, you must first know the Song of Sorrow. For this song is truly how Aerluin came to be with us and how the legend begins." The old

woman's voice grew solemn in deep melodic tones as she
began the Song. The images upon the stained glass
glimmered and seemed to move in harmony with the music
as it filled the whole room.

Countless harmonies were bound as one
From the endless skies to the resting stone.
The Song carried low as it had once begun
Then It lifted high; a sweet harmony intoned.

The alluring music did yet own a task:
It encircled the dark chaotic barrier between
the heavens and earth; Chaos, a palling mask
Struggled vainly against the song serene.

Amid the harmonious chords that spun
Two voices rang clear and bright.
Ever they had been since the music begun
Lithe-shadowed Aerluin and pure Llian of light.

In the course of their enchanted flight,
Aerluin pondered upon the world beneath
Whilst Llian - eyes cast toward heaven light -
Tired of her watch and sought relief.

Llian strayed from the bounds of the song,
And parted from Aerluin of enchanting night
Who failing not to chant sweet music along.
It was longing Llian who drifted from sight.

Llian ascended upward, till she was afar.
Aerluin called out from the barrier below.
And as Llian's light became as a star,
All Chaos was set out to overthrow.

After long imprisonment, in all were contained
All the horrors, agony, sorrow and fear.
Formless creatures, wrath barely restrained,
Drew to the barrier, opportunity near.

The marvelous song which Aerluin formed
Grew strained and pained in great dismay.
So with the weakened song, Chaos stormed;
A dark and bitter cage to repay.

Late did Llian fly to her sister's aid.
Alas, Aerluin sang out in awful despair,
As all Chaos swarmed her in a vicious raid -
Falling deep into the land Aerluin fair.

Weeping her tears, the luminous kin did cast
A sorrowful rage upon the Chaos wave.
The savage horde was consumed to the last
Swept violently into a restless grave.

Thus deep and wide the distance spans
Between Llian and her silent kin.
Neither can breach the great expanse,

An emptiness where unity had been.

Between the stars and skies Llian cries
A lament for her kin and the song they lost.
For Aerluin is silent. Within the earth she lies.
Their melody broken at a terrible cost.

Now ever so often, from within the land
Hales a haunting whisper of a forgotten tune.
For the listening heart it is grand
Yet, never comes to Llian beyond the moon.

The echoes resounded in the large room even as the singing ceased. The old woman turned her face back toward the young girl, for as she sang she had cast her gaze heavenward. Tears traced along aged lines and coursed downward until they fell silently and were gone. The young girl looked on, rapt in amazed silence.

"Will she ever see Llian again?" she asked softly. The grandmother moved her calloused and wrinkled fingers through the golden weave of hair that cascaded along the bright face of her granddaughter.

"If the weave is strong … she may yet … if the weave is strong when the time of the Sapling comes."

Her voice became suddenly distant as she turned and gestured toward the large circular window the girl had seen earlier. "Our world, Aeredia." Suddenly the girl perceived the collection of small intricate images as one. Her grandmother discerned her discovery and continued. "With the coming and passing of countless cycles, the world has seen much of toil and suffering. Countless wars waged upon its soil, the cries of thousands as they fall under sword and fire. Yet for all the turmoil upon the world's surface, the land grows lush and vibrant in her care. The times of all the world are known to Aerluin, for her power is bound to all living things. Though seemingly silent within the land, her works of spinning soft patterns of life are like whispers throughout the world. Slowly and gently she weaves the strands of life together, entwining them to adjoined fate. While she has no governance over life or death, she guides the weave with great care. All things connect upon the mystical loom to form the wondrous patterns of life. Yet always in her mind is her long separation from her heavenly sister. She is always in search of the means to return."

"I know she will grandmother. I just know it," the young girl whispered. Her grandmother nodded politely and then continued.

"Perhaps, dear. Perhaps. Yet, after countless years a fell stain appeared, consuming portions of the weave, and Aerluin wept for the darkening of her bright patterns. Always she could see them all, each strand bright and unique, and yet many were turning grey, blackened with a dark pall. Aerluin knew that if unchecked the shadow would engulf the whole weaving. However, she did not despair long - for, while the fabric held together, there was hope. She took her brightest and sturdiest threads and wove them carefully into the pattern. Individually, they seemed insignificant against the shadows. However, whenever the chosen threads mingled there came signs of brightness and strength.

"So it was - the pattern was woven, the threads moving ever closer together ..."

THE THIEF IN THE STORM

THE HARSH RAIN beat down upon the sodden ground, and the surface of great pools of water danced to the percussion of the heavens. It was late into twilight and the streets of Lenhir were especially vacant. All the residents waited with a subdued acceptance, being holed in against the relentless storm. For many days previous the weather had supplied a welcome sun and little in the way of moisture for the folk of Lenhir. This night, the storm's wrath seemed focused upon the little town in Mehnin Province. Every layman and serving maid exclaimed that they had never witnessed such a torrential downpour. "Llian in the Heavens is trying to cleanse the land of its stains," some said. It was all penance for the misdeeds of a previous Cycle of tyrants. The scarring upon the land and people was slow to heal. Myths of the past had persisted which spoke of peculiar beings who wielded wild potent energies. The stories were as diverse as the profiles upon the peaks of Tamers Reach which shadowed the town now at the end of the day. As such, regardless of any former strange workings in their country of Kenhar, life passed in relative peace in the mountain haven.

✵   *Splish, splish, splish.*

Firah danced across mud and cobblestone deftly, skipping over particularly large puddles. She laughed gaily as she moved through the storm. The droplets were chased from her exposed skin as swiftly as the wind that rushed about her form. This kind of weather was what she enjoyed, smelling the fresh falling rain, arms outstretched and truly free. In her joy she ignored how strangely the deluge had come, where no cloud had been. The light was slowly failing and with the curtains of rain it would soon be too dark for the girl to work.

Firah had never known a proper family and she relied on her own two hands to get what she needed. Her mind slipped away to the past even as an inner voice pondered upon the memory. 'The life of a thief is not glamorous, but I'll never have to resort to begging like the others! Those waifs have no dignity, and I'll never be like them.' Firah shook her head in disgust, her mind a flood of justifications, each one bolstering her resolve. She had seen the suffering of those wretches in the winter months. I was clear in her mind, as she took from others (without their approval or notice) she would give back to the community in other ways. Did she not assist in removing part of the rat infestation only last harvest season? The thief had counted herself proud to have slaughtered a considerable portion of the rodents. Firah recalled as well the Dryke skirmishes in early spring where she actually killed one of the reptilian migrants herself. Well, barely, and she still had a scar to show where the poisoned spine missed her heart. When it all weighed out, Firah was a survivor.

Movement caught her quick eyes through the thick deluge. Careful perusal revealed a lone figure walking slouched in the torrent. With a twinge of avarice she determined anyone who was foolish enough to travel about in this weather deserved a good dose of reality. Slowly, like a sodden cat, Firah moved ever closer to the slowly moving form. She drew out her small knife from her belt and performed a quick check to cover all contingencies. To the left, she had an escape route through the alley under windows which were shut up. No one else was about in the greying dark which was setting in. Firah glanced back up the street to mark her 'patron'. The rain distorted figures so badly that Firah could not make out any distinguishing features. She concluded her check with the most critical part: raising the small blade to her eyes, she ran her finger across the cool steel. It was sharp, and it would need to be so every time. Firah knew that she needed only one swipe across the leather straps and she would be gone ... melding into the night. The young sneak-thief moved in and out of shadows and slinked ever closer to her target. The person seemed in no particular hurry, which struck Firah as odd, but she deemed such distractedness would work to her advantage. Working in the rain had its bright side. With the thunder roaring and lightning flashing most senses were disorientated. However, it also meant that her target would be wearing extra clothing.

Soon Firah was behind her prey, just to the left. She observed that the cloak was not a full piece pullover but instead it opened at the front. The belt had to be accessible for her plan to work; and were it not so she would have stopped right then. She was gambling on which side to hit from. It was possible a money purse was worn on the right, for this was most common in her experience. Occasionally, her 'patron' was armed which complicated things, but an attack from the left usually disrupted any removal of weapons from the left hip. She usually came in low and twisted around completely while making the cut through the spin. Her exit came from another complete spin which ended behind the baffled prey. Thus, if noticed, she had a head start as the patron reoriented himself and figured where to go to chase after her. She had thrown dirt into her patron's face on drier days to improve her odds and further disorient her prey; however, she always felt guilty afterward and thus only resorted to using that tactic on down-days when she felt ill. During this storm, however, none of that would be necessary; Mother was being kind with the elements and so she would remember Her in a prayer.

Firah began to breathe deeply and shut her eyes. She shivered as the water flowed slowly down her lithe form. The thief became one with the rain and felt it weave like a pulsing blanket about her body, distorting her figure to the point where she had taken the rain's appearance. She was a shimmering shadow fully enveloped in the night. All thoughts and feelings were centered on the task at hand which caused her skin to crawl. It always did this when she focused her mind to create the strange effect. She embraced the feeling and steadied herself. The girl's eyes opened slowly.

The traveler would never see her.

The moment had come. Creeping slowly, Firah moved next to the form, her body shifting with the rain. The plan was fixed firm in her mind. She waited for a moment when a great flash pulsed overhead. Like a coiled tendon, she snapped into action. In one swift motion she twisted herself around beneath the person's arms. As the thunder boomed and shook the ground, she lightly flicked the cloak open, then coming around espied and cut the threads of a leather purse, all within mere heartbeats of time. The leather straps barely twitched as the keen edge whistled through them. Continuing to spin, she returned her knife and caught the falling pouch in one motion. Without a glance she dashed catlike and unseen through the shadows, her mind completely focused. Her chameleon-like skin shimmered as her heart pulsed with adrenalin and excitement.

Finally, she paused behind a wooden midden-house, her breath coming hard after such an intense burst of effort. She glanced back and saw the form continuing along seemingly unaware of the crime committed upon its person. She laughed within herself gleefully, and let her focus go. It was so easy some days … she felt elated and completely free. It helped her forget the hard days of virtual starvation. She tossed the leather pouch lightly into the air, feeling the weight as it fell into her slender palm. About two and a half weeks of eating she estimated, possibly even some repair for her leather vest … life was good. Smiling, Firah moved down the alley towards the forest path which would lead her home.

⊥   The man did nothing as his money pouch was removed. He continued his slow methodical steps as he listened to the nearly undetectable taps upon the ground grow dimmer. His mind pondered over the girl's unwitting demonstration. She was fast, he thought, calculating and certainly showed talent in accessing the Root but she was still young and unpolished. He could feel her breathing; she was watching him now and most likely full of herself. She had no way of knowing that others would be looking for her as well. Her raw skill and connection to the Pattern was potent which made a desirable prize for the Defilers. They masked their actions skillfully and went unnoticed by common folk.

So many had been taken swiftly and unseen. Families left in awful anguish of loss. It was now clear the girl was their next target. Upon her capture, they would use her innate ability to fuel one of their foulest rituals. They had done so in the previous month with the others like her, bound within secretive holdings all throughout Kenhar. The Defilers masked their true purposes under the guise of academics and politics. On the surface they could be pleasant and genial. Many of those taken were led away carefully through guile rather than through force.

Yet none of these could escape his notice. Their foolish dabbling was dangerous and threatened life on all of Aeredia. They could not hope to control the potent forces of the Chaotic Void by attempting to bind them. He shook his head sadly; blinded by ambition, they were foolish and unwary. They could not fathom pure destructive energy of that magnitude. Nor could they see the outcome of that act. The Defilers were power hungry and blind, and would soon lose control of what they unleashed. One thing was certain, as a whole world, Aeredia would come undone with the clash of potency of both Aerluin and the Dark One within the Void.

The man pulled himself from his dark sentiments. They would make their moves just as he would now make his. He had heard the whispers upon his soul. The direction from Mother was clear: to stop the Defilers from reaching the girl at all costs. They saw her as a mere binding link for their demon, but she was much more than that. No one but Aerluin could possibly know her potential.

He would assist the girl as she walked the path of fate, though to which end he knew not. The road of corruption could be chosen as easily as that of truth and discipline. One could hardly know how such things would pass. The choice would be hers ultimately, for good or ill. Fate was like that. He continued moving slowly through the flooded streets.

ө   *The tender plant had only begun to grow - sprouting heavenward with potential despite the oppressive downpour. It was shooting forth from its native earth with determination into the waiting darkness.*

TREASURES

THE MORNING *was still as the sun prepared to peak over
the crags of Tamers Reach. From within the lands of
Jandor, a quiet evil was stirring. The slow and guttural chants of
many voices grew in cadence and intensity. The voices wound
their words together forming like a fabric of the blackest kind. As
the web grew and took shape, the crescendo seemed to penetrate all.
through the rocks and forest glens to empty city streets. It stirred*

every heart in the land, even into dreams. Finally, in one terrific shout, the black seething mass awoke. Methodically, every chanting voice was silenced one by one; a cruel and agonizing payment for service. With every death, the entity found more life. Then suddenly, it was over. The chanting ceased and all became still. Certain people woken from the strange event had wondered what it was that moved in them and then within a moment it was gone. There were some however who knelt and prayed for the mercies of the Mother to be with the people of Kenhar. It was those few who sensed the change - evil had found new form in Aeredia. The memory of the dream entrenched itself deep into their minds. It was a foreboding sense of fear and helplessness that latched itself to the shadows of the subconscious.

Firah awoke screaming, drenched in a sweat. She cursed her mind. This horrific experience had happened once before, equally potent and disturbing. She shuffled over to the wash bin, now full with last night's rain. Splashing the water across her face she tried to remove the stained memories of her sleep. They would not depart. What were they? Every time a large dripping mass of blackness, an utter abomination against nature! It frightened her to her very centre and yet it was strangely compelling at the same time. She always felt drawn towards it. In her dream, the more she tried to flee the grotesque and overpowering form, the closer it would come. It was a frightening experience. She felt that only by giving into the darkness would she find peace. There were moments when she would almost falter and consider embracing the seductive nightmare. It was at those times that she would see that same creature. It was four legged and seemed to shimmer and meld with the dream. It was an animal spirit, but it was unlike any that she knew. Always it would latch onto her with powerful jaws and pull her back from the brink.

She splashed more water on her burning face. It was like this too afterwards. She would feel ill and catch fever. Some would say that running about in the rain caused her illness but she knew better. She wandered about in storms all the time; she cherished the rain. No, this was always after those nightmares ... always.

Firah glanced at herself in the settling water. Her green eyes sparkled in the new day sun which reflected off the water's surface. Her hair was a mess of dark brown tangles, and frowning she tied it back with a leather strap. Firah was in her seventeenth year but she was often regarded as too young to be on her own. The older townswomen reminded her constantly that there were predators and evil men about who would abuse her youth and purity. 'Well, I can handle myself, thank you very much' she mused within. Turning slightly she looked upon the water's flowing surface; Firah knew she wasn't an eyesore. Many a man had cast a glance her way, and yet she had no interest in choosing someone to be with. Such things complicated life. She touched the shift she wore and admired the way it accentuated her features. Still, it was getting a little thread bare. 'It might be time to invest in some new clothes ...' she thought to herself.

She groaned and slumped down ungracefully into her makeshift chair. Cloth was very expensive in the country. Not to mention that she had little skill in sewing or patching. Those services were available in town but once again at a high price. The big cities were cheaper, but she could not abide long in those places. She needed to be outdoors and free, not caged within large city walls. It seemed to be a part of her very soul and something she could never understand nor explain. It just felt right living out here in the forest. It was about a half hour walk to the town and they generally supplied all her needs. It was in the big city that she had bought her knife and then in a flash, had quickly departed the odours and entrapping walls. She had considered stealing one but the other fact about cities was their tighter security and harsher laws. Once she had been caught pilfering in Lenhir and she spent half a day in the stocks. 'Thank goodness Tohm was there' she admitted. She knew the penalty for thievery would be much more severe in the city. Yes, country life was certainly more relaxed and appealing. Rubbing her eyes and yawning widely, Firah rose to take a moment in meditation outside. It was then she remembered last night's lift and decided to see exactly what fate had brought her.

She dumped the contents of the pouch on the wooden table. Slowly, she filed through the effects, humming to herself as she sorted. There was more gold than silver in the pouch which surprised her greatly. A purse like this would typically belong to a nobleman who was usually escorted and relatively untouchable, at least for her anyway. It seemed like a great stroke of luck to the girl as she placed the coins into her own pouch. Still, Firah found herself questioning more and more as she dressed, and later as she ate some berries and dried meat from her storage. 'Was that man a thief like me, or did I just happen upon his path' she wondered. Because of the rain and his rain cloak she could not determine whether he was a local. 'It could have been anyone.' The thief idea left her quickly. If he had been one, he would have certainly noticed her and if the coin was a measure of his skill, he could have stopped her too. Yet here she was assuming it was a man as well. 'I'll never know' she supposed. There were other assorted trinkets which remained upon the table. She hadn't time to spend with them and so she placed them in a small wooden box near the bed for nighttime contemplation. Firah picked up her bundle of to-be-mended clothes. She said a silent prayer of gratitude for fortune past and present, checked her personal inventory and made for the town. Smiling to herself, she exited the small cabin. Thanks to the unexpected haul, she would not be working this day; today she would celebrate.

The local pub was dingy and a bit musty but well known for excellent ale. Firah walked down the short dirt road toward the welcoming building. It was neighboured by the smith and farrier, whose ramshackle structures always made the sturdy bar stand out. Not only was the structure solid but the keeper also; he maintained a tight ship and required no bouncer for unruly patrons - he left that pleasure to himself. The young girl had not acquired a taste for alcohol, so the keeper, Tohm, had invented a "special" blend more to her liking. Even still, he would always tease Firah about her age as if she was too young to do anything. But Tohm had always been like that. Firah had trusted the large jovial man since she was a little girl. He always looked out for her, and even though he was embarrassingly nostalgic at times, she counted him a good friend (she always remembered it was he who had fed her when she was in the stocks). After all, it was Tohm who constructed her cabin; which she took ownership of when she was old enough. The pub door squeaked in defiance as she slowly pushed it open and tentatively peered into the common room. Her wariness was a habit she had learned from hard experience and, while this place usually had no trouble, someone new could always be in town. It paid to be cautious.

The room felt more spacious than the outside shape of the structure implied. Within the cozy common area were various tables of sturdy make. Many of them were still in a state of use from the previous day. The light through the windows was enough to illuminate all but the deepest corners. The atmosphere in the pub retained the joviality of its patrons like gentle ghosts. It could be felt in every breath and touch upon worn wood. Most of all, it was a reflection upon its owner's candor and courtesy.

"O' there ye are, Firah! Be a nice girl and grab me some of those glasses on the tables!" Tohm was in his usual jovial manner. It was rare to find him in any other mood, and his mirth was often contagious. Firah had only seen him mad twice. Needless to say it was unsettling to see a mild mannered man become enraged and terrifying. Tohm was built stocky (a little over-girthed) but he was powerful. He stood over most people, and yet all that stature seemed to disappear inside his peculiar joviality.

"Sure thing," Firah replied. "I suppose it's drinks on Tohm today then?" She smiled as she went swiftly around the room cleaning up.

"Keep dreaming, lil' girl!" He laughed loudly in his own odd way while Firah grimaced at the youthful comment. "But then, ah well - last night was quite a haul and most of my stock is down. Everyone wanted to be indoors at least; most everyone, I think," Tohm trailed off with a certain knowing in his tone. He winked at Firah as she approached with the glasses. Blushing slightly, she averted her gaze and said nothing. "Don't worry, Firah, I've got hired help today to help out with dishes and with moving the 'eavy stuff. So just relax." Tohm placed a large mug frothing with her special blend upon the counter. He had a warm smile upon his weathered face.

"Thanks, Tohm," Firah said warmly. Then she spied a familiar look forming in his face. She smiled at first, and then sighed. Her friend was a creature of habit, and memory dictated what was coming next.

"Ye know, I remember when ye were wee tall and sneaking around here looking for scraps," his words slowly faded as he descended into the cellar. Firah shook her head. 'He'll never change will he?' she thought with another sigh. She made her way through the room and slumped into a table by a window.

The door to the kitchen opened and someone stepped through. Firah's eyes shifted in a heartbeat from the window to the newcomer. Immediately, she took in his near-naked wiry frame. Aside from a gird about his nether regions all he was wearing was a service apron which was splashed and soiled from dish work. He had a somewhat agreeable look with a short cut of brown hair which was flecked with grey. She was drawn to his deep blue eyes which were intense and mysterious. Sweat glistened upon his muscled frame and trickled down his brow. Facial hair, trimmed shot and neat cut across his jaw line, accentuating his driving eyes. Upon noticing Firah, his head bowed in a respectful gesture.

"Excuse my lack of dress, madam. I have finished my work in the kitchen. Perhaps have you seen the master of the pub about?" His formality threw her off. He was definitely not from Lenhir or anywhere else in the area. His accent certainly suggested his origins existed outside the community. The uncommon use of civility had truly shocked her. She felt at times she was condemned to live among uncouth barbarians whose greatest achievement in life was learning how to wipe properly in the midden house. The man waited upon her expectantly.

"He … he went to the cellar. I'm sure he'll be back." Firah averted her eyes, surprising herself. She found herself blushing but it was not out of attraction for the man. Rather, it was the clear piercing gaze that seemed to be appraising her, even her thoughts, if it were possible. He simply stood and gazed at her calmly; meanwhile, Firah fidgeted under the weight of his stare. She stood and peered out the window in an attempt to disrupt the awkward moment. Despite her efforts, she found it nearly impossible to avoid his presence. The hair on the back of her neck rose slightly, tickling her skin. A tremor of fear shivered through her which she could not entirely hide. She considered the door and flight from the room.

"Firah! How about a lil' trip into the city tomorrow?"

Firah jumped slightly from the floor. Tohm's voice boomed from the depths of the cellar. Slowly his shaved head appeared, then the rest of his body carrying a large keg of his noted ale. Tohm had entirely missed the moment between his two patrons but upon seeing the man, regarded him heartily.

"Well, Zyr! Done already? Y're the best help this place has seen in a long time; silent and 'ardworking!" Tohm cast a side-glance at Firah who threw a disgusted face back at him. "'ave you met Firah? She's the local tom-boy and troublemaker. You may want to check your pockets before ye leave." Firah's eyes flared up with anger at the comment and she stood up violently, dislodging the table. First, the nightmare, then this unnerving stranger and finally Tohm's unbearable candor; it had all culminated into a burst of frustration that stole her sense.

"Why don't you shut it, Tohm?" she lashed out venomously. Her face flushed even deeper crimson after she observed the newcomer's brow raised in response to her outburst. She swung her arm in Tohm's direction midst the rant. "Why do you say that to everyone? You have no consideration for me or how hard it's been! I've had enough, you hear me? Sometimes you really ..." Her eyes watered slightly as her voice trailed off. How could she take this teasing so seriously now and why did it bother her so much? There was no answer she could discern yet she stood her full height and glared back at Tohm.

Her words clearly cut him, and in shock Tohm began to falter. "I'm sorry, Firah, I meant no 'arm. You know I always mean well for you. It's just that…that being the case … I ..." Tohm seemed to squirm under her gaze. Secretly she relished the moment, though it was a fleeting feeling. He quickly recovered and attempted to restore order to the uncomfortable scene that had infiltrated his bar.

"Well anyway … introductions! Ah, bless me! Firah, this is Zyr, the 'elp I mentioned to ye … Zyr, this is Firah, a fine lass of the 'ighest caliber, if I do say so m'self!" he laughed weakly and only then did Firah release him from her gaze. She sat back down to her now overturned mug and sighing slumped her feet onto a nearby chair. She was confused for sure and that annoying tingling on her neck was still lingering.

"Oh … yes, as I was saying, would ye like to join me for a short trip to the city?"

Firah glared again, frustration threatening to spring her from her seat.

"I know! I know!" Tohm backpedalled quickly, "ye 'ate the city! It's just that the ride gets so lonesome and some company would be nice. Listen, I know there are a 'undred other things ye would rather do…but, for me?" He put on a heavily exaggerated face so pitiful that Firah just shook her head in embarrassment.

"I hate your face more than the city." The girl shrugged her shoulders, defeated. The anger was abating but her hackles were still rankling. "Okay, I suppose a quick trip. I do have some mending to be done and the shop can do it faster and cheaper there. Still, I'm not too keen for long talk, Tohm." Her voice trailed off. Her gaze was upon the unlit fireplace in the wall and suddenly she felt drawn into the sheer blackness of the soot within. Slowly, she was drifting off to other places, darker than the soot amidst the coals. Memory of the previous night's dream came creeping back into her mind.

▼ The stranger piped up. "That's all the dishes and kitchen work; I assume standard pay is a just payment?"

"Not for ye' sir!" Tohm retorted, "You've been of such great service, I'm doublin' the standard." He made his way over to the strongbox, designed to store the various coins and precious items that were traded for drinks and food.

Tohm invited the younger man to the various spirits that lay racked overhead to which the dishwasher declined with a raised hand. As Tohm made to grasp the coins for payment, Zyr put a hand out gently upon the larger man's arm. "Instead of money, perhaps if you would permit me transport? I need passage to the city and logic dictates that group travel is safer, particularly with the unusual array of creatures prowling about in the area. I would consider payment in full in exchange for passage." Tohm stroked his chin and harrumphed a couple times.

"Well … I don't see a problem with it. Some extra protection would be nice, 'specially for Firah. I would hate to have her injured in any way, if you catch my meaning." Tohm stared hard into the deep blue ocean that was in Zyr's gaze.

"While I am aboard, I can guarantee her safety and health, sir. She will be guarded from predators of any sort." He nodded to Tohm and collected his clothes from behind the bar. He moved through the room, past the girl.

"Dishwasher and mercenary … mmm … how very … convenient." Tohm muttered beneath his breath. With one glance back at Firah, Zyr stepped to the door. She appeared still lost in thought and unaware of the conversation. "I'll be here at sunrise sharp."

Thwack. The wind draft closed the door firmly, snapping Firah back to the world with a jolt. She grasped the table to stop her spilling over in the rickety chair.

"Huh? Did he leave?" she enquired, looking about.

Tohm leaned up against the counter and scratched his chin thoughtfully. 'He is an odd one, Zyr.' he mused inwardly. "Ye can bring me more of those used glasses, daydreamer." As Firah turned to walk slowly to her friend, Tohm looked her square in the eyes, "I've got something to tell ye." He set two full mugs upon the counter for each of them; two very different blends.

θ   *Last night's storm had given way to a compelling calmness in the land. The sway of the trees and grass grew motionless. Freedom beckoned and from deep within the world a restless will was calling for the Sapling to grow.*

PAIN AND PARAFFIN

Y THE MORNING DEW gathered softly upon the
leaves of the thick forest boughs. The sun rose sharply
in anticipation of the new day. Firah awoke to a morning
chorus orchestrated by the local Thrushtal population. Their
song was exquisite and lifted the heavy heart, and invited
her to a new blessed day. It was said that the song held

mystical qualities, a myth that many naturalists had tried in vain to verify. Firah appreciated the family that had nested just outside her window and enjoyed when she was treated to a musical awakening. It was the infrequency of these moments that made the experience warming and unforgettable. She remained still beneath her goose-down patchwork-cover and drank in the ethereal melody. The harmonious birds seemed to always have a new song to sing and Firah joked that the space of time between recitals must be spent in coming up with new and exciting material. Eventually the notes subsided and all was still. The wind rustled the branches of her tree outside and the sweet smell of morning enveloped the room.

It was at this minute that Firah realized she was late. Snapping out of bed like a blinded Gnarel, she attempted to pass through the morning ritual of cleansing rapidly. She eventually abandoned that and attempted to accomplish many tasks together. "Tohm will kill me!" she muttered furiously. As Firah crammed down food, she tried to control her vast bramble-bush of hair. Either endeavour was ultimately unsuccessful. She grimaced uncomfortably as food jammed at her stomach while stealing a glance in the settling surface of water. Her hair had seen better days.

Firah was whisking out the door when she heard a familiar sound. One of her Thrushtal neighbors had appeared and perched upon her bed post. Though a small bird it boasted a bright array of red and orange swatches on its wings. The colours were accentuated by its soot-black body which shifted this way and that. It looked at Firah inquisitively.

"Well, you finally decide to visit when I am in a desperate rush," Firah said tartly.

The Thrushtal's head cocked a little. "I'm afraid I have no more time to spend with you. I have to go!" She turned to leave when she felt a small pinch on her hand. There was another smaller bird there and it had nipped her! An irritated chirp rang out and she looked back to the bed post to see the first bird still there. It cocked its head again, almost as a signal, but Firah was beside herself. "Fly away!" she urged as she flicked her hand gently to remove the smaller white and black speckled visitor. The striping on its breast seemed to flow with the motion of Firah's hand. The bed-post Thrushtal made a forlorn note and turned its head from right to left.

Firah sighed deeply. "What are you doing here? What are you trying to tell me?"

The one on her hand nipped her again and then flew to the small wooden box beside the bed. It cooed with a flustered tone and then preened its colorful secondary feathers.

"Hmmm. Is this what …?" Firah trailed off as she approached the small wooden box. She remembered yesterday morning that she had placed trinkets inside. The box held the few precious keepsakes of any value Firah owned. It was ornately carved, with bands of wood encasing the perimeter. It almost seemed that braids of hair were etched carefully and masterfully along the surface.

As she reached down to open the lid, the smaller Thrushtal climbed back onto her hand. Firah allowed it stay as she lifted the lid and then withdrew the contents. She discovered a small brooch, which had a distinctive brilliance and deep green color which sparkled brightly in the light from her window.

Firah held the brooch lightly and considered the small stone wrapped in golden braids. As she did so, the small Thrushtal on her hand pecked deeply into her thumb so that blood seeped from the skin.

Firah yelped and flicked the bird off her hand in surprise. She examined the small wound, as her blood flowed down her thumb onto the gemstone. Suddenly, both Thrushtals struck up a haunting melody which weaved through the room. It began first with the smaller female with a single piercing note which echoed eerily. Then together the voices grew in a complex weave of sound, and Firah felt a strange power growing in the room touching upon everything she could see. The surface of every object seemed to illuminate and glow. The light grew in intensity and Firah lifted her hand to shield her eyes. The Thrushtal chorus rose to a brilliant crescendo. It was a masterpiece of sound and deep within the score was a hidden longing.

Then the music stopped.

She withdrew her hand from her eyes. The Thrushtals and light were gone. No sign of bleeding remained, though she located a small, near-invisible scar on her thumb. The brooch had changed shape it seemed, the braids had become more like brambles and entwined themselves about the stone. Firah did not know how to take what had just occurred, but instinctively she raised the brooch to her leather tunic and slid it firmly into place.

"Whoa ..." she breathed out after an age. Coming to her sense, Firah looked at the rest of the items quickly: a small white stone of no apparent value, a strange set of dice, and a signet with a symbol of an open hand gesture completed the search of the new items from last night's catch. She scooped up the items and dropped them in her inside pocket for future perusal. "I suppose I'll have some time on this trip ..."

A sudden flash of fear shaded Firah's face. "I'm late! Tohm! He'll ... Oh no!" With reckless abandon she tore the door open and sprinted down the path. She intended to set a new time record today.

☙ Tohm tapped his foot in irritation. He would tan the hide of that irresponsible little ingrate. She knew how critical an early departure was. If he could get a head start in the morning he might just get a better spot in the ridiculously long line of merchants into the city. Now where was she? He tapped a thick paddle against his shoulder. Well, the last time he used it was quite a while ago. Maybe she forgot how it felt. Still it hurt him to do it. He felt he had some responsibility to watch out for her. She was not his daughter in any sense, but their relationship had evolved over time. He was her conscience despite her attempts to ignore his promptings. Left to her own ends, she would likely have little if any moral sense. This small correction today would prevent certain disaster tomorrow. 'No, it's the right thing to do' he thought as he steeled himself for the task. Sometimes the firm hand was best, as it certainly yielded short term results. His foot and paddle tapped in unison. He detested waiting.

A soft even voice broke through his annoyance. "She seemed quite distracted yesterday, Tohm. Perhaps something held her up today that we are unaware of?"

Zyr was there and on time as promised. Not that he would ever consider chastising the man if he happened to be late. Zyr appeared to be well past his thirtieth year and he was no slouch physically. Tohm had let him know yesterday in no uncertain terms what kind of conduct he expected of strangers in tow. His fears were alleviated and yet he had many questions for the man which he intended to ask along the journey. Zyr was introverted and said little, which made him a mystery, still Tohm felt at ease around him.

"I expect more of 'er, Zyr. She's a young woman who needs to learn responsibility. The whole day yesterday she spent frolicking about from place to place. Finally she 'eads 'ome late! She 'ides out there in the woods and does little for this village except to lighten the people's load in unwanted ways." He smacked the paddle vigorously against his shoulder.

Zyr grunted in response. Tohm did not know if it was in approval or whether the man simply acknowledged the statement. A sweat droplet trailed from Tohm's brow. He cast his gaze heavenward. To the east, the sun was lifting off the crags of Tamers Reach, and the heat of the day was setting in. Another reason to leave early and an opportunity wasted. Tohm harrumphed and tapped some more as thoughts of the previous night returned.

"What do you want, Tohm?" Firah asked as she sat down upon the stool adjacent to him. Tohm filled her mug and leaned against the bar, flipping the copper coin over and over between his fingers.

"I'm not sure 'ow to begin. Things have been very strange lately. Very strange. There is an ill feeling about and I can't describe it. You know I'm no naturalist like Lady Zymka. I don't know anything 'bout that. It's just that I can't get this odd feeling out of my mind. It's somethin' unnatural." He sighed and placed the coin down and looked at Firah. She was staring off into nowhere again. Her obliviousness finally got the best of him. "Are ye listening?" he snapped loudly at her. Firah jumped out of her seat and splashed her second mug over the counter.

"Tohm! For heaven's sake, don't do that!" Firah hurriedly mopped the counter with a cloth nearby. Tohm merely stared at her. "I am listening, really. I've had ni... that is I have been feeling kind of odd recently too." Firah chose not to discuss the nightmares; he would only worry more.

"It's bigger than ye or I, Firah." Tohm's expression softened. "I wanted ye to come with me on this trip for more than a companion to chat with. I feel that something migh' happen if ye - if ..." His gaze fell away from her.

Firah was watching Tohm carefully. He tried to mask the feeling of fear upon his face as he hurriedly wiped his brow free of sweat. "I can handle myself, Tohm." She folded her arms subconsciously and watched the older man breath in deeply. Her face immediately betrayed the chiding she was giving herself for her brash comment. Tohm was preparing to blast.

"Ye have no idea what is coming! Ye think you will be able to resist the evil that has been infesting the land recently? Firah, get down off yer horse and take a sensible thought for yerself! You almost died during that last Dryke 'gration and I won't go through the torture of seeing ye cry out in poison-fever again! Now ye listen plain. Ye'll get yourself here at sunrise sharp or I'll paddle yer backside so hard ye won't sit straight!" His breath came hard and his face was burning. Firah backed away and stood up.

"Fine." She said dryly. "What, you want to play parent now? I don't care what you think I can handle. I said I'll go on this trip with you, but don't think I owe you anything! Don't even think about using the past against me!" She crossed the room vigorously towards the door and wrenched it open. After stepping outside, he heard the familiar thump of her hand smack against a wooden pillar.

Inside the tavern, Tohm slowly counted the coins with trembling hands, placed them in the till and deposited them into the safe box. He stopped working and braced himself against the sturdy counter. His toughened gnarled hands, worn with years of *labour, slowly raised up and softly cradled his head.*

An eternity in Tohm's mind passed before Firah came racing around the corner of the smithy at top speed. The dirt kicked up fiercely beneath her boots while her arms pumped and her loosened hair flowed behind her. She came to an abrupt stop in front of Tohm and immediately rested her hands on her knees, while leaning over gasping in dreadful racked breaths.

"I ... it's just ... you see ... birds ... not ... my fault," Firah wheezed out. She glanced in terror at the paddle in Tohm's hand. Tohm waited until the broken testimonial was complete. He looked down at Firah with a calm steeled expression. Firah's mouth moved wordlessly and then she slowly shuffled off behind the tavern. Tohm waited a moment, considering the wooden device in his hand. Then, head hung, he slowly shifted away to where she was waiting. At the last minute his head raised, steps resolute.

Zyr waited and listened to a breeze which rustled the trees gently. To the girl's credit he heard naught but silence from her. He rolled the end of the cord that held his robe together between his fingers thoughtfully. His robe was white with dyed red columns that descended down the front. The hood was lowered, his hands protruded from beneath long sleeves. His feet were shod with worn leather boots which stirred the dust as he shifted. He listened as footsteps approached. Both heads were lowered, Firah's face red from embarrassment and exhaustion. Tears lined her eyes which she quickly wiped away upon seeing Zyr for the first time. She climbed gingerly into the back of the waggon, settled down onto her side and said nothing.

Tohm climbed upon the waggon, loaded full of empty ale barrels - and situated himself in the driver's seat. He quietly replaced the paddle behind the seat. The ponies shifted anxiously upon feeling tension on the reins and in the air. He sighed heavily and looked away from them into the distance. "Shall we leave now?" he asked quietly. Zyr stepped up lightly to take the place next to Tohm. The reins' sharp crack sent them off.

❄️   The ride was no picnic for Firah. Her sore backside made any degree of comfort impossible to find. She had little choice but to lie in the back of the uncomfortable waggon, near the end of the wooden carriage. Between the bumps, shimmies and lurches of the wooden wheels upon the uneven earth below she cursed those forsaken Thrushtals. In reality she knew that she had slept in sufficiently enough to merit a paddling without the birds delaying her, but her young mind needed to lash out at something. She simmered and sulked as she lay beneath the shadow of the large kegs. She was still feeling the stinging of the paddle but her conscience was stinging her worse. Still with every shift in the waggon she forced those feelings down with thoughts of self-pity. For hours she remained in the back of the waggon

while her pain and discomfort gradually subsided.
However, her mind remained stubbornly fixed upon her
misery.

She was somewhat surprised to find out that Zyr was
along for the entire ride to the city. What was with him? She
had many questions about him, because he seemed so
different. For a moment, she peered carefully but painfully
over the lids of the kegs. Tohm and Zyr were engaged in
quiet conversation. She slowly shifted back to her most
comfortable position (which wasn't saying much). 'Well, let
Tohm figure him out then,' she grumped.

It suddenly occurred to Firah that the waggon had
slowed. She propped herself up to look ahead past Tohm
and Zyr. Tohm was peering around the near road and treed
hills with a look of apprehension. His hand was resting
upon something just behind him; Firah could not see what it
was. Zyr simply stared ahead without moving.

"Hey, what's …?"

Tohm silenced Firah with a quick gesture. He put his
finger to his lips. He pointed far down the road. A lone
figure stood there waiting. Firah hunched low and
considered the situation. Meeting other travelers was not
uncommon but somehow she felt uneasy as well. Their
passenger Zyr showed no sign of any emotion, his hood was
over his bowed head. To the onlooker he might appear
asleep, but Firah could see his one visible eye coolly focused
upon the road.

"We'll play ignorant and stupid. It could turn out to nothin'," Tohm whispered softly. Firah's vindictive streak laughed within. Tohm's plan of action described how she felt about him perfectly. Quickly she chastised herself for such a thought. There was real trouble ahead and time for anger and grudges was past. She nodded and lay down again, staying low and very still. The waggon slowly made its way up the road towards the lone stranger ahead. "G'day, sirrah!" Firah heard Tohm bellow jovially. She waited and strained her ears.

"Hello there, m'good man," a deep voice penetrated the air. "Off to Khyvla, eh?" The stranger was close to the waggon now. Firah felt her stomach drop as they jolted to a halt. Normally, lack of movement would be a godsend, but presently she wished to be gone from this place. Despite the wagon height blocking her from view, the terrible stirring in her gut had only magnified in proximity to the stranger.

"Just takin' some empties up to the city. Time for a refill." Tohm's voice never wavered but maintained its mirthful tone. He was good at theatrics, Firah noted.

"Empty, you say?" The voice seemed to falter slightly as if in consideration of something. "Carrying anything else?" Firah's throat tightened. The voice was closer and she heard footsteps scraping upon the ground approaching the waggon bed. It was during this moment of alarm she realized, that in the morning's haste, she had forgotten her knife.

"Nothin' of interest to you," Tohm's voice now carried a note of warning. The footsteps ceased. There was a palpable moment of dead silence, where voice, wind, all nature seemed silenced. Firah wondered if they were regarding each other. For now she could only perceive the inside of the waggon around her and portions of the trees standing upon the hills on either side of the road. Firah's thieving experience told her that they were caught in a disadvantaged position, considering all the difficulties of maneuvering a cart as well.

"Well then, you'll be needing to get along! G'day!" the man announced.

Tohm snapped the reins instantly and muttered a quick "Mother's blessin'upon ye" and the waggon was moving. Firah remained low. Something wasn't right and the apprehensive feeling remained. They passed into a wood and after a minute, the waggon stopped again. "Curses!" Tohm shouted. Firah felt the wagon lurch as Tohm dismounted. She chanced a quick glance down the side of the waggon. A large tree had been felled which blocked the path completely. Tohm tested the weight of the tree, but it was evident that it was too heavy for one man.

An arrow slammed into a keg above Firah's head. She jumped in fright. Several forms leapt from the trees on both sides of the road. They charged down the short hills shouting indistinctly, weapons drawn. Firah knew she was exposed prey so she climbed off the back of the waggon and

crawled beneath. She felt so useless. If only she hadn't
forgotten her knife!

✢   Zyr had other more efficient ways. He glanced both
to the right and left as the assailants charged towards the
stranded waggon. Ahead, he spied Tohm quickly taking
stock of the situation; however, he also appeared indecisive
due to foes on either side. Concentrating inwards, Zyr
moved his arms in a circular motion, and weaved a central
focus of energy from the land and his own reserves. He
projected a portion of it outward.

Aside from the three of them, he detected sixteen healthy
bodies in the area, fourteen visible and two hidden. Zyr
stooped and picked up a large weapon that Tohm had
brought along. Its haft was about four feet long, while a
massive double ended hammer was fastened firmly upon
one end. "Here!" he shouted to Tohm, and tossed the
weapon to him. Tohm caught the weapon with surprising
ease and flourished it towards the nearest enemies.

Their full charge was stalled, and for some their
exuberance caused them to stumble to the ground. The
weapon was intimidating.

Zyr leapt from the cart to an adjacent side and assumed a
defensive stance. "Firah, stay put," he whispered to the
waggon undercarriage. He directed a small portion of
energy from his central focus down through his arms until
his fingers tingled. They emitted a pale glow which was

masked by the morning's rays through the trees. He waited upon the charging mass patiently.

One came at him swinging a short sword in a low attack. Zyr hopped lightly over the blade arc and swiftly struck out, gripping his fingers beneath the attacker's jawbone. Zyr sent a quick charge of power though his fingers into the nerve cluster located there. The man collapsed on the spot without a whisper of pain. He was unconscious; Zyr would not kill the ignorant. The next attack came from above, a wide arcing swing from a club. Zyr dropped his stance into a partial leg split and shifted under the man, where his thumbs found the nerve clusters just inside the groin. Then there were two down with fourteen left.

⚑   Tohm eyed the seven assailants warily as they slowly advanced. The hammer looked unwieldy but it had significant reach. They had a mix of weapons: a sword, two clubs, a make-shift mace, and three rough-hewn staves. The grizzled bandits jeered on, casting insults and calls to fight. Tohm focused upon himself. He had not fought in years. The Dryke skirmish ... yes that was the last time. He tried to forget, after all the pain and sorrow he witnessed. Somehow, he felt he could escape all the violence in the world. His was a gentle heart, and it still ached from this morning. He wished he could leave all this now, but Firah ...

One of the attackers with a staff snuck a poke at Tohm's leg. With one hand Tohm swung the hammer hard and smashed the cudgel to pieces. The bandit's arms shuddered from the blow upon the staff. He stared dumbfounded at the short stalk of wood in his hand. He glanced at his fellows, threw the bit of wood down and, shrinking away unarmed, ran for his life. The others glanced at each other, and the jeering stopped. Each assailant had imagined what such a blow could do to them. They hunched down and circled slowly. Then, on a signal, they attacked as one.

Whirling the hammer, Tohm's body became one with his weapon. He altered its momentum and switched the trajectory, but the attackers still came. When possible, Tohm pulled the hit, glancing blows only, while the group gave no such ground. Tohm connected with an assailant's hip with enough force to knock him down and dislocate his joint. He followed up with a downward blow to break another weapon. His hammer struck dirt and he felt a blade bite into his calf, just missing the hamstring. He roared in pain and swung the hammer in a sweeping motion above his head. The mob pulled back and he slumped to one knee breathing hard. With one down, and two fled disarmed, he waited for the next to come.

Firah watched the battles ensue. Zyr was incredible. His speed was such that his attacks rendered his opponents prone and incapacitated before they could react. Amazingly, his weapons were his hands. She stared at her own; she wished that she could say the same. Tohm, on the other hand, was struggling. His sheer strength was impressive but already he had suffered several small wounds which were taking a toll on him. She wished now that she had not let him down and felt sorrow for every bad thought she entertained that day. She prayed within herself, "Please Mother, do not let Tohm die!" She watched Zyr dispatch another man swiftly; would he be able to help in time?

Suddenly she felt a warm grip around one ankle. She was jerked out from under the waggon. Her head struck hard on the undercarriage. Dazed and with her eyes blurring from pain, she turned herself about to see the man hauling her up to her feet. He wrapped one arm tightly about her midsection trapping her arms. She was only just recovering from the blow to the head, when she felt a pinprick upon her neck. She looked down to see a knife at her throat. She felt the warmth of his body uncomfortably against hers, his breath rasping in her ear. "It seems we found somethin' of interest after all. Don't think about calling out." In an instant, she recognized the voice of the one who stopped their waggon earlier. Firah looked desperately to her friends but they were caught up in their own battles. She struggled but immediately stopped at the sharp point pressing upon her neck. The man began to move her toward the wooded hills and whispered frightening things in her ear. "Please … don't do this …" she pleaded. The man laughed and prodded her on.

Within her heart, Firah found courage as inspiration flowed from her companions, who were fighting to save her. In one movement, Firah twisted her slim body which caused the blade to gouge into her skin, though as she turned she brought her head around to meet her captor's head sharply. As the blow collapsed the soft tissue in his nose, his grip loosened and she reached up and tore at his eyes.

The man screamed and fell to the ground clutching his wounded face.

Firah sprung like a white-tipped fawn out of the thicket. As she ran, she thought about seeking shelter in the far trees.

A sharp pain impacted upon her right leg, dropping her to the ground. She howled out in her highest volume as she attempted to cope with the pain. At first she felt it was the man she fought off, but peering down at her leg she gaped in horror. An arrow shaft had driven clean through her right thigh and protruded out the other side. Though it had missed bone, the leg was immobile, as her muscles entered into traumatic shock. She tried to stand but with no leverage she only aggravated the injury. Cursing with pain, she cried out again. She was down and open to any attack, and horrified she saw the man she injured stumbling for her, with intense hatred in his reddened eyes. Slowly she dragged herself from the approaching brigand, blood beginning to flow down into view from the gash in her neck.

ᛞ   Tohm stared in horror as he saw Firah. He had turned to look, after her piercing cry. He saw her on the ground - partially obstructed by the waggon - languishing and terrified. Deep within his heart, a caged animal was released from its long imprisonment. He let out a deafening roar that shook through the grove. Energy filled his frame as his mind, body and spirit became one.

He swung heavily down upon the shoulder of an assailant's sword arm, completely severing the limb.

He swung twice and two more fell under bone shattering blows.

The unprecedented ferocity had taken his foes unawares. His mind shut off the pain from his wounds, and crouching low, he sprang out from the bodies surrounding him. In a few short leaps he was instantly upon Firah's stalker. The bandit sensed him and slashed out with his long dagger. Tohm raised the handle of the hammer and the blade notched itself into the haft. Tohm ripped the dagger from the grip of his opponent by twisting the haft roughly. He then hurled the weapons away, his massive frame pulsing with adrenaline. Firah's attacker stuck out at Tohm, which Tohm simply took in full measure in the face. His head shifted slightly from the blow. Tohm looked back at the man and wiped the spit and blood from his mouth. Scowling, he leaned back. The man's eyes flashed with dread as Tohm laid full into his opponents face, returning the blow a hundred fold. He felt teeth dislodge and bones shatter under his attack. The bandit flew through the air several feet and came to earth motionless. Tohm looked around hungrily for the next opponent only to feel Zyr's arm on his shoulder.

"Enough, Tohm ... enough." At the touch of his ally, Tohm's body collapsed under forced strain and exhaustion. The animal retreated back within, and Tohm looked around wearily. Firah sat whimpering upon the ground. The forms of unconscious and deceased men littered the road. The day was theirs.

ᛉ   "These wounds normally would take a while to mend," Zyr spoke as he prepared a strange smelling paste in his hands. "Luckily for you both, this paraffin does wonders." He applied portions of the mixture on both Tohm and Firah's wounds. Firah felt a tingling as the medicine was applied by the hands of the healer. Surprisingly, it relieved most of the pain and discomfort almost immediately. She was impressed but grimaced in pain as she shifted weight on her leg. "Ah yes. Well, I'm afraid that wound isn't going to be as simple." Zyr capped the ointment and placed it within a pouch on his hip. He put a hand upon Firah's arm. "I need to be honest. This will be very painful. Tohm, if you're up to it, I will need your help." Tohm grunted in approval and moved around inside the wagon to get a better position. "You will need to hold her down," Zyr instructed. Tohm stared into Firah's eyes which now betrayed some fear and apprehension.

"Firah, you know about this morning …" his voice faded to a whisper. "I am so sorry. You are no' a girl anymore. Have I been too blind to see it?" He shook his head and looked away.

"Oh, Tohm," Firah's vision grew blurry, "I guess … I need you now and then. Right now I just need you to hold my hand, okay?" She lifted the chin of the older man so that he looked into her green eyes.

"Aye, lass. I'll do that." Thom grasped her hand firmly with his own, and she settled herself against his sturdy frame. She smiled at him softly and then glanced to Zyr and nodded. Zyr squeezed her arm one last time and removed his hand. Firah began to breathe long deep breaths and tried to focus as she always did when a difficult task was at hand. Zyr began to collect the potency within himself and the whisper of a prayer was upon his lips. He would need to be steady, and quick to stem the blood flow. He wished he did not have to perform the mending weave but there was little choice here. Infection, even tissue decay, would be her fate if they delayed longer. He silently prayed that his enemies would be far from here and unable to detect the weaving. He breathed in deeply, balancing and focusing the energy within. Small cuts were one thing, but this would require much more effort.

"Ready," Zyr called out. Tohm and Firah braced as Zyr in one motion broke the arrowhead clean off the shaft. Firah violently bit back the near-overpowering urge to scream. She wasn't strong earlier, but she could be now. As well there was a quiet strength in Tohm's warm calloused hand. His other arm had come around as well to hold her tight to himself. Zyr waited for Firah to catch her breath before he continued.

"Extracting." Again Firah clenched Tohm's hand, who welcomed all of her strength. The shaft was pulled cleanly and sharply out of Firah's thigh. This time the quietest scream Firah could utter escaped her clenched teeth. Immediately Zyr's hands went to the entry and exit wounds which began to flow red. Firah felt a strange tingling swell and surge up and down her leg. Within moments, Zyr removed his hands and breathed out long and heavily. The skin had sealed over the wounds, though the surface was still raw and sore. "That is all I dare risk for now, "the healer said, "Now you should rest. I'll deal with the bodies and the tree." Zyr stepped down from the waggon and stripped down to his loincloth, a sign of heavy labor ahead. He folded his robes neatly and precisely, and set them on the waggon bed. As he moved away from the two companions, Firah rested her head in Tohm's lap. Tohm stroked her hair and began to hum a tune from the village.

𝒱   Tohm was not sure what he felt at this moment. Disgust of the beast he had let loose upon those men, relief for Firah's stable condition, or grief for bringing her into this mess. Either way, he was sure he did what was right. He closed his eyes and continued to hum the soothing melody.

⁂   Firah closed her eyes and let sleep overcome her. One stubborn thought carried her into the land of peace; she would become stronger and never be a liability to others again. Sweet darkness overtook her.

θ   *Slowly nature breathed as the wind blew across the land and all things living rejoiced under the gentle sun. The breath of nature caressed the Sapling. The young seed had grown under adversity and now was blooming for the first time, revealing the beauty and strength within.*

THE BLADE UPON THE BANNERS

⊖ THE TOWERS OF KHYVLA rose high above the outer wall, stretching into the darkening blue sky. The royal standards and the colors of the most renowned cadre of the province were displayed upon the capital's shining pinnacles. The city was operated and maintained by a local civil government which was appointed by the Kenharian king. The civil leaders interacted regularly with the representative and master of the cadre, through the "One Seat" or the position of power over all other organized groups. The position was created in a forgotten time as a way to appease the rise of powerful cadres. They had a voice in establishing policies and in turn honoured existing regulations.

Relations could land on rocky ground whenever the governing chancellor and cadre master disagreed on public policy. To add to the confusion, the One Seat could change at any time. Such shifts in power created difficulties for the ruling monarch to establish favourable relations with the cadre masters. In earlier times it was more simplistic, with cadres exchanging places only every few years. Of course, there were far fewer organizations then as well. However, times were shifting as new cadres sprung up everywhere replacing the "old traditional organizations." This year alone had seen two new cadres rise to significant power and claiming the One Seat. Due to the influence the ruling cadre had upon the city, small changes in governmental policy were included to keep the One Seat appeased and stocking the local coffers. Needless to say, the local citizenry were often confused as to which rules were in force and what was illegal. The best they could manage was to keep listening for announcements of any change, and for sake of convenience, new cadres would include codes of conduct to be read along with the notice of change. It was said that the local criers had the most interesting occupation, as information was dynamic and constantly changing. Their role was quite unlike the endless grind of typical professions.

𝖄   Outside the wall, a line of carts and waggons loaded full of all assortments of goods, spanned well into the distance. Somewhere in the middle of the endless trade procession, sat two silent figures. One of them, a man and the larger of the two, gazed upward at the drifting banners upon the pinnacles. He shook his head and shifted the reins in his hand. There was another change in the cadres. Or had it changed more than once since he was here last? It did not matter in the end, he supposed. He was still too far from the criers who would announce at the merchant gate the newest rules of conduct. Announcements came every hour without fail.

Stiffly, Tohm shifted his large frame and stretched his back. This would be some wait until they would gain access to the city. Tohm thought of the time and money investment involved in each restock run to the city. He cursed inwardly at the thought of the customary tribute. Luckily, the amount required was typically the same, which was a relief to the traveller who counted on some semblance of regularity. This was preferable to travelling for miles and finding you were short of money and could not get into the city. Usually, the ruling cadre horded nearly the whole sum for their selfish purposes, with little returns to the common folk. He shook his head again. A girl's voice brought him from his musings.

"How much longer do you think, Tohm?" Firah looked at him dully, evidently bored. She yawned and stretched herself like a cat, pushing her arms well above her head and linking her hands. Joints crackled as she breathed out slowly while lowering her arms. The noise rankled Tohm.

"I wish you wouldn't do that around me," Tohm said as he shuddered. She laughed as their eyes met. He felt happier when she smiled, especially now. Gratefully, she appeared to be feeling better and back to her normal self.

"This sounds odd coming from you, the vigorous, roaring ox who came to my rescue." Her expression turned playful and her green eyes sparkled mischievously.

Tohm subtly weaved the threads of the discussion to her original point. "The reason we're here," he said pointing at their general location, "and not up there," he motioned to somewhere well up the crowded line toward Khyvla, "is your tardiness." They fixed their eyes upon each other and stared hard. Still, within those stares was a shared understanding of certain lines not to be crossed. The moment was broken by the waggon shifting slightly, while shuffling sounds came from the waggon bed.

"He's been asleep for a while," Firah noted of the form in the back of the waggon. Their third companion became still and the sound of slow breathing was barely heard.

"Well, he certainly earned it, the good man." Tohm considered the early day's events. It was now well toward dusk, many hours after the ambush upon the road to the city. The battle was pitched and furious, at times uncertain

… at least Tohm felt in his own case. Zyr was truthful when he stated that no harm would befall Firah. How grateful Tohm was to the strange Ashori, who did for her what Tohm could not. His heart sank when he realized that he could not protect her sufficiently. If Zyr had not been there …. He chose not to dwell on it; the thought of Firah coming to harm was unbearable. "Let him sleep as long as he needs." Firah nodded grimly in understanding. Both were grateful beyond words.

"I wonder how he did all those things?" Firah mused out loud.

"I don't know much about it," Tohm replied in straightforward talk. He could never fathom why the clarity of his speech improved when it came to certain topics. Perhaps it was a reflection of his rational mind overcompensating from the pain of the past. Maintaining control of the beast was sometimes difficult. Tohm checked his thoughts and came back to the conversation. "Years ago there was a place spoken of where people like Zyr gathered. It's rumoured that they swore oaths and dedicated themselves to the strictest training. Perhaps he came from there."

Firah nodded in response. "What training could help somebody do what he did? I mean, you saw him lift that tree. Such a weight would have taken several men!"

Tohm gave her a shrug. "I don' know darlin'. He's full of mysteries. All I know is that to move like he did takes work, whether he has tricks to do amazin' things or not. Wouldn't surprise me if he slept through into morning. I'm not sure yet, but we may all have to camp out here tonight and wait for entrance into Khyvla tomorrow." Tohm considered the line ahead. It spanned for a way and movement was slow.

The barkeep was unaware of any festivals or holidays, events which impacted upon the planning of his city supply runs. While the massive rainstorm had necessitated the trip be ahead of schedule, he was fairly certain that he was still between festivals. Those were times that any wise merchant would either plan to come beforehand or not at all.

The city only had so much space and the population was monitored closely. An innovative signal system from either end of the city walls was incorporated, thus maintaining incoming and outgoing traffic. Tohm felt sure that they would be fairly close to the merchant's entrance by sundown when the gates were locked. He stared over at the main entrance where the rest of the folk entered. That entrance was taxed as well, but the process time so much faster. Only a few persons waited outside the gates that he could see, most likely peddlers.

Firah smiled. "I guess I'll just have to wait then." She rested her elbows on her knees and leaned her head onto her hands. He had known her long enough to know she wasn't in any hurry to go inside that stone cage. Yet her body language declared that waiting was tiresome. Tohm knew that any movement would be welcomed by her even if it meant cramming along inside city streets.

"Do you really wish to see the city?"

Firah jumped in her seat while Tohm whipped around instinctively. Zyr stood high upon the tops of the empty ale barrels, shielding his eyes from the setting sun as he gazed to the city entrance. His brown over-cloak tossed gently about in the wind. He looked down at Firah with that cool gaze which always unnerved her. Yet, she no longer mistrusted him.

"I've seen it," she replied. "It's just that I'm getting bored sitting around and Tohm and I have talked each other blue in the ears." She stood up from the passenger seat and stretched again which caused Tohm to shudder.

The monk was placid as he spoke. "There is nothing to be gained by entering the walls tonight. I recommend waiting outside until morning." There was something deep and troubling in his eyes which was nearly missed by the others.

"Stay out here 'til morning?" the girl's voice was mixture of shock and whining antipathy. Tohm's senses shuddered under the thought of an endless night of complaint and woeful angst.

"The city has its diversions which will keep even this one occupied," Tohm replied thumbing toward Firah. "She'll avoid any trouble with the City Watch close a' hand. I have no misgivin's 'bout it."

Firah was visibly ruffled. "Like I need either of your say in this. I'll make my own decisions, thank you."

Tohm cast a wary glance at her. The earlier events of the day were still near the surface.

"It seems my counsel is overruled," Zyr sighed in resignation. "I understand your wishes, perhaps more than you realize. Even so, please permit me to accompany you." He looked to Tohm, "trouble will not avoid the unwary."

Firah piped up at his request. "I trust you, Zyr. You should know that. I accept your offer." Her face drifted from a sincere cast to a more mischievous variety. "As for Tohm, I don't think that we should leave him here in line by himself. It could be dangerous."

Tohm looked at her squarely. "Darlin', your absence might allow me to think without all the chattering." He grinned smugly and winked. "Be off with ye! I'll be fine here, besides it's of no use wearing two holes in this bench when you could be doin' something productive. Shoo! Shoo!" Firah mocked a confused and perplexed look, but jumped off quickly with a grin at the sign of Tohm's hand being raised. Zyr was waiting below to help her down but she cleared his head and hand with a leap, landing softly into a crouch.

"It appears your energy and movement are fully restored. Shall we?" He started towards the main road at a brisk walk.

"Bye Tohm! I'll head to the merchant gate in the morning, okay?" Tohm's head wagged in affirmation as she glanced over her shoulder. She stepped into a trot beside Zyr. He had raised his hood once again and was staring intently at the banners upon the towers. His eyes narrowed slightly and his pace picked up considerably.

"Hey wait!" Firah shouted. She had to work to keep up to the pace of the healer.

Above, the wind tossed the red and black banners to and fro, as if intent on dislodging them from their supports. The blade emblazoned banners resisted the wind's every attempt. The sun slowly sank low on the horizon.

*　　　*　　　*

Deep within the confines of the central tower, the sun gave way to candlelight which cast dancing shadows upon the walls of stone. Tapestries were freshly hung about the halls, displaying a silver blade against distinct red and black patterns, masterfully woven from the best silk. Silent cloaked figures moved about from room to room, heads bowed in submission. They moved up and down the tower steps in pious cadence. Occasionally, through openings in the stone walls, they would peer down into the streets below and all throughout Khyvla.

The entrance to the tower was guarded by massive Blackstone sentinels. They seemed a part of the tower masonry, except for the shade of the rock from which they were hewn. The midnight black hue contrasted with the grayish tower stone and yet details were difficult to discern in the figures. They resembled grotesquely twisted human forms, towering over the door; as such their presence was enough to keep most curious folk at bay. The remainder of the people avoided the doorway, due to stories they had heard about unfortunate curious folk who walked where they should not have. In addition to the sentinels, the door itself was quite sturdy and was capable of resisting almost any attack. From the door frame, the tower's smoothly joined stone flowed upward, making an ascent all but impossible. In general, the tower was an effective fortress against all enemies of the cadre which inhabited it.

Echoes of approaching feet sounded across the cobblestone. People walking past parted quickly, making way as a procession of dark cloaked figures approached the entrance. The sentinels seemed to leer down upon the silent visitors as they paused in front of the massive door. Slowly, the front most member of the group lifted his hand toward the door. The door slid open silently and the group moved through the entrance. It closed with a solid clunk echoing up through the spiralling structure. The figures slowly but steadily ascended the stairs without stopping to interact with others. A profound silence prevailed within the tower, only broken by the sounds of padded feet upon stone. The hooded visitors halted their climb at the highest floor in the tower. Again, they stood before a solid wooden door. A gesture released the lock and admitted the cloaked party. The room was lavishly decorated and sweet smelling fragrances lingered in the air. From deep within, a lone form sat in the confines of shadows. The party moved into the room and assembled into a broken line near the entrance, heads bowed. All was silent for several minutes.

"Where are Murghath and Alsyr?" A voice called out, sweet, exquisite and alluring. It echoed with soothing tones and yet it commanded fealty. All who heard the voice were enticed and fearful in the same moment.

The foremost member, who had opened the passageway, replied in a suppressed voice, "Alsyr had not returned from her search to the east into Tamers Reach. As for Murghath, he remains hidden still, my lady."

"Alsyr's absence is forgiven. No doubt Murghath heard of the attunement at Jandor. At first, I assumed his prolonged absence was for the purpose of gathering information; however, his cowardice has been unveiled." The woman moved silently into the soft candlelight. Her beauty was intriguing to the unaware. However, none of the men present had ever remembered having lustful considerations, or making them public in any event. Lady Nuril was considered exalted above the base passions of the rank and file. Her demeanor simply carried a guarded and venomous warning, one no reasonable man dared cross. With the limited speculation that prevailed in the halls, no one knew if she ever had possessed or entertained the thought of a companion. Ultimately, she was the cadre master and such matters were beyond their concern.

The mistress moved around a black obsidian table centered in the room and slowly toward the waiting subordinates. She moved down the line, brushing each member gently with a silky shift that trailed behind her. Her hair was lustrous ebony, which was pinned up into an intricate weaving by long and slender stiletto daggers. A thin black veil was fastened within her dark locks and fell across her face, shadowing every feature. Her shift was crimson red and woven intricately with black symbols and patterns, leading all the way down to the hem of the garment. Her skin seemed creamy white against the blackness within the room. Her skin's whiteness glowed in the candlelight. As she passed each of her bond-servants, her scent floated just behind, capturing each of them within her web. She stopped in front of the vacant space in the line and stared intently into the void. All present felt trickles of sweat form and trace down their faces. No one stirred as she stood motionless. Finally, the cadre-mistress spoke.

"Each of you are linked to me by oath, by bond, by blood." She raised a slender hand and withdrew one of the shining blades from her hair. She raised her arm above the gap in her solemn line of servants, where Murghath would have stood. Slowly, she drew the knife across her arm, letting the blood flow in tiny streams, dripping through the vacant air upon the floor. She then began to chant a haunting chorus of guttural sounds and moved her hand in a slow rotation in the air at about the height of a man's head. A strange luminous glow pulsed from her hand to the floor, dancing along the falling droplets of crimson. Once, twice, thrice her arm circled in the air. Following the last rotation her hand clenched to a fist and she jerked it back with one swift, violent movement. She stopped chanting and lowered her hand. The greenish glow faded. The shift slowly concealed her elegant but bloody arm as it returned to her side. "The departure of Murghath is irrelevant." She turned and slid gracefully towards her sitting chair. As she took her place, beneath the veil a small smile touched upon her lips. "The prize, our key to success, is near. The Jazyn smelt her at midday approaching the city. She is young, perhaps seventeen years of age. Each of you is a weave in the net we cast tonight. Begin at your starting points and collapse the search upon her. Do not arouse suspicion. Go now and fulfil your oaths to me."

θ   "Yes, mistress." Ebyn chanted in unison with his blood brothers. The lesson was plain and the message was clear to them all. The price of failure and betrayal was deep and final. It was disturbing imagining an enemy writhe in pain from this curse and find only death as a comfort. The curse was fuelled by the terrifying pact they had solemnly sworn. While somewhat disturbed at this dark form of punishment, he felt that for the time being, he had the confidence of his Lady. Nuril was a terror, of near-infinite power in the art of Nexism. Occasionally, she would unveil sweet morsels of her knowledge to him. He intended to stay close to her, and outwit these other buffoons for the position of First Seat. Now there was one less to compete with. He turned toward the door, and his heart raced in anticipation. His ascension was so close! Now, he must be the one to find the girl and return to the cadre-mistress with the prize in chains. The target was being drawn to them by subtle forces and all they needed to do was collect her. The reward for faithful service would be beyond comprehension. Ebyn smiled quietly as the group descended the long winding stair.

*   *   *

θ   The serving maid at the Three Quarters Inn checked the door to the room again. It was still locked and no one had come in or out for days. It seemed that the occupant had skipped out of paying overdue fees of service. Grimacing, she dreaded the cleanup that was coming. It was likely that the room was in shambles and completely unsanitary. It was usually that way with dead beats. Grumbling to herself, she raised the spare key to the lock.

Absently, she opened the door, which ground out a slow, steady squeal upon rusted hinges. The room was dark and musty. She raised her candle to the blackness. Suddenly, the candle tumbled to the floor and the maid collapsed in a stupor of fright. The fading flickers of light illuminated the form of a man lying upon the wooden floor. His mouth was open in an expression of pain. The pale eyes betrayed the look of horror. All of the exposed skin was marked by tiny pinholes from which blood had escaped. His neck had traces of scars from some sort of strangulation, but no weapon could be seen. The room was pooled in blood, which shone in the fading light. The flame ceased, and the maid's gentle sobs carried into the early night air.

*   *   *

🌱   "Citizens all! Hear my words!" Firah watched the city crier project his eloquent voice among the thronging mass. "This is the last news of the day! Hear ye!" Zyr deposited some coins into the hands of the gate collector and stepped over to Firah. She looked at him inquisitively. He was strange. He had nearly sprinted to the gates and, despite being physically fit, she was hard pressed to keep up. Even now as she steadied her breathing, he seemed calm as a summer's morning.

"Where to now?" she enquired. He held up a hand, signalling for her to wait, and then pointed it toward the crier. She nodded slowly, folded her arms and leaned against the near wall. With the teeming masses, compounded with the disgusting odor from the sewage troughs along the road, she was reminded of her distaste for city life. Glancing upward she saw one maid deposit a tub of excrement out of a second floor window into the street, which scattered folk nearby. 'Disgusting' she thought. The city was a haven for disease and vermin. She looked toward the young crier, whom Zyr had focused his attention upon. His voice rang out clearly for all in the vicinity to hear. Some continued on their way ignoring the crier, whether informed or not. Other interested folk gathered round to listen to the news.

"Lend your ears! The season of the governance has turned again. The Red Watch are no longer stewards of the province of Mehnin. All hear! The laws and governance of the province, under the direction of the King - May he live - will be conducted under the High Chancellor with consultations with 'The Blade of Ahtol', who have acquired the One Seat this very week. All hear! The code of civil conduct for Khyvla remains firm with the addition of these terms. A twilight curfew is in effect and will be enforced with great diligence and harsh penalty. Religious gatherings will not be tolerated within the walls of the city. Personal grievances will be dealt with judiciously, with all higher appeals being settled by the High Chancellor. That is all."

Firah glanced at Zyr, who stood as still as a mountain. Dislodging herself from the wall, she walked toward him, slowly circling him until she could peer past the hood and into his face. His expression was peculiar, one she had not seen nor expected from the man. His lips were tight and his eyes narrow, his gaze upon the highest tower. His mouth moved but no words escaped. A great sadness was palpable in his demeanor. Suddenly, his piercing eyes flashed to Firah, who twitched under the shifted gaze. He seemed unaware of all else and seemed to look beyond Firah, but not necessarily through her. After a long moment of silence, he closed his eyes slowly. Upon opening them, his typical expression was back, non-confrontational and unassuming. He nodded to Firah and touched her shoulder gently. She felt a warm sensation flow through her at the touch of his hand.

"I suppose you will be passing up the tour of the city?" He asked quietly. She stared at him puzzled. He was strange, no doubt about it.

"Yes, but never mind that. What was with the serious expression earlier?" She placed a hand on her hip and cocked her head a little. His gaze caught her eyes momentarily, then slipped away. 'What is he thinking?' she wondered.

"We can chat on the way to an inn. We need to secure lodgings before this new curfew sets in …" Zyr shifted his faded cloak and hood and lifted his gaze to the heavens as he finished the thought. "Which should be just outside of an hour or so." He looked down the main street and then a side street. Pausing briefly, he observed the pathway, buildings and alleys, and then motioned her to walk with him down the smaller cobbled thoroughfare. As they walked, Zyr surprised his young charge by commenting on her attire. Firah felt he was making small talk and avoiding the previous subject, until he made an unnerving enquiry.

"That is an interesting brooch. Was it passed onto you?" He looked at her intently, his eyes inquisitive. She had forgotten the jewel but now recalled all the previous events that had brought it to her.

"Oh, it's just something I found. Sometimes you get lucky finding stuff lying around." She chuckled less sincerely that she would have liked.

"I had one just like it, but I lost it not too long ago." He stared down the road as they wove a path through the local people.

"Really? I'm sorry to hear that …" Firah felt a ballista go off in her guts. Could he be the one? No, he couldn't. It would be impossible. Still, she felt the conversation taking a dangerous twist. It was time to divert to other topics. Any topic. "So, I'm curious, what were you and Tohm talking about on the way here?"

Zyr paused, then continued. "We discussed the weather, the land and the people, but generally, we talked about you. His concern for you runs deep, Firah, as I'm sure you know. He is a man of exemplary character with a heart and mind attuned to peace, a quality truly unique among men." Zyr's expression softened. He looked at Firah. "I consider it a blessing to have worked for him."

"Oh yes, work …" Firah trailed off. She was becoming somewhat speechless. The conversation was turning dangerous once again. As a confirmation of her intuition, somewhat uncharacteristically, Zyr continued the conversation.

"Imagine, one moment you are travelling the countryside without a care in the world, and the next you are copper-less. I have never given much thought for trivial things, such as money. My philosophy is that 'it comes and it goes'. However, having no place to stay or no food to eat was difficult, although it's not the first time it's happened. Master Tohm was good enough to let me work for food and pay. Quite an honest man, Tohm, with a heart the size of Llian's Spire."

Firah was now intimately inspecting the local insect life upon the cobbled road. The ants scurried as rapidly as her frenzied mind. Her face was burning, and she tried desperately to hold onto her dignity. He knew. Somehow he knew and he was testing her to see how she would handle the problem. Curse his probing! She couldn't live with herself now, especially after what he did for her and Tohm on the road to Khyvla. She opened her mouth to speak.

Zyr was one step ahead, as usual. "Of course, whoever ended up with all that worthless money would probably be better off with it than me; all it does is gather dust in my purse. It would be better drinking money than not to be spent at all." He laughed softly, and then pointed in the general direction of a shop farther down the street. "Didn't you mention you had clothes to mend? That looks like a reasonable shop."

Firah came to her senses, suddenly dumbfounded at being offered an escape. He had reeled her in like a fish and she still had the proverbial hook embedded in her gaping mouth. Zyr's last words about clothing took hold in her mind. She realized that she had forgotten everything due to yesterday's events as well as this morning. She had left her worn out clothes at the tavern after her argument with Tohm. Certainly, after being tanned at Tohm's hands, clothes were the last thing on her mind. Then she remembered the Thrushtals, the remaining money and small items in her leather vest. She looked up at Zyr, watching him tentatively as she spoke.

"Uh … I decided to get some new cloth and have some clothes made … the old ones are pretty worn … been through a lot of repair … you know how it can be …" She looked at him desperately. At a moment's word he could unveil her whole crime, even have her arrested right here. She was fated to this man whom she barely knew. Justice demanded a punishment and it seemed to be consistent with his disposition to expect nothing less. A sickening feeling swirled in her stomach. Zyr reached over and touched her glistening brooch. He smiled gently in response to her foolish, young and reddening face.

"I'll be down the street a bit, securing our lodgings. Don't be long." He turned and moved down the street with that same methodical pace he carried the previous rainy night in Lenhir. Firah scratched her head and breathed out very slowly. True, he might be odd, but she doubted that she could find a more compassionate soul than this man named Zyr. She turned and trotted off to the seamstress, grinning foolishly and wiping tears all the way.

*   *   *

θ   Ebyn watched the cloaked one disappear into the crowds and the girl just afterward moved toward a shop. Two targets, but which to follow? Lady Nuril wanted the girl; following her would be the obvious first choice. Yet he was feeling subtle energies surrounding the man, which was worth considering. To lose sight of him while trying to capture the girl could lead to complications later. He would follow her companion and determine a location of residence, if any. At that moment he considered whether he should warn his blood-brothers. But share the glory with them? It was too much to bear, to think of being considered on an even field with those simpletons. Ebyn swelled with pride considering his combinations of the most potent dark abilities with powerful Arcane Lore. His assaults left opponents in his wake, sending them to the afterlife. Or to the Underworld. No, he was all the Lady Nuril would need for this task and his reward would be great. His mind caressed the thought: First Consul to the Dark Lord Ahtol. With his dark cloak shifting about his legs, Ebyn stalked slowly after the nearly vanished man and smirked at the thought of great expectations.

*   *   *

ᛏ   Tohm finished pulling the large canvass across his
cart and inspected the spring bars and body loops at the
front of the waggon. Satisfied they were soundly fixed, he
proceeded to rub the ponies down, eased their whickering
and made for the makeshift camp he had erected. Tohm was
no stranger to hardship, many a day he had spent on the
trails of this land. Most of the other merchants had hunkered
down for the night, and he considered that they were as
disappointed as him to be in such close proximity to the now
shut gates. He saw a lantern swinging toward him in the
failing light, and squinting saw another larger man in
traveller's attire approaching.

"Lo' there, good man!" Tohm cheerfully stated as the
man grew close. "How about sharin' a fire with a lonely
soul?" The visitor extended his hand which Tohm took. He
looked to be in his middle years like Tohm, and the wrinkles
around his eyes betrayed many a winter, in merchant's
terms.

"Actually, I was about to offer you the same courtesy.
Some of us are gatherin' up a few waggons ahead. You're
more than welcome to join the group. There'll be singin' and
tale spinning if you don't mind the company?"

"I'll bring the ale." Tohm smiled as he took the man's arm
in the embrace of meeting. Tohm secured his camp and
made for the gathering.

After a few jokes and songs and many drinks later, the group of merchants were becoming fast acquaintances. All were pleasantly surprised at the quality of Tohm's special blend. It had a nice bouquet and, being powerful, was not meant to be consumed in vast quantity as with so many other typical ales. Although Tohm usually charged a significant price for his own special blend (it took many working hours to culture it to perfection), he decided this night he would forgo with business. The group was a merry bunch and recited every song common to all, at considerable volumes. The sun had dipped below the horizon when the group settled down to small talk.

Tohm sat next to another fellow who had been somewhat quiet that night, though had partaken of the hospitality. His face was shrouded by a hood and the growing darkness, which further hindered the inquisitive eye from discerning detail of the man's appearance. He sat upon a barrel with a small cup of Tohm's ale, which was barely touched, the surface of the ale reflecting the flickering fire that burned in the center of the cheery merchant circle. Tohm looked fuzzily at the man and the nearly full cup.

"Whasha matter? You don' like my ale?" Tohm weaved slightly and waited upon a response. The man's head turned, though the fire did not illuminate his face. It was a few moments before the reply came.

"You came with two companions today." The voice was hollow sounding and barely audible. Tohm's mind was addled with brew and his thoughts swam through oceans of molasses trying to connect and form ideas. The voice had a palpable soothing effect upon his senses. His already sodden brain began to slow its synaptic processes.

"Yeah ... I did." Tohm's arms and legs felt heavy and his mind slowly turned the conversation around in his head. Somewhere, deep within the recluses of his conscious a voice was screaming. "You fool! Be careful! Where's your sense?" Tohm's eyelids slid downward across his now bloodshot eyes. It took every effort to lift them again. Another unseen whisper melted away his defences.

"What were their names again?" The cowled head was now focused upon Tohm. His head was sagging and burdened by an unseen weight. Tohm looked into the darkness within the hood with pleasant interest. He was unsure why he had sat down, and overly perplexed as to where he was. The hidden face in the dark consumed his whole mind and body. He felt peculiar, as if caught in the clutches of a sensual, comforting beast and having no desire to escape. Slowly, his mouth formed words as the screaming voice diminished into whispers and shadows.

θ   "Fira' ... and Zyr." Gaeth stood slowly upon hearing the names and paused in front of his incapacitated prey. He felt he should end this miserable speck's existence, and normally would; however, there was a specific charge to avoid suspicion at this critical phase of the plan. More importantly, this news merited haste. *Zyr*. Lady Nuril must be informed without fail. For, it seemed that the 'prize' had arrived at last, but with an unexpected and dangerous companion.

'Pity to have to leave him alive' he thought as he passed his hand over Tohm's now glazed-over expression. Tohm's eyes closed slowly. Would he leave a small present with the man, a 'possible future' which was in store for his precious charge? Why not aggravate the conscience? That was a far more effective and demoralizing punishment. Yes, that was worse than death in many ways. Gaeth smiled within himself. As Cerephor, his ability to manipulate the mind combined with significant advances in Nexism would make him a fit First Consul. Nuril would reward him greatly for this information. Gaeth placed a hand upon the brow of the entrapped simpleton. Just a small delay would be sufficient, and then the nightmare would begin. Gaeth's body pulsed as he transferred a small portion of energy from the Root within the land. It twisted and convulsed under his masterful control, shifting into a horrific scene that burrowed itself in Tohm's memory. Then the Ashori whisked away into the dark, unseen by the merry drunkards. His body moved smoothly through the night, and slipped through a small enclosure in the stone wall, which sealed itself anew without a sound.

🜊   "Nooooo!" A distorted scream broke the night air
replete with agony and utter despair. "Firah!" Tohm lurched
to his feet and being inebriated promptly fell over into the
fire and searing coals. The agonizing heat of his demented
mind far outweighed the physical pain of scorching flesh. At
first, he sluggishly tried to regain his footing out of instinct,
but failed. Finally, he rolled from the fire and extinguished
his clothing. Tohm's entire right side was sore and blistered
from severe burns. His mind was completely aware now,
sharpened by the horrific scene in his memory. Tohm
sprinted from the campsite, knocking over gaping
merchants who witnessed the peculiar scene. He charged to
the city wall and rammed his fist on the rigid wood beams of
the gate. "Firah!" Tohm's voice was harsh now from
damaged vocal cords, which were pushed to their limit. He
slammed his large knotted fist into the gate again and again.
Tohm kept calling out her name, knowing that there would
be no answer. She was inside, the subject and sacrifice of the
darkest ritual the Defiler filth could invent. His hand was
bleeding profusely and his body ached painfully from the
intense burns. Tohm seemed disconnected from the pain
while his mind could not escape the scene in which it was
entrapped. It kept playing over and over, as real as any
memory. Whenever the dagger in his mind would fall upon
her, his hand would smite the wall vibrating the cool,
unforgiving beams. Guards atop the wall looked down and
jeered at Tohm in disgust.

Those within the city, who listened intently, heard the most peculiar sound but could not pinpoint it. The noise which sounded like soft distant thumps or taps carried on into the night.

8   *Nature had been kind to the Sapling; it had grown unhindered, soaking in the sunshine and rain. Now, an unforeseen shadow was cast across the Sapling's path. Blocking Nature's sweet nourishment, it threatened to choke out the life of the tender plant …*

DRAWING THE GLYPH AND DAGGER

TAMERS CRAWL provided the means for all travel and connections in Southern Kenhar society. It was first born from the chilling heights of Llian's Spire. From thence, coalescing from the vast ranges of Tamers Reach, the mighty Tamers Crawl meandered ever westward to the shores of the sea. Though wide and deep, its flows were calm and trustworthy. It was upon this great river that all traffic passed continuously through the land. The talk and trends swirled about the nobility, who were centered in the great capital city of Syrion. The Royal city's walls were last to touch the river before it emptied into the sea. From those great ageless towers rumours would endlessly flow, nearly as swift as the Crawl, coursing back upstream through the provincial lands.

Khyvla was positioned conveniently along the banks of the Crawl as it passed through Mehnin Province. Local businesses made great lucre servicing the nobles and social 'acrobats' seeking to climb ever higher toward glory and fame. One such establishment was the Gilded Scabbard, which took pride in its noble patronage. For most of the public house residents, any news was welcome to reignite forgotten and faded rumours. For some, it was the opportunity to discredit a rival while spreading their own accolades. Naturally, this all required a certain degree a tact and timing. The Scabbard was such a place; far enough away from the royal hub to be free of recourse but fertile enough to plant the seeds of lies and sedition. Certain information, in skilled hands was as valuable as any finely crafted weapon or royal treasure.

✖   Shien was the newest resident at the Scabbard this fortuitous week. The paths of fate were converging and, at any time, fortune would shine upon him … after so long.

The entrance admitted a pristine woman, who glanced around the room, her eyes brushing over Shien. After whispering something to the owner (who waited upon her), she proceeded into a private room adjoining the busy common area. Shien took a moment to survey the small crowd growing from the arrival of the last transport. The vessel was requisitioned by the Blade of Ahtol and as such it was prestigious to book passage along with the new cadre. It was past dusk and more and more pompous, snobbish looking patrons entered and began to mingle and acquire lodgings. The river transport was a charter direct from Syrion which was a haven for the stuffed up, high-born folk. Shien listened in disgust to their mindless prattle. The people were so transparent to him. He slowly rose to his feet and straightened his own fine silk outfit. It had cost him significant wages and he was hard pressed to "throw away" his money on things that served no tactile purpose. 'Well' he thought 'at least it helps me pass as one of these idiots.' Shien slowly but gracefully wove through the crowd into the private room occupied by the woman.

Upon stepping to the threshold, he observed the woman. She was sitting quietly and staring lazily out the window. Her demeanor was somewhat haughty, but Shien figured that was probably an act. He could sense that beneath her attractive allure was a quiet fear, kept well hidden. He never wondered why he had such impressions, only that he was always right. That was why he had come to her. She was an easy target.

"Excuse me, my Lady ... the room is becoming quite full and I don't do well in crowds. May I impose upon your hospitality?" Shien played a sincere smile as he addressed her. He knew that he was regarded as handsome to the opposite sex. He toyed with the emotions of women, finding them opaque and easily manipulated. Men were harder to figure at times because they seemed to be more calculating and logical, while woman tended to think with their emotions. He sensed trepidation mixed with amounts of interest. Good.

"I was waiting for the rest of my companions ... they will be here shortly. You may share the room until then if you wish." Her tone was guarded and sent an obvious message that any potential assailant would not miss. He took the bench seat across from the regal woman and bowed his head to her.

"You have my gratitude. I find crowds to be uncomfortable and stuffy." He chuckled within himself; that part was completely true. He looked into her eyes which quivered slightly as she caught his gaze. Her feelings were shifting to curiosity. "I was wondering how you felt about the ride today down the channel. I can't abide the swaying motions. Even now the very thought of it ..." Shien gripped the table and put a hand to his mouth. The woman looked alarmed and her soul exuded concern.

"Are you quite alright?" She put a hand on his wrist. Her gloved hand squeezed his arm gently. 'Perfect' he thought. Now he had to choose his words very carefully.

"I would be fine under normal circumstances … except that I was removed from my quarters upon departure due to the safekeeping of some *special cargo*. I would like to know what was so important to cause me so many days of discomfort in their *common* rooms. I doubt any of my friends knew of my presence on the boat, being overcome with boating sickness." Shien sniffed and dabbed his nose with a kerchief. The woman's eyes flashed while he read a mix of excitement and uneasiness. She glanced around the room and then leaned forward and spoke quietly, her grip tightened.

"We were forbidden to even speak about it." She lowered her voice even further, "however, I could *suggest* what it might be. The cargo is supposed to be for the new cadre, you know … The Blade of Ahtol. I haven't seen what it is; however, the talk is describing the goods as enchanted trinkets or even weapons. I also heard that they have something that will control the will of all the citizens here," she quickly gestured towards the city outside. Shien mocked a look of horror and surprise. His entrusting confider drank it in.

"Surely there could be nothing that could bind the mind and will of those of us here," Shien indicated to the patrons of the Gilded Scabbard. "However, perhaps the mindless rabble could be affected …" Shien trailed off with a whimsical look and he gazed out into the darkening night.

"Yes, perhaps." Her hand gently moved along his arm. He looked from the hand to her longing face. Her emotions were shifting to the slightly hot variety. She stared at him intently and spoke again in almost the same whisper as before. "How comforting it is to be able to rely upon others … for strength." Her hand caressed farther up his arm. Shien was amused slightly. Her elegant beauty would be an intriguing prospect at another time. On this night, however, his mind was set upon one purpose and he would not rest till it was accomplished.

"It is well then that your companions are expected shortly. Here I have delayed you with such impertinence. Forgive the intrusion; I should take my leave of you," Shien stood and bowed low to the woman, who was visibly put out. He moved toward the door.

"Wait … my friends aren't …" Shien slipped from the room as her voice trailed off, "coming at all." She stared longingly at the seat he had occupied with a simpering scowl. Sighing, she looked back out the window and fanned her now flushed face.

Shien stalked through the shadowed streets, after taking a moment to change his garb. The goal was in sight. After all his endless searches and an eternity of waiting, it had come full circle. Now what was taken would be reclaimed - The Spirit of Vyn-shi: Isil and Kiros.

*   *   *

🌱   The material was perfect. Her night gown would be deep cobalt - the silk shone in the lamplight with a sensuous luster. Somehow Firah did not feel guilty choosing the finest material. Zyr had helped her feel at ease with the uncomfortable situation she had landed herself in. He was so kind to her, and that was the strangest thing of all. This world seemed so cold and cruel at times. Everyone looked to themselves (except for Tohm of course) and hardly gave a thought to the suffering of others. There were dangerous folk about too, and one could not rely upon the mercies of bystanders in the advent of being assaulted. Aeredia was a different world than the one recited in worn-out old songs. Somehow, it had changed in a short period of time. Firah felt the change even amongst the country folk of Lenhir. The change scared her.

She came to from her musings and folded the material over her arm. The tailor of the shop who waited upon Firah, kept a close eye upon the girl. That annoyed her, but Firah realized that she was young and others would hardly expect her to procure coin enough to purchase such luxurious material. She lifted her head slightly in an aloof way as she approached the shopkeeper.

"I will take this material; please take the measurements now so I can collect the garment in the morning." The woman regarded her with an air of mistrust. Angrily, Firah withdrew her purse and jingled it sharply in the face of the startled woman. "What does this sound like?! I'm paying here or somewhere else!" The woman snapped into action, either by the sound of gold or the rebuke. Either way, Firah smiled broadly as her every care was attended to with the utmost speed. Money was useful in many ways.

A yawn escaped Firah's mouth before she could catch it with the back of her hand. It was getting late now and the shops were all closed. In the distance she heard a crier announce that the city-wide curfew would begin shortly. She shifted her shirt about her shoulders and subconsciously touched the glistening brooch pinned to it. She was having her leather vest mended and was having a couple shirts tailored in addition to her night gown. All would be prepared for the morning.

It was odd not wearing her vest, and she almost felt naked without it. She still wore her brown breeches and sturdy knee-high boots. Yet, her mind could not ignore that her body was certainly more pronounced in the shirt. Considering her attire, she wasn't sure how she felt about hinting what nature had blessed her with, but under the circumstances, she had little choice. The vest had conveniently held everything in place, which was ideal for vigorous activity. The items and money were now secured to her belt within a well-built pouch. She tightened the cloth cinch that corralled her long curling brown hair and sighed. The day was over, and for once she had actually enjoyed the city; well, the shopping anyway. Then she remembered that

Zyr was waiting for her. She moved deftly along the cobbled stones towards the inn Zyr had indicated to her. The soles of her boots tapped softly upon the stone as she ran.

⊥ It was night and still no Firah. Zyr wouldn't have minded but for the fact that he was uneasy. The feeling had come the moment he spied those cursed daggers upon the cadre banners. Somehow he had to know if she was here. It pained his heart to think about it. His mind could not focus with his thoughts dwelling in the troublesome past. The silent monk pondered whether bringing the girl to the city was wise, considering the imminent danger. Khyvla had its guards, but the Defilers were really the power in the city. He was sure that the curfew was imposed by them so they could maneuver about in the night, going about their evil works. He spat upon the ground in vain to remove the images of past experience. If she was here … Zyr closed his eyes sharply and his left hand gripped his right which was clenched tightly. He raised the fist into his field of vision. Slowly, the hand uncurled into an open-handed gesture. If it came down to it, would he have the strength for vengeance?

He stared out into the street from his perch upon the steps of the inn. In the faint distance, he detected the sound of footfall upon stone. Reaching out with his will, he detected her presence. The curfew was good in that way. It was dangerous running about alone, yet he had taken steps to keep her reasonably safe. He hoped that if the need arose she would find shelter in the attunement of the stone. As she rounded the far corner of the street, his sense of danger intensified. He glanced about the street surreptitiously, examining the shops and houses. Nothing. She slowed as she approached and gave Zyr a guilty look and mouthed 'sorry' as she came toward him. He partially regarded her and continued his survey of the street. There was a definite increase of power in the area. Zyr wasn't sure what caused the change, but it was certain. Followers of any path possessed the Sense, and experienced the sensation in different ways; for some it was like ripples in a still pond, others interpreted it as waves of wind or heat that washed over the mysterious Sense. The stronger the power drawn forth, the hotter the feeling burned in anticipation and warning. Currently, Zyr's mind was on fire. He saw Firah's mouth moving, but he heard nothing. All of his senses were stretched out and desperately trying to locate the source of power which was building steadily. Most weavings would have stopped building by now; clearly the unseen enemy was connecting potent reserves.

❀ "Are you listening to me?" Firah half yelled at the quiet man. He seemed as if in a trance. The creepiest aspect was in his eyes, which were obsidian black; the pupils had dilated so far as to remove all trace of blue. His head never moved and his body was still. She would have guessed Zyr wasn't breathing except for his eyes pulsing ever so slightly at odd intervals. She gave up and just watched the strange behavior. Something tickled the back of her mind, a feeling of alarm, but she ignored it.

Suddenly Zyr took hold of her arm firmly and pulled her into motion. "We have to move. Hurry, Firah!" Before she could say anything she was being pulled along in a near dead run. She could see they were heading for the city gates. Shadows seemed to appear in the darkness under the gate archway. Zyr turned their course down a side alley and Firah fought desperately to keep the rigorous pace. Her mind was full of fear as she coursed through the labyrinth of stone and wood. Their unseen foe seemed to be closing in through some elaborate web, and she wondered if there was a way out. In the commotion she had not noticed that Zyr had opened her belt pouch and hastily removed the small white stone. He pressed it firmly into her palm.

Suddenly, something caught her attention in the corner of her eye. A glowing spike of red heat and ash flew swiftly toward them. The form resembled a fiery lash which hissed through the wind like some strange serpent of flame.

"Firah! Don't let go of the stone!" Zyr shouted and pulled his cloak around him while falling to the ground and sheltering his face. Firah had less than a moment to react. As the flying mass of heat snapped about them, she clamped her fingers hard around the stone. The wave of fire struck them and exploded into a cascade of flame and sparks. Her eyes closed instantly from the brightness and impending blaze which threatened to consume her. She waited what seemed many moments before she dared open them again.

The whole area around them was scorched black, except for a small circle of untouched stone at her feet. As she examined herself, she found she was unharmed. Zyr's cloak lay upon the cobblestone burning in flames. She shrieked suddenly in fear that he was consumed by the lash of fire, but then saw him sprinting at full speed down the courtyard. "Find the Watch!" he cried out as he ran into the distance.

✚ Zyr had braced himself for the stinging heat which overwhelmed him. It had been painful but he could mend that later. In an instant, he had rolled out of his cloak and was sprinting towards the source of the attack. The order to Firah served two purposes. Mainly, he wanted her away from the area, where dangerous weaves could fly unchecked. Also, he wanted her under the care of capable guardians, which the Watch were. He could consider no other options as they were quite alone in the city. He was up against a powerful and calculating foe, more dangerous than most physical combatants. Tonight, it would be a contest of wits and weaving. Zyr had no connection to the elemental paths of the Root but he had studied many long hours into the nuances of those disciplines. Hand gestures, glyphs and some verbalization all sufficed to enhance an Ashori's attunement and focus. It was a boon to have an attuned stone to counter Ashori weaving; however the protective item lay now with Firah. He would have to make due with

Alacritor counter-weaves to avoid damage from offensive strikes.

As the healer rounded the corner of a house, a writhing ball of fiery threads exploded upon the wall beside him and sprayed flames throughout the area. Zyr winced as his skin scorched and trembled under the heat. His opponent was just up the alleyway and likely elevated to gain the advantage of sight; probably three floors or more up. Just then, Zyr caught movement in a stained window above him. It was the Ignitor and he was weaving another attack. Zyr noted the movement of the hands. "No! Don't do that here!" he shouted out in desperation to his enemy. His mind was a blur of thought. He had but moments now to weave a counter, before the whole area would erupt in a conflagration of flames. People would die if his skill was found lacking.

Zyr relaxed his body and began to draw a large circle in the air. Traces of blue energy lingered from his fingertips and remaining suspended where his hand passed. He could not miss a step. Carefully and deftly he traced the counter-glyphs for the weave of fire. The monk's mind raced through memories of his past studies as he worked feverishly. The blue patterns glowed in the air surrounding the pulsing circle as Zyr painted them. In the last moment, he felt the massive surge of power from above. In a blur, he embedded his fingers into the center of the protective glyph and, wielding it as a shield, slammed it forcibly upon the ground at his feet.

The air around him exploded into a consuming inferno which coursed through the alley and street. For a moment it licked hungrily at the motionless kneeling monk. Then the circle's pulsing blue energy began to overwhelm and consume the flames. Zyr could see the patterns within his threads of power twisting and snaring his opponents work, choking the flames. The effect spread rapidly through the area, waves of Alacritor power rippling outward from the circle. As quickly as the inferno began it was ended, all the collective energy being drawn into a vortex at the center of the circle which glowed white hot under the strain. The ground rumbled in protest as the energy was released into the land. Slowly, the glyphs and lines faded away.

Zyr summoned energy through his arms and into his hands, while simultaneously triggering his adrenaline. With great exertion, he leapt high onto the wall of the building, just below the attacker's window. His strengthened hands crunched into the sheer surface, supporting his precarious perch. With one movement, he released one hand and twisted his body around, re-anchoring the hand, his back now pressed against the wall. Finally, he thrust his legs upwards over his head, while pushing off the wall with a shout. Zyr's body arched toward the window. His legs crashed through, shattering glass and splintering wood. The healer rolled into a crouch and spied his enemy fleeing through the bedroom door. As Zyr sprang into pursuit, he passed the occupants' lifeless forms upon the bed, twisted and charred. Zyr vowed that such an unmerciful demon-sworn could not be allowed to live.

*   *   *

Firah's breath was coming hard as she sprinted with all her strength down the main street. She wished she knew the city better; it was impossible to tell where she was going or where she came from. Every alley, every home began to look the same. Finally, Firah lurched to a halt and collapsed against a shop wall, sucking deep racked breaths. She was frightened and looked around desperately for the city Watch. The problem was she had no clue where they were. In the distance, she saw flashes of light which sketched strange dancing shadows upon the near walls. 'It must be Zyr' she thought. She uttered a silent prayer for his safety. Meanwhile she looked around hopelessly. He was counting on her! She kicked down hard against the wall behind her and then grimaced in pain. 'Standing here is accomplishing nothing' she chided. The best bet would be to keep going the same way and pray she would bump into someone, anyone who could help. Setting herself, she ran into the darkness at a quick pace.

*   *   *

⚔   Shien cast his gaze upon the strong box before him. He kicked the lifeless form of the guard over to access more room. The struggle had been quick but tricky. Suffocation proved the best tactic as it prevented cries for help from his opponent. The guard was strong and the cramped, confining quarters on the lower decks of the transport barge did not help. The barge gently swayed and rocked as he carefully examined the box. Traps were notoriously unhealthy for the unwary. Methodically, he examined the container which rested upon the floor of the cabin. It was about five feet in length by a couple feet in depth and breadth. The light of one candle was limited, so he was doing most of his searching by feel and experience. He moved his hands slowly along the edges of the chest. 'There, got it' he thought as he heard the click of a spring being released. He slid a slender needle out of a small narrow compartment along the box's frame. His hands were gloved for good reason: the poisoned surface glistened in the low light. He pressed the small weapon into the leg of the motionless guard. Best to get rid of it now than risk having someone else die accidentally; besides it wasn't going to hurt the guard. Only one thing remained, something Shien had accounted for but had no skill in disarming. The chest belonged to a cadre comprised almost wholly of weavers of every sort. Odds were good that another surprise awaited him. He looked back to his improvised stick-pin cushion.

"Hmmm," he mused quietly, "I may need your help once more, my stalwart friend." Dragging the stiffening body upward, he glanced into the pale face. "You don't mind do you?" he asked as he patted the pallid cheek. Shien draped the body over the strong box and extended a collapsible metal rod he had brought. Everything was going smoothly and according to plan. He flicked the tip of the rod at the latch. A bright flash of light illuminated the cabin and the body flew off the chest and tumbled to floor, visibly damaged by some sort of charge. "Well," Shien chuckled softly, "that's it - Ashori are fairly predictable." He raised the lid of the strong box and gazed silently upon the contents. Without a word he scooped up two long and slender shapes which were wrapped in ornate cloth. He bowed his head and touched the cloth to his brow, whispering a silent oath. Never again would the honour of his family be violated. Never would these ancestral symbols of power come into unworthy hands. Shien raised his head and paused in thought of past memory. No one would ever understand the cost of these two swords, what blood had been exacted from his family. Now, the spirits of his fathers could find peace. "Be at rest."

After finishing the oath, Shien made to leave. But something else within the box caught his eye. He did not regard himself as a thief since what he had acquired tonight was stolen long ago. Still, curiosity overwhelmed him and he glanced further into the depths of the container. A simple dagger lay sheathed within a rather plain scabbard.

Seemingly worthless, Shien doubted it would fetch a silver in the market. Likewise, it would not be missed either. He needed a dagger as his last was gambled away in attempt to pay for those blasted silks. Slowly, his hand grasped the blade.

A sudden surge of pain shot through his body. Shien reacted by dropping the heirlooms and dagger and stood up sharply, where his head connected soundly with a support beam along the cabin ceiling. Wincing in pain, he stumbled over the dead guard and crashed into a desk and chair in the corner, further smiting his head against the wall. "Curses!" he swore aloud as his head and hand reeled in pain.

"Someone's below!" The voice penetrated the foggy chasms of Shien's mind. Scrambling to his feet in a dazed panic, the young man stumbled over to the items upon the floor. Shien quickly removed his large pack and tossed everything within. Strapping the pack behind him and around his shoulders, he heard voices being raised in alarm. 'So much for stealth' he thought to himself. 'Idiot.' Shien had chosen to come as lightly equipped as possible to avoid detection; however, he now had a serious problem. He glanced to his fallen enemy and spotted a metallic glimmer of hope. Stooping, he picked up the guard's discarded broadsword. Quickly he tested the weight; it was somewhat decent and fairly well balanced. Footfall was thumping closer from the main deck. He steeled his nerves for what lay ahead. It was going to be a fight for survival tonight but Shien remembered his silent oath. He would not fail them now. "I'll prove my honour," he spoke to the blackness, to his forefathers. Taking a deep breath, he burst from the room into the waiting dark.

*   *   *

ϴ   The huddled forms melded into the blackness of the night. The 'prize' was near and moving swiftly. They retained one advantage which allowed them to keep her within reach and still remain in shadow: Namely that her movements were erratic and for every three steps forward, she retraced two. They had the advantage of knowing the city and all the detours and passages. The girl was lost and calling out for help periodically. They would ensure that no help reached her, and when the opportunity was ripe, the Defilers would spring their trap upon the little mouse. Returning her to Nuril would please the mistress greatly. The final ritual of Mehnin would seal off this part of Kenhar against the holy orders and their meddling. Slowly the shadows melted in and out of the streets toward the fleeing and fragile leaf. It was so close now ...

*   *   *

The broadsword whistled through the air as if in a dance. Shien dipped and weaved, stepping around the mast and hanging ropes. Anytime an enemy sought to gain an upper hand he would move to a better position. In vain they struggled to surround him, which resulted in them being hewn down, tripped or catching some object full in the face. The frustration was beginning to show upon the guards of the boat. A rather large man with long straggled hair charged him like a boar. Shien launched himself over the ox, curling his body. At the last moment he stretched his right leg out behind him, adding momentum to the already lunging lummox. Head and body crashed into the cabin entrance and fellow guards alike. No one moved from the twisted pile of wood and limbs. Shien had used the same leg to spring off the large man's shoulder, onto the netted rope which ascended the primary mast. He climbed swiftly to the sail's cross-beam and released the enormous sail with a few hacks from the sword. All below cursed as the large sheet of sturdy material settled over them and made movement next to impossible. Shien wrapped a foot around an anchoring rope which led to the prow. His gloved hands grew warm as he slid rapidly in descent. As he landed upon the deck he looked to his struggling opponents and felt grateful; he did not have to kill many tonight.

Shien stepped from the prow onto the gangway and peered into the darkness past the admitting gatehouse. The sounds of muffled struggling from the ship played upon his ears, but all was quiet past that. He stepped gingerly, sliding along the wall of the gatehouse, straining his ears. Only a fool would assume the danger had ceased. As he cricked his neck around the corner of the building, he jerked it back suddenly.

A large bolt of wood impacted into the wall where his head had been. He took off down River Street in a near sprint. He couldn't run full out, as he carried a sharp blade and tripping could be hazardous. Also, he would need strength when the Watch cornered him. They knew this city like no other and would exploit the unwary, slowly closing in the gauntlet. He occasionally altered his course to discourage any other trigger-happy soldier. He would not underestimate these men. They were leagues ahead of those imbeciles on the boat as far as training and skill. Deadly accurate and swift of blade would describe their creed. He had tangled with other Watch in other cities; however Khyvla seemed to take pride in the rigorous training of their marshals.

Shien dodged toward a house and paused, briefly listening above his steady breathing. His sword arm slumped and rested his weapon upon the cobbled stones. Sweat trickled down his cheek; still, he was far from exhausted. The cold sweat, chilled from the night air, seemed to accentuate his thoughts. Shien wasn't sure he could win against these men. He listened as they called out their signals to each other. It was ingenious; the language resembled sounds of animals or birds in flight. Shien had heard enough to know the intent. He pulled the straps of his leather pack firm and felt the objects shift upon his back. He closed his eyes and lifted his head toward the starlit sky. Breathing deeply, he crouched slightly in preparation to run again. 'May the blessings of Aerluin be with me' he thought. He paused momentarily. 'That was weird' … he had never prayed before. His body snapped into a swift step around the house wall.

"Aaaaaaah!" a high pitched scream was all he heard before something smashed into the side of his head. Shien was brought to the ground in a heap. Between the flashes in his brain he could detect that something lay across him, but in the dark he could not make out anything. His head felt like it would split in two, from all the abuse upon it that night. He shook it to clear the fuzziness. Then his senses returned.

"Damn it! Can't anything go right?" Shien shouted as he shoved the smaller form off his torso. He leapt to his feet and glanced around. It was all shadow here on this street, but his eyes were slowly adjusting. He detected movement on the ground. He raised the broadsword and made to strike.

"Owwww." The person moaned in pain. Shien's sense awakened as he realized it was a young girl who had collided with him. She slowly stood up, holding her head. Both of their skulls had connected and Shien instinctively touched the thumping area by his temple. Blood came away with his hand.

"Get out of here, girl!" he whispered sharply to her. Well, his position was a dead giveaway now. A ten-toed bird chirped nearby and Shien cursed again. He started to lope down the alley that she had run down. If he could make the merchant court, maybe ...

"Wait!" she yelled after him, "I need your help ... I ... look out!" Shien narrowly dodged a dagger which slashed out of the shadows at him, but it tore at his thick vest. His arm moved in a fluid motion and struck deep and hard into the shadow.

"Urk ...gha ..." A voice grunted as the shadow tumbled to the ground at his feet. Shien looked closer as the black cloak of the assailant spilled open. The clothes revealed dark red embroidering upon black cloth. His mind worked fast and suddenly his jaw dropped as a thought crashed upon him.

"No! You're not dead! Get up!" He grasped the arm of the motionless form and heaved. "No, no, no ... why did you attack me, you fool?" He threw the body which collapsed as a rag doll upon the ground, the life completely gone from it.

"What's wrong?" the girl's voice spoke beside him. Shien ran a trembling hand through his damp hair. His hand came away slightly red but he wasn't focusing on that anymore. He stared at the body upon the ground, his head shaking slightly in denial.

✴ His words washed over Firah like a tempest. "What's wrong? That's a blasted Defiler from their cursed cadre! I've killed one of their own! They are going to find me and exact a penalty in blood! They are going to suck out my soul and feed it to their bloody demon! I'll be worse than him!" He was now shouting at her. Her green eyes flicked on every accentuated word in his tirade. However, her mind was still reeling from his mention of the demon. Her thoughts raced back to her horrific nightmares. He knew about that? That black terror which haunted her mind?

✕ Shien was getting anxious and regarded the girl. She was going to get him killed. He pressed his finger against her forehead and prodded her firmly. "Bother someone else, girl. I'm leaving." As he turned, she pushed her foot firmly into the small of his back which sent him tumbling to the ground.

"Thanks for your help," she cooed. Her face was set in a smug grin.

Shien growled as he shot back up. He didn't need intuition in empathy to divine what she was thinking at that moment. Utter contempt and frustration was seething from her every pore. Her pathetic display of effrontery ate at him. The nerve of the girl! The feelings of pure disdain were mutual now. He strode over to her and gripped a fistful of her shirt, drawing the young girl up to his face. "You little brat!" Her eyes narrowed just as a slight snort mocked his actions.

"You think I'm scared of you ..."

"Hold there!" The voice caught both of them off guard. Then Shien realized that the command was not meant for him. He heard muttering of voices in the street outside their alley. He released the girl and moved his body tight against the wall until he was able to peer around the corner into the dark street. Several members of the Watch had stopped more cloaked cadremen. They were engaged in a heated discussion. Apparently, the cloaked ones took offense at being accosted, and the Watch were enforcing the very curfew the Blade of Ahtol had imposed! The irony was too rich, but Shien knew better than to stick around. It was his window of opportunity. He sprang into a run, back up the alley past the annoying waif. His mind focused 'Forget it. She means nothing'.

🌱   Firah watched him leave and considered herself lucky to be rid of the Gnarel-bred oaf, but the dream question poked at her mind. The Watch was close now, and Zyr needed help, but somehow all she could think about was getting answers to her dreams. This man knew something of it and her whole soul hungered for information, anything to help her solve the puzzle. There was something else too - a tugging at her heart to follow the young man. The feeling seemed to wind itself around her completely in comforting reassurance. Though her logical mind protested with Zyr's desperate plight, she reluctantly sprinted after the brash man. Although he had a head start, she was able to catch him moving down an adjoining street. She was chasing the trailing threads of fate.

✕ Shien saw her moving behind him quickly. He groaned within himself and rounded behind a small wooden shed. There was an open entrance on one side which he sidled into. Crouching low, he saw the girl stop and look about, visibly frustrated. He chuckled and decided to wait till she was gone. Deep within, he felt a pang of guilt which stirred like stone in his belly. He drove away the feeling and continued to survey the street.

*　　*　　*

θ "You have no business outside past curfew!" The captain of the Watch roared at the seething man before him. The cloaked persons were lined up before the six Watchmen, and all appeared quite put out.

"You meddling fools, make way in the name of Lady Nuril!" the one screamed back into his face. The argument had raged on and all tempers were flaring. The headman had been through countless of these encounters with cadre upstarts thinking they were above the law. Finally, they were going to receive justice at the hands of true public servants. He thought the curfew was a ridiculous notion and every Watchman now worked longer hours to enforce the new code.

"You're in violation of curfew, and believe me, Nuril will hear of it." He made to apprehend the man before him and his companions followed suit. The group of shrouded men withdrew several paces and flourished their hands. The captain smiled. "If that is your choice, I'll accommodate you," he spoke slowly while unsheathing his short sword. The sound of sliding metal from his squad echoed in his ears. The criminals were saying something and faintly he could make out movement of their dark cloaks. Suddenly, fear came over him. In his mind it never occurred to him that they would go this far. "Defilers! Stop them, quickly!" he shouted out desperately.

"Thank you for assisting us, gentleman," the dark figure spoke acidly. As the Watchmen rushed toward the shadowy figures, they screamed out in agony, falling to their knees. They felt their life essence slowly draining away, which seemed to flow as wispy trails of red towards the enemies' now elevated hands. The captain struggled to regain his feet and wearily slogged toward the lead Defiler. The others screamed and writhed as the glowing trails of essence were being pulled from their bodies to the fingertips of the dark Ashori. The captain growled loudly, willing his body to move a little more. He slowly raised his sword up and made to strike down the closest fiend with all the strength he had left. Suddenly, he felt a hand over his face and a searing pain coursed through his head. He dropped his sword as he collapsed, twitching in agony. His last thought was to look to his foe, who knelt down beside the immobilized fighter.

The captain's expression filled with horror as whispered words entered his ears.

"Your bodies will do nicely."

*   *   *

‡   Zyr leapt down five stairs at a time, almost overtaking his enemy. His mind was as hot as the attacks which had been flung against him. His only concern was to end the threat that this man posed to Firah and all the people in Khyvla. He was a Defiler, and Zyr had sworn to fight against their kind until his days were ended. They violated all which was pure through their demonic rituals for the selfish pursuit of damning evil power. He rounded the last stair and stopped abruptly. His enemy was vainly working at a locked door to the street. He stopped and whirled around, his face full of anger and frustration. Zyr stepped slowly into the room moving in a circle around a table in the center of the room. His enemy hopelessly mirrored him, trying in vain to keep the monk from engaging in close combat.

Zyr stopped and regarded the scowling man. Likely, the Ignitor's strength was somewhat depleted, especially after such aggressive weavings. Zyr knew he could make the end quick, which was the most merciful way according to his creed. However, something was bothering him, which ate at him since he entered the city. It was the burning question which would cause him to abandon even the most sacred charge from Mother herself. It was a matter of honour; yet that sympathy was merely the rippling surface of the deep recesses of his soul. He had come to see her. He had to know, even if it meant risking everything. His conscience chided him to the last - it was a foolhardy and selfish gesture. Yet it was the only choice. Firah's safety pricked at his conscience in a battle with past feelings. He assured himself that she was capable of reaching the Watch. With that assurance he sprung the trap.

He quickly prepared a pulse of detective energy and delved outward; his intuition was right. Another waited outside in ambush, as he detected the faint tell-tale imprint of an Ashori. He would never be able to gain access to the tower of Ahtol through force; its defence was too formidable. There was only one way in. He picked up a chair and brandished it at his opponent. He moved so as to position his foe next to the entrance. Zyr sent the chair flying toward the door, but it appeared to his wary foe as a near miss. The door crumpled under the force of the blow, exposing the street. Zyr cursed out loud in a convincing volume.

Not missing a beat, his enemy flung himself through the opening. Zyr paused and prepared himself for what fate held in store and burst out of the door, roaring some senseless war-cry he heard used by Tey'ur long ago. His plan had worked. He felt a sudden unseen weight come over his whole body. He felt as if he barely had energy to move his feet. 'So it's a Cerephor' Zyr thought. It was a simple illusion and could be countered with some degree of effort, but he let himself bend under the weight of the illusion. Next, he felt hot bands of fire encircle his arms and torso. The heat seared his arms and body, while the unseen burden forced him to his knees. Good, they were not going to kill him. However, he could not give up easily; that would spoil his ruse. As he struggled to rise, he saw in his peripheral vision a glint of metal rise above him. 'The moment has come' he thought. His hand lay open, 'Will I have the strength to do it?' The handle of a dagger connected with the base of his skull. A whisper escaped his lips as blackness stole his conscious thought.

"Tehsa."

* * *

Firah searched in vain throughout the street. The uncouth Reykal had actually got away from her. She let out a scream of frustration from behind clenched teeth. Why were men like that? Why was the whole world full of those bone-brained idiots? She knew that she could not find him in the thick darkness. Sighing, she realized that she better try to locate the Watch again and get back to Zyr. She had spent too much time on her own foolish whims, and she wondered how her friend was faring. Zyr was quite resilient and she felt he could hold on until she got help.

As she paced down the street she noticed some forms moving toward her slowly. In the dark she could not make them out at all. They made little sound in their advance. 'At this time of night, it must be the Watch' she thought. Elated, she moved toward them and raised her hand.

"Hello! I need help! A friend of mine is being attacked! Please help me!"

As she drew closer, she could make out armoured torsos and the movement of swords upon their belts. Their lack of sound was unnerving; they continued to move in a slow and steady pace toward her. Firah strained her eyes and looked at the closest figure advancing close to her. Slowly, her eyes opened wide. The man's face appeared to be melting or rotting, and she could see portions of his skull beneath the putrid skin. The sight was such a fright to her that she hesitated to move. In a quick movement, the disfigured man thrust out a cold fleshy hand which grasped her throat. Desperately, Firah struggled against the chilling fingers, twisting and clawing, but the hand held firm. His expression (what could be read in his ghastly face) revealed no emotion or evidence of care as she grasped at the horrid fingers. She felt her breath fail as the grip collapsed her windpipe. Grunting and screaming faintly, she writhed and worked against her dispassionate adversary. Gradually, her movement slowed as her strength ebbed. Her body struggled for air which would not come. Firah's eyes closed slowly, her vision blurred … 'Oh Mother, please help. Not yet. Please.'

Suddenly, her body collapsed to the ground. She struggled to open her eyes. There was someone moving over her body, charging into her attacker. In the recesses of her mind she could hear the sound of someone yelling. It gave her strength in a strangely spiritual and passionate way. She fumbled at the hand around her throat and found it gave way to her prying. Breath rushed into her body as a great wind of nature. After a few gulps, she raised herself upon her arms, coughing violently. She slowly became aware of what was happening around her.

Some person was moving about around her, swinging a weapon and shouting forcefully. "Get up! Get your butt off the ground and do something!" It was him. She was filled with hope and disgust all at once. Firah slowly pushed up to one knee, her head still reeling from lack of oxygen. Her rescuer was moving in and out of the swinging limbs of the Watch. They hadn't bothered to draw their swords, and strangely their movements were stiff and lacked fluidity. Regardless, the sallow limbs moved fast. Their relentless attacks were also potent, their grazing blows causing him to reel. Yet he would recover each time, his weapon countering like the wind. His sword play was amazing and she stared in awe for a moment.

✕ Aware of her gaze, Shien lashed out at the girl near his feet. "What are you doing? Grab that sword!" He pointed to a downed guard's weapon which rested in the scabbard upon the body's hip. He barely had time to dodge a knotted fist before slicing upward and relieving his foe of that limb.

"I can't use that!" the girl shouted back to him, gaining strength and pushing herself up to her feet shakily. There were still four Watchmen left and Shien was slowly fading from exhaustion and pain. His mind was near irrational as he grimaced between strokes.

"Useless, good-for-nothing ..." Shien's irritated voice was cut off as he was pounded soundly in the gut and dropped him to a knee. He rolled backward by the legs of an advancing attacker, poking his sword out as he passed. He felt it enter flesh, but pain was beyond these men now. Shien had a clue as to what had happened to them. Poor souls; it was like hacking at deadwood. Thrusts with the blade would have no effect now as they were beyond pain. He had to completely adjust his technique to incorporate heavy slashes to dismember the animates. It was an exhausting task. As he swung again and again without remorse, he stole a glance at the trembling girl who moved here and there trying to avoid being grasped again. He noted that the assaults on his person differed significantly from hers. Shien had only one option; this pack was slowing him down, limiting his technique. He might lose his life if he couldn't swallow his pride. Quickly he removed a strap and threw the pack toward the girl. "Look in there!" he stretched low under a knotted fist. Then a thought hit him harder than any blow. "Don't touch the swords!" he shouted into the night air.

☼   Firah's heart jumped at his vocal command. Her temperature boiled at the absolute crass of this man. "I already told you I can't use them!" She ripped open the pack and saw two large slender objects she assumed to be the cause of his distress. Hurriedly, she looked further and saw a small weapon. She grabbed it and quickly removed the sheath. An abrupt feeling entered her whole soul as she stared at the midnight black blade. The feeling of clawing, tearing, vicious energy shot through her whole system in a moment. The shock was such that she almost dropped the weapon, but something caused her to hold on. Then the sensation ebbed and she dizzily lifted the dagger up to her eyes. There were no features upon it, only a blade of the blackest kind. The feeling while holding it was a peculiar rush - like taking a thousand breaths at once. Another shout broke her train of thought.

"Wake up, idiot!" She turned in a blur of movement to see a massive limb slide through the air she had just occupied. She lashed out with the black blade. The arm of the attacker sizzled as it contacted the strange weapon. Her cut drove in and then upwards, completely removing the arm above the elbow. It was strange ... she felt little resistance as she slid the blade through. As the other limb came across to maul her, she dived low and spun repeatedly striking the midriffs of her foe. The remains of the dismembered body fell at her feat, the torso twitching and struggling but having no legs to carry it. She stared in wonder at the incredible dagger in her hands. Then she saw in the corner of her eye another assault. "Watch your back!" the tactless man warned again. Firah had had enough.

"Watch your own back, you Gnarel-brained, pig-faced …" She slashed out at the remaining enemy with ruthless efficiency, each stroke accentuated the words she spoke. " … clumsy, selfish, midden-head!" Firah stopped suddenly. All was quiet around her. She was smattered in a sticky substance that smelled putrid. She looked around her slowly. Her companion rose quietly, holding his left shoulder, grimacing as he limped toward her. His expression was different now. He regarded her with a degree of awe and some wary revulsion.

"You done?" he said as he pointed to her downed foe, what remained of him. Many of Firah's attacks had been exacted in a brutal fashion, long after her opponent was incapacitated. Her mind had been so clear and lucid. Now she felt disgust and attempted to throw the black blade away. Her hand would not open to release the horrific tool of death. She stared dumbfounded and tried to pry her fingers apart. Nothing seemed to work, as her hand maintained a sticky, vise-like grip upon the hilt.

Shien watched her with a look of strange curiosity. His eyes were drawn to the strange dark blade. The surface of the blade was clean and devoid of the gore which splayed across the girl's arms. There was no light reflection at all upon its surface. He stooped down and picked up his pack. Shouldering it, he took a few painful steps away from Firah. Glancing back he saw she made no attempt to follow; she simply stood there staring in horror at the soiled blade.

He spied movement down the road, shadowy forms moving silently from building to building. So, they were coming back to clean up what was left of him and the girl. He sighed deeply, and resigned himself to what would come. He couldn't outrun them now and he wouldn't be able to fight effectively at all. His fighting partner had not moved. She could still run if she could just focus her mind. He felt perhaps she had never seen combat like this - at its grisliest. Limping over to her, he touched her arm. Her eyes flashed to meet his; even in the dark he spied a trace of red within the gaze. It was cold like a tomb.

"Listen, "he began, "you need to leave here. There are Defilers coming this way. You aren't hurt and can outrun them still. Go before you can't escape."

"You underestimate me." The voice was strange, cold and full of malice. He was taken aback by her statement and strange tone.

"It doesn't matter anymore. We won't be leaving here." He pointed to a house near to them where several dark forms were moving in the dark. Soft scraping of sand penetrated through the deathly calm of the night. "It's too late for both of us now. They are moving in to finish it." Shien slumped down and resigned himself to Fate. Well, he had tried, but she seemed beyond reason. Bending down she brushed his arm, and, as he turned instinctively from the touch, blood from his clothes smeared against her. The girl picked up a fair sized stone that had come loose from the street in the fight. Her hand now hefted the dagger so easily he wondered what caused her previous struggle.

"You simpletons think you can control me?" Her voice was strangely altered, like acrid blackness, pure evil. Slowly, Firah leaned back and cocked her arm as if to throw the stone.

θ   The Cerephor had reached out to his cadre-men and drew them into one sphere of thought. A linking of minds was underway and the Defilers were prepared to take the 'prize'. They were preparing a complex and potent effect.

The multiple weave would entrap her mind and body into a death-like state. Her body would stiffen and her mind would weaken, taking away any will to resist. They uttered the words infallibly. In unison, all would aid the weave's effectiveness and duration. As such, she would remain in the dormant state long enough to bring her to Nuril. Tonight would be the final stroke upon Mehnin.

However, while completing the complex weave of strands from the Root, disaster struck the shadowed group. Their Cerephor took a large stone straight to the forehead, crushing bone and flesh. The Cere-Ashori collapsed dead in an instant. This sudden assault broke the critical link between the cadre-men in a terrifying way. The mind-Weaver's last thoughts of fear and agony twisted back upon each of them binding them mercilessly. In the span of a breath each of the Defilers lay upon the ground, completely immobile from horror and shock. It was impossible to move and in vain they struggled against the effects their weaves had sown. Groaning and wailing they writhed helpless upon the street as the two figures moved slowly away down the street and eventually out of sight. The prize had escaped. Tragically, the duration of the weave remained consistent, and the hapless Ashori lay prone and powerless upon the ground until the late morning hours. They were found by the change of the Watch lying next to the scene of massacre.

SAPLING

The Shadow had narrowly passed over the Sapling but fled. The sun rejoiced and sent its blessings down upon the tender flowered plant. Yet, something was different, amidst the Shadow's assault, a black seed had sprung up alongside the Sapling. They grew together now, winding about each other - the Sapling strongest in the day, the noxious weed in the night ...

A Mihyl's Dream

 "Tehsa."

DARKNESS enfolds me. Suddenly, a light forms far within my mind. It is growing ... growing. The light splits across my lucid thoughts. The colors of light are so brilliant ... It's blinding ... Prismatic patterns of the flow pass me, while I soar through the chasms of my mind. Where am I traveling to? I am weightless ... I move about on a whim. All is below me, yet as I look up ... What is that? A vision of her is forming in the phantom clouds of my mind. My thoughts coalesce into a memory from the hidden past. I know this place. The images sharpen and become clear ... the marbled halls of the Order.

I see my young self hurrying up the even steps of the Hall's front entrance. The stone is warm beneath my bare feet which tap softly across the marbled surface. A Convert of the Order moves slowly toward my young form. I dodge deftly around him, drawing a small frown from the robed superior. Piety and humility are the bulwark of the Order's creed. I still have much to learn of such things. The look on the Convert's face reflects a commonly held sentiment: here passes the next dropout. As the Convert gazes upon me, he shakes his head. Turning, with head bowed, he continues down the marbled steps into the garden.

No one thought I had potential ...

I follow the small boy into the nave. The massive pillars flow upward in the hall; they are magnificently polished and clean. Just like the surface of still water ... Many shimmering reflections dance upon the floor. I move about the main concourse, suspended in the air slowly becoming one with the memory and the past.

The sun coursed through the clerestory windows as sharpened blades of light struck deep into the nave. Several robed figures entered the room, the light bending around their forms.

"Where have you been Initiate?" A tall figure inquired as Zyr moved toward them at great haste. The addressor cradled an ornate scepter upon his arm. Zyr stopped in front of the bald man and looked up into the emotionless face. Stylized patterns traced along the hems of the smooth hung robes of the group of elders. The hemwork was carefully embroidered and bound as a testimony of service. They were an identification in the Order and everyone received a basic weave upon coming of age and gradually they became more complex as each member rose through the Order. The scepter carriers' robes were simple without hemwork.

"Humble Servant," the boy began in the customary greeting," I was practicing in the south woods and lost sight of the sun behind the trees and …" The man raised an eyebrow at the explanation. Zyr noticed the subtle movement and ceased speaking, his youthful voice echoed softly in air throughout the immense chamber.

"Initiates have specified time for training and study," the tall man replied, as he gazed down with hazel eyes, which were endowed with the wisdom of age. They had seen many seasons. "You have neglected your books; I saw dust upon the covers as I inspected your room For-Mena. Meanwhile, your Kota have worn through at the palms," He indicated to the lad's padded hands, which were quickly hid from view. "It is the responsibility of every brother and sister to uphold high standards, especially for the benefit of our junior Initiates."

"Yes, Humble Servant." the boy half-mumbled. Zyr was puzzled at the statement, as he was not aware of any juniors since his arrival.

Slowly, the group parted to make way for a small robed figure whose head was bowed. Gradually, the head rose, revealing a child's face. It was a girl, and even at a young age her features were striking. Her eyes were a deep and radiant hazel which stared indifferently back at Zyr. Her face was smooth and near white; her lips delicate and supple. Dark brown hair was tied back into a simple bun upon her head. His eyes caught upon a shimmering green brooch encased in golden braids that served to clasp her tunic below her neck. She simply stood there regarding the lad.

Finally, the Servant spoke. "Tehsa, you will follow the lead of your Mihyl," he took a deep breath in and closed his eyes for a moment. "Zyr will instruct you in our ways. The role of a leader is an efficient guide toward humility and someday, Tehsa, you will have your turn." The girl bowed low and all the robed party moved away. Soon the main hall was silent.

How I hated her at that moment. I hated the new responsibility ... All images blur while the players change, as if in some forgotten play. Why have I been brought here, into strange memories long buried? My form floats like a mist over the still lake of recollection. The motion ceases and I see it again as if for the first time ...

Zyr knelt uncomfortably on the stone. He leaned slightly against the wall and barely looked about the impressive room. His indifference was not indicative of the splendor of the Order's most noted enclosure. The decor of Initiate's Path was legendary. Indeed, not many places in Kenhar could boast such craftsmanship. There were intricate symbols carved upon the walls and floors. Each a story of countless hours spent in painstaking honing of stone and wood. It was a priceless treasure all bound within the confines of the majestically pillared chamber. The purpose of the room was simple but profound. New Initiates would face a crucial test that revealed their aptitude toward the power within the land and to which aspect they would become attuned. Yet, it was much more than a simple examination. Character, motivations and discipline were all determined as well through observation. It was a dignified occasion and all in attendance adopted a candor of the most heartfelt respect and solemnity.

Zyr snorted loudly to clear some phlegm that had lodged most annoyingly between his throat and sinuses. He ignored the looks that were cast his way by other designated witnesses of the ceremony. He detested waiting for most things, but to wait upon the elders was most agonizing. He vaguely recalled the ceremony upon entering the Order as an Initiate. He felt as uncomfortable then as he did now. He glanced at Tehsa kneeling quietly in the center of the circular room with eyes closed. She was perched atop a cylindrical dais that rose several feet above the floor level. The dais was surrounded by a series of stone steps that branched out from the center in eight directions. Each stairwell pointed to a small mat several feet away which together circled the dais.

Tehsa's expressionless face itched a raw sore in his mind. His crash course as senior member or Mihyl of the Tetsu was a disaster in his opinion. His careful regimen was disrupted beyond reason and she was all to blame. He glared in disgust as the Elders finally strode quietly into the room from the council antechamber. He maintained the stare for those whom he hated the most. Tey'ur received a particularly sincere dose of pure optical spite. Of all the Elders, the Warmaster was the only one who returned in kind - if briefly. The Council took their seats which were stationed evenly about the room, forming a circle about the Initiate seat. Tehsa kept her head bowed through their approach. 'She doesn't know them yet, or she would be running from this room' the young Myhil thought ruefully. If not for the binding oath he took upon his Acceptance Day, he would have stirred the dust mightily in his rapid departure. His glum musings were broken by the tap upon the stone by Greil, the senior member of the Council of Masters.

"It is time to proceed. Is the Initiate prepared?" Tehsa dipped her head slightly lower in affirmation. "Very well. Brethren, please bring forth the Seeking Crystal." Two robed figures bowed and stepped into a small enclosure. A new spark of insight shot through Zyr and he abandoned his misery. The crystal was unique: hewn from a Deepstone cache somewhere within Tamers Reach. It was said each imbued stone held specific properties quite unlike any other material. The men appeared hefting a sizable load and shuffled carefully toward the near stairs to the dais. The crystal shimmered in the midday beams which streaked through its transparent facets. It was roughly three handspans in breadth and two in depth. The general shape was somewhat rounded but still somewhat abrasive and jagged along the surface. It was also rumoured that to attempt to alter a Deepstone may change its properties or destroy it all together.

Zyr still knew little about Deepstone but he knew it was connected to the same power deep in the earth that he had attuned to. Any information on how to gain advantage over his peers was a top priority for the young monk. He paid close attention to the proceedings to gain any useful information. The senior Master of Arcane Lore nodded to the others and as one they assumed the Arc of Weaving. It was a traditional position made to access the potent energies from the weaving threads within the world. It was said to originate from some inexplicable being of power, but Zyr had difficulty believing such things.

Each Master had claimed attunement to a different aspect of the raw power, all except Tey'ur. For some reason, he did not access it, but rather it was part of his whole being. His whole frame was imbued with it from birth. This was a rare occurrence in present times and it certainly afforded the recipient considerable abilities: enhanced strength, longevity, heightened perception to name a few. All of this served to create an indomitable war machine in the now Master of Arms. Truly, he had no rival in the field of war, which aggravated the ambitious Initiate intensely.

Zyr felt the hum of power through the room. The Deep Root it was sometimes called, and to have users of all aspects accessing it created the strange noise. The feeling permeated elements and flesh alike. The flows were directed through outstretched arms toward the crystal, now resting in front of Tehsa atop the dais. All she had to do was to reach out and touch the crystal and her path would be determined. Tehsa stare into the now pulsing light that emitted from the crystal. The light reflected upon the glistening brooch clasped to her garment. After a few moments she withdrew her arm from within the loose cloak and touched a finger lightly upon the luminous surface. For a span of time there was no change in the throb of energy in the room.

All at once Tehsa cried out in what seemed like a sound of fear and terror. Some in the room looked about uncertain with the sound, while the Masters maintained their solemn vigil. Zyr saw the expression fixed upon her face, and puzzled. This was nothing like what he had experienced. Beads of sweat coursed down the young girl's face, even as her hand was now pressed firmly upon the crystal in a strange snare. Finally, the crystal changed. It sparkled and shifted in distinct patterns of colour. At once the Masters relinquished their connection to the Root. Tehsa slumped down upon the dais in exhaustion. Tam, Master of Diplomatics, stood slowly with hands clasped in front. It was the sign of traditional respect.

"Categor." Her voice was firm and rigid, like her demeanor. All in the room stood and bowed their heads in unison. Zyr hardly noted the motions; he was still puzzling over what he had just seen. He had never heard of any Initiate struggling in pain through the ceremony. Just then his gaze caught upon Greil who had for the briefest moment a most peculiar expression on his face. Then the High Master's eyes flickered to Zyr. There was a knowing in that gaze, like the observer of pieces upon a game board. It was most unnerving and Zyr averted his own eyes to another location in the room. The room began to empty with the low buzz of whisperings from the attendants. Zyr chanced a glance back at Greil who was now making his way through the room to the other Masters. Zyr debated what to do at the moment. The spectacle was over and his old biases were setting in like the late tide. He noted the girl upon the dais and the slight shuddering of her form. She was crying silently. Strange workings in his conscience pricked against his mind.

 *In the end I turn from her and slip out quickly past the others. The colours begin to swirl my memory. Moving fast ... transcending time, another scene - as a door in a multifaceted room - is opened to view. Darkness seeps through a forest glade.*

"Wait, Mihyl!" the young girl called out between gasping breaths. The two youths dashed through the trees, dodging here and there. Tehsa was falling behind the energetic boy. Upon his face was a mischievous grin. Zyr sprinted ahead even faster completely leaving the girl alone in the dark. As she lost sight of her Mihyl, she slowed down to step tentatively through tangled webs of branches. Fear began to show upon her face. "Mihyl! Please … come back …" She slid down against a tree and buried her head into her arms. Small whimpers and sobs were swallowed up by the dark trees which loomed in upon her.

I forgot about this … Tehsa … please forgive me …

Zyr looked for a suitable tree to climb in order to get a favorable view of his pathetic charge. She was a thorn in his side since the day she arrived. Useless girl! She was always around him. He had never had a private moment to train in two years. He had just about enough of her. Up ahead he spotted a large tree whose branches would conceal him perfectly in the darkness. Directing his personal store of energy toward his hands, he felt them tingle and shiver under the strain of the mysterious power. In a great leap, he flung his body upward, focusing his energy to his fingertips. His hands grasped the tree, fingers penetrating through the bark. Then slowly, he began to climb, slamming his hands forcefully into sturdy tree, securing handholds as he ascended.

He had almost made the branch he wanted when he felt a thudding impact near his body. As Zyr attempted to move, he felt his clothes restrained. He let one hand go to feel about his person. A shaft of some sort had pinned his training robes to the oak. He tugged at the arrow (he determined its identity as he felt feathers) but it was to no avail. Zyr prepared to break the shaft and began to focus his thoughts. He was suddenly seized by the leg and hauled off the tree trunk. The initiate landed upon his backside; stunned, he looked at a frightful set of yellow eyes at his feet. His foot was grasped firmly, by some sort of beast! Zyr breathed in quickly and, in a fright, made to strike at the terrible yellow eyes. As his hand moved back, it was caught in a hidden grasp. Grunting and squirming, he was forced to the ground upon his face. A strong pressure rested upon his head.

So naïve …

"I don't know what I'm more offended at," a quiet voice whispered in his ear, "your defacement of a sacred tree, trying to smite Nisa, or your tormenting of that girl." Zyr could not move his head and his mouth filled with grass and dirt as he opened to speak.

"Rhagal, you meddler, release me!" Zyr sputtered out the dirt in his mouth. How he loathed the Wilder. He often interfered in Zyr's physical training, which was so precious to the young man. What infuriated the student the most was that Rhagal was not an official member of the Order, and thus was not bound by the code of brotherly conduct.

"Such strong aggression from a fool, and an incapacitated fool at that. Remember my words, young one …" He wrenched upward on Zyr's arm, producing a cry of pain from the youth. The arm was fully removed from the socket. Suddenly the pressure on his head and limbs was gone. Zyr lifted himself off the ground in a quick thrust from his good arm. Rhagal and his creature were nowhere in sight. Zyr peered into the blackness. All was quiet except for the sound of weeping from farther away. Glancing around, he noticed that the tree no longer bore his finger gouges nor the arrow. He shook his head and growled within himself. Finally, after a pause, he walked slowly toward the direction of the girl.

 *How much I wanted to prove myself. It always led to folly ... My body moves swiftly away from the dark foliage. Light flashes across the land; all the trees now appear taller and lusher. I fly across a small plain near the forest of the Order. A terrible battle ensues below me. This was a dark day ... the blood ... so much blood. The day the Order's third war ended and my own conflict began.*

A blade deflected off of Zyr's palm as metal would off a stone surface. The grotesque creature twisted and thrashed out again and again. Zyr was on the defence, his hands blocking the blade, but occasionally he would get nicked across the arm where his skin was soft. The creature screamed and bellowed, its rank breath washing over the young Seeker, flecks of spit smattering his bloodied face. Zyr feinted low and leapt up high to head level. His opponent fell for his move, its upper body descending to where Zyr could make contact. Twisting sharply, Zyr's legs whirled around and slammed into the head of the undead warrior. After both limbs struck in sequence, he landed directly in front of his stunned prey, following up with a knife hand under the chin. His hand sunk deep into the head of the monster. Zyr amplified his strike through sound focus, his voice an emblem for powerful energy, surging through his arm and fingers into the creature's head. The decapitated torso slumped to the ground as the remains of the head sprayed throughout the area. The Seeker looked around quickly to assess the battle. Four foes lay dead at his feet, and many more lay in the wake of the disciplined ranks of the Order. Yet for all their cunning and sheer skill, the enemy was pressing them back. He looked to his right; Tehsa was swinging her Gé with intensity and utter ferocity. It was like that with her now in battle. She became someone different and he found it unsettling.

"You okay!" he shouted above the cacophony of pitched battle around them. She turned and flashed him that grin, which meant much more. Not only was she on top of things, she was enjoying herself. He watched as she entangled the Gé around one her attacker's necks and sent a shocking blast along the metal wires that connected the weighted balls. Her foe toppled twitching and convulsing as the remnants of the blast fizzled through the body. He had to admit, she was incredible with that weapon at times. Slowly, over time, she had earned his stubborn respect. She had opted to forgo Zyr's love of hand-to-hand combat and adopted a weapon that suited her knack for the Categor attunement. Despite their success, however, things were turning for the worst.

Zyr watched as one of the Masters fell under the swarm of a dozen bone creatures, animated by their relentless Defiler enemy.

Aragil ...

It seemed a fruitless battle as their opponents were mindless minions of a more dangerous enemy. The call came for the valiant warriors of the Order to fall back to their established defensive position. Zyr finished off a rotting monstrosity with a snap of its neck and dodged his way through to Tehsa. She dispatched her closest foe and nodded her head to him. As they started to make their way back to the stone foundations, gasps were heard from fellow Initiates who moved nearby. Zyr turned to look and his jaw dropped. A gigantic mass of bones was rising up from the ground. It had a strange configuration; it was supported by a massive serpentine vertebra, which flowed into a spiny tail. It had large skinless wings, which spread menacingly above it. The jaw snapped and hissed while within its eye sockets flashed a pale green light. It was unlike anything Zyr had seen.

It was the broken remains of the Crimson Serpent of Elhil.

"Let's move it!" Zyr called out to Tehsa. "We can't handle that thing!" She appeared to have either ignored him or she was frozen with fear. "Didn't you hear me, Jyril?" he shouted as he made to grab her arm. This was no time for stupidity. As his hand touched her arm, he jerked it back in reflex. His hand was numb for a moment. He realized that she was preparing a potent weave. He could feel the power swelling within her. Looking into her eyes, he saw clarity not fear.

Suddenly, an animate swung at them clumsily with a dulled sword. Zyr reached across, disarmed the abomination and impaled it upon its own weapon. He knew he would have to keep them off until she was finished. However, as their allies fell back, more and more enemies swarmed in upon them. It seemed an eternity waiting on Tehsa, and Zyr was tiring fast. Finally she spoke the weaving-words which enabled the power to move.

Pulsing streaks of white energy flashed from her outstretched hands. A lightning strike jumped from enemy to enemy, struggling in vain to find an arc towards the ground. He watched Tehsa's concentration upon the jumping lights. She would not allow the deadly bolts to follow their natural course, but they continued to blast through one undead after another and under her direction, the walking-dead were blown apart mercilessly. Finally, she directed her assault upon the massive serpent. All the white-hot energy converged on the terrifying beast as it mauled one Initiate. Whatever tainted energy inhabited the bones screamed out in pain as the bolt danced along the spine and shattered the serpent at the hip. Large pieces of bone blasted from the creature upon all nearby. Zyr had jumped in front of his Jyril to shield her from the onslaught of bone shrapnel. A large fragment impacted upon his arm and embedded itself there. He winced but made no sound. Then, he looked around slowly.

Tehsa had cleared a significant path through the enemy, but they continued to surge forth from the distant hills. She slumped into his body, visibly weakened from such a potent weaving.

She always pushed herself too far ...

"Come on!" Zyr shouted as he helped her move from the scene of mutual destruction of the living and dead. As he pulled her away, he heard a wrenching, grinding sound from behind him. He stole a glance as he attempted to quicken her pace. The massive Serpentine was only partially destroyed. Impossibly, it was dragging a portion of its upper body along the ground with an enormous claw. With great sweeping motions the jagged limb fell and clawed the earth, dragging the partial torso and head directly toward the weary youths. "Tehsa! Hurry, please!" It was no use; her feet were dragging through the bloodied earth. Zyr's arm prevented him from carrying her; the best he could manage was to support her body as they stumbled in vain from the monstrous demon-skeleton.

Zyr saw the entrance to the forest, where the foundations lay just beyond. They could make it! Everyone else had fled in haste to the rendezvous point. He tried to shut out the crunching and scraping sounds in his ears, growing louder and louder. His mind raced in frenzy. He saw the trees just ahead and felt the ground shake beneath him from the weight of terrifying, bony claws.

Tehsa screamed out in pain and was wrenched from Zyr's good arm. Turning in horror he saw that the dragon had impaled Tehsa straight through and now she was pinned down to the ground through her midsection. The pain would be too great for her. Her mouth was fixed open and shock had passed swift across her face only to reform into unconsciousness or oblivion … Zyr knew not which. All time was still before him. Her crumpled form lay motionless upon the ground as the massive head reared for one last brutal assault upon the girl.

"No!" The boy screamed out in anger. Ripping the bone shard from his arm he wove his remaining power throughout his frame. He was pushing the limits, he knew, but simple reason was far beyond the young man's mind. His body pulsed and burned with an icy blue aura, the ground around him rippled and seared from the potent energies thrust down upon it. All of the undead warriors turned their heads toward the small form which gleamed intensely, a beacon for all creatures magically attuned. It all happened within an instant. A blinding flash of holy energy - a massive concussive wave - swept the battlefield.

My body is moving away now, riding the wave of lethal, forbidden power. All the sound of battle grows silent to my mind's senses. I am moving to a quiet glade. All is darkness. A small light entices me as I trace through the darkness. Two forms huddled together.

"Tehsa, hold on, damn it!" The boy shouted out in fear and alarm. The front side of his robes were dyed red in her blood. Patches of grass within the glade gleamed in the full moonlight, reflected by the lifeblood of the girl. Desperately, Zyr pushed one hand into the gaping puncture hole coming out her back, while pressing down upon her wounded abdomen. Her eyes were glassy and her breath shallow. She looked up at him, oblivious to any pain. "Do not think of leaving. Do you understand?" The young man looked about in desperation and finally to the heavens. "Please ... What should I do?" he shouted out in frustration. With every small breath, warm fluid bathed his hands. He hung his head and whispered low. "I can't ... help you. ... I'm losing you ..." He never had felt so powerless. She lifted a cool hand up to his cheek and smiled softly.

"Mihyl ... you mustn't allow emotion to ... don't forget the first statute ..."

Conquer the body and mind.

The moon lit upon small streams of emotion coursing down her cheeks. Yet, her eyes were dry. His head hung low, almost upon her bosom as he desperately sought the discipline that served him his whole life. The search only enhanced the rain upon her face. Zyr felt a touch on his shoulder.

"You have learned to care, fool." The voice was not harsh or commanding. It was soft and temperate, like the breeze that rustled through the glade.

"Have you come to mock me, Rhagal?" The boy never moved, but sat holding his dying comrade. He felt a nuzzle against his arm, and his heart calmed upon hearing quiet soothing purrs.

"I have never assisted any man or woman, regardless of the circumstance. Guardian of Mother is my call, not that of people. However, I have been directed to you specifically … it seems that Mother has heard your plea. Nisa felt the call and led me here. Your friend may yet survive, but you must trust me." Zyr raised a wearied head towards the solemn Wilder. As usual, his features were all but impossible to divine in the darkness, but he felt the cool gaze and sighed heavily.

"I'll never trust you, but … I would give anything now …" Zyr stumbled over his words. His heart had changed and his mind had just come to realize. Rhagal stooped down and lifted the girl easily in his powerful arms and led her to a familiar tree. The sacred Darkwood tree. Rhagal placed her at the foot of the tree and looked at her for a moment. He turned his head slightly and spoke. "You will remove yourself from here for the time being. Not all the secrets of Mother's servants are for your eyes, Ashori." Zyr raised himself shakily to his feet, and turned as Nisa's dark form led him from the glade.

"This changes nothing between us, Rhagal, but if she survives, I'll bond myself in a debt service to Mother for payment." Zyr limped away in exhaustion, as he felt potent energies flow from all living things around him, streaming toward the glade. He never looked back, but uttered a silent oath inside. 'I'll never rely on him or anyone else for help again.'

 *That day, I left the boy in the glade. My mind's eyes cannot focus upon the blurred scenes before me. I am moving in and out of time and space. Within my memory I am a specter of thought. All images unite into a bright Blackrill day, upon a tall hill bathed in flowers of every colour. The sun sends its blessings upon two familiar figures that stand together gazing out over the endless range of green. I am moving around them ...*

"Zyr, you are an insensitive, callous boor! I ought to ..." Tehsa raised her hand as if to gesture a potent blast in his general direction.

"Tes, I'm sorry. I thought you would want to know. Leaving the Order isn't an easy decision to make, but I promised my service and ..." He was cut off quite soundly by a slap across his face and a stern rebuke.

"Duty! Promises! You are leaving your only home and abandoning me to what? Servitude to a bunch of insensitive and blind fools who wed themselves to books and a life of fruitless fighting until death comes for them. That isn't living! You were the only one who ever respected me ... who knew me! You can't leave me here!" She was shaking in rage. He touched his hand to

his face where the sting lingered.

He was not sure what he was feeling. After all these years since the war he thought he understood her and now this. His studies had drawn him away from all others but her. Only in her had he confided the deepest desires of his heart. Their relationship had passed beyond mere familiar bonds. No, parting was especially painful for him now on the eve marking the summit of all his aspirations as a Master in the Order. The tetsu had been through so many trials and triumphs, and feelings. From broken memories of over a year ago, upon the snowy climbs of Racur, he felt he suddenly had met her for the first time. Since then she had grown into such a beautiful young woman, now of eighteen years, blossoming into full allure. He had to leave, for many reasons, for he dared not violate the strictest code which existed between Mihyl and Jyril. The last year had been difficult for him, to stay focused upon his studies while thinking on her endlessly. When the call came from the Wilders to fulfill his oath, his mind rejoiced and his heart broke.

Her chest was heaving up and down. Her training robes hung loose about her shoulders. Her hair was tossed about by a gentle breeze. He turned to leave, sensing danger lurking within the dammed lake of emotion in his soul.

"Wait … Zyr. I shouldn't have …" As her arm touched his, a charge coursed through his body, stronger than any she could have woven. He struggled to maintain a crumbling mental fortress. He turned to gaze into Tehsa's eyes; the light brown hue glowed softly in the noon-day sun.

Her face was close to his, peering upward into the taller man's gaze. "I know I can't force you to stay … I also know why you have avoided me recently. Ever since Racur, you have changed. I know it's my fault for everything I said to you then. Even if your mind can't remember my pleas, your heart does." Her pale skin started to redden slightly. His heart skipped a beat as she moved to find his other arm. "I won't let you escape from me without giving you a token of remembrance." Zyr's guts clenched in knots and twisted inside him violently. All his training screamed out at him, all the dire warnings raged and all the logic moved to bolster his resolve. It was too late; the dam had burst into pieces.

Almost mystically their lips had met, mingling upon sweetened brushes of desire. Both held their breath in a surge of fervor, embracing each other passionately while sailing upon the tide of emotion. Zyr was about to drown happily in her waters when a lingering remnant of sense stabbed through his passion. He pulled himself from her caressing arms and withdrew a pace. Tehsa stood there, visibly moved and perturbed. Zyr tried to speak, but every attempt was in vain. Finally, he ran from her, charging through high fields of grain, running scared of himself and what may have been. Tehsa stood for a moment and then sunk to her knees. Her head bowed low and all was silent but the wind moving through the grass and her long hair.

All is moving now around me. A strange sensation is coming over me. All the color is turning to blackness. Suddenly there is only one image shrouded by all the black. She is before me, beside me, all around me. All I see is her. Her face is burned upon every facet of my memory and her breath, her lips, they call to me from the depths of the consuming darkness.

"Zyr?"

Hidden Truths

THE SUN lit upon the glistening spires of Syrion. Each slender pinnacle rose upward struggling to reach the stars. Their height was unimaginable; their beauty breathtaking. The view from the highest point of the tallest spire always stirred Toryn. He stared out at the massive city which was the country's capital. Beneath the towers were various constructs; homes, guilds, industries, schools of thought all filled in the area below. It was always invigorating for him to take in all his subjects and their holdings. Far past the horizon toward the east, his country spanned to Tamers Reach. The mountains shielded his country from the fell wastelands beyond. Little accounts emerged from beyond the barren waste, but horrific rumours abounded. Toryn turned his gaze to the sea which also expanded past the horizon. How he wished at times that the burden of leading a country would ease, and that he could pursue his heart's desires upon the solitary sea.

A flash of light from below caught in his peripheral vision. "I knew it wouldn't last." Sighing heavily, Toryn stood and stretched his large frame. For a king there was no time for rest, especially in troubled times. He started down the steps which wound round the outside of the spire. There was little to hang on to in the descent, but he was accustomed to the path. Pushing his foolish whims behind him, Toryn set his mind to other matters. Finally he descended into the council chamber. As he walked through the gilded doors, a man in eloquent robes of deep blue approached the king hurriedly. Toryn noted that his face was set with worry.

"My Lord, many thanks for answering the summons. The High Council has just arrived from Jandor, and there are pressing matters to attend to." The chancellor was wringing his hands and fidgeting as he stood before Toryn. The King knew that the news would be unwelcome. He had already felt the doom in the nightmare that shook his subconscious mind. Another Defiler guild had cinched power over another of the old traditional guilds. Sadly, the news was far too late. Trouble was stirring in Kenhar, and the young monarch could not evade it nor even stop it. Darkness was spreading like a disease across the land. The people would never be informed. It was better to let them live out the remainder of their lives in peaceful bliss. Perhaps that explained his wanderlust of late. The prospect of opposing the unstoppable was overwhelming and wearisome. He put a hand to his head and massaged his temple gently.

"Let us proceed as quickly as possible; time is working against us now." He moved down the corridor swiftly, the chancellor stepping in a pace behind him. The doors of the inner sanctum swung open with a dull clanking sound which echoed in the hall. All the High Council was seated and heads turned to Toryn. Every minute required action and the evil must be resisted even if it was a useless gesture. The king of Kenhar moved slowly into the room and to the Head of the Council's chair. "Shall we begin?"

✕ Shien's eyes bolted open. It was still early morning and he found himself in the soft hay of a stable loft where both he and the girl had collapsed earlier. He had used this location before and in his wounded and weary state he had to rest. Many thoughts buzzed through his mind which refused him the sleep he desperately needed. The girl sleeping beside him was a mystery; quietly he leaned over and stared at her. The light was low where they were, and the sun would soon peek over the Tamers Reach. He considered for the first time her youthful beauty. Despite being soiled from last evening's exploits, her cheeks were illuminated slightly, and reaching out to remove the hair from her face he found her skin creamy smooth and warm. The dark brown hair spilled around her shoulders, and lay loose upon the golden straw. She breathed in slowly, her forehead furrowed and her hands clenched. She began to shift and whimpered in her sleep. Shien was astounded that this seemingly unassuming girl could be so brutally lethal only hours ago. It was terrifying and yet there were other questions as well. How did she know to throw the stone at that moment and with such accuracy? Her resolve was so sure, so much unlike the trembling youth he bumped into (literally). She became so cold and calculating, and what disturbed him further was when she was in that state, he could get no reading from her emotionally. It was as if she became another person altogether.

Her eyes flicked open and she caught him looking at her. She sat up quickly and instinctively moved her arms to her shirt as to cover herself. She fidgeted with the buttons while shooting an accusing glare at him, her brow furrowed. The shirt was smattered in a foul substance and dirt from combat, but it was done up, as was his clothing. She bit her lower lip suspiciously and looked silently upon Shien. After staring at her for a moment he broke the silence in the loft.

"So nervous … this is hardly a fair assessment of the person who stuck his neck out and saved your life back there." He shifted as to move slightly away from her. The young girl seemed to ease a bit at the gesture. Her brow smoothed out and her body relaxed. Shien could tell that she was feeling a mixture of many emotions. Some were understandable: disgust, fear, uncertainty. However, something else was mixed into her sea of sentiments, something that wove through it all, but it was impossible to tell. She carefully regarded him and shifted her legs together underneath her. "It's a funny thing …"he began suddenly, "I don't know what to call you." She was silent for a moment.

"I should say it's a funny thing," the girl began, "you've called me many things already …" Her voice lowered into a near whisper as she finished her thought.

"Can you blame me if I get a little anxious in a fight?" Shien was not about to feel guilty for anything. "Besides, what possessed you to run around looking for help after curfew; you know where the Watch tower is, don't you?" He knew she could question his violation of the civil code as well, but his reasons were personal and he had prepared meticulously for last night's operation. Almost subconsciously, his hands slid over to his pack, and comfortingly he felt the objects within.

"I'm not from around here. I come from Lenhir, to the south east. The name's Firah." She said the last part with some trepidation; she still did not trust him completely.

"Shien." He produced a small smile and groaned out as he rubbed a sore shoulder. It would require looking at by a physician. "I've heard of Lenhir. Wonderful ale ..."

"Oh, that's right, Tohm ... Zyr!" She started to get up but struggled against cramped muscles. Finally, she gained her feet and began descending the ladder to the ground.

"Are you out of your mind?" He said to her as she stepped gingerly down each rung. "Those magi weren't all that belong to their cursed guild. They are still roaming about out there!" He started to move down the ladder, and then remembering suddenly reached and snatched his pack and then continued downward. Each step was painful and he nearly stumbled.

"My friend still needs my help ... he could be hurt or even dead!" She was hurriedly fixing herself up, but it was in vain. Both of them were a sight and Shien knew that they would draw undue attention and questions if they were seen. He reached out and grabbed her arm roughly.

"Would you just stop and think about this!"

She snapped her head around to meet his troubled face.

"First of all, there are going to be more magi stalking around out there. Second, you think anyone will help you when you look like that?!" he emphasized his argument by pointing to her garments which were a mix match of dried substances. "Finally, how do you think your friends would feel if you turn up dead?" Her resolve ebbed with every stinging piece of logic that he forced upon her. Her shoulders sagged and her head slowly dropped down.

Finally, Firah slumped down onto a small wooden bench and put her hands to her face. Shien could feel the waves of emotion cascading inside her. At times he wished he could ignore that intuitive ability.

Her voice came ragged and broken. "It's just that I … He asked me to …" She sniffed and let tears fall amongst the hay strewn across the floor. He could tell that there was more than just the concern for a friend tormenting her. He fixed his gaze upon the sheathed dagger, secured upon her belt. He moved to sit down beside her and put a hand on her shoulder. She did not shy away but continued to sob quietly.

"I can imagine how you feel … We can move in a couple of hours when curfew lifts. We'll get washed up at the rain barrel just outside, and then cover ourselves with those horse blankets over there." Her head lifted up and she looked at him gratefully. Tear trails streaked through the dirt on her face. "It's the best I can do; I wish I could do more …" He was mildly surprised at his response. He typically used those words to win over a woman, but they couldn't be more genuine. There was a significant passage of time when neither spoke but sat in silence.

Firah broke the respite. "Do you want to know the true reason I followed you?" Her head did not move; she merely studied a part of the hay-strewn floor. Shien thought he knew but now he wasn't so sure. He nodded his head quietly. Firah continued her confession, sighing slowly and staring out into the dissipating darkness. "I remember when you were upset after killing that man … that necromancer."

Shien's stomach twinged with the reminder. "You mentioned something about a dark demon. I want to know what you meant about that." Her voice was a little shaky and quivered subtly with fear. Shien's heart now beat against his chest harshly, and his mind lapsed from a vivid memory. He glanced down at Firah, who was now looking at him intently. "You know what I speak of," she spoke softly, "I can see the same fear in your eyes that exists in my heart."

Shien stood up quickly and rubbed a hand through his blond hair which flowed free across his neck. His eyes twitched toward her and away again. He had tried desperately to forget everything about that blasted demon! Though it had been just been one night - one dream - the memories had attached themselves to his very soul. He thought at times his mind would burst in sheer terror. She knew about that as well as he? He paced the floor trying to sort out his thoughts. His sanity recoiled at the prospect of reliving such horrid events, but he had to talk it out. He didn't know why he trusted her either, after only a few hours of acquaintance. Perhaps encounters with mortality created powerful bonds between people.

"It's only happened a couple times, all in the last six months."

She nodded her head in affirmation which gave him a strange sense of security … he wasn't insane after all. Yet, something needed to be sorted out.

"I can't describe it ... something like terrifying darkness, alive and growing ... still it is more than horrifying it's ... it's ... " he paused for words.

"It's like being seduced or enticed."

Shien's throat constricted; that was exactly what it was like. Perhaps that was the most disturbing element. He could handle fear and entrapment, but this was far beyond the scope of those feelings. He walked over to a stall of a workhorse, whose occupant nickered softly. He reached up and stroked its neck absently. She stood and walked slowly to his side and greeted the massive beast. Shien's felt full of tension and he stared intently into memory. He was deathly quiet and rigid. The same terror she recited unnerved him and the memory gnawed at his conscious mind. Now bereft of any ego, he stood open as a book before her. He turned a frantic stare to her.

"How can you be so calm now? The very thought of those dreams cast a pale of dread across my mind so great that I can't remember hope or happiness." His voice trembled. "Perhaps it's the feeling of helplessness ... I don't know." He turned back to the stallion. "I can't talk about this anymore." Upon feeling her consternation, he quickly added, "At least not right now. We can talk again later ... this evening seems a difficult burden to handle." She nodded. After a moment he turned back toward her.

Her unlikely rescuer turned a cool gaze upon her which made her feel a little uncomfortable. In the growing light she could make out his features better. Shoulder length blond hair and piercing grey eyes. His build was wiry and firm. He wore a strangely embroidered leather jacket and breeches. Her assessment was detracted with all the grime crusted along his arms and across his body. Despite the twinging of her cautious heart, she admitted that he was not quite the boor she had made him out to be the previous night; he did seem gentle now. Who could understand men anyway? She rubbed her brooch absently. What would happen to them now? When the morning broke she would have to make for the merchant gate to contact Tohm. She had so much to tell him, and he was liable to tan her for a solid week. Shien's voice interrupted her musing.

"I think it's fair that you answer a question of mine now?" She looked at him guardedly and considered for a moment what the question might be. Eventually, good sense won the conflict in her mind; he had certainly earned her favour the previous night. Firah nodded in affirmation. "Thank you for your trust. What I have been puzzling over all night is your connection to that." He pointed to her hip. She looked down in confusion and gazed upon her belt where her knife was secured. It was her turn to be puzzled.

"What's so odd about a common knife?" she asked incredulously. Was he feeling alright? His expression was certainly one of utter bewilderment.

"What are you saying girl? There is nothing common about that blade. It's as black as midnight and was the cause of all my troubles. It gave me a nasty shock when I first found it. As soon as you took it from my pack you were doing things that … well made me shudder."

Firah gaped in utter amazement. He must have hit his head in the fight. She had been there at the battle, but she simply watched her rescuer hack the guard to pieces with his sword. It was he that did all the killing, not her.

"Look … I don't know what had possessed you to link me to anything that happened last night. I saw you kill all those men. I'm grateful for your help." Her leg shifted backward instinctively. Shien closed his eyes and ran his hands through his hair and then pressed his fingers to his forehead, massaging the area. 'He is strange' she thought, 'completely out of his mind.'

"Okay … okay. Listen. I'm going to talk through what happened, okay? First, you nearly got strangled by that zombie Watchman. I couldn't bear to watch you get killed so I charged in … right?" She murmured in agreement and waited. "Okay, next we had a discussion while I was fighting (Firah scowled at the memory). I asked you for help and threw you my pack." Shien's fingers gripped tightly around the straps of the pack he now wore. He seemed never to be far from the pack.

"Yes, yes. I couldn't find anything so you took care of the rest of the guards. Then we left after they were all downed. You led us to this horse stable and here we are." She was getting tired of restating the obvious.

"Wrong! That's where you're mistaken Firah! You grabbed that dagger and used it in the most brutal and vicious manner that I think I've ever seen a knife used. It was terrifying." Firah was nonplussed. Was she talking to the same man? How could their memories be so different?

"Are you mad? Look, I've had this dagger for a long time. I bought it here, in Khyvla, two years ago. I always carry a dagger with me for protection … and, well, for other things."

"It's not just the dagger! You threw a stone into a crowd of Ashori and broke their power! With a stone! How could you forget about all this?!" He stood there and stared at her with a determined if not sincere look on his face. How could their stories be so different? She was sure what she said was true. Something was wrong about the situation. One thing Firah knew for certain: she was no killer. She felt bad enough when she had to hurt people when stealing from them.

"I don't understand what is happening, but maybe this will help. Look, its silver-iron as it has always been, not black." She removed the knife from the belt sheath and showed it to him. The dagger blade gleamed silvery metallic in the early morning light. His expression changed again to intense concentration. He was clearly trying to piece together a puzzle that she knew nothing about.

"Do one thing for me then." He stood away from her and continued, "Try to throw it away, even to drop it."

"That is a ridiculous request, but if it will ease your mind and stop all this confusion." Firah held the blade outward, her hand gripped tightly around the hilt. She slowly opened her fingers and the blade tumbled to the floor in a clatter. He stroked his chin thoughtfully.

"May I hold it?" She picked up the blade and held it out for him to take. Cautiously, he held the slender weapon. His body seemed to relax somewhat, although his brow remained creased in thought. He passed the dagger back to her quickly. He paused for a moment and then paced about the floor. The young girl replaced the dagger and stretched her back; suddenly the activities of the previous night were catching up to her. Firah yawned and slumped down into a pile of hay. For a long while she watched Shien move this way and that, which made her feel even more tired. Her eyes drooped and she decided to rest them only for a minute. It would only be an hour or so till curfew lifted. After a few moments, she was completely asleep.

Her companion did not stop his pacing for the remainder of the morning. Nor did his eyes leave her or the blade.

* * *

⊥ "Zyr?"

The inviting voice was sweet and alluring. The monk slowly blinked his eyes and tried to focus. Darkness gave way to blurry soft candlelight. His mind was slowly unfogging from the effects of unconsciousness. Zyr focused his mind and began reviewing recent events as they occurred in his memory. As a physician, Zyr knew that

154

blows to the head, particularly around the base of the skull, were potentially irreparable.

He hoped that his gamble had paid off, and it seemed it had. However, judging by the situation, he knew that every contingency could not be planned for. Even his best laid plans had been fraught in ruin before.

Gradually, things began to take shape around him as he quickly began to appraise the surroundings. He was in a large room which was decorated with all sorts of wall hangings and tapestries. Small trinkets or artifacts adorned different parts of the room. There were two windows set into stone encasements, each easily as tall as a man and ornately decorative. He was lying on a large black stone table at the center of the chamber. He tested his ability to move but found himself firmly bound. Off to his right side, several cloaked forms stood in quiet readiness. He assumed they were all Ashori and would form powerful weaves at any sign of aggression. Beyond them lay the only exit from the room.

He reached out to the Root lightly and found nothing there. He felt a strange feeling lying upon the black table. It was a total absence of life and spirit.

He turned his head slowly, looking for the source of the voice he had heard earlier. From the shadows a form appeared and moved smoothly towards the prone healer. As it moved closer the form became more defined. It was a woman whose beauty was commanding and seductive. The very sway of her gliding steps reminded Zyr of a bird of prey or stalking Gnarel. He observed her features with a mixture of intrigue and disdain. It was possible that this woman was her, but it had been over fifteen years and many things would change. No, he would hold his judgements until he was certain. An examination of their motives would be most telling. The woman's face was veiled from view, which intrigued Zyr more as to his suspicions of her identity. If only he could be sure.

"It is Zyr, isn't it?" she spoke as she moved ever closer. "Your name is not unknown in the city. I am Nuril. It appears you have taken a wrong turn this evening. What is your business in Khyvla?" Zyr stared hard at the veil in silence. The voice was very different but his senses were still alight like the storms over Tamers Reach.

After a tense moment, a form from the right broke ranks and raised a hand to strike the monk across the face in payment for silence. In one blurred motion, the woman had moved and the Ashori was staggering, choking back a scream of pain. A long slender stiletto blade had passed through his hand and imbedded itself into the man's shoulder. The aggressor's limb was now pinned uncomfortably and he stepped back quickly, nearly retching in pain. Zyr noted the wisps of smoke trailing from the blade.

"No one touches him." Her voice was suddenly commanding and harsh. It carried a warning so palpable that the cloaked ones knelt to a knee and sought forgiveness in unison.

She regarded the ritualistic display briefly, and then spoke venomously. "You will leave, now. If I see another foolish upstart this night, I will rend your hearts in the utmost agony." After she finished, they quickly departed and closed the door behind them. No one questioned her motivation for being alone with the monk. If they had they would not have dared to vocalize it.

"Well," she said in a mocked cheerful voice, "those are no longer necessary, I believe." She nodded her head subtly toward Zyr and the fiery bonds dissipated. He reached over and touched the raw flesh where the bonds had made contact. The bands of fire were meant to be painful and to hold the enemy, but not to kill. He sat up slowly and swung his feet over the edge of the dark tablet.

"An interesting way to inspire fealty," he spoke as he slipped to the floor. Blood rushed through his body and he stepped gingerly as his equilibrium returned. She remained at the foot of the table, observing him behind the veil.

"It is the only way to motivate the simple minded. Come, sit with me by the window." She turned and moved towards an ornate seat at the end of the room. Next to it was a deep-set, gilded window which overlooked the south eastern domains of Khyvla. A small candle rested upon the casement and illuminated the gilded framework. The soft glow of the early morn silhouetted the peaks and foothills beyond the city.

Zyr remained standing next to the table. He reached for the Root again and detected the faintest thread. The effects of the table seemed to be fading. He was not sure now what to expect. So far, she had betrayed no foreknowledge of knowing him, much less a familiar greeting. True, she had spoken his name, and yet, it seemed that she avoided any connection to him. An empty seat sat across from hers, which he likened to a cozy thread in a spider's web. Slowly, Nuril untied the threads which bound her deep red robe across her shoulders. As the stool had no backing, she let the robe fall across the top and settled down comfortably upon the lush material.

Though her face was still veiled, her delicate shift revealed much about her beauty. It was a thin form-fitting garment and hinted at every curve and line beneath. The neckline was cut low, and soft white skin glowed in the shadows. Despite the charms she was initiating, Zyr was intent on the features beneath the veil more than upon lusts of the flesh. She turned her head toward him slowly. They simply stared across at the other, the moments sliding by like a dagger across a whetstone. Finally she broke the silence.

"There is nothing to gain from refusing the hospitality of your host. Am I so dangerous to a man such as you?" Her voice was light and sweet. Zyr noted the contrast from her earlier words with the cadremen. He chose to remain silent. "Very well, if you wish we shall disregard the formalities." The cadre leader turned and faced her guest. She rested an elbow upon her crossed legs and lifted a finger to her cheek. "What possessed you to attack the Ashori of this cadre?" Her voice had changed again. It was sharp like a blade and cut through the space between them.

"I had no idea self-defence was indictable." The monk kept his responses short to avoid giving any leverage to his opponent. Her hand lifted from her cheek to emphasize her next words.

"Surely you cannot lay blame upon the men of this cadre. Their actions have always been in the best interests of the city."

Zyr's retort was quick to the task. "Perhaps you mean for themselves or you. Regardless, the true issue at hand is why are you here, leading this cadre?" Her form was perfectly serene sitting there regarding him from behind her veil.

"The business of the Blade of Ahtol is none of your concern. Know that you interfered in the apprehension of a dangerous individual. Once you took it upon yourself to harbour her, you became an obstacle to be removed. Count yourself fortunate to have survived the incident. Now, with a formal statement of apology you shall be released with a reprimand. Leniency, you will learn, is not outside our creed." He studied her carefully. She was turning the conversation away from his enquiry. Bluntness, it would seem, was called for in such times.

"Defence of those outside the Root is something you should know …" Zyr stabbed a knowing glare towards the woman, "Jyril." Her fingers which had been pressed together in thought separated for a quick movement. He thought he had scored a subtle strike in her verbal game.

However, her fingers slipped together into a vice like grip. She peered just over her clamped hands and emitted a small laugh.

"You speak in riddles, sir. Is that some sort of title or a slander?" Her body had straightened and she regarded him with a cool air behind the dark veil. She was resisting his attempts to unmask her. She was manoeuvring as well; he could sense the game changing. She concluded her entrapment. "Know that if you refuse our attempt at treatise then you shall be released to the Khyvlan authority and endure the full weight of law." She sat in perfect stillness as her words trailed through the air. She was weaving a web to ensnare him, and he sensed her dark approach through the shadowy veil. It was obvious; no proof could be garnered for his defence. First, there were no witnesses and, second, there would be no evidence of a fire thanks to his counter-glyph and she would have cleaned up the rest since the attack. Her position was solid and near flawless. Either way, she was attempting to steer the conversion away from his investigation.

"I regret that you feel my dealings had intent of malice," he began slowly. He had to be extremely careful now. "I assure you my actions were unselfishly motivated. I would be sure to note my gratitude for your stopping your servant from striking an innocent and unarmed man; I'm sure he also thanks you for the favour, instead of being investigated by local authority. After all, I am sure the authorities would have no reason to want to investigate the Blade." His face was dead calm and expressionless, revealing naught but innocence. Her two pointer fingers flicked upward and met. Pressing them together, the pale skin grew white under the pressure she exerted. Zyr knew he routed her argument, but she was merely testing the waters.

"Clearly, it was better for him to suffer judgement now than bring disgrace to the cadre."

"Indeed," he responded. Her poise was so delicate and her voice like sweet honey; the monk knew lesser men would have been ensnared by her conniving charms. Her every quality centered on the game of acquisition. She was skilled in the art of deliberation and hidden truths. When he had heard rumours that Nuril was Tehsa he had no choice but to act. Nuril was fully ascended through the ranks of the Defiler cadre, and she had survived the destruction of the marbled halls of the Order, years past. Yet, more alarming were the implications of betrayal. The information was sketchy and yet, full of implications if it proved true. That was why he had to be sure. Mother help him if it proved true.

Nuril sensed his lapse in concentration and manoeuvred quickly. "Now, considering the matter of your attack on my bondsman..."

"It is not a concern," he interjected, "considering he was not harmed. Yet, I am caused great pain by these obvious marks left by the fiery bonds of my captor. Really, was such force required? I would have gladly come upon receiving summons from one so familiar to me."

Her head cocked slightly. He sensed tension in her limbs, and he knew she could feel the victory slipping from her. She abandoned the line of questioning and shifted to a full defence.

"Whatever gives you claim to my acquaintance? We have never met before this night." She tilted her head to the side and cast her gaze toward the dark horizon which was shifting low to purple-blue in its anticipation of the morning sun.

"The Lady Nuril is well known in these parts to everyone, especially as the occupant of the One Seat, which honour I believe has never before been bestowed upon a woman. Surely, only a true Convert or Seeker of law and justice could succeed where you have. Your training must have been rigorous." He accentuated his references to the broken Order through a simple open-handed gesture. It was a common acknowledgement amongst those of that place. He had her against the wall and was ready to land the final blow. He began to move slowly through the room, around to the long black tablet where he had awoken. Tracing a finger across the cold stone, he could feel the rage and heat emitting from the woman. She would know now that he suspected her true intent here in Khyvla. Her web had failed. It was no mere fly she had caught. Tehsa would have remembered. It was time to strum the last chord.

"Listen well, Nuril. The plans of this cadre are known and will not be ignored. You cannot control a power as potent as this Ahtol. You will bring our world to ruin!" He brought his open hand down in emphasis upon the cold stone. He opened the faintest weave to the Alacritor aspect. He found the stress line within.

"Spare your simple-minded rhetoric. You have no idea what true potency is. It's because of naive thinking such as yours that we scrape by upon the whims of an unseen and crippled entity. You wander the land following spectres, mere whispers! We shall mete out power as we see fit and not limit ourselves to fragments. Think of it! The possibilities are limitless!" She was looking not directly at him but at a woven map which hung upon the far wall.

Zyr was not yet certain of her identity. However, he was fixed upon his purpose and opened his mouth to speak a final time. If it was her, he would leave no doubt to his purpose. His mind mused briefly upon the symbolism nestled inside his leather pouch. The die was cast.

"You say I am misguided and of a simple mind. How presumptuous to think you know all the workings of Aerluin. Your lust of power draws focus away from what is real and what you lost. You should know I have wandered these many years in search of someone who disappeared. I have had strong confirmation that she exists, and dwells here in Khyvla. I promise you she will be found. I also swear to you that she will come to answer for the grievances of the past. That I swear in blood!"

Opening the floodgates of the Alacritor Root, Zyr felt a massive surge of power thunder through his body, almost taking him over the verge of consciousness. He let the power course through every muscle and aspect of his soul. Nuril's eyes shot wide as she turned suddenly to face him. The power shattered his stalwart resolve, as was the case when he opened himself unguarded to the pure fragments of Aerluin's might, that tears flowed from his eyes. In a quick movement he brought a glowing fist down upon the obsidian slab with tremendous force. A massive crunching sound vibrated the walls and foundations of the tower. The table split across the middle cleanly, the massive slabs crashing to the floor. The echoes of tumult seemed to multiply upon each other, reverberating around the circular room endlessly. The backlash of released energies and splintered stone had lacerated his hand and lower arm. Zyr stood there bowed, his hand dripping seeds of lifeblood upon the dark remains of the altar.

Green tinged energy flows surged throughout the room which had escaped upon the rending of the stone. Nuril was now standing and moving toward him slowly, her hand outstretched. The green flows began to move and twist toward the master Ashori. Sensing the danger, Zyr leapt over the altar remains straight to the window adjacent to where she had sat.

All at once, all things seemed to move slowly.

Twisting through the air, the green trails snaked rapidly toward Zyr. He knew he had one opportunity for escape, and it was a risky, possibly fatal venture. Yet, his luck had run out in the oral skirmish. Death awaited the unwary, and he had overstayed his time here. As he readied his final manoeuvre, he looked to Nuril. Her veil was fluttering from the energies which curled and wrapped around her slender body. He saw her eyes flash in fury toward him. They were blood red and shone with intense hate. It was his Jyril's face but with the eyes of a demon. Then time remembered itself. Everything moved quicker than a heartbeat.

Zyr shot through the tower window, glass exploding while grasping at the tapestry curtain as he passed through, blue-white energy trailing from his fingertips. Deep jade energy struck through the space he had been like great tentacles, then coiled about to pursue the monk. Clinching the curtain tightly, Zyr twisted himself around and swung his legs hard toward the sheer tower wall. The tapestry slowed his momentum and then finally gave way to the exertion, but it had served to bring the Monk close to the vertical surface. He reached out with his pulsing hands and pulled himself to the stone. The green bands streaked after him in a flash, altering course through the shattered window frame. With moments to react, Zyr knew he would not survive without the ability to counter the opposing power; for that he would need his limbs which were currently engaged in preserving his life. There remained only one painful but obvious choice.

Steeling himself, he let go of the wall and felt his stomach lurch under the effects of a free fall. As he dropped he remained in line with the wall, as the structure was perfectly cylindrical. The green strands fell behind unable to match the speed of his descent. The wind was whistling in his ears as his tattered robes flailed about his head. Zyr watched the ground fast approaching with intense concentration. One small slip and Nuril's problems would be solved. At the moment of decision, he slammed his hands into the sheer surface of the tower which sped past him. Grunting in pain, he squeezed his eyes shut attempting to discipline his mind to avert the overwhelming pain. Heat and pressure threatened to disintegrate his hands upon the stone yet he struggled to maintain the enchantment which strengthened his hands like unto iron. The pressure was also great upon his arms, he had to keep his fingers imbedded in the stone and the friction of descent and rock were resisting. He could not risk using his feet for it would upset the already tentative balance he fought to maintain. With no counter leverage to push against the stone with he had only his strength to thrust his hands into the stubborn stone with all his might. Finally, in order to keep the alacrity focused he abandoned discipline and gave way to the impulse to roar out in pain. It echoed the wounds in his heart. As he plummeted on, he was slowing, but the ground was approaching fast. He spied the most adequate escape lane and breathed deeply. At the last moment he dislodged his hands and kicked off from the wall, stretching his body full out, his arms pushed out above his head. As he came swiftly to the ground he tucked his body and began to roll, each movement had to be precise, no body part exposed to the significant force for more than an instant. He rolled hard and felt his body groan against the shifting vectors. He continued to revolve his body like a thundering wheel, as he desperately tried to hold the tuck together. His body slammed into barrels and dragged over stone and wood, rending his garments and flesh, all of these helping to slow his inertia. Finally, he smashed into the wall of a nearby building, completely knocking the air from his body. Gently, Zyr rolled himself over, gasping and retching for recovery of breath. His watering eyes saw the mystical bands of green retract back within the tower window now high above him.

In his daze he thought he saw her standing at the window far above, peering down at him. "Tehsa," he mouthed wordlessly. He let his head slump down on the ground, his eyes closed again from the agony of the night's abuse upon his body; its nerves screamed at him in disdain. His mind, however, was stoic and cool with the bitter coldness of vengeance. She was here and she was a blood-traitor, a Defiler, and the enemy. She would find her end among the others of her kind now. There was to be no mercy for the corrupt and vile abusers of all that was pure. His heart was rent in twain; deep within he felt a pang that overwhelmed all his physical pain. His breath returned at last. A raspy whisper escaped.

"Tehsa … why?"

ꚩ   She watched in cool disbelief as he lay there for many moments. He was always reckless, but this display completely unnerved her. 'Why did he come here' she

thought. It must have been as he said, to find her. But to risk
so much, on such a foolhardy and near-fatal venture, she felt
there must have been another reason. It had been so long
now; the years had melted by since he left her. Her head
slumped against the stone wall and she sighed in frustration.
Nuril slowly removed the veil and the daggers carefully
from her hair. As each blade slid from her tresses, dark
waterfalls spilled across her breast. She ran a hand absently
through the shining locks and looked on at the stumbling
fool. He slowly gained his feet and limped off into the night.
She watched him carefully, with glowing ruby eyes. Before
he completely faded from view, he turned and glanced at
her. She felt a tremor in her heart which unsettled her and in
frustration she struck the stone with a clenched hand. The
plan of the Order of Cadres did not permit this needless
delay. There was much to be done, now that the meddler
had set back plans. She glanced at the broken black altar. It
would need to be repaired or replaced. Neither option was
easily achieved. She shook her head angrily. He had set her
back at great expense in time and resources, and the Order
would certainly be enraged. She detested Zyr so much, and
yet her hate was not centered on this morning's havoc. It
reached further back than that. She cursed the day she met
him, or became his friend. She wished she had not let him
go. She looked at her hands which were trembling and
folded about her midriffs, gently caressing her skin. She was
bitter, but could not stop her feelings from surfacing. In the
end, deep inside she did not want to stop them. She

remained lost in time while gazing down at the empty street, surrendering herself to the pleasurable memories of the past.

A soft tap upon the door dragged her from her private escape. She smoothly replaced the bladed veil and a fragile mask of civility.

"Enter."

The door opened slowly admitting one of her cadre. He approached, as always pausing just past the darkened threshold. Nuril noted that the sun was now peaking over the far mountains. How long had she stood there? "What merits this disruption?" she demanded.

The man hesitated for a moment. Perhaps it was seeing his mistress for the first time so informally. Perhaps it was the state of disrepair in the room, or the broken alter. Either way he remained speechless. "Speak or I'll kill you where you stand!" Her voice came strangely high pitched and fast, uncharacteristic of her demeanor.

"Forgive me my lady, I have news to report." He faltered again, at a loss for words and it seemed to be related to the information he brought. Struggling on, he spoke cautiously, "My lady, the prize has escaped."

Her face darkened upon hearing the devastating report. Pacing the room she pondered to herself. This would create more difficulty, more setbacks. Her thoughts were interrupted. "Excuse me, but I must … I have to report that the Blade of Ahtol … has been stolen." He barely whispered the last portion of the account.

"What?" She wheeled around and swept over to him, grabbing his cloak roughly. The hood fell from his head from the violent motion and she glared into his fearful eyes. "That is impossible. It hasn't arrived in Khyvla yet. The cargo is expected today." He trembled as he started to slink backward; however, she maintained her grip and prevented his escape by crushing him into the wall. Her veiled face was but a breath away from his and her chest rose and fell in the anxiety of the moment. He struggled to maintain a sense of composure.

"The shipment arrived late last night. It … it appears that the thief moved almost immediately following the docking. One man overwhelmed the entire armed escort stationed on the boat. The cadre representatives from Jandor are surprised as well …"

"Of course they are! Idiots! They should have hired professionals, not common street rabble to protect it!" She ground her fist into the herald with increasing pressure. He was having difficulty breathing. The thought of retaliation would never cross his mind. She could wink out his life in a moment. "Be gone from my sight. Warn any who wish to disturb me this day." She turned from him and paced to the broken altar.

His final words were a bellows to the inferno of her mind.

"But … my Lady, I have to tell you, the authorities are approaching the tower as we speak with demands to see the One Seat. Several of our numbers have been taken into custody, accused of witnessing or aiding in the slaughter of six Watchmen last night."

*   *   *

Θ   Ebyn perched upon a bench in the lower regions of
the guild tower. He shook his head in memory of the
previous night. To be bailed out by Gaeth was beyond
imagination. That bumbling oaf had the audacity to follow
him and assist in taking the prisoner. Yet deep within, he
sensed that the battle had slipped away from him, and that
he should be dead. His mind played over and over the
sequence of events. Clearly, he underestimated the monk.
The speed in which Ebyn was overtaken was unthinkable
and frightening. He had stared his mortality in its merciless
face and came out victor. His mind grazed over the chair
flying at him; he had closed his eyes for the briefest moment.
It should have hit! Did the monk miss intentionally? His
troubled thoughts were broken asunder as agonizing
screams, drifting through the tower, reached his ears below.
So the monk was suffering. It was well then that he had
risked his life to capture him. Earlier, all had paused in
alarm as the tower doomed like a gong, the thundering
resonance coming from Nuril's chamber. None dared to
enter and seek answers. No one would go unless
summoned. Earlier, a comrade had climbed the steps
hurriedly and seemed intent on passing on information from

the previous night. Ebyn had kept to himself, marred with the stain of defeat. He hadn't spoken to anyone. Perhaps he could acquire information from the cadre-man when he returned from Nuril.

At that moment, he jumped back in alarm as something flashed past his vision. He moved quickly from the antechamber to the stair which spiralled downward around the tower perimeter. Looking down in horror, he saw the same guildsman crumpled upon the floor below, blood pooling steadily around his head. He had fallen from the heights of the tower. Everything was thrown into confusion and the magi stalled in their impulse to ascend the stairs. Ebyn wondered to himself whether the man had fallen or was thrown. The entrance to the tower sounded the dull thumps of a visitor. 'Who would dare such effrontery?' Ebyn wondered as he peered down to the sealed doors. One of his blood-brothers moved cautiously to the door and gestured his hand to temporarily unseal the binding weave. As the doors opened he moved back a step. A formal looking entourage accompanied the chancellor of the city. A large uniformed guard stepped forward but, careful not to cross the threshold, his deep voice booming through the tower.

"You will summon Lady Nuril to meet with this delegation without delay."

Despite adversity, the tender plant had taken root and was growing strong. Other more mature growth surrounded the

Sapling in attempt to shield it from danger. The black weed was deceptive and near invisible in its entwining around the stem of the Sapling. As well, the young tree would soon pass beyond the shelter of the surrounding foliage and would have to weather the storms alone.

QUELLING DEMONS

THE CITY awoke from its induced slumber. Every house spewed forth its occupants into the streets. Within moments after the end of curfew was sounded, the thoroughfares became bustling rivers of activity. The streams of people rushed here and there, moving intently to their destinations. The gates would not open for another half hour, allowing merchants and tradesman to prepare somewhat for the influx of visitors. It also allowed the vagrants and less fortunate to set up for begging, stealing and any other shady business that powered a lucrative market. A typical day in the city greeted the people of Khyvla. None were aware of events that took place in their city the previous night.

It was through the swarming masses that two inconspicuous forms wound their way. They moved together, clothed in blankets, which were wrapped around their heads and draped down past the waist. To most of the city folk, they appeared as street vermin, and many steered a wide berth around them. The two continued on their way slowly to the merchant gates in the south-east corner of the city. One of them, the smaller of the two, moved quickly and stopped periodically - waiting for the other who limped after. It was slightly before gate opening time that they arrived at the heavy wooden structures.

The immense doors of the gate were hauled open by use of a pulley and chain system. Several men stood half naked, preparing to exert themselves in the strenuous endeavor. At the sound of a loud whistle from far off into the city interior, the men took places around a pinwheel on either side of the gate (one for either side). The massive chains were stretched taut to the gate doors from the pinwheel gears. The workers exerted all their energies upon metal shafts which protruded outward from the wheel, and slowly the chains began to spiral around the gears, while the doors slowly parted. It wasn't long before the gate entrance stood open, and the labourers wiped slick sweat from their bodies. A long line of merchant carts and waggons spanned into the distance, their owners prepared to move the procession ahead. They moved to where they could see the merchants as they approached.

The gate marshals readied the admitting and inspection booths, as they did, they spotted a body strewn across the path where the gate had been closed. Angrily, they moved to the still form, and bent down to inspect the problem. As the two covered figures watched on from a distance, they saw the marshals recoil in disgust, standing and pushing the form over with their boots. The body stirred dust and grime as it flopped, until it came to rest against the stone walls adjacent to the merchant gate. As the marshals returned to their post, the cowled pair heard them mutter curses and profanities.

"Forsaken merchants! Drunk and filthy … Seems every morning there's one."

"Looks like he's been messed with; still it's one less drunk to deal with today. Let 'em rot! …"

"That's fine until the Captain arrives, then guess who gets appointed cleanup. Bloody merchant!"

The two blanketed persons regarded the still man who lay in a cloud of dust. Slowly as the dust filtered to the ground one of the shrouded figures screamed out, "Tohm!" As she sprinted toward the gate entrance, the blanket swept from her shoulders. The marshals went to block her path, but upon seeing her state of apparel they made way and scowled as she rushed past.

"Tohm? Tohm!" She cried out in alarm as she fell to the ground beside him. His chest was moving and the dust swirled from the breath in his nostrils. It was then that she gasped in horror. His whole face was severely burnt on one side. Then upon closer inspection, she hurriedly discovered that his whole right side above the knees was blistered and scarred brutally. His hair was mostly gone and his face was contorted in the most desperate and sorrowful expression. "Oh … Tohm, why? Who did this?" She laid her head upon his chest as tears began to fall in despair.

"Firah, who is this?" The voice came from her companion, standing just behind her. The merchants had already begun moving slowly through the entrance, completely ignoring the desperate scene.

"This is the friend I was going to meet, Shien, but something has happened … oh, Tohm." She brought his head up and placed her discarded blanket beneath his head after Shien passed it to her. She brushed his good cheek and shook her head slowly.

"His hands … they're practically black from bruising and blood." Shien remarked as he bent down to inspect the man. Tohm's clothes were also tattered and scorched black from fire. He felt the left wrist; there was still a heartbeat. "Well, I suppose we will have to get him to an inn. He needs immediate care from a physician." Shien sighed; his little discomforts would have to wait. He moved to the gate, and was stopped short by the marshals.

"This is the merchant gate, and unless you have wares, you must remove yourselves from here." The look from the marshal was pure disdain.

"We just passed through here! We had to assist that man, and he requires help now!" He moved toward the marshal, who put a hand upon the flustered man's chest.

"Use the main entrance and see if they will accept you there; any more talk and the Watch will be called." He turned from Shien and continued his work.

Shien was livid. "You heartless Vikyral-slave! You absolute vermin! Do you think we can possibly carry him that far?" The marshal glared at him and made a motion to another worker farther in, who disappeared quickly. Shaking his head angrily, Shien limped back to Firah. "We need to move, encountering the Watch right now would be well … you know." She nodded quickly. Shien unrolled the blanket beside the large man. They took two limbs each (Firah on the legs and Shien the arms) and shifted Tohm's massive frame onto the improvised lift. "I'm sorry," Shien murmured, "I should have held my tongue … I just can't believe the utter callousness of some people."

✲✲ "Don't apologize," Firah grunted out behind gritted teeth as she clenched wadded rolls of blanket in her hands; it was all she could do was to move her end of Tohm's body. "I felt the same … your words were right." She thought about last night; she had felt the same about Shien. She marveled how fast things could change. Suddenly, she stumbled and a blanket corner dropped from her grasp. The momentum tore the material out of Shien's grip, and Tohm crashed to the ground. "Oh no! I can't do this, Shien. He's too heavy for me, even together. Look at you too; you're hardly able to walk straight on your own. What are we going to do?" Her face began to fall again in hopelessness.

"We're not giving up, that's what!" He came around to Firah's side. Placing a hand on her shoulder, he looked squarely into her eyes. "I know it's hard to do this, but if we just move a little at a time we'll ..."

"Take the rest of the day and that will take too long." A familiar deep voice remarked behind them. Shien whirled and Firah yelped. "You, grab that corner and, Firah, take the other. We're moving to Tohm's cart." Firah had turned to see Zyr preparing to hoist Tohm's massive torso. She gasped again.

Zyr looked similar to Tohm, his body burnt in places as well as bloodied, bruised and cut, not to mention his robes that were tattered and sullied beyond recognition. Zyr favoured a leg as he set himself to lift. Shien was still gaping in shock; the man had completely caught him off guard. "Grab a corner!" Zyr snapped them from their shock. "I don't have energy to waste!" Firah jumped into action. It was the first time she had heard the monk raise his voice in irritation. Shien grabbed the other side wordlessly but continued to watch the new arrival carefully. Together they hoisted Tohm on the heavy wool, all muscles flexing and knotting from exertion. Luckily, Tohm's cart was not far away. He had almost made the entrance the night before. However, it was many slow, painful and agonizing steps until they reached the waggon. The line had moved around the dormant cart and merchants rode by wordlessly.

Gently, they placed Tohm down just under the waggon chassis with a rolled blanket under his head supplied by Shien. There was no room in the waggon for his large frame, not to mention the dead lift would be near impossible for them in their depleted states. At best, shade was provided this way. "We will need water, but judging by our attire, none of us should try to gain access to the city right now." Zyr unbuckled Tohm's belt and unbuttoned the remains of the shirt. After a quick inspection, he moved the large man to his side and adjusted Tohm's arms and legs in odd positions. Firah was perplexed watching the procedure. "I'll return soon." Zyr instructed as he took up a long water skin hanging from the side of the driver's seat, which appeared mostly empty.

"Wait right there!" Shien demanded as Zyr made to move off. "Who are you? What's going on here?" He looked from the new fellow to Firah.

"She will tell you. I have work to do." Shien watched as Zyr set into a limped trot towards the river, which wound away in the distance. He looked at Firah, who sighed and sunk down by Tohm's side. Shien slowly followed suit, his body screaming out for a break from the punishment without respite. He looked at the diminishing figure incredulously, and waited.

"His name is Zyr, the other friend of mine... the one I was trying to help last night ..." His face lit up in understanding.

✕   "I see." Shien considered how much his life had changed in just one night. Previously, he felt carefree about life and he hadn't taken much responsibility except for securing the heirlooms which where his by right. He fingered the pack strap; his heart ached to see them and yet he knew if wasn't appropriate at the moment. Now that he had acquired the weapons he was unsure as to what he should do. This passion to reclaim the swords was all consuming for so long. Now his life seemed to open as a broad road before him. It was an odd feeling to have. Looking down at the large man, who lay unconscious and infirm beside them, he felt the pangs of sorrow exuding from the girl. Her delicate face was intent on the wounds and scars the man bore. He also felt a degree of concern within himself, and he marvelled at the foreign feeling. Shien continued to ponder as he watched over the poor merchant. There was profound silence until Zyr returned some time later. He examined Tohm again, this time rolling him gently to his back.

"Firah, prop his head up a little; keep him comfortable. Try elevating the feet slightly ... that's it ...," the healer directed "and you ..."

"Shien," the young man interjected briskly.

"… prepare this water by boiling it; I can't afford infections. I'll be assessing the extent of the damage. Luckily, we are close to the city and my curing should not draw out any aggression upon us." Shien looked at the cleric with an air of offense. He did not take well to orders; however, the circumstances were dire. He would swallow his pride, for now.

"You could try behind the seat, Shien. He usually stores his cooking things there." Firah cast a quick smile at him. If anything, he would do the task because of that small act. Stiffly, he willed his frame to move upward and gradually around the waggon.

≠   Zyr's hand passed slowly over Tohm just a fraction above the skin. With his eyes closed, he sought to trace the map of the human body in his mind. That was all there was to delving really, once a person understood how the body worked. Each pass with his hand revealed vital information regarding the muscular, nervous, and skeletal and blood systems. Strangely, despite the massive hurt upon his large friend, Zyr discerned that there was no bodily harm that should necessitate such incapacitation. As his hand passed over the skull he felt something odd. Zyr stopped and lowered his hand to his side. What was that feeling? He closed his senses off to all else around him and searched deep within his mind for an answer. Suddenly he recalled a vague memory, a case concerning a member of the Order long ago. It seemed the victim had been assaulted by Cerephor weaves which had caused severe damage to the cerebral functions. It was a vicious lashing which required significant efforts in healing. Sadly, the man was never the same. Personality changes, emotional damage, longevity diminished. Zyr pulled himself from the induced meditation and opened his eyes slowly. He cast his soft blue gaze upon the poor man. He could do something for him, but would it help? Glancing to his right he saw the girl intent on her old friend. Her eyes full of concern, she brushed the uninjured skin of Tohm's face. Should he let her know? It would only cause her more sorrow and pain.

Zyr closed his eyes again, this time they clenched in anger. There was one clear answer for this perpetration and crime. It always came back to those who inflicted evil for naught but sheer pleasure. After this morning's encounter, he was struggling to maintain his calm composure. Already, he had been short with others because of the diverting battle raging through his soul; now the hurt was building upon itself. Somehow he must suppress it for Firah's sake. She would need a strong support soon. Sighing deeply, he touched her arm. She looked to him eagerly.

"The physical damage is not severe, despite what it may look like. Those burns while seeming grave, are generally superficial. I may be able to help cure such injury. His hands are crushed and splintered, but I can certainly remedy that." He decided to stop there. He would never lie to the girl, yet he could not tell her what he suspected. He would need to talk to Tohm first, following the nerve repair. She brightened upon hearing the news and cried softly in relief. She placed her head on Tohm's breast, her matted hair spilling over his torso. He would give Firah a moment before the mending.

Zyr stood up and walked toward the other man. Shien was busily tending a small fire, and had to his credit performed the task with great efficiency. Zyr would need to speak to the young man, to glean any knowledge of the previous night and determine the character of the Firah's escort. Shien lifted his head as the monk approached. His face betrayed mistrust; it was understandable. Zyr crouched down beside the stalwart fighter. He could tell that Shien was harbouring some pain and hurt, but was choosing to keep it to himself. That was admirable. "Forgive me. My introduction was poor, as I had to determine how our colleague was faring. I pray, accept my apology." Zyr held out a calloused hand smattered with dried blood and dirt. Shien grasped the hand tightly for a moment and smiled. Releasing the grip, he looked back towards the fire.

"I understand your apprehension about my involvement with the girl. I merely helped her out of a sticky situation and apart from that, I have no other agenda." Zyr gazed upon the young man with a degree of awe. He had discerned his thoughts; was it luck or something else? He put those thoughts away for later.

"I was wondering if you could tell me what happened last night? While we wait for the water ..."

🜚   The air was still. The sun burned high in the midday sky. Clouds would occasionally bring fleeting respite to the people below. Tohm's eyes fluttered open slowly, the pupils gradually focusing. He lay there for a time shifting his gaze from person to person. He let the air flow into his nostrils, passing in and out. He looked at a man, who sat nearest with his sleeves rolled up his arms. He was preparing some solution in a bowl which brought herbal scents to his nose. The man was preparing to cure him of some injury. It seemed to Tohm he looked like a water-golem; settled and still as a mountain lake. Tohm's memory was foggy and occasionally lapsed into voids of thought. It was as if his mind was a wooden puzzle with pieces carved and plucked out. He saw hands moving toward the swollen flesh on his face. Suddenly his mind exploded from some distant shaded memory. He swatted the hand away from his face. Sitting up swiftly, he grasped his bare scalp with a trembling hand.

"Nnn ... uh ..." He whipped his head around quickly, his eyes wild. All perception of things had changed suddenly. The beast wrestled with reality as it twisted into strange perceptions. One creature trembling like a fox kit gasped and stretched out a hand slowly. The beast saw the kit reaching ... like the hand which seared its mind. "Rhyaaa!" Screaming violently, the beast slammed a fist into the kit, knocking her back several feet. She tumbled upon the ground and pulled her arms and legs toward her body, whimpering softly in pain. Another shape like a wolf immediately reacted by attempting to secure the beast's massive arms, but this only enraged it further, unleashed and completely untamed.

"No, Shien. Wait!" the water-golem shouted out, as the beast easily outstripped the wolf's strength. It was too late. The feral force grabbed the struggling wolf's neck and wrenched the throat violently before pounding him into the dirt. The wolf stopped moving. Tohm shot up sharply into a feral stance, his eyes darting and shifting while saliva dripped hungrily across his chin. The golem shifted slowly - water flowing through a low combative stance. Tohm felt his prey edging away and the choice of action was clear. The prey must die for the harm upon the beast.

⸕   Lashing out with massive limbs, Tohm raged and howled. Zyr moved quickly and evaded the desperate attacks. Within the Ashori's mind, logic flowed as steady as the power from the Root. What was done was required, yet Zyr never imagined the outcome would be so severe. Tohm's condition must have run deeper and more complex than he thought.

Suddenly, the monk's defence faltered under a flurry of attacks from his deranged friend. As he dodged low, Tohm's foot rose up sharply to connect with his groin. Zyr leaned forward with snaking hands intent on snaring and trapping the leg. It was part of a sequence he learned long ago, yet, it had risks. In that instant, the healer's mind read the flows of combat that told him what would happen next. His weary body, fatigued from hours of strain and abuse, would not move as fast as he willed it.

▽   It was in that moment of weakness that the beast struck out. Its head savagely hammering the healer with all the force of a battering ram. Reeling, the water-golem attempted to compensate, but primal instinct altered the attack and brutally gnashed teeth down upon the monk, rending his robes and tearing the elusive fluids away from the healer's lower neck. The living water creature cried out in pain while the beast howled within the frenzied blood lust. As he did so, his hands came around battering his prey's body with several thunderous blows. The golem collapsed to the ground and struggled weakly to rise as the giant linked both his fleshy hammers and bashed them across his foe's back.

⊥   The monk's mind told him what would happen. Tohm would not stop until he was dead. Tohm picked up Zyr with seeming ease and threw him mercilessly into the side of the cart, splintering wood and grinding the metal chassis. Lying prone, the monk squinted upward at the relentless animal which stalked toward him. 'How could I have misjudged so badly?' he thought wearily, just as another torturous hail crashed upon his broken body. Zyr fought desperately in spirit for his life-force to remain within his body.

"Tohm, stop! Please … stop this …" Firah was upon her knees a few feet away, her hand outstretched toward the massive beast which was her truest friend. Her breath was short and voice ragged.

♈ "F … r … ah …" His voice came in a guttural drawl. Slowly the anger was ebbing, recognition was returning, yet his blood was hot and the beast fought for control. His hand was raised in a final mortal strike across his enemy's neck. The beast snarled in protest. The prey must die. Tohm grabbed his head again and screamed out in a twisted fit of rage. He beat upon his skull harshly to stop the pain.

"Tohm … stop … you'll kill yourself …" Her faint pleads were cooling winds across the scorched desert of his mind. He pressed upon his head so harshly, he felt it would burst. His mind was slowly ebbing, the beast was tearing and lashing within, but slowly it was retreating behind a fragile, veil-thin barrier. Tohm slumped to his knees and continued to moan while clutching the vessel of his storming emotions. It was after several moments that his hands fell to his side and his chin dipped down to his chest. All was still as the sun burned down upon the scene of conflict. Silently, a cloud slipped before the burning orb; as if from an unspoken signal, the girl moved slowly, upon her knees, toward the subdued warrior. Tohm's shoulders rose and fell with his tense breathing.

♓ "Firah … don't … touch him …" Zyr had somehow rolled away and he clutched his savaged neck, where gushing blood had soaked down through what remained of his robes. He seemed barely conscious, trying in vain to move. Tohm eyed the girl intently with a gaze of suppressed rage. His eyes pierced the air between them, deep brown as the earth beneath his fingers, which tensed and released at his side.

"It's okay ... he won't. I just know it," she whispered as she moved close to her friend. She looked at him with such pity. His mind was still chaotic, and he struggled for a semblance of sanity. She was next to him now and he watched as she stopped and breathed in deeply. A hand rose up in front of her body, not moving toward him; it simply floated there before him. Firah turned her hand and slowly opened the fingers. It was an open hand. Timidly, as a wolf before the shepherd, the beleaguered man moved his own hand to take hers. As he felt her gentle warmth, the last of his anger left and he pulled her to himself. Firah wrapped her arms around Tohm and held him as he began to groan again. The older man simply wept tears of pain across the girl's neck. Hers was a soothing presence; the beast had been quelled. Yet, it lingered in the shadows of his mind and growled low in anticipation of freedom again.

✕   Tohm lay upon the ground, eyes closed in deep slumber. He would suddenly toss and stir where he lay, his forehead creased and burning with heat. Shien had only been rendered unconscious, and luckily escaped with only a bruised and painful whiplash in the neck. Gingerly, he rubbed his neck to try to take the stiffness away. Time had passed by so quickly and the sun was heading in its downward march through the western sky. After the frightening episode with Tohm, they had removed themselves as quickly as possible from the merchant entrance. The struggle had been short but all the traffic had moved quickly away from the terrifying scene for fear of being swept up. Moving Tohm around proved as difficult a challenge as it had been earlier, especially in their weakened states. It had not been the only dilemma; they had all waited patiently for the monk to overcome the injuries inflicted upon him. Then much later, after significant trepidation, Tohm successfully ingested some herbs in a drink prepared by the monk. This had appeared to quell the man's emotions sufficiently. He had fallen into slumber quietly, and the hapless group, weary and fatigued, were afforded a respite. Finally the cart and companions rested under the shelter of a small grove of trees to the south of the city. To Shien, it seemed that fate had completely abandoned all of them to long dreary roads, which offered no relief from harsh pain and suffering. He was amazed at the recent chaotic events which had come into his life, all he felt he could do to cope was to chuckle to himself. Firah was walking by when she heard him emit the suppressed mirth. She turned on her heel and moved to him angrily.

"How can you laugh … after all this?" She had her fists planted firmly upon her hips and carried a look so dark that

Shien was sure it would repel the fiercest Gnarel. Firah had been storming like a typhoon about the camp for the last hour or so. She was frustrated at her inability to receive an explanation for Tohm's sudden behavior shift. Once Zyr had sufficiently tended to all their injuries, only then did he slip into an induced trance without offering any information to either of them. Shien wasn't about to be critical, after being selflessly healed by the good man. He found out later that Tohm had abused Zyr like a butcher tenderizing a fresh shank of meat. He shuddered as he watched the still form of the Ashori against the tree. 'He should have died' Shien mused.

He realized that he was ignoring the girl who loomed overhead. She was completely unreasonable in this state and no amount of talking would help either. Every emotion was centered on impatience and anger. Everyone dealt with the situation in their own way; for Shien, he had to laugh … the only other option was to grieve. He looked to the massive frame of the slumbering merchant. He was still scarred in severe burns. One thing Zyr had made clear was that only life threatening injuries could be attended to initially, as his energy was waning. Firah's voice cut through Shien's vain attempts to shut her ranting out.

"Stop ignoring me! Curse your silence and his too!" She waved toward Zyr's location. Her whole spirit was now livid and seeking an outlet. She slammed her fist into a nearby birch. "Oooh …" Firah waved her bruised hand about in fits of pain.

Shien laughed again. This time the laughter was unsuppressed. "What are you doing? Are you trying to kill the healer or the tree?" He stood up slowly and scratched his day-old stubble thoughtfully. He could sense the heat from her rising to dangerous levels. That was good; she needed to channel her anger toward something. He could sense her taking the bait.

"You … you …" Her face welled up crimson as her body burned like a furnace. 'Any second now' he thought.

Something unusual was happening. The brooch Firah wore on her shirt had started to flash brilliantly. Shien watched as wispy trails of energy began swirl about the troubled girl. They shifted amongst every colour, illuminating her body. Her face contorted in anger while the streams of hot energy pulsed in rhythm with her blood within her veins. Shien began to consider that he had erred in a bad way.

"Now, Firah, just wait …" He was backing away. Firah was watching the streams intensely with a mixture of alarm and curiosity. They were swelling now in intensity and speed, and bizarrely resembled large vines or brambles replete with pulsing thorns. They snaked around her small form, searching…searching. Suddenly, fear flashed across her face; the energy was starting to overwhelm her.

"Shien, help me!" She cried out as her body was beginning to disappear behind the bands of power. The young man was at a loss as what he could do. She was slowly being swallowed up, cocooned by the very energies she had started in rage. It was as if the brambles were seeking a target and chose Firah. Shien watched helplessly as the energy engulfed the girl. She screamed out in terrified alarm while he shouted to her in vain.

Suddenly, Shien was pushed roughly aside. It was Zyr. The monk rushed over to Firah and set himself in a low stance, his legs square to the ground. He spread his arms outward to the sides, hands open and palms down. Drawing a deep breath he began to weave while moving his hands close together in front of his bare torso. They were positioned strangely, like holding an imaginary ball. Then, Shien saw the mystic, with a flurry of movement, create a strange effect. The hands were moving too fast to see, but he could make out the semi-transparent circle, which could be seen from the passes of Zyr's hands. Shien could not discern what it was exactly; he had no knowledge of magic or its nuances. The best he could determine was that he was weaving some sort of siphon. Twisting trails of white hot energy began to slowly peel off the colorful nexus swirling around Firah, drawn into a mystical ball which the monk had created. The strange man had not shifted his stance, even his head remained perfectly still. His demeanor was cast in grim solemnity, his blue eyes shining hard in reflection of the passing trails of white power. Finally, as the last strand ripped away, the girl was flung to the ground by the force of the twisting energy.

Zyr gathered in the remaining strands and raised the shimmering ball above his head. His whole body glowed from the resonance of the power within his grasp. Shien watched in amazement. Clearly, he had underestimated the humble man. During their talk, Zyr had been very polite and courteous. Shien had measured the meekness as a flaw, perceiving Zyr as weak. How different was his assessment now, as he watched the man wield staggering amounts of energy.

"You two! Get back now!" Zyr shouted out with a strained voice. Shien ran quickly to Firah and helped her up. She was as limp as a weeping birch. Yet, her expression showed alarm as her thoughts remained coherent. She nodded to him as he steered her away from the proximity of the hunched Weaver. Then at once, Zyr brought the energy sphere to the ground in a swift direct motion. The ground reeled and pitched beneath the blow; everything was thrown into motion. A massive fissure opened beneath the monk's legs. Violently it began to spread apart, one side of the forming chasm rising high over the other. The land groaned and rolled in protest to the disruption of its slumber. Shien struggled in the tumult, clutching a limp Firah in one arm and grasping a tree firmly in the other. The ground continued to struggle in anger as the power dispersed throughout the area. Time passed beyond recognition as all waited for nature's tirade to cease.

After a time, the earth ceased its fury; all became still. The land had changed significantly. Green flora had sprouted up for a great distance around, blooming in maturity. The grove had become a substantial wood, thick and lush. Waterfalls of foliage now decorated the sides of the cliffs and spilled over the enormous crevice into the depths below. Then Shien's heart skipped a beat; Zyr was nowhere in sight. The ground had opened right beneath his feet! Surely he could not have ...

Shien placed Firah down and rushed to the precipice, quickly scanning the chasm for any sign of the fallen Ashori. He spied a slender crack in the fissure wall and then noticed the hand grasping tightly just inside the breach. Jumping into action, Shien leapt across a negotiable gap in the chasm. He dashed to Zyr's location and lay flat while extending his reach. Stretching, he secured the healer's hand and began to heave upward. With some effort he pulled the monk out of the chasm. Zyr slumped to his knees, and shook his bowed head from side to side in apparent antipathy. He looked up slowly to the two young fools, his eyes a shade of frozen blue. "It would seem I cannot even find a few hours of peace, can I?"

⁕ "I'm so sorry," she pleaded quietly as she knelt beside her silent protector. He had been quieter than usual this evening. He stared into the fire they had created here in this wondrous new garden. The night sky was cloudless; the stars were all present, flowing waves of light particles across the blackened sea. "What else can I say? Zyr, I don't even know what happened … I wish I knew." She gazed into the dancing flames and sought for understanding.

"I have not been ignoring you intentionally, Firah. I have been putting a lot of thought toward the situation we have all placed ourselves in. I wonder if you ever considered that I sought you out that night in the village." She nodded affirmatively; obviously she had thought there was more to his presence than he initially led them to believe. "I wanted you to take my purse. It was an assessment of sorts." She began to flush in embarrassment, and seeking to rectify the situation she reached to her belt and undid the snaps to the pouch there. She withdrew the contents and held them out in the firelight for them to see.

"I guess you'll want all these things back ... oh and this too," she fingered the brooch pinned to her shirt. Zyr held out a hand, but it was vertical, suggesting a refusal.

"I only request the dice to be returned. You may keep the rest." She placed the two six sided items in his awaiting palm. He squeezed his hand shut and closed his eyes tightly. She watched his manner, and felt a pang of guilt.

"I really am sorry, they must be incredibly powerful, and you could have made use of them today." She hung her head slightly.

"Actually, they have no power at all." She snapped her head up, her features alight in confusion. He smiled slightly, for the first time she could remember. "It's a keepsake from long ago ... about how lucky one can be." He paused in thought, his eyes were distant. "They also remind me of a promise; actually ... no ... it's more like opportunities missed, lost moments which drifted away in the winds of time." His voice now echoed the look in his eyes. He seemed so far from her now, even though she could lift a hand to touch him. He stared into the distance for a time. Firah dared not disturb him. He seemed so peaceful and somehow remorseful as well. It was a perplexing and uncomfortable moment.

He turned his eyes to her and opened his hand again. "You see, they are quite ordinary, except for the fact they are made of Serpentor bone." Firah wondered how such strange bone could ever be categorized with normalcy. Zyr placed them within his own pouch.

"Are you sure about these? I mean this stone ... It was incredible! I didn't get touched by the fire at all. It was really scary. I'm sure you will miss this!" She wondered about what the monk's priorities were in life. First money and now this. Common sense did not seem to be particularly high on his list. Zyr read the telltale signs upon her face.

"Don't misunderstand me, Firah. While this Deepstone is extremely rare and a potent protector, I would rather you have it. I feel more at peace when I know that you are safe. That peace of mind goes a long way in a conflict as it allows me to focus easier on what is required. Also, I do not want you to think that all things always go according to some plan. I had a hunch that a possible attack would be attributed to an Ashori; however, if it had been a different sort of weave ... well ... I suppose we wouldn't be having this conversation. Fate is like that sometimes." She was dumbfounded, but it soon gave way to curiosity.

"What is Deepstone?" she asked inquisitively. He nodded in acknowledgement of her question.

"An excellent question. Deepstones are a fascinating study. This particular stone looks rather plain and ordinary, doesn't it? Actually, it is an unfathomable merger of natural element and untold altering-capacity. You see, Aerluin's power extends as great threads throughout Aeredia. They are always in motion and sometimes come near the world's surface. Needless to say, it is a rare and potent occurrence. When two or more of these threads intersect, a peculiar reaction occurs. The substances which happen to exist upon these crossings become imbued with Her great potency. There is a potential that any being could become attuned to the material in question; to wood, water or, in this case - to stone. Each substance is unique in its ability and certainly there are no two alike. Deepstones are also called Bloodstones for earthy substances are often attuned through the interaction of a person's blood. Once it is attuned, the Deepstone is generally loyal for life, and it can adopt the properties of other energies temporarily as you saw in the city."

⟂ "Bloodstone … oh, I see." she replied. Her face was a picture of illumination and puzzlement as she connected the teacher's words with her experiences. "And this?" She touched the brooch lightly.

"I cannot tell you much about that other than it is made of Deepstone as well. I knew it was for you when I saw it on your vest the morning we left Lenhir. I am certain it has something to do with the form of energy we saw today. I wish I knew more about it, but curiously, we do not understand all the properties of altered elements. It seems they can be as varied and unique as people and the many races upon the land. For example, that gemstone seems to only respond to females. I have tried in vain to delve its full purpose many times. I suppose discovering its significance will come more on your own. I am sorry; that is all I can tell you."

"I really don't know much about all this talk of power and those amazing things you do. How does it all work?" Firah looked to her friend more attentively than perhaps she had ever been.

Zyr smiled inwardly as a memory of his youth flashed across his mind. She was like him, thirsting for knowledge of the wondrous workings of the world. Her curiosity and youthful candor was a forgotten melody echoing in the halls of memory. "First of all, it hasn't always been this way. Ages ago, before the reckoning of time, a wondrous event occurred that changed the fate of our world forever. A great being of immeasurable power came to dwell within our world." As the monk paused, the girl whispered in awe.

"You mean Mother, the giver of life?" Zyr nodded in affirmation, to which Firah merely blinked in astonishment.

"You have deduced correctly, though the title of 'life-giver' is a false notion passed on through generations. Truly Aerluin is not a creator nor was she born of this world.

Think of her as a visitor, a weaver of existing threads of life. This power which emanates from her is constant and cannot be ended more than you or I could decide to stop our heart from beating. Nothing is truly created or destroyed in this world. No, we would never have known of her except for an event that is only hinted about in legend and song. Something so momentous, so terrible occurred that it drove her from her ancient home and ethereal pathways and bound her here, within all the lands. Many have doubted her existence, but there is one potent fact that cannot be discounted. There is real power radiating from the land which cannot be explained nor was it there before, according to primeval records.

"All living things touch upon it in different ways. Some originators have suggested that this power is what led to the sentience of many races, like the Dryke, Gnarel or Vikyrl. Truly there were no primal record of such species. For many who merely brush with the power, it is expressed as inspiration or powerful surges of talent. However, for those who dedicate and link themselves directly to this power, it becomes much, much more. These were once called the Ashori, and the untrained, Ashori-tar. I belong to that same order."

The girl was bursting with questions, so many that her words stumbled and collided in effort to be made. "Does she ever speak to anyone?" her young face was bright with excitement.

"She does not speak, if you mean forcing air from your lungs through a muscle to manipulate sound. Her impressions are felt, more than heard. Declarations of such events are rare indeed. For those who have felt her influence it is interpreted differently. Our minds struggle to comprehend the communication and organize it into some form or another. I once heard it described as a musical form that would shake your emotion to the core. For another it was sweet harmonies of songful lyrics. One report even stated that it came as a soul rending wail. I wouldn't wish to fathom what message was intended then."

Firah struggled in vain to form coherent statements. "Then … wha … bu … how did … I mean … urgh!" She finally growled in frustration at her lack of sense. The teacher merely chuckled and raised a hand. She noted the gesture and stopped her struggling.

"Stop. Focus. Clear your mind and think about what you want to say. You will surely pass out before our conversation is concluded." Firah shook her head and laughed softly. With her cheeks burning slightly from her outburst she took long, drawn breaths.

"Okay. I got it … thanks, Zyr." The monk merely nodded politely. "So Airloon …"

"Aerluin," he corrected her quickly but with some emphasis to mark her speech.

"Aer … lu … in, right. Anyway, so she came from somewhere outside our world? How is this possible?" The monk placed a finger on his chin and closed his eyes for a moment. His hands found a stick laying on the ground and went to a patch of dirt nearby. He traced a large ring into the loose earth. Firah looked on in interest.

"Many scholars have suggested that our world is shaped as a large ring and that the realms or space within and without are occupied by entities, forces and powers beyond reckoning. Mother or Aerluin was one of these strange beings who came to dwell within the ring itself," Zyr pointed to the different parts of the diagram to emphasize the words. The girl nodded her head in understanding but her brow was furrowed under the weight of questions still unanswered. He detected her bewilderment and paused the discussion. "May I borrow a coin," he asked simply.

"Well, of course … they're yours when it comes to it." Zyr chuckled and took the coin from her hand. He spied a flat topped rock nearby and brought it back to her.

"Imagine this is a ring." She nodded as he took the coin and spun it on its side. Her face lit up immediately in understanding.

"Oh! It's round!" He nodded simply and passed the coin back to her. She looked up into the heavens with significance. The crackling sparks chased and danced ever upward.

"But, how can anyone claim to know such things? I would have thought the world was large and flat, that's what I see when I stand on the peaks of Tamers Reach."

Zyr nodded at her words.-"Well, the spinning ring world is only one theory. More perspective would certainly shed light upon truth. Largely, your position is likely one that most would agree with. Still, none of this changes the fact that She exists."

"So how does a person start using the power? Does everyone have the same abilities?" Her eyes betrayed some strange stirring, the shimmering shade of jade was fading. Zyr knew time was short but he had to occupy her through the transition.

"Think of the mystery of attunement as a newborn river weaving its way through the land. The water follows a path of least resistance. For each weaver, or Ashori, the path is defined in a similar way. As he develops his ability, he slips into a flow or aspect of the energy that offers the least resistance. For those who try, to learn otherwise often leads to frustration or even death as the potency of the Root is great indeed. Each taps into the power differently and the effects are diverse as well. We have determined to date certain tendencies and conveniently named them according to the strange effects the power yields. For myself, the Alacritor, a studious journey of the systems of life was a lengthy course, but it has afforded me the ability to manipulate and detect the workings of living patterns. Each body, be it animal or floral is open to me to delve, shape, sustain … or destroy."

Firah's face retracted slightly at his last words. His eyes had shifted to her keenly to emphasize the word. "Of course there are those who access Her power and alter it for their own needs and gain. These we call Defilers, and they remain carefully hidden, for it is expressly forbidden in most lawful realms of the world to corrupt Mother's powers in such a way. To be a Defiler is to live hunted and alone. In the past there existed those who would expressly hunt these down but those numbers have dwindled. Now the forsaken Ashori seem to multiply unchecked in the lands. Sadly, there are no Ashori today who are trained under a strict code of discipline to govern their choices. Lesser developed beings arise - Ashori-tar - with new names for the same origin of power. Sorcerers, magi, alchemists and such. All novices with limited potential."

She nodded and he continued the conversation. "Firah, you have a special gift, a true connection to the Root that is wondrous and yet potentially dangerous as we have seen tonight. I sensed that gift within you even before we met. You might say I was led or guided to you." She watched as he closed his eyes and breathed in slowly. It was as if he was summoning courage for a task. "Your gift has attracted the attention of others, those who would use it for evil, diabolical reasons. They would use you to bring forth darkness so real and terrible that no man can envision it. Only you seem to fit the mold for which they seek, at least in Mehnin. I am sorry, for I have kept this to myself, thinking I could protect your ignorance. I should have known that you would have dreams of the demon Ahtol. I misjudged your inner sight - your resolve and resilience. That display of power earlier is but a small insight into your potential, but you will need to learn how to control it." She was staring in disbelief at his words. She was needed for some terrible evil? She was just some street waif, hardly worth a glance by most people. What made her so special? And to servants of a demon?

⸸ Zyr watched the girl as she took in the information. Her face was trembling, growing darker. It would happen soon, by his best guess. "How did you know about the dreams ...?" she spoke weakly.

"Shien told me about your adventures, and a few particulars. I also understand you have come into possession of a dagger?" He looked down at her belt. Her eyes twitched slightly.

"I have always owned it. You must be mistaken." Her voice was slurred and, as she turned to look at him, her eyes were fading. Zyr passed his hand slowly over the dagger hilt without touching it. "Do you want to look at it?" she mumbled while slowly removing the clasping belt across the hilt, her hands faltering.

"No. I have a hunch about some things. I can tell you now, with certainty, that your dagger is a cursed weapon. I sense within that blade a heart of malice and guile. Something in that dagger is twisting your mind, thwarting your attempts to understand what is happening. Firah's eyes suddenly flashed red. Zyr stared back with a guarded air.

"You think you understand anything at all, meddler?" Her voice was low and grating, much like a man's; it seemed to echo upon itself, resonating in the dark.

"I know enough. You will not succeed here demon. She will overcome your will; her spirit is too great, even for you."

"That remains to be seen. Will you foolishly give of yourself for this girl ... assuming you can afford the price of my ownership?" Firah's arm withdrew the cold black blade from the sheath. It reflected no light at all.

"I have come prepared," Zyr said, raising a smaller blade to his arm. He cut deeply across his skin and allowed his blood to flow over the cursed blade which Firah held out. The black surface drank in the monk's essence, gleaning from the droplets which had been spilled. The healer never flinched but maintained a quiet vigil of the girl.

"Ahhhhh. So sweet. I wish that I could taste this the preferable way, and yet time will bring me what I desire." The girl's face was contorted into a sickening display of ecstasy. The monk watched her closely. Her red eyes traced back to find his own. *"You cannot keep me suppressed this way fool. There are others who will be drawn to you. You know nothing can slake my thirst, and with each offering I am closer to this realm."*

"I will do everything in my power to quell you, demon. However, it will be the girl that will eventually beat you. Be gone! Your selfish blood-price is paid." The girl's mouth quirked in mirth and laughed softly and long. Then the fire reflected a pale green colour passing into her eyes, though not as bright as before.

"Zyr, are you alright? Do you want to look at the blade or not?" She stared at him with complete ignorance of the last few horrifying minutes. Zyr's eyes glistened in the fire light.

"No … thank you."

θ	*The noxious weed was growing stronger with every passing rainstorm. The glade around the small tree continued along its life cycle, near oblivious to the conflict within its heart. The Sapling was growing unimpeded as it began to unfold the buds of its most precious flower. Thorns jutted out along the stem … precious and deadly.*

REFLECTIONS OF DUTY

ALL WAS QUIET and still in the deep foliage. Nature had completely overrun the silent courtyard with twisting vines which wound around shattered pillars and crept over high broken walls. Foundations and footings were smothered in moss; shrubs burst through cracks in the marbled floors. No human touch had attended the Halls in decades and the forest had become the caretaker, enshrouding the whole monastery in a green veil. All was at peace within the Broken Halls, every living thing coexisting with the ancient architecture. As events passed in the world outside the forest, time seemed to have abandoned the monastery. Completely hidden from view, the Halls had passed beyond reckoning of most men.

Leaves shuffled and crunched beneath soft leather boots which pressed upon the spongy ground. It was midday and the sun shone down through breaks in the lush canopy overhead. The cloaked trespasser moved slowly through the tranquil copse with deliberate, careful steps. Stopping and glancing upward past the ceiling of branches, the bristles of a graying brown beard escaped the shadows of the cowl. After sniffing the wind, the stranger glanced over his shoulder. A large animal stalked from the undergrowth. Its pelt was black and melded with shadow as it moved across the mossy bed. Moving more silently than death it came alongside the lone figure in the center of the copse. The newcomer's deep green cloak fluttered in a passing breeze while staring down into the golden gaze of his feral companion. He nodded slightly and took a seat upon the top of a mossy stone located in the center of the copse.

Stroking the black pelt of the purring animal, he stranger spoke softly, "now we must wait, Nisa."

*   *   *

✖   The waggon rolled gently across the soft ground. A
rain shower in the early morning had soaked everything
thoroughly. As muddy as the road was, the group had
avoided getting mired down by choosing careful paths
along the road. Their progress had been staunched by the
mire as time squelched and splashed on its way. Shien sat
across from Firah in silence, under the cover of a tarp
erected above the waggon bed. He watched water drops roll
lazily off the side of the cover into the pools below.
Conversation had run as dry as their water supply, as the
road was long to their eventual destination. No one really
knew where they were headed except Zyr, who chose to
reveal only strands of information, like morsels to a starved
pack of dogs. Shien preferred the quiet as he looked over the
small booklet in his lap. They were on the third day of travel
and still he had only caught up to their final visit to Khyvla.
The writing was a habit born from his youth. He had always
kept a journal of sorts. It helped him settle his thoughts
when life grew complex, like the previous week. Having
been through more than most people in his limited years, he
still couldn't remember when his life had been more
eventful or hazardous than it had recently. He glanced up
from his fresh black marks to peruse his traveling
companions. Firah was stretched out along the opposite side
of the waggon, with her head flopped backward over the
side; her arms were thrust out, grasping the wooden planks

which comprised the short walls of the waggon bed. Looking over his left shoulder he saw Zyr driving the cart with Tohm at his side. The enigmatic monk would occasionally whisper things to the large man, who hung his head down perpetually these days. Shien looked back to his writing. He had started a new chapter of sorts upon meeting the unusual group of companions. He flipped backward in the book to peruse his thoughts of previous days. He shook his head in wonder. They were all alive and mobile, not to mention freshly clothed and bathed. He set the thin charcoal stick to the paper and prepared to commence their experiences within the city.

"What have you been scratching into that book all this time?" Firah had lifted her head, and the look she gave him was pure desperation. She was bored beyond reason. The girl loved the outdoors, so she had told him, and she wanted to be up and moving about. Unfortunately, muddy boots and a stranded young woman is all that would result of her walking beside the waggon for the time being. The sun had not shown itself since the rain, hiding behind dark clouds which threatened to break again over the land. The ground would not dry up soon. Firah had been so lethargic recently that she could have passed for one of the worn planks of wood she flopped over.

"Just words and more words. It's rather tedious actually." He dropped his head back to the page and sought his memory for the details.

"You must be good at it. Your scratching has been carrying on for hours. I want to see ..." She shuffled over to him on her knees and stuck her face around his book to peer at the characters he wrote inside. "I can't read it," she remarked disappointingly and slumped back against the side of the waggon next to him.

"Not many can read this kind of writing. It comes from a far country, where writing evolved differently than in Kenhar. Here, I'll show you." Firah moved next to him, crowding the space in front of the small book. "See this one here; look how the lines here make a square and the lines above intersect?" She nodded in understanding. "That means city ... and well I'm just going over our trip into Khyvla."

"So you are writing about our adventures?" Her face brightened as she found this new information exciting and diverting.

"Our mishaps is probably more appropriate." He scribbled down some characters and immediately Firah was engaged in the process.

"What did you just write?" She looked up to him, her green eyes fixed in anticipation. He smirked and humoured the now animated deadwood.

"Uh ... okay. It says 'Firah and I successfully passed the gate and retrieved my equipment.' He watched her face drop in surprise and then grow somewhat irritated.

"That's it? That's all that happened?" She spoke in heavy sarcastic laden tones. "We just went in and grabbed our stuff and called it a day?"

"What else do you write? I wrote what happened." He was taken aback by her criticism.

"What about all the danger? Remember we didn't know if the enemy were lurking around corners. You probably didn't mention how difficult it was getting into the city, wearing blankets to hide the muck we were covered in? I remember how nerve racking it was as I thought every eye was on me!" She was speaking so rapidly, Shien's head spun. She poked at the book for emphasis as the lecture rolled on. "How about stealing those clothes so we could pass for normal people in the shop and inn? Remember how furious I was at you when, after all that and after a clean escape, we forgot to collect the clothes I had made? Then we had to go back again! How could you forget all that?" She was fuming, but lightheartedly or so he divined. She was happy to stretch her mind from days of stagnation.

"That's all superficial. Besides you're getting too far ahead." Her face was uncomfortably close to his. She was pretty, even when in a huff. Her voice echoed in his ears.

"Hah! Superficial … what's that? Anyway, I have an idea. I will tell you what to write and you just move that black stick around okay?" She had a gleam of triumph in her eye.

"Okay…" He shifted his position to relief some cramped muscles and prepared the writing tool. She watched impatiently and fidgeted around. "Alright, dictate away, young herald." She laughed brightly at his comment.

"Firah and Shien moved ever so close to the gate and waited for the necromancers to jump out and set them on fire …"

Shien was moving the pencil while his mind twinged in mirth. On the pages his characters were written down steadily in cadence with her words, though the words were far from her narrative. He dared not disrupt her story while maintaining his ruse. He checked his last sentence - 'Next we acquired Firah's clothes, bought some for the others and safely exited the city.'

⊥   Zyr listened to the lighthearted scene behind him in silence. At least they were able to receive a reprieve from the seriousness of the situation before them all. His mind could not detract for a moment from the task that was placed upon him. The weight was almost too great to bear; the thought of what must be done seemed impossible. He was faltering on the slim precipice of despair. Tohm and Firah depended on him for their very lives. The terrible irony was apparent. Firah would have no recollection of the night activities, except for what the demon specter would create in her mind. Over the last few days, her episodes had grown worse. Her body would actually change subtly for the time that the demon had control; and those changes would only grow more severe. He had kept her hidden from Shien and Tohm, while he dealt with the demon each night. They must not know yet. And still, how could he keep the transformation secret? He knew what would come in the end, how it would play out. Breaking the black alter had only bought them time, not a victory. Everything seemed uncertain.

This journey to the Broken Halls was an attempt to buy time, to try to figure out what to do. Removing Firah from the vicinity of those who would take her was paramount, and losing the dagger was not an option either. If she became separated from it, she would try to search it out in the night, causing many difficulties. Besides, being able to keep the blade under surveillance was strangely comforting. At least The Blade of Ahtol was not using it on another victim, somewhere else. He only hoped that the answer to the dilemma would come soon. Somehow, the solution would depend on his ability to conquer himself, his emotions, fear … all the old tenets. Yet for all his preparations, cursed dark fate had drawn Firah to the dagger like a moth to flame. He felt caught up in a wind that was unassailable, and the sense of powerlessness infuriated his mind. Zyr hung his head sadly; he truly doubted whether the forces of purity assisted those few who fought against evil.

"Zyr … they are coming for her …" Tohm's voice rumbled beneath his weather resistant hood. His friend's voice echoed what Zyr had tried to dismiss.

"No, Tohm. They are far away; please try to focus as I taught you earlier." The man's head drooped down again, and no more was said. It was enough to make Zyr weep when he thought about Tohm, for the damage that had been inflicted upon his friend. His heart ached as he could do nothing more to aid the once gentle giant. He watched powerlessly as fate played out its course in this good man's life.

A hungry beast lingered beneath the surface of Tohm's weakened resolve, and was constantly trying to claw its way to the surface. Zyr had to remain ever on alert to detect the signs of Tohm's mental resistance faltering. The monk had guessed what had occurred. The beast had always been there and Tohm had kept it hidden for years in the darkest pits of his psyche. A glimpse of that terrible force had been seen on the road to Khyvla, during the ambush. Somehow, the attack on his mind had disrupted the careful balance. Tohm could no longer resist the raging anger and lust for combat. With frustration, the monk clenched the leather reins tightly. Zyr knew that he could not calm the starving beast within Tohm and monitor Firah effectively for much longer. In both cases, conditions were worsening. It was these things that were wearing his resolve threadbare. How could he care for others and have no room in his heart for her? She still played upon the far recesses of his mind, ever lingering. Recently, those thoughts had become more real and touched upon emotions long dormant. Zyr shook his head to arouse his faculties. Such nonsense!

He was grateful Shien accepted the invitation to come with them. It gave his mind some reprieve to know the young man would watch over the girl. He felt there was something special about Shien worth investigating, but there was far too much bearing him down to consider such things. For now, he was content to place a degree of trust in the newest arrival to the ill-fated group.

*   *   *

Nuril glanced over the legal documents strewn across the table before her. The guild had come under significant fire following the failed attempt to capture the girl. Yet it was possible to overcome the feeble charges pressed upon Ahtol's guild. She picked up each parchment and carefully perused the accusations against them. The advantage leaned toward the guild as the evidence was vague and relied heavily upon assumption. Eventually, her subordinates would be released on lesser charges, though she was inclined to simply let them hang until dead. As pleasant a thought as it was to entertain, it would not do for the guild's reputation or its resources. For all the trouble these fools had caused in their bungling of a relatively simple task, they still had their uses. Could she trust them to maintain affairs while she was away? 'Will the tower remain standing?' she mused dryly to herself.

It was the worst time to leave, but it was never more dire a circumstance. The blade and prize were on the move. Her body shuddered subconsciously at a nightmarish thought. If those two should somehow unite for long without the suppressing control of the Deepstone table, all would be undone. Ahtol's fury would spill out upon Aeredia unchecked and unquenchable. It had been three days now, and she could wait no longer. With images of the slender blade upon her thoughts she looked down to the table edge. Her hand was trembling. She quickly clenched her fingers tightly to control her body's yearnings.

The blade had been so close. She had thought she could handle its presence, after all the years that had past. Now foolishly, she was preparing to pursue what she feared and craved the most. Her road was clear, an obsessive and terrifying duty. Thus, the trip would need to be quick and efficient with no room for errors. That was why she was going personally. She would travel fairly lightly and move as swiftly as possible.

The direction the blade was moving was the most disturbing. Surely, he would not take her there. She paced around the desk coolly, stopping in front of a map of Mehnin. No one had returned alive since the Breaking. Yet he would be one to do something so rash and clearly illogical, to throw ignorant trackers off the scent. Still her Jazyn were more than mere ignorant animals. Being fostered from birth toward their eventual end, they were completely loyal but lived independently. They were attuned to the subtle shifts in the Root and could sniff out the slightest imbalance. They were a strange breed, sharing features of man and beast and yet something altogether different.

Something occurred three days ago that had knocked the three Jazyn that lived in the area completely unconscious.

She had felt it too, as many in the tower had. It was some
time later, when she visited the energy-hounds, that she
discovered the cause. A major spike in the area just outside
the city had caused the disruption. Nuril had dispatched
grey rangers to investigate and the news was somehow
unsettling and predicable. A massive labyrinth of
undergrowth and towering trees had burst forth from the
land. The whole affected area was a mysterious and bizarre
upheaval. Nuril had seen it before in some instances and
guessed the monk's meddling as the cause. The town was
buzzing with wonder ever since the ground had ceased
shaking.

It was clear that Zyr had united with the young girl, 'the
prize' who would fuel the ritual, and a couple of
mercenaries. They were moving at a decent pace in a south
by south-west bearing. Nuril knew that only one significant
landmark lay in that direction, and most mortals knew
nothing of it. She moved all the documents off her desk into
the enchanted compartment along the wall. Any forced
entry and search would meet with disappointment. Only she
could unlock this compartment.

A presence was at the door and she turned herself to
admit the visitor. She was dressed in her best riding gear
beneath a sweeping dark cloak which she had prepared with
a fur lining. The last summer moon was growing old and
hidden. Soon the first Autumn phase would begin to show,
illuminating nights that would grow steadily cooler. It was

best to be prepared. The door swung open slowly admitting two subsidiary cadremen, adorned in sturdy riding cloaks.

"Ebyn. Gaeth. We leave within the hour. Is the tower readied?" She kept her veil lowered for the lesser men. The monk was the only one alive who had seen her face, her new eyes. She would see to him soon enough.

"Guild mistress." It was Ebyn who spoke. The Ignitor held a slight advantage of ability over the Cerephor which Nuril presumed was infuriating to the lesser of the two. "The tower stands ready to send us off. All the paths are clear and ready for a smooth exit." He kept his head bowed and would do so until commanded otherwise. They all would.

"I'll make that judgment myself at the rendezvous. You two will leave first with the escort and assemble for combat at the specified location. Proceed according to what we discussed and break away from the escort when you can. I will meet you at the rendezvous point. Make sure all is readied for immediate departure when I arrive. That will be all." They bowed their heads low and moved out of the room. Nuril went over to the window that she frequently gazed from. Something inside told her that this trip would not go as planned. All of her preparations could not help when it included confronting the man she desperately hated.

*   *   *

✕   Night had fallen and all was still on the roadside. The slender moon shed a fuzzy light upon the land through the clouded heavens. The canopy now extended over the whole waggon bed, sheltering all from the weather. It was too damp to set a fire and the heavens continued to drizzle upon the land. The group rested in silence and huddled under blankets seeking in vain for warmth. Shien sniffed softly and watched as Firah huddled beside Zyr. It was an odd feeling, and he really couldn't decide how he felt. It was partially curiosity and something else … what was that feeling? Jealousy. It was impossible, and yet he had become so used to reading other people's emotion that he had forgotten to recognize his own. He had enjoyed his association with the young girl, finding himself taking pleasure in their banter and private moments. Somehow, he was growing enamored with her, to the degree that he despised himself for almost leaving her to those despicable demon spawn in the city. He felt grateful now that he had endangered himself to help her. It was a blessed ray of warmth across his chilled mind that she was here with him now. The attraction was strange in some ways, and yet not so in others. He had found that she was not much younger than he, about five years. These days, that was not such an issue.

He watched as she shifted her weight against the monk, who sat in silent meditation. How he wished … he turned his eyes away. It would not do to go on like this. Shien didn't even know how she felt about him. He suddenly reeled from thoughts long dormant. He had completely surrendered the passion for his family's heirlooms for whimsical fantasy. The weapons were reality. He cast a second gaze around the waggon bed; all were asleep or resting. The young man's eyes lingered upon her once again and then moved to big Tohm who snored lightly under a patchy covering. He briefly wondered why the healer had not taken liberty to cure the large man's severe burns, which were scabbing and mending slowly under the body's normal processes. Shien stopped himself. He had become distracted again; how things had changed!

He slowly pulled his pack near and untied the straps to the pack. With some trepidation he pushed the material down to expose the two slender forms. Each was wrapped neatly in intricate, delicately thin fabric. The material felt smooth under his fingertips, like the texture of silk. He slowly unfolded the character-embroidered cloth. He felt strangely connected to the symbols. He knew what each symbol represented but together they weaved a strange pattern. He traced his finger over the threads from which they were formed. They were a puzzle to be solved. He took a few minutes perusing both pieces of fabric. Both were fashioned from the same material but the characters differed greatly. He would put serious thought toward that enigma.

He hefted the first slender weapon.

Kuros.

The ornate hilt of the long-bladed rapier was plainly inscribed in his native writ. The counterguard wound round the hilt and tang, a brazen serpent contorting upon itself. Upon sliding the scabbard from the hilt, Shien discovered the metal glowing with a red luster. The blade seemed to shimmer hotly though it felt cool to the touch. He felt uneasy as he grasped the hilt, his fingers clenched as if in fear from the serpent's venom. The vibrant hue struck the chords of a woman's voice which sang gently from the recesses of his mind. It came in the form of a song which was sung to him every night as a child. The words slowly formed upon his lips, in harmony with thoughts which sung low in an ancient and noble tongue …

Born from the searing fires of the deep,
The heart of Kuros.
Burning through the lands which weep,
The wrath of Kuros.
Thy fury bright with terrible might,
The will of Kuros.
The child will weep upon the breast.
The cold dark thy fury will contest.
Rage and Sorrow fuel passion bright
The fires of Kuros.

The melody paused and Shien's mind was caught up in a thousand threads of thought. The simple rhyme now laboured his mind; years of memory sought for understanding in that singular moment. He had no inclination what it could mean. Yet his heart was burning within, swallowing up the chill of the evening rain.

He picked up the next weapon which was as unique as the first. It too was masterfully crafted, the metal taking on a pale hue, whiter than the purest ivory steel.

Isil.

The blade gleamed as a pallid spike, almost transparent in appearance. The hilt and guard formed strong rigid patterns, which suggested firmness and instilled a sense of trust. He felt safe as he held it to his body, letting the cool steel brush across his cheek. The haunting melody continued to flow through his mind. He could not stop the next verse from forming, this time his voice sung low in accord with the unseen woman who sang softly as she stroked his hair.

Tempered and still are thy strains,
The song of Isil.
Thy steady reprieve for all remains,
The mercy of Isil.
Evil's thunder is torn asunder,
The justice of Isil.
The child shelters under thy care,
As evil throes in awful despair.
Compassion stays the perilous plunder,
The aegis of Isil.

Shien paused as the haunting melody ceased. What was the next verse? It was there upon the distant climbs of his mind. He struggled silently to retrieve the chords. It was essential to hear them now. He cursed himself for his childhood inattention. Perhaps, he always passed into sleep at this point of the lullaby? It was infuriating to be so close to a clue which would lend understanding to the weapons' purpose.

The soft voice he heard was his mother's servant, Yyriha. He barely recalled his mother. He remembered that it was Yyriha who had raised him and schooled him in the formal arts, who taught him fencing and warfare. She had taught him how to live, to respect all nature, and his place in the royal courts. At night she lay next to him, providing warmth. She had been adept and wise, and ever so gentle; and yet, firm and immovable in training and many a scar had been caused by her unyielding hand. It was customary for the first servant to instruct in all areas of learning, while the arts of war and fencing fell to the father. Shien had no recollection of a father and thus learned those skills in private from Yyriha. He also remembered that she often came to practice with bruises that were not caused from his weak attacks.

It was during his youth that Yyriha had made an escape from his native lands, with him at her side. She continued to care for him along their endless trek, till her death upon the fell marches of the Wastelands. Shien had found his way to the outskirts of Kenhar, living off the land as he had learned to do in his sojourn. Men had found him as he passed an outpost along the Serpentor March at Dryke. Life had passed so quickly since then and yet Yyriha's teachings remained so strong within him. Her last words of counsel were etched into his soul. Reclaim what was lost, retrieve Isil and Kuros, and revive the Spirit of Vyn-shi. Was it fate that permitted him to hear of their existence and brought the swords to him? Perhaps it was her will beyond the grave driving the winds which carried him down many rivers. Either way, her will was achieved and now he felt useless. How could he forget that last verse?

"That was nice singing, Shien." Firah whispered to him from across the waggon bed. Shien glanced over at her, and lowered the sacred weapons to his side.

☼   She suddenly felt pangs of guilt. "Oh … I'm sorry," she whispered, "I shouldn't have interrupted you." She looked away into the dark night and sighed.

"Please … don't concern yourself with that. I'm not offended," he spoke in low tones. "Actually, I wouldn't mind talking right now. I need a break … there's so much to think about, I feel my head will burst." There was something in his voice, like calling across a wide expanse. He ran a hand through his hair, something she noted he did when he was under certain duress. She moved apart from Zyr and sidled softly over to him, blanket in tow. Firah saw his eyes watching her as she moved toward him. What was he thinking about?

"You silly, you haven't even got a blanket." She felt his hands and withdrew hers sharply. "They are like ice!" she hissed. Without an invitation she threw the blanket around him and moved against his side, adjusting the cover over their legs and bodies. She slid down slightly and wrapped her small arms around his torso, trying to transfer some warmth to him. What was he thinking, the Gnarel-brain? He could have caught a serious chill and fever. What use would he be then after that? His body shifted slightly beneath her arms. She looked up at him and smiled. It felt good to be here, next to him sharing his warmth. Her heart began to pound as she felt his arm lower over her shoulder. She placed her head against his abdomen, which felt reassuring and firm. He released a long breath as she felt the tension slip away. Many moments passed between them, paced by the gentle patter of rainfall upon the protecting shelter above. His voice broke the silence.

"Where do you come from, Firah? I mean, how did you come to meet Tohm and Zyr?" His voice still sounded distant to her and she felt her old guards going up. She had pushed others away for so long. Except for Tohm, she could not name a friend. Oh, she had tried when she was younger to reach out to the other children. She couldn't explain to them what made her different. Her mannerisms were all wrong and uncivilized. By the time Tohm had schooled her in the rudimentary norms of conduct, the damage was done. She was never accepted. Ever teased and bullied she slowly laced the emotional and physical scars into a stoic bulwark. It was then that she chose the woods for her home and ultimately thievery for survival. Tohm had long pleaded, chided and at times threatened to end her retreat. His will wasn't strong enough to break her defences.

She had made it clear at twelve years old that if he treasured their friendship he would know to stop his meddling. 'You are not my parent. I care little what you think is best for me!' She remembered his face as the words came as swords and knives thrusting out from behind her toughened shell. A terrible wound she inflicted with a sickening sense of relief. She didn't do it because she knew he could handle her pain. She did it because she wanted to … because she could. His look was one she could never describe or forget.

Now, here was a man whose relationship with her was still in its infancy. He sought to push past those careful boundaries she had erected. A tremendous struggle began within her heart. A desperate conflict between fear and trust waged as she closed her eyes and held to his body. After a few moments the battle was over. She took a deep breath and plunged into the unknown.

"Well, we're from Lenhir. Except Zyr, I don't know about him. Tohm found me as a little girl, maybe four years old. He says I was like a stray cat, wild and untempered. I have dreams sometimes … I dream I'm surrounded by strange creatures or animals. They walk in shadows on all legs … I don't fear them … in fact I ..." Her mind suddenly detected what she had felt for some time. She turned her head around toward him. "Shien?" His eyes were closed and his breath was coming in slow, steady cadence. Firah slowly turned her head and lay it back where it had been. The hardened sphere around her heart had broken and peeled away like flowers petals from the bud. Now, as the fleeting sun, her resolve gave way to darkness. The fading glimmers of hope illuminated the perfect, impenetrable sphere which refolded around her heart. Shien slept on unknowingly.

☥ Tohm's eyes snapped open. Danger was approaching from the west, from deep within the trees. He moved his head slightly and read the shifting smells upon the wind. The airstreams reeked from a foul bestial odor; the scent was closing fast. That wasn't all. He sensed their foul essence. He looked to the young kit who nuzzled the new one. His mind was racing, 'She must be protected ... she is vulnerable!' He sprung up from the waggon bed and crouched lightly to determine any other danger in the area. Tohm seized hold of the kit's coat and leapt from the waggon, landing carefully in the wet grass. He heard a startled yell behind him. Let them fend for themselves; he had to protect the young one. It was engrained deeper than any instinct or habituation. Both the master and the wolf were chasing. He could outrun them easily ... yet they needed to hide. The scent was getting closer. Blood was spilling; their bodies were being torn apart. Yet still they closed.

Tohm leapt high over a massive tree which had been unearthed. He listened to the faint cries of the young one in his grasp. She was flailing at him, but the young were often like that. He hunkered low beneath the tree, but held her fast in a knotted grip. The master landed lightly in front of them. His face was stern and he approached slowly.

"Tohm, why did you leave the waggon?" He crouched down and stopped just short of the large warrior. The master was wise. He knew the boundaries.

"Danger comes." Tohm lifted an arm toward the trees which lay westward. The master's expression changed to one of exasperation. Tohm glared back at the master as the wolf gazed into the dark wood. At least the young had some sense. Why did the master not sense the obvious?

"I have told you, Tohm, the danger is far away from here. You mustn't react so; it can lead us into real danger ..." The master's calm voice wavered slightly; he carried great burdens. Tohm was sorry to bring more hardship, but she needed to be safe.

"Tohm ..." The kit spoke quietly, "are you sure that ..."

�֍   "Get down!" Shien shouted out harshly. He dived beneath the large tree as he called out and at that very moment the wood was thrown into chaos. Firah gasped as large forms crashed through the brush, growling and panting from exhaustion. Surprise did not stay long as the travellers ducked into nearby cover. The creatures leapt and dashed through the trees, passing perilously close to the small concealed party. After several of the animal like forms thundered by, arrows smacked into the trees and thudded into the ground at their heels. The whinnying of horses was drowned out by a crunching clatter that penetrated through the wood.

"They overturned the waggon, and the ponies have bolted," Zyr spoke just above the noise. The monk looked puzzled.

"Don't worry, Zyr, those boys will stick around. They never drift far from Tohm," Shien replied in an equally low tone. Firah watched him in the low light. She barely had a moment to consider what he was feeling before something else caught her eye.

More forms raced into the limited view, dancing through the shadows. All was dark and made it all but impossible to discern detail in the wood, but Shien appeared to be able to make out shadows moving toward them.

He watched the beast-like creatures leave the wood and halt in the ditch at the far side of the road. The sliver of a moon barely illuminated their steaming bodies. They were growling and gesturing to one another, and he watched as they set up a rudimentary defense behind the cart. He wasn't absolutely sure, but he thought he saw one prepare a bow.

"They are Gnarel," Zyr whispered to them. "Human warriors pursue them, though they appear to be equal in number. We need to stay down so not to be mistaken for targets in the dark."

Firah tried to move even closer to the soil, but found her tunic still firmly grasped by her old friend. She looked up into Tohm's eyes. They were so alive and almost smoldered in the darkness. She wasn't sure whether she should be more afraid of being so close to Tohm in his present state. He had done terrible things days earlier. He had simply lost control of who he was.

Footfall passed by, leaping the large trunk near their location.

All four remained deathly still.

The sound of crashing metal filled the air, as the pursuing forward-guard encountered the Gnarel riposte. Flashes of light peeked through the low brush as weapon met weapon. Cries of war were meshed with snarls of fury. It was a cacophony of rage. Human archers were sniping from behind the near trees and occasionally Gnarel arrows would skitter close by the party. Firah kept her head low to the ground, seeking some comfort from Mother, silently praying they would escape this terrible clash of warfare.

A terrible scream of agony pierced above the rest, and a howl of triumph followed slightly afterward. Zyr turned his face to the others. It was grave and full of hidden burdens. "That's it. They will not survive a Gnarel counter-attack if we do nothing. We must help, even if we are complete strangers. Tohm you stay here and guard Firah." The big man nodded slowly as Zyr started to fasten the long sleeves of his robe.

✕   "Hold on Zyr," Shien interjected. "Why should we risk our lives, there is no logic in this! On what grounds do you casually place our lives in harm's way? You must answer that!" Shien was speaking loudly, but none of the near combatants would hear. They now fought for their very lives. The monk appeared anxious but took a moment before answering.

"I can't help you, or even force you to understand. It's something I must do, till I meet the end. It's the duty of a promise, nothing more. Somehow, life would not be worth living if I did not heed that duty. Do as you wish but I leave now." As the magi prepared to move he spoke low without turning. "By the way, didn't you leave something in the waggon?" Zyr crouched low and moved away slowly from their hidden refuge.

"Damn him!" Shien cursed harshly. "What was I thinking? For all the cursed luck, I can't believe it!" Shien struck out at the rough bark harshly. Running his hand through his hair tensely, he peered just over the tree toward the waggon. There was no question in his mind now. He would need to recover Vyn-shi's emblems at any cost. That would mean defeating every last Gnarel; unless they ran, of course. He slammed his hand again into the tree in anger. In his haste to follow Firah and Tohm, not only had he abandoned his lost heritage but also his own dueling weapons. Now he would need to think fast and cautiously to avoid coming to harm. It was not a simple task. The Gnarel were strong fighters; even the weakest of their kind exacted respect from the most seasoned veterans. Shien had faced them before along the Dryke-wasteland borders during his youth. They were incredibly savage and their fighting style was unpredictable. Many images of massacre resided within his brain; they would suffer that fate now if they faltered.

Shien shifted slowly away from the downed tree. Firah was watching him with an odd expression. A malevolent grin had spread across her face and her eyes, which caught glimpses of the dimmed light, seemed to be on fire. Yet he was moving and hadn't time to think about such things. Shien stalked low to the ground, and determined a flanking maneuver was best, yet as to how to actually fight with the beasts, he was uncertain. He looked for anything to use as an advantage as he moved. His foot caught against something unusual and he quickly inspected the ground. It was a crude Gnarel arrow; it would have to suffice, as it was better than mere hands and feet. Yet it would be one shot, one attempt and then … he chose not to dwell on it. When it began, he would have to react as best he could.

Shien purposely moved apart from the direction the Monk had taken. It wouldn't do to get caught up in his battles. The young fighter admitted that Zyr was a man who could win a war with his limbs alone. What concerned Shien was the safety of the rapiers, and preventing a Gnarel looting in a potential withdraw. He would keep an eye out for his heirlooms as best he could, but what use would they be if he were impaled upon the claws of the enemy? He moved slowly but stealthily around the faltering rear guard of the pursuing party. He came through the trees and gazed out from behind cover down the road to his right. He was several feet away from the now diminished battle. The conditions had not improved at all, and in all the cover of the trees he had forgotten the drizzle. He felt the mist brush his neck as he brought his head around a trunk into the slight wind. 'To fight on that road will be suicide' he mused. The muddy quagmire may have led to the downfall of the fighter who cried out earlier. The Gnarel were much more adapted to this sort of environment and took advantage of the situation. The archers in the human party were wise, staying off the road, but their vision was very limited. The Gnarel were well holed in on the road, and covered sufficiently from the woods behind. He would need to skirt across the road and flank upon the opposing grassy side.

Taking a quick breath and clutching the arrow he sprinted to the limit of the grass and leapt hard over the mud. He needed one step to help clear the remainder of the road. As he placed the foot down, muddy water splashed across his leggings, and echoed in his ears. He tumbled to the grass, and lay there in dark as the sky shed wetness upon him. He heard the Gnarel growls and barks. They sounded different. It was possible that they heard him. What would they do? Rather than mindless beasts, the Gnarel had proven to be shrewd adversaries. Shien shot up and barreled into the trees. He picked up a stick in the other hand. It would have to do. He quickly hurled it away from him into the woods. He strained his ears in the dark for any sign of movement. In a moment of alarm, he thought he heard the soft padding of feet or paws from within the trees. His eyes scanned the dark feverishly. He had heard something but as to which direction he was not sure. The sounds of battle were still there, with the occasional yell or taunt from either side. Neither group wanted to make a move, as both had holed in sufficiently with good defensive positions. The Gnarel may not have realized that they won a certain advantage felling the warrior on the road. The men had been too overzealous in pursuit and fell into the Gnarel counter.

A massive claw swept through the air and nearly sliced through Shien's face. In a moment too brief to measure, the young man's fighting sense had reacted quicker than his mind. Instead of being gashed by the assault, he was caught further up the limb and hammered across the head by the sheer force of the blow. He stepped back groggily, as a massive Gnarel warrior crashed into view, spreading its massive limbs apart and roaring an invitation to battle and death. In the right claw, a massive Gnarel war axe dripped tendrils of water from the rounded blade edge. Clenching the wooden shaft firmly in his grip, Shien wondered how the creature found him. His mind responded in a chastising matter-of-fact way. 'The Gnarel are downwind, fool.'

≚ Zyr moved quickly through the trees. It was possible to go undetected in the dark, but he knew better that to underestimate the enemy. He had mixed feelings about the Gnarel. Generally, they hated everything outside of their culture, and at times extended the conflict within their own circles. However, their xenophobia would often be the catalyst to band together to fight against any aggressor and also strike out to acquire wealth for their tribal families. They were a slave race but generally nomadic. They could also be dangerous as they sought rudimentary but effective links to the mystic realm. He had fought many in his time, and each time learned something new about them. Zyr doubted a lifetime of study - if one should live that long in such a bizarre science - could reveal all the secrets of the Gnarel. Either way, the monk felt he was well on his way toward that end, and not just concerning the bestial warriors, but many creatures. Based on that expertise, Zyr had concluded long before that the Gnarel were not necessarily evil but terribly introverted. Yet, evil found its way into every species, and the Gnarel were known to engage in strange rituals bordering upon threads similar to Defiler lore. This night he would have to use careful judgment with these creatures.

Dodging around a slender tree, Zyr assessed the battle. Several Gnarel archers had set up position in the woods just behind the waggon. Blade warriors were established behind cover at either end of the waggon to counter a head-on attack. It was a fair defence for the often underestimated intelligence of these creatures. The men who opposed the Gnarel had a similar setup in the near trees, yet they were having difficulty hitting anything effectively on the road or in the far trees. In the event that their arrow supplies diminished, they would be overwhelmed by the aggressive warriors. The monk considered the options. There was no indication of how many Gnarel resided in the trees across the road. Perhaps four to six was his best guess. He estimated that the combined force of the men was about seven. He dared not attempt a probing at this time in fear of being detected. Only use of his own reserves was safe at the moment. The Gnarel would have near ten. It was difficult odds, especially as he considered the loss of the burly fighter who lay in his gore near the waggon. Arrows protruded from his chest like a porcupine coat, creating a disturbing if not unusual silhouette in the darkness. Zyr briefly considered raising the man. Perhaps if he coordinated with the human archers … no. It was regrettable, but the man was probably too far gone. The danger would be great as he would expose himself to attack for a significant period of time. The best would be to attempt a flank against their rear guard. The danger lay in the uncertain numbers he faced and the near blackness of night. Gnarel had exceptional senses and often fought in packs which made combat tricky and hazardous. The wind was blowing across his face, which he determined would give him a slight advantage to avoid detection. He hoped that Shien was ready to act, but he could not rely heavily upon the young man. All their weapons were now thoroughly immersed in muddy pools of water next to the now vertical bed of the waggon.

Zyr directed power into his legs and skipped over the road easily. Clearing the road had not proved a difficult test as it was a maneuver he had developed as an initiate and mastered since. Moving through the trees with careful steps, he heard guttural chatter coming just ahead. Scanning the surroundings, Zyr moved forward carefully and stayed extremely low. From his perspective he spied upon a small gathering of the tribal beasts. There was a strangely dressed and rather morbid looking Gnarel conversing with two stocky and seasoned Blade Warriors. He had never encountered the likes of the odd one, but the tattered robes and bone ladders suggested the beast was a mystic of sorts. The others were armed with tribal weapons, ornamented with the spoils of war from their tribe. They were armoured somewhat but chose the freedom of movement over heavy protection. Their hides were also naturally tough, which aided them more than the skin of their human opponents. After a small moment, Zyr knew what to do. His mind created the battle as it should transpire many times as he slowly moved closer. It was a very small clearing which held the sweaty and rank snouted warriors. Their silhouetted bodies rose and fell in anticipation of battle. Muscles were tensed and ripped across their furred skins. Suddenly, the smaller clothed one snorted sharply and gruffed to one of its larger kin. The large one sprung like a cat into the forest with a growl of battle lust. The moment was set; the battle plan weaved its patterns through the monk's mind. Zyr's body drove swiftly into the clearing, from stance to stance. The Gnarel spun and howled the moment they espied the motion of Zyr springing from his hands into the air. Almost floating upon the winds, the monk closed the distance - fluidly twisting his legs into the first critical move in a long dance of death.

ᕆ   Urshaak breathed in the night. It was hunting moon and the feint had played the humans into their jaws. Following the token ambush, the retreat was good. The intruding men were so foolishly predictable. He personally felled the strong one, and taking a moment he drank in the fumes of death which rose from his fallen enemy. It had been a good battle. Now he waited for the humans to waste their puny little attacks. Soon, he would hew them down … just a little longer. He twisted the grip of his heart blade in his massive claws. The rush of battle was sweet as the rain upon his brow.

His ears perked slightly to a familiar sensation. Death. From the enemy in the trees. Perhaps one of his brothers … no it wasn't that … something smelled wrong. His mind began to burn, pulsing in warning. Danger … foul danger. It was seeping through every pore. Urshaak moved his horned head slightly to catch sight of the woods where the enemy … the evil lurked. What he saw chilled the blood which once ran hot within. Shadows. Living shadows. They were slinking, creeping, melting through the wood. The shadows struck out like a writhing blade. Screams, gargled and torn. Now it was coming, dancing from the trees. Urshaak felt the tip of his most precious blade touch the ground. His resolve was faltering, his mind broken. All of his instincts roared out at his inaction, at his fear. Yet it was the shadow descending upon the proud warrior which drove all his courage like the deer before the wolf. The red-eyed shadow ...

The Sapling's thorns now flowed into blackened tips, both elegant and venomous. The glade remained oblivious to the changes as the heavens wept. The furtive weed had grafted itself to the young tree and grew steadily upward, choking the heart of the Sapling, corrupting the sweet nectars within.

SHADOW AND FIRE

THE NIGHT OF SHADOW AND FIRE, that was what the old folk from southern Mehnin called it. For those who remained alive to recall, it was a memory that would never fade. No one could really explain what happened that night. From one moment to the next, the world seemed thrown into chaos. All the heavens withdrew their light; the slash of a moon fell into shadow; the stars extinguished. A dark shroud fell over the land like a chilling mist. It was spoken of rarely by those who fought for life and spilled the same upon the lonely border roads from Khyvla. Neither Gnarel nor human could adequately recall the dark bedlam which spilled upon their battle. Mercifully, their memories were vague and limited. It was enough to know that a great wickedness, a presence both foul and alluring, had caught them up in a void of fear and dread from which they could not escape. The conflict which brought them together was quickly drowned in darkness. Then the shadows fled, melted away under fervent heat which blazed like hellfire across their skin, dispelling the gloom which tore at their minds and bodies. Most who survived soon abandoned the paths of war, their bloodlust quenched through the insanity of that night. Now for those aged and decrepit who waited for death to take them, life remained full of dark memory and endless fear of gleaming shadows. A lifetime of shadows born from one night of shadow and fire.

X   The Gnarel axe-blade cut through the air and spitting rain, wedging itself into a near tree after passing deathly near its target. Rain was pounding furiously in the area. Somehow, in a few moments everything had changed. It was all Shien could do to dodge and roll to avoid decapitation or some other grisly fate. He had no battle plan and faced a foe determined on one obvious course of action. Not to mention the Gnarel were certainly adept with their weapons of war. The beast growled in frustration and tugged sharply on the long handle, freeing the slick axe-blade. Shien's opponent glared in disgust, to which Shien merely shrugged his shoulders in response. He wiped his soaked forehead with the back of his right fist, briefly removing hair, dirt and rain from his vision. He still retained the arrow in that hand, for all the good it had done him. Anytime he felt he had an opening to strike, the Gnarel recoiled to the defensive making any assault near impossible. The young man had tried every trick he could remember, even inventing a few on the spot, yet nothing was working. Worst of all, he could feel his muscles slowing, losing energy. Soon he would lose his edge and he would miss that critical dodge. Upon his death, the emblems of Vyn-shi would fall into other hands and be defiled by the unworthy. His face contorted in anger as streams of water poured down his brow; it was so frustrating to be without a means to attack effectively. He felt absolutely naked without his precious instruments of war. What he would give for even an unwieldy broadsword at this very moment.

A thunder crash cast the ground into turmoil, overwhelming the relentless cacophony of pouring rain that dulled the senses. The Gnarel moved suddenly, swinging twice, the first a feint to draw Shien into the second brutal cut. The beast was certainly intelligent. It had adapted to his defensive style. The young man made to draw into the feint and reversed his stance at the last moment. The Gnarel, committed to the attack, drove its swing through with violent intent. As Shien moved slightly off the path of attack, he rolled under the long arc of the axe-blade. As he came up to the side of the beast he struck out with his leg at its knee. Connecting solidly upon the bony limb, the Gnarel grunted and brought its talon-like foot upward and then forcibly down upon the grounded fighter. Shien pulled his leg back in time to avoid the worst of the blow, but the sharp claw edges sliced through his skin. Wincing, the young man fought back the pain by focusing his mind.

Taking the initiative, the Gnarel sprung forward, throwing its body downward upon the prone man. Shien twisted quickly as clawed hands impacted upon the earth next to his head. Thinking fast, he took a clump of sopping mud in his hand and slung it into the face of the beast. His attack succeeded in diverting the creature momentarily, and Shien divined his moment of opportunity. He sprung upon the hairy and spine-laden back of the dazed Gnarel while slamming the arrow into its neck. Howling in rage, the Gnarel staggered to its feet and with massive arms flailing, it tried to grasp the wily prey on its back. Shien hung on with one arm, and twisted the arrow around, driving it deeper through flesh and muscle. If he could just connect with the spine, it might paralyze ...

In a crazed contorted and writhing motion the furious creature shook the young man off, hurling him into a tree. His grip had faltered upon the Gnarel's slick fur. Shien grunted in pain as a sturdy branch pierced into his back. The Gnarel slumped to one knee and was howling and shaking in agony. Shien had got the arrow close, and his enemy was hurt significantly. However, he also knew the Gnarel were beasts of passion. They would not ask for quarter. He would need to kill or be killed by his opponent.

The Gnarel suddenly ceased its convulsing and regarded Shien with a sideways glare past the bony protrusions from its head. It seemed to nod slightly to him and it laid the axe blade down gently upon the sodden grass. It slowly rose up and extended a clawed gesture to him. Slowly and methodically it turned its claws upon itself, driving them deep into its abdomen. Its small black eyes never flinched from his through the torrential rain. The beast withdrew its claws slowly and extended a fist toward him, dripping wet with rain and blood, which flowed upon the ground in great drops. Shien caught the meaning. The creature was not to survive the skirmish, but it would fight him with all of its soul. It honoured the battle and so had marked where it would meet its end, either at his hand or from slow death. Shien was strangely moved by this simple yet powerful sentiment. The Gnarel tilted its head upward, spread its massive jaws wide and proceeded to howl out a cry which moved Shien to the core. Yes, this would be an end for one or both. Standing himself, he prepared for what was to come.

It was then that the heavens were consumed in gloomy shadow, and all was thrown into darkness.

⊥ Zyr stared across the small clearing at the smaller clothed Gnarel. It snorted in disgust while gripping a long spear in its claws. The larger of the two warriors had proven a stalwart fighter, but the beast had been clearly outmatched by the monk's skills. Zyr felt a small degree of pity for the downed warrior. It was not his intent to kill, but the blood lust that flowed through the dark veins of the Gnarel would permit nothing less than mortal conflict. The robed Gnarel moved slightly, casting a quick beady glance to its fallen comrade. The downed Gnarel's body lay sprawled face down in the mud, with an immense blade protruding through its back, blackened slick with blood. Zyr had neatly turned the gnarly-toothed sword upon its master with quick precision. The monk had to be efficient as time was precious, and so it was that the conflict ended with one lethal motion.

As the two remaining foes regarded each other, the heavens broke down upon the area. The drizzle made way for a torrential downpour, which soon saturated the small wood. As if from a cue, the remaining lone Gnarel drove toward Zyr in a fury that rivaled the storm. It threw the spear with terrible accuracy and force. Being caught off guard the monk leapt backward, deflecting the spear to his side with his palm. The spear point struck into the ground and the shaft quivered for a moment. It was neither the storm's distraction nor any lack of readiness which put Zyr on the defensive. Simply, the creature had not shown any sign of aggression previously, in the limited time he had to observe its behaviour.

He followed the movement of the creature. Weaponless, it had moved to its fallen clansman after the failed attack. It rolled the larger beast over and withdrew the wet blade swiftly. Zyr marveled at the actions of the strange animal. It had chosen rashly for an all-out attack, which lost the Gnarel its spear, and now it would fight with an unfamiliar weapon? Perhaps it felt a degree of fear and was reacting out of panic. What puzzled Zyr more was how the creature had shown no evidence of actual prowess in combat. Its physical presence was of no apparent comparison to its war brothers; so why was it here? It stood slowly, hefting the blade and snarling in warning. Zyr marveled as he prepared for an attack; 'what is it hoping to accomplish?' he mused to himself. It was hardly a blade warrior by the way it held the weapon.

Then, in the space of a small moment, all the mystery became clear in an amazing display of cunning which awed the stalwart monk. The robed Gnarel dropped to its knee and placed a claw upon its fellow. There was a quick exchange of energy, of life essence, and the Gnarel suddenly collapsed. Zyr's mind sparked in instant awareness; Alacritor weaves. In the place of the primitive Ashori, the once dead warrior Gnarel snatched up its sword and hurled itself toward Zyr. Swinging the jagged blade with furious strokes, it pressed the monk, who dipped and darted his body to avoid each potentially lethal blow. Rain was pounding upon the combatants, yet both bodies moved lithely through the pools of water and torrent sheets which assailed them. Zyr's mind was still processing what had just occurred; the smaller Gnarel had sacrificed itself for the larger. It had pushed the weaving beyond the safeguards without a thought of self-preservation. He felt that he never really understood these creatures.

The warrior struck out with its shoulder which was set with spiky bone protrusions to impale its enemy upon. Zyr twisted his body to avert the attack and then reached up and grabbed hold of the great horns of the Gnarel's head. Then he launched himself up and over the Blade Warrior while grasping the slick bony shafts. He twisted his body around sharply as he cut through the air and rain, and heard the familiar grind and crunch of a crumpled spine in his ears. Releasing the horns, he turned his head, the body of the Gnarel lay a second time upon the ground in a twisted abnormal way. "You better stay down, my friend," the monk said as he began to stand.

He had a fraction of time to react, but somehow Zyr
narrowly averted a blade from penetrating his ribs. It
skittered across his chest, ripping flesh and tearing his
pectoral muscles. Gasping in pain, he clutched his wounded
chest, searching through the cursed downpour for the source
of the attack. It was all but impossible to see now; between
the rain which came so thick and hard and the lack of light.
All this, combined with the constant echo of the rain in his
ears (like thousands of hands joined in ovation), created a
sensory state of deprivation. The best the wounded monk
could manage was to await another attack. It would appear
his enemy was relying upon senses other than sight or
sound. Another attack came, this time to his abdomen. Zyr
struck downward and broke the haft of a large spear; the
healer's spear! Still holding his chest, he sprung forward and
came across whipping his body around with a knotted
backhand fist to the temple of the crouched Gnarel. The
blow stunned the already weary beast, and was followed up
by two swift debilitating kicks to the Gnarel's vital points.
The beast fell helplessly to the ground, groaning savagely.
Zyr pressed his boot to the neck of the dying Gnarel and
mercifully ended its life with a quick twist of his leg.

The monk shook his head in anger, water spraying from
his brow. 'When will I learn not to underestimate the
enemy?' he thought in chastising tones. He thought the
strange healing beast had incapacitated itself. It was a ruse
to draw his attention away. The Ashori-tar Gnarel must
have made its way over to the spear it had cast away earlier,

while he was preoccupied. He certainly could not have seen it move through the rain. The monk contemplated his enemy as he surveyed the bodies, blurred by wet darkness. They were fearless and cunning and had caught him at a moment of opportunity. Standing in the rain, while his blood mingled with his foes' upon the ground, he honoured the departed warriors in a moment of silent regard.

A strange sensation was suddenly gnawing at his mind. He wasn't sure of the cause, but the feeling was growing steadily deeper and heavier. It was a feeling of dread and weariness that he had never before experienced. He struggled with his will; it became weary from carrying heavy burdens. Somewhere in his brain a small seed was spreading roots of wicked dissent. Surely, it would be easier to give up, rest this weary body ... you cannot win this war, Mihyl. A cloud was settling over his rational mind, suffocating and entrapping the spark of life. Zyr rubbed his temples slowly, feeling the great weight of responsibility and the seductive thoughts crushing his will into dust. 'Perhaps ... it would be easier to ...' Zyr slowly fell to his knees with his head bowed in defeat. His broken mind began to dim just as a great black veil settled over the surrounding area.

ϴ   Far beyond the monk's hearing, terrible cries of anguish were lost in the downpour and rain. A great mist more deep and palpable than any fog fell upon every living thing. It swarmed and swirled around every soul. Gnarel and human alike wailed in misery and despair. Slowly, the voices were being silenced one by one, in brutal agony. Being separated, no being in either group was aware of the great slaughter that was commencing among them. The darkness was consuming their wills and eventually their very lives. With every cry of despair, the great gloom seemed to grow ever more terrible and profound.

✕ Shien stumbled about in a dull stupor. He collided with a tree trunk, and then slipped to a knee upon the watery ground. He was unsure about what to do, or what to think. A great war was commencing in his mind. The side of his rationality was utterly perplexed and employed logic as its great ballista in the mental struggle. 'This cannot be! It is all wrong! Come to your senses!' Equally strong and relentless was the opposing thoughts which hammered upon his mental fortress as a great battering ram. 'Fool, you cannot see, hear or sense anything! Stop this foolish struggle! Be still … just a little longer … all this will pass …' He gripped his head and cried out in anguish. He could not bring his thoughts to any certain cohesion. Yet, somehow through all the chaos came a sound that broke the struggle. It was an enchanting and profound whisper that pierced through the raucous turmoil in his mind. In all its power it was strangely melodic and haunting …

"Awake! Awake! Ahtol has come!"

Shien slowly stood as if bolstered up by an unseen mighty arm. He felt his body moving, guided slowly through the wood. The war slowly ebbed in his head. He sensed something deep within his soul strengthening his resolve, causing his legs to move steadily and swiftly through the wood. Finally, he saw something in vision or in mind, which one he knew not. Two burning lights, one searing red and the other a brilliant white, parting the sea of shadows. The Spirit of Vyn-shi! Though the darkness clawed at the bright intrusion it recoiled at every attempt. The brilliance shone out like a beacon and Shien moved slowly toward them. As he came up next to the dazzling radiance, his hand raised to cover his eyes. From utter blackness to a luster beyond the noon-day sun! Now his whole body was illuminated by the glow. Shien stooped down slowly and slipped his fingers through the counterguards. His whole being became consumed with the energy flowing from the two swords. His legs quivered as he made to stand erect. The darkness was alive and all-consuming trying desperately to choke the very life from his lungs, yet the power of the Vyn-shi was on him, within his whole frame. Trembling, he felt his right arm raise the fiery standard through the murky cloud above his head.

All at once the Heart of Kuros began to beat. Beginning slowly at first, it gradually grew quicker and stronger. Shien felt the thumping sensation from the tip of the hilt to the deepest recesses of his soul. With each pulse, the rapier gave off a tremendous burst of scorching red energy, which spread outward from the weapon in great ripples. The shadows retreated from the washes of flame and fire, and tried in vain to regroup after each pulse. Shien stood in awe at what was transpiring. It was as if his soul was linked to what was occurring. The flames never harmed his body, but slid over his skin like a breeze.

As the pounding fury of Kuros dispelled the darkness and illuminated the area in red hues, Shien saw the terrible cost of the weapon. The land lay barren and scorched in the crimson light; where neither a tree nor blade of grass stood above the ground. A blacked wasteland remained; the fruits of the wrath of Kuros. The blade called Isil lay still and firm in his other hand, content to let its counterpart's fury swath paths of destruction across the land. So this was the secret of the Spirit of Vyn-shi. It was terrifying and breathtaking all in the same thought. As the shadows dispersed, the sword replaced its thundering fury with a brilliant red aura that cast everything in a crimson hue. It was then that things began to move very slowly, almost as still moments in time.

Shien saw something move in the corner of his eye, a blurred motion which swept toward him rapidly. He turned his head slowly to see what his soul was reviling. A horrific form filled his vision. Looming before him just off the ground was a creature beyond description. Illuminated in Kuros' red glow, it appeared to be draped in black liquid shadows. Ghastly slick and almost tar-like, the shadows dripped in bead trails off its massive black form. Its towering shape was somewhat humanoid, with great black arms which hung outward from its body. A gleaming and twisted blade flowed up the sleek right limb, from clawed hand to shoulder. Its head was a mass of flowing strands, thick and vine-like. They twisted and curled through the air riding on winds of dark energy. The most soul-wrenching sight was the deep red orbs that lay within the tangled mass of black filaments. They were a gateway to a void of misery and torment, now fixed horribly upon the lone fighter. Shien felt that without the cooling wind Isil was forming around his psyche, he would easily slip into that hateful searing void. The rapier handle felt reassuring in his grip.

The demonic creature lunged toward him in a fluid and graceful motion, while shadows trailed in its wake. Shien moved faster and lighter than his body had ever permitted. He stepped in alongside the enormous creature, stabbing and slicing with Kuros in blazing motions. The monster twisted and stretched its body in an exquisite spiral, deflecting the flaming blade across the razor surface of its limb. The two combatants moved apart and then engaged again in a heartbeat. The demon's arm danced in a flurry of motion in which Isil was employed for a solid and remarkable defence. Shien marveled at his precision in battle. He did not feel his body being controlled, but rather a perfect union had been forged with the weapons, bypassing the usual limitations of response and reaction between body and brain. It was if a direct link from his mind to the rapiers gave him power to move his limbs as swiftly as the speed of thought. That was fortunate, as the demon matched him in every movement. The battle had become pitched, an intricate and deadly sweet ballet. The mêlée spanned all over the scorched ground with neither combatant giving way. Shien wondered what fate had in store for him, as he contemplated the eventual limitations of the human body. How long could he go on? He stretched his thoughts briefly outward to the unseen voice and pleaded for any assistance. The battle raged on with increased fervor, demon and man in fragile deadlock.

"Shien, be ready!" It wasn't the same voice he had heard earlier. It seemed an eternity since he had heard another's voice; he had thought he was the only one left. Yet, there was the monk, clearing the low rise just to the south in a dead run. Zyr's body was churning and swirling with pure white energy, equally as brilliant as Kuros' red aura. The demon did not falter and immediately adjusted itself to meet the monk's attack. Zyr weaved large crackling patterns of pure alacrity which surged from the ground and entwined about his outstretched arms. Shien had not eased his assault, and with renewed determination, focused his every thought to move his body faster. They could end this!

Zyr came upon the demon swiftly, joining in the perilous dance to which Shien was engaged. The nimble healer navigated the seas of combat despite the flashing of rapier and demonic blades. The great black fiend screeched in frustration as it was forced to defend against the unyielding assaults of its enemies. It dared not be struck by either the monk's hands or Shien's formidable blades. The two mortals were pressing harder and harder while each moment was as fine crystal, so delicate and clear. One slip would mean the end for either side.

"Now!" Zyr bellowed as he snapped the two energy weaves free of the Root simultaneously. Shien sensed the plan and responded within a fraction of a thought. The shadowy lithe frame slipped clear of the monk's twined alacrity strands, its body elongating to impossible heights as the great threads surged past. Kuros thrust passionately forward, its will thirsting for impact. The great fiery weapon sliced through the midriffs of the shadows, flames scorching and searing in a great conflagration. Ghastly screams filled the air as the black specter writhed and thrashed upon the purifying pyre of Kuros. Zyr sprung powerfully upward to the head of the demon and drove a pulsing hand through the many lashing tendrils and seized its skull. The other hand he stretched out as shimmering threads snapped to his call from the Root. Radiant streams of energy coursed the shadowy form like silvery veins, all at the monk's command. It sank to the earth screaming and convulsing.

"Curse you, impotents! One more - just one more!" It cried out in mighty discord.

Shien had thrown himself clear of the thing as it sunk slowly to the ground. Leaning on Isil he wheezed from exertion, watching the impossible play in its final act. The monk perched atop the demon's shoulders, hands thrust downward around its head as his face was turned heavenward in great pangs of exertion. Relentless power coursed now like great white rivers through the whirling

shadow and across the ground. The demon slashed in vain
at the monk, but Zyr would not relent. As it repeated its
previous lament, the monk's voice echoed through the air in
reply. "Be gone! Cease your thirst. The blood-price is paid!"
The great shadow was diminishing, slowly gathering into a
mighty spinning vortex above the demon. It shook its head
in violent protest, but the monk held firm.

"*No, I won't yield to you again!*" it screamed defiantly.

"Withdraw, I say!" the monk's voice came more
forcefully, and if possible, the great streams of power came
more potently, causing the monk to gasp in great agony. The
vortex swirled faster and faster and funneled downward
into the rift the monk had opened upon the shadow's brow.
The strange entwining of dark and light energy rushed
downward with the force of a gale wind until in one great
moment, all was calm. No power was felt, all force had been
extinguished. Kuros slumbered.

Shien stood slowly and shakily. He was unnerved by the
great transition: a whirlwind of power beyond reckoning to
complete and utter silence. He shuffled awkwardly toward
Zyr who still remained motionless, hunched over a form on
the ground. In a daze, Shien barely reckoned that the land
was illuminated by the stars once again, while the moon had
passed on. With weapons in hand, he stumbled to the
monk's side. His senses were still adjusting from the
overwhelming surging of power, yet his ears detected an
unexpected sound. Zyr was weeping audibly, his head
bowed over the form upon the ground. Falling to his knees,

Shien released Isil and moved to brush away the tangled hair of the shadow's fell minion. He prepared Kuros to strike, but it too fell from his grasp.

Firah's face glowed white pale in the heaven's light.

THE BLIGHT

III THE EXPECTANT SUN was transforming the horizon from black to deep blue shades. In the first morning light Tey'ur surveyed the destruction around him from his saddle. His grey eyes took in all the land, while he drew in his cloak around his armoured frame. The chill of the night still lingered and the mail contracted the cold. His graying shoulder length hair spilled forward as he leaned over rubbing his mare, Calista, with the leather undersides of his gauntlets. He shifted in the saddle; it had been hours since he set out to recover the ill-fated recon unit. The Gnarel had baited the guild hall and the White Guard had responded. Yet he could not fathom what would cause such devastation. The barren land, scorched to the very roots stretched for miles and miles.

This whole area which he had roamed for all memory was once a lush and vibrant land. It was a mark of dedication to the service to the Order which was situated in southern Mehnin. Throughout the south-lands thriving forests spilled into rolling plains and endless waving fields of grain. Creatures small and great filled the scene with a variety of colour and joy. Some of his fondest memories were the in the quiet times, in solitary walks through choruses written and performed by the wind and grass, the carefree cricket and jubilant sparrow. It was a lovely memory - a stark contrast with the blight that lay before him now. He had to determine the sheer size of the disfigurement upon the land. Sounds from the company pulled him from his thoughts - there would be time for such things later.

The forward sentries were signaling. Tey'ur pulled in Calista sharply, causing her to wicker in mild protest. Motioning a halt to his troops, he spied upon a small camp in the distance, amongst the rolling hills, close to the road to Khyvla. He signaled for two rangers to inspect the site. As the two lightly clad infiltrators moved silently away, the grizzled veteran checked his vanguard and equipment as was his habit.

He sat tall in the saddle (as his height was well above that of typical men) which was an advantage when surveying the troops in combat. Despite being well acquainted with his winter years, Tey'ur's body was still robust and healthy - the gift of Symian blood. Whatever age had taken away from youthful strength, he had made up for in wiliness in combat. That was not to say he was frail by any stretch; he was still feared in the Dorgyn Circles and was more than a match for any man.

He stretched his tall frame and felt the straps of his shoulder plates dig the chain mail uncomfortably across his lateral muscles. Unfortunately his large frame also necessitated customized armour which was molded to his body type. While customizing was not unusual for some folk (most armour required some modification), Tey'ur's was a completely different situation. It took ages to receive work back from the smiths and usually not to his satisfaction. He demanded perfection, as shoddy work could easily turn the tide in a close skirmish. He tugged on the vambrace absently. Intricate symbols lay etched beneath scars and dents from the old days. It was the only armour he retained from the Halls. The rest had fallen by the wayside, irreparable from countless battles since the Breaking, now faded into memory. He glanced at the white stained cuirass and checked his thoughts.

The White Guard was under his stewardship now, and presently they needed culling. Evidence of this was ample and ever-present, as shown with the rashness of the recon guard! Hot-headed folly most likely led to their doom. Recon was not equipped for a strong defence. Instead, he had designed the unit to move swiftly; delivering quick death and handling light engagements.

He guessed what had occurred. The Gnarel likely devoured the recon within an hour, if they foolishly fell into difficulty. The White Guard had been itching recently for an outlet to their restlessness. It had been particularly bad when some of his men had reduced themselves to enforcing provincial laws upon the hapless peasantry in the area. When the Gnarel attacked the White Guard, it was a mother-send to some of the younger men, and the recon guard had left without orders.

Tey'ur supposed the Gnarel had effectively culled his forces for him. He sighed quietly and surveyed the encampment in the growing light. The scouts returned swiftly across the scorched earth, and reported to their superior. Chain of command was essential in the guild. The scout lieutenant strode up next to Tey'ur's brawny warhorse. The stealthy man hefted a great bird of prey on a padded arm.

"My Lord," his lieutenant spoke in hushed tones, "the camp consists of our recon unit, minus one, who are all resting. There are no other marks in the area. Gnarel tracks lead away from the camp, in a northerly direction, about three hours old."

This was strange news indeed. The scorched earth presented new challenges for the scouts but they had adapted. There was no mistaking their report and he hadn't expected to see his men gathered in such a way. He suspected they would find the survivors of the conflict straggling along on a return journey home. But to have them all gathered together with camp unbroken this late in the day? Indeed, it was most unexpected and mysterious. The Gnarel tracks were even more perplexing. Normally, Gnarel tracks would have passed through this area, and in the worst case been the only tracks remaining. To have his men alive and to have departing Gnarel tracks made no sense. The Gnarel rarely retreated. It was beyond peculiar. It merited caution. He dismissed the ranger curtly with a gesture.

"Corbin."

A solemn hooded figure in white robes moved his horse up from his position to his Lord's back right. He halted the animal next to Tey'ur and spoke quietly.

"My Lord?"

"What do you sense from the camp ahead? Is there any evidence of Ashori activity?" He waited as the brow of the Ignitor wrinkled slightly.

"Not presently; however the lingering residue of the weaves we have been tracing is strongest here." He said nothing more. Short and to the point is what Tey'ur demanded.

"I see nothing that bespeaks danger, and yet my instincts will not rest. They have not let up since we left." Tey'ur calculated the options aloud. Corbin's face drew into a sardonic smile.

"You should have considered a career as Ashori," the hooded one commented, "Your instinct is as shrewd as any acquainted with the arts that I know of. Perhaps it's not too late …"

The Lord of the White Guard Hall glared at the man with tempered disdain. Corbin simply nodded and moved his mount back to position. Within himself, Tey'ur smiled. That man was destined to lead the White Guard, he was sure of it. Mild effrontery was tolerable, if not evidence of the winds of change. Corbin's words were nothing but a heralding of the winds of fate. Besides, his aging bones were closing in upon their last war. Soon he would leave the defence of the land to the young. Tey'ur raised a weathered gauntlet and signaled the advance.

As the company of a hundred grew closer, the forms that huddled around in small circle took shape. He recognized the men under his command, most sat hunched over their knees with bowed heads. The one thing that did catch his attention immediately was the absence of wounds. If they actually survived the encounter, there should have been bandages and dressings to cover all manner of trauma. He did not equip most units with adepts in the alacritor arts, as healers were in short supply. He glanced to his left, and watched their guild healer look on with apparent concern. The healing role was a demanding one. Often when situations became perilous or hopeless they would suffer the greatest. The inability to solve every dilemma sometimes broke their resolve and they withdrew into themselves, never to heal again. Sadly, they did not live long after.

The company vanguard spread out to form a perimeter head, while the rear guard moved to fill in the gaps. The maneuver would guard effectively against any outside attack, at least long enough to regroup into formation. He moved through the center of the expanded configuration, and guided Calista toward the circle of motionless guildsmen. After moving close, he slid carefully from the saddle to the charred earth. He felt his muscles complain under the stress of the dismount and grimaced within; truly, it had been some time since he had been on the hunt. Tey'ur moved steadily in the half plate mail to the foremost soldier who was already being assessed by Menhol, First Alacritor of the Guard. The graying lord crouched down and placed a hand upon the hunched shoulder of the man.

"Yohen." He whispered to the man's ear. Slowly, the subordinate's head lifted and stared with a dull expression into the older man's eyes.

"My Lord Tey'ur ..." He seemed at a loss and struggled to find his words. "The shadows ... guard yourself ... it'll destroy us all!" Moisture was forming in the corners of soldier's frenzied eyes and mouth. He seemed to be in a daze, or trance-like state. Menhol was silent, slowly delving the man for injury. "Lord, how did you …?" the soldier spoke frantically. Reality suddenly settled upon the soldier and he began to sob silently.

"Easy, Yohen." He eased the weeping man's head against his armoured chest. He leaned slightly toward the monk. "Tell me, Menhol, what's happened," he whispered. The monk frowned and stroked his chin thoughtfully. After a moment he responded.

"I am not exactly sure. There is no evidence of injury, and yet …"

"Something's happened inside." Tey'ur tapped his own temple softly. The healer nodded.

"I have little expertise in this area as it's a highly complex and developed form of lore. My initial assessment is that there may have been alterations through parts of his psyche. Yet, I have my doubts. A mind master would know for certain if another of his craft were tampering. However, Cerebors are extremely rare in the land, most are known and accounted for … and they are hardly numerous. As you know, there are none in the White Guard who can delve into the mind." His mouth frowned sternly in concentration. The old warrior stood slowly and cast a gaze into the glowing horizon. His eyes, which witnessed untold wars, gazed to a faraway place to the south.

"I have known many … seen their work. None have ever been capable to act on this scale." He stared unflinching as a northern wind tossed his cloak about his massive frame. The

Gnarel trail was a false lead; a greater mystery lay in other paths. He breathed in deeply and listened to his innermost feelings. They were drawing him south, inevitably connecting to his past. It was either sentimentality or a distinct impression. Perhaps She was guiding him … No, that would be impossible. He closed his eyes and then turned to face Menhol. "Get these men loaded into the equipment transport. We move within the hour."

*　　*　　*

☯　　Tohm's brow dripped sweat across his exposed barrel chest and upon the dry ground. The morning sun shone high overhead. The southern passes of Tamers Reach loomed ever nearer with every passing hour. Plodding on, Tohm adjusted his grip on the shafts. His muscles were taut and strained from hours of labour, yet he never uttered a complaint. His eyes never veered from the vast field that spread before him. His mind was set on one goal, to deliver the motionless monk he carried to safety. They had pressed on for hours with short but otherwise merciful rests. Though they had emerged from the scorched land some time ago, the southerly winds harassed them with debilitating dust. Zyr now lay cocooned within the waggon tarp, shielded against the foul particles of charcoal-like dirt which swirled about them.

Following the terrible struggle where Zyr and Shien had subdued the demon, the monk had performed some last acts of complete compassion. After reviving any survivors from *both* sides of the conflict, he healed them to the last combatant. His last instruction to the three of them was to head in a strictly southerly direction and tend to him as his body recovered. He collapsed after that, completely immobile. An improvised bed had been formed from the remnants of the cart. The terror of the previous night had driven the ponies away and no one looked for them. A sense of uncertainty had settled over the group.

Tohm was concerned; Shien had not spoken to anyone, not even Firah. He walked ahead of Tohm several paces, checking the direction of their travels against the sun and hills. Previously he had eliminated evidence of their tracks for a significant distance. After fording a steady stream, which fed from the southern peaks of Tamers Reach, Tohm's inner logical mind began to be at ease. Rivers were difficult to track through, especially with Shien taking care to replace rocks and stones to hide footfall and tracks etched by Zyr's bed. A pack was slung across the young man's back which he clung too tightly, while weapons on his hip swayed in cadence with long strides. The young girl walked behind, head down and feet dragging through the grass. Her hand grasped the grip of her dagger constantly. The whole mood of the group was somber and withdrawn. He shook his head and pressed onward with renewed fervor. He knew that his mind was weak; he would at times lapse into fits of rage and animal-like lust, yet he could not fail his most precious possessions, the friendships he treasured more than life itself. He could not fail, and strangely, his mind was stable as he focused on the singular task of dragging the litter across the ground.

Suddenly, Tohm's instincts exploded into fire. He reeled as his conscious mind screamed in protest. 'No! Not again! I am in control!' Yet that same consciousness watched in vain as his body released the shafts and crouched low in a feral stance. It was if the limited conscience was trying to control a raging tornado by shouting feeble words; it was utterly useless. Tohm scampered across the ground swiftly toward the girl, his large frame defying logic as it flowed across the ground. The girl looked up suddenly, her red eyes full of alarm.

"Tohm, wait!"

Tohm felt his body lurch to a halt beside her. He sniffed the air. Strange smells filled his mind as his brain interpreted the odors. Horses, men, energy, and excrement mixed with endless smoke and ashes. The weakened mind that was Tohm's strained to rein in the beast, to prevent it from acting rashly. It might as well have tried to blow out an inferno with a breath.

"Danger approaches." His arm lifted to the north and he watched as his hand moved slowly to hers. She snatched it away quickly.

"Not this again. Shien!" The young man slowly stopped and hesitantly turned himself around. His face betrayed no emotion, as he walked over. Tohm watched the young fighter's eyes. They were hard and impassionate.

"What is it?" He said coolly. She flinched slightly at his terse address but quickly continued.

"Tohm says we're in danger. Normally, I would say it's his mind but I was thinking about last night and ..."

"Tohm. Where is the danger?" Shien interjected. Firah fell silent and her head lowered slightly. Tohm felt his hand rise again.

"There. The danger comes. We must go." He was beginning to fidget where he crouched, his keen eyes locked upon the horizon where the enemy would appear.

"Where are we going to go, Tohm?" Shien's voice was steadily increasing in volume and force. "What in Aeredia's name are we going to do? Zyr is half-dead, and you think we will be able to do anything? Look at us. Despoilers! Beasts and demons! We should be running from ourselves!" His face was red in anger and frustration.

The wind blew harshly across the land, scattering black dust which caught upon the girl's dampened cheeks, marring her complexion. Her eyes squinted sharply. She turned her head away as raven black hair was tussled by the wind's unseen hands.

Tohm's rational mind ached to reach out to Firah. He sensed something was happening to her, but he could not piece together all the clues. He found it difficult to focus on keeping control of himself, when he did have control. 'I'm sorry, Firah' Tohm whispered quietly in the dark recesses of his mind. It was clear how much the monk had helped them, now that they were without his aid. No one knew how long he would remain in his state.

Shien's light-colored hair shifted slightly as he pressed a hand to his face. He had sunk down to one knee and bowed himself low. "It doesn't really matter …" his voice mumbled from his lowered head. "Do as you wish. In some ways, a quick end is preferable to all this." He fell silent and remained still. Tohm's body shifted anxiously but stayed beside the girl. His mind determined that it was probably useless to run, as there was no cover for miles. It was futile.

Two thundering columns poured over a far hill spreading rapidly apart. They branched outward and extended around the four companions. Tohm crouched lower, emitting snarling, guttural sounds. While Firah stood upright and faced the nearest arcing line of horses and men with stoic pose, Shien simply raised his eyes slightly and waited. The two columns intersected and then slowly turned inward, settling into various formations. In a few moments they halted thirty Spears distant from the small group, completely enveloping the four companions. The riders were adorned in shining armour and their weapons gleamed in the early morning sun. Their white cloaks and tabards flowed in the cool breeze.

One large rider dismounted and was followed by two others, who smartly stepped up next to either side of the first. The three armoured men approached the small group. As they grew nearer they slowed and stopped just out of reach of any potential attack. The large one considered the weary group for a time from behind a sparkling helm, his eyes moving from person to person. Tohm continued his low growling and seemed to be coiled tightly as a spring, with Firah's hand on his shoulder the release mechanism. She stood boldly and waited upon the visitors to speak. Shien had not acknowledged the troops, but glared out from behind locks of hair which had been blown across his face. No one dared move.

"You seem to be in some distress," the large one spoke finally. "Perhaps we could be of some assistance?" He seemed at ease, but Tohm could tell that the leader and all his men were wound as tightly as he. One false move would bring a quick end. Desperately, he tried to cool the beast which hackled with anticipation of attack.

"We have things well in hand." It was Firah who addressed the commander, which visibly took some of the surrounding troops aback. The large man displayed no emotion, but focused his gaze directly on the girl. She brushed the dark hair from her face. "Thanks for your concern, all of you," She looked around at the massive force, "we'll continue on our way."

"So it will be." The large man assented. Firah's crimson eyes widened. Clearly she did not expect this.

"However, permit me to solicit some good will. It is our duty to assist those in need. I am Tey'ur of the White Guard, caretakers of Southern Mehnin and all its rural holdings. I have a healer with my troop who might be able to help your downed companion." He indicated the resting pallet to which Zyr was secured and covered. Firah faltered. Tohm remembered well her philosophy about most men in the world, and it was not conforming to the demeanor of this stalwart warrior. He was intrigued to learn what was at the root of this request. The beast sniffed the air anxiously.

"I need a moment to talk with my companions."

The large man bowed in simple courtesy. It was neither patronizing nor overdone, and the massive soldier withdrew with his guard to allow them room to converse out of earshot. Firah stared at them with her blood-like gaze and spoke quietly. "What do we do? Can they help Zyr?"

"Don't be a fool, Firah." Shien spoke quietly. Apparently, some sense had replaced portions of his indifference, perhaps in the event that they might yet survive another day. "Never trust soldiers, even ones who dress in white. Look at the emblems. These belong to the same group of men we helped last night. They have a reason for being here, more than just emissaries of good will. Judging by the size of their army, they are clearly engaged in more than a refreshing morning ride." He was speaking to her, but his gaze never met hers.

"Well ... I trust the leader. He seems ... or rather feels trustworthy. I think we should take their offer."

Tohm would have loved to contribute many things. It frustrated his rational mind that he was reduced to a passive observer. He sensed his body relaxing somewhat, but the beast was still on guard. He looked to Firah and Shien. They were both standing firm in their opinions. The horses were shifting restlessly around them, reflecting their riders' mood.

"And on what sense are you basing your judgments?" Shien retorted.

"What is that supposed to mean?" Firah replied hotly. Tohm groaned within himself. Not now.

"You don't exactly have an outstanding record in judgment calls!" Shien fired back.

"Obviously, since I am talking to you, an ignorant meathead!" Firah scowled and put her hands on her hips in defiance.

"Oh, what's this? A nice repayment for ... fine ... you know what? You started this, you can finish it!" Shien was glowering in anger. Clearly, there was much more the young man yearned to say, but he was fighting the impulse with all his resolve. He turned himself from the girl again, which she reciprocated with equal disdain.

Firah signaled the commander who walked back to conversing distance.

"We have agreed to accept your request." She said confidently.

ᛞ   *The Sapling had shown the true colours of its blossoms. Peace around the small glade was thrown into disarray. The buds had not grown splendid and bright as anticipated, rather they wreaked a foul odor and cast uncomfortable shadows over the surrounding foliage. The Sapling was changing and all near the corrupted young tree grew apart, desperately trying to avoid mingling with its wretched pollens.*

THREADS OF THE PAST

THE WINDS from the north countries stirred the remnants of a memory. The strands of thought were shifted about by the subtle breeze, which entered through the nostrils of the resting and tranquil healer. The sensation coursed through every limb, organ and fiber. Somehow, there was something familiar about the land and the wind which plucked at the strings of hidden memory. Slowly, gates long shut, swung open upon the gentle breeze. The secrets of the past began to flow outward, drowning the monk's mind in terrible, frightening truths. Pieces of memory now fell into place for the first time.

*　　*　　*

⏚ "Both of you stay put. You caused enough delays." Tey'ur growled in frustration, his breath steaming through the air. Crouched low in a small snowy ditch, the three paused for a moment. The morning was coming fast and still they had only partially infiltrated the mountain fortress called Racur, or *cursed* in lesser tongues. Zyr's face tightened. 'What? Does he think we are Initiates?' he thought to himself. Tey'ur's hard eyes flashed to the Convert. He grabbed a handful of the young man's Chota and hauled him up to his weathered face. Zyr knew better than to resist the veteran. Tey'ur had been on the Council of Masters longer than any other, even surpassing the Servant's time. All respected the wisdom and battle ferocity of Tey'ur, and Zyr knew he was clearly outmatched in every technique. That one fact served to anger the young monk more than anything else. He hated being inferior to others. Zyr's eyes burned with all the fury of his heart. "I can't stand reckless upstarts like you," the white clad warrior spat. "As a matter of fact, I've always despised you ..."

"At least the feeling is mutual, Tey'ur." Zyr replied through gritted teeth. A long notched blade slid up the side of Zyr's face, which felt cool against his skin. Tehsa gasped and made a movement to her Gé. The larger man's eyes darted to her, piercing through the near darkness. Tehsa's hand hesitated and then remained still. When the grizzled master returned to Zyr, a small smile had crossed the Convert's face. Tey'ur pressed the blade edge against the young man's face harshly. Zyr chuckled low. "You just can't stand the fact that I have been promoted, even though you voted against me every time." Zyr's face was full of smug self-righteousness. A trickle of blood slid gradually down the blade edge. Tey'ur's teeth clenched together visibly in silent wrath.

"You have worn my patience thin. I warn you, *Reykal*, my blood is running hot. Act outside of orders, or cross me in any way again and I'll rid the Order of your idiocy." He withdrew the blade and pushed the young Ashori away roughly into the snowy embankment. Both men held a deadly gaze for a brief moment before the larger man broke the silent war. "Now, both of you will remain here. I'll check the third ring perimeter." In one quick movement the stalwart warrior leapt from the low trench and was gone. Tehsa moved quickly to Zyr's side. She had pulled some cloth from her neck which covered the breast gap in her Chota, and applied it to the thin slash across her Mihyl's cheek. Her brown eyes stirred with concern while she pressed softly upon the wound.

"You always pick the battles you cannot win," she spoke with a soft chiding. He turned his gaze to her and smiled a wily grin.

"That is an odd thing for you to say. After all, it was you who moved against that guard and I had to bail you out as usual. Too many risks and too little skill. You still fight like an amateur with that thing you know," he said glancing to the balled weapon at her hip.

A small frown fell across her face. "I should hold you down so Tey'ur can end it quickly." She jammed the cloth down hard upon the wound.

"*Lliankor,*" he cursed. "Mind yourself, Jiryl!" He shouted as he smacked her hand away. In an instant the skin sealed itself, leaving no trace of a wound.

"How bold, Mihyl, to slander the Heavenly One." Her voice rang in a chastising tone but her face was set in a small smile. Zyr ignored her and stared up at the looming mount.

The heights of Racur were enveloped in snow and ice, and while snow presently covered the land, white patches adorned the summit year round. Racur was known for its impassible rings of defence, home to a variety of creatures and beasts. Most of all, its name was spoken in the Halls with the greatest disdain. The mount harboured the most detestable demon spawn, causing all who ventured too near to meet a terrible and unspeakable end. It was said by the locals that any who lived in its shadow would inherit an awful curse. The Hall had always considered Racur a black blemish upon the beautiful veil of Aeredia. It had remained untouched due to its formidable walls which wound upward around the mount in an endless coil of death - until this night.

Tey'ur slid back down into the small trench. He was breathing fast, and quickly regarded the two waiting Order companions. "We must move quickly. There is a troop of blasted axe-wielding spawn coming this way," the warrior whispered between breaths. "Remember, both of you, we are trying to infiltrate, not conquer, this mountain. We need to find information, not needless death. Now make ready. There is a break in the watch thirty paces to the north-west. Ready ... Let's go!"

Zyr collapsed against the wall, clutching a nasty stitch in his side. The fifteenth ring had proven to be the worst yet. He calmed himself and performed a quick internal check. His energy level was decreasing with every conflict. Around the tenth gate or so, he had come to terms with Tey'ur's harsh wisdom. There was no way they could beat off the whole mountain, and at times it seemed the only option. The key was eliminating the enemy quickly, before hue and cry could spread to the next gate. That usually required expenditure of energy, and it was taking its toll on his body.

He slammed his fist against the cold stone in frustration; despite all his training he still wasn't powerful enough. Recently, he felt he had reached a wall in his soul as immovable and unscalable as the heights before him. He had not been able to increase his internal reservoir of holy power. Every attempt to increase in spiritual stature was unsuccessful, and this mission only served to accentuate the failure. To make matters worse, he had become separated from the others.

He looked about quickly, and searched in vain upon the countless drifts. The sun had risen behind murky grey clouds which stretched across the sky, horizon to horizon. The white Chota had proven invaluable in avoiding detection. This had saved his life more than once. Zyr wondered how he would ever get off this cursed mountain, not to mention ascending to whatever heights were necessary. He looked off to his left toward the sheer cliff face. Through howling wind some strange sound caught in his ears.

Rising into a low crouch, Zyr worked along the cold stone wall toward the mountain climbs. The passage around the mount comprised of endless walls and defense points, which surrounded the jutting crags that drove upward at impossible angles. The only way to ascend safely was to pass through the gates, but safety had little to offer for that route as well. The young monk was pressed against the walls of the gate and the side of the mountain and looked to what had caught his attention. Low thuds echoed off the sheer surfaces from deep within, beyond a small gap in the rocks. Touching his ear to the frigid surface he felt the vibrations.

Zyr could not resist investigating the cause of the anomaly. There was barely enough room for one to press through, between rock faces, but it was possible. As he moved to press through the small space, a gauntleted hand caught his arm. He twisted that arm sharply around and stepped in low, knocking the legs out from his attacker. The armoured form crashed to the ground heavily. Pinning his enemy, his hand flashed to deliver the killing blow, but stopped just short of the target.

"I can't believe I fell for that again!" A female voice cursed. Zyr slowly removed the helm from the head of a familiar face. Tehsa's fuming visage appeared, and then it slowly shifted to mirth. "You should see yourself, Mihyl." She laughed softly, her dark brown hair spilling across the snowy ground. She made to move, but Zyr slammed her down to the ground, strengthening the pin. His face was flushed and hot.

"Do you know what I ... you could have been killed! What is this?" he demanded, looking at the heavy breastplate he leaned upon. Her face was also flushed but strangely she was not angry at all. Tehsa looked up at her superior in a strange way, a look Zyr had not seen before. She placed gauntleted hands upon his shoulders and pulled him down next to her face. Her voice came in a whisper.

"I call it infiltrating. What exactly do you call this?" Her voice was as soft as her pale skin which radiated heat upon his face. They remained motionless, staring into the others eyes, everything else dissolving around them into white. For

Zyr, all that remained was the sea of green - caught up in a pair of eyes that burrowed relentlessly into his soul. He felt her hands on his shoulders tighten, which caused him to suddenly sit up. The young man paused and then slowly moved off of her prone body. Zyr held out a quivering hand to her, which Tehsa took. They rose together, neither speaking a word.

After a time, Zyr turned his face toward the small hole in the rock face. "I ... I was heading in here to check something out. Where is Tey'ur?" His voice found a steadiness as he focused on the task he had so easily discarded. 'What just happened?' he wondered to himself.

"Tey'ur is down at the thirteenth ring. He's been tagged by a couple of arrows and suggests it's futile to go on," Tehsa reported.

She also sounded calm and resolute, but what was that he detected behind her voice, something new and alarming. "He sent me to get you, and I figured it would be easier to put this junk on than try a man's way of getting up here ..." She was smiling now, which put things more at ease in his heart for the time being. "What do you want to do, Mihyl?" she inquired softly. There it was again, that same feeling from her, the way she addressed him. After countless conversations, he knew something had changed between them forever. He knew because it was planted deep in his heart; a small seed which had finally sprouted. Zyr knew that it had always been there, and despite anything he would do, it would always remain.

"I want to check something out before we leave. You'll need to rid yourself of that cursed armour if you want to tag along." He moved to the rock and made to slide his body through. Yet, he hesitated. His peripheral vision was burning, his mind aching. In a silent struggle, his head turned slightly enough for his eyes to catch a fleeting glimpse of the beautiful vision that stood next to him, armour folding away like petals off a rose. She was strikingly alluring, captivating his mind and soul. He marveled how he had never seen her before, like this. Then he considered what his mind was deliberating and reality in its cruelest rebuke came crashing upon him. He belonged to the Order of the Open Hand. The Council of Masters would never condone such thoughts. It was strictly forbidden, to love or lust after another disciple within the Order, particularly where training tetsus were concerned. For a brief instant, Zyr considered life outside the Order, and what it would be like to awake beside the warmth of an angel each morn. His heart was torn, and as the companions slid through the tight rock cavity, a great war had begun within the confines of the young man's mind, for which both sides struggled for victory.

Zyr stopped and listened intently from between the close rock faces. The split in the rock had continued for a ways and the tapping had slowly turned into a faint pounding. They were moving through the interior of the mountain, through a natural opening in the rock and warm air was caressing their faces as they moved steadily inward. Light was giving way to darkness, but the path remained true without deviating left or right. Tehsa moved up next to him.

"Can you hear …?" She whispered.

"Shhh." He interjected with a tap from his hand. From within, he detected the direction of pounding which echoed through the crevice. "Let's go." He led them between the small enclosures, and gradually the opening widened as did the intensity of the pounding. Metallic ringing filled their ears as they came next to a large opening in the rock, at least twice a man's height and breadth. The constant pounding echoed from stone to stone. It resembled the sound of a smithy shop, with several anvils being used at once. Now in closer proximity to the source, other sounds were mingled with the hammering. They sounded like the screams of human souls, wracked in torment. Cautiously, Zyr slid his body alongside the rock face and shot a quick glance toward the opening.

He briefly considered their orders. The land had been under attack from fiends from Racur; however, there was no evidence of the usual pillage and massacre. People were being taken without bloodshed or death. It was most unnerving, as the enemy would sweep down upon a village and leave nothing but ghosts to haunt the abandoned houses and shops. Entire counties lay completely unpopulated and deserted. The Order had determined that an investigation of the mount must be undertaken, despite the incredible odds against them. Tey'ur was the most rational choice, with Zyr and Tehsa chosen as the most efficient Tetsu or combat team. Tey'ur had obviously objected; 'he would have teamed up with a Gnarel before choosing me for his squad' Zyr considered glumly.

The rock felt smooth and cool despite the warm breeze issuing forth from the opening. Zyr peeked around the edge of the rock he clung to. A vast cavern extended well into the mountain, full of shadows. Stalactites and stalagmites notched the crown and floor of the cavern, jutting out like teeth in a monstrous mouth. Fires were scattered throughout the wide expanse, illuminating certain areas of the massive cave. That was all Zyr could determine from the quick look.

He looked back to his companion. She was watching him expectantly. He nodded his head and hand-signaled his instructions; move quickly through the opening, advance to the left for a few paces, and then hold behind cover. She understood and adjusted her combat dress beneath the wide weapon belt at her hip. The Gé was secured to the belt by a sturdy leather strap which she could remove quickly. Zyr had only teased her concerning her fighting style; truly, she was unmatched with that weapon, and gave him room for pause when sparring. His eyes lingered on her a fraction longer than usual. When he looked to her face, the young man saw that she had been doing the same. He signaled for readiness, which she responded back in the affirmative.

The two lone fighters moved swiftly through the mouth of the cave.

The beast snarled savagely as its great breath washed over the bound fighter. Things had gone from bad to worse in a short period of time. The beast's rider being fully armoured and clenching a long slender thrusting spear, would jab the weapon into Zyr's back occasionally to move him onward. The chains were wrapped effectively around his torso and limited any degree of movement. This was one of those times where Zyr questioned his judgment, or big ideas.

They had observed long shuffling lines of shabby and pathetic-looking folk, who trailed away through a small opening toward the sounds of hammer blows and screams. Zyr had determined that the only way to get through was to become one of the bound commoners and investigate. It seemed reasonable at the time, seeing as they had fought and stalked their way so far up Racur's height. There was a mystery that needed solving and there would have to be another group sent later if they failed. Not to mention that the security would be heightened significantly upon a return trip. No, it made sense at first, and yet the fledgling healer debated his sense as he felt the sharp tip of the spear enter his flesh.

The trail of people wound around rock outcroppings and steadily the hammering was getting more severe, to the degree that any conscious thought was scattered with every pound. It was relentless in its cadence. Zyr watched the people cringe and moan for mercy. It was disturbing for the young man to watch, but he needed to see more before he could act. Ever since they began their ascent he had detected potent energies which grew ever more intense with each step. Even now his senses were buzzing with great alarm. He could not determine the source by glancing about, but pondered on what he would do upon its discovery. He would have to keep his intent hidden for the time being.

Tehsa had remained back in a bad temper. She clearly wanted to be next to him, assisting him. Yet when he tried to explain how one more bound fighter would be counter-productive, and at least one of them would need to return to Tey'ur if things went sour, it fell on deaf ears. Her constant badgering and concern necessitated a direct order, something he rarely did. She conceded, but just barely, and when he left her (bound with some chains they had 'borrowed') the scowl on her face rivaled any Defiler's worst sneer.

The plan had proceeded well until an unusual amount of guards suddenly slipped from the shadows beyond the small opening, escorting all the people along their weary trek. Now it seemed that to escape, he would need to fight off at least a dozen beastmasters and anything else that lurked in the surrounding shadows.

Zyr rounded a wall of stone and came into a vast chamber. The source of the pounding became painfully clear. He looked upward to a high shelf where a strange contraption moved in rhythm with the great deep booms. From his vantage point, he could discern two large gears that smote violently downward in steady cadence. There seemed to be a thick hide or cloth that was collapsed and then stretched under each gear, like a large clumsy bellows.

It was unsettling to hear screams of terror mingled with the overwhelming booming; the great cacophony echoed throughout the large cavern endlessly. The people were being escorted along a high precipice, climbing steadily upward upon roughhewn stairs in the rock. The stairs ascended through a vast opening in the ceiling of the cavern just above the massive machine and all its churning gears. Screams followed, trailing off gradually and then became silent.

Sensing something from above, Zyr focused his mind, employing the sacred training from within the Halls. He detected chaotic dark energy pulsing and dripping from the massive opening. It seemed to grip the people upon the stair, drawing them along a winding ascent to oblivion. He could not determine what lay beyond the stair. The whole scene was very unsettling and created difficulties in determining a course of action.

Zyr considered whether to act or not. People were dying, but he was unsure of endangering his own life for strangers. He had risked himself for Tehsa and other Order disciples countless times. Yet to sorrow and lament for the common and weakest? Zyr had always taken great pride in his ability to rise well above the commoner and rejoiced as he surpassed his rivals. He had never been placed in such a predicament. He was here to observe and not engage in battle, and yet as he was herded with the rest toward the stair he knew he would have to act soon. At that moment, words that the Servant had spoken years ago, swept through his mind.

"Have you finished your duties, Initiate?"

"No, humble Servant."

"I understand your presence in the kitchens is for violating the code of behaviour again."

"Master Aragil was being …!"

"Be still, Initiate. I have heard this story many times before. You were unfairly treated by a superior, who demanded too much of you. A common complaint in the Halls, and yet this particular event caused a creative outburst of words that, quite frankly, gave me pause. Such clever vocabulary."

"… well … he didn't …"

"Listen well, Initiate. There comes a time when we must choose for ourselves what course is best, when we stop reacting to the forces which act upon us. The day you begin to see the greater picture and think beyond yourself is when the true path to ascension begins.

"I'll give you this one key to true understanding. It is our selfish pursuits of talent which ironically block the path to our greatest potential. That is the greatest mystery of all.

"I perceive that you fail to understand presently, and that is expected. Someday, young one, your day will come."

"Yes, humble Servant …"

"Now, pass me that other scrub brush. It's time to work - time to act for ourselves."

The words echoed in the Alacritor's mind even as he caught hold of the thought of preserving the file of strangers about him. The young man's eyes flashed once, a bright blue spark which ignited great untapped flowing oceans of power deep within his soul. The physical chains seemed to melt off his body, as did the ones which bound his soul's potential, which now burned bright, illuminating the cave in a cold blue flame.

Twisting sharply, he seized upon the enemy's spear which prodded him, and slammed the blunt handle forcefully through the armoured breast and the body of the rider.

Zyr grunted and leaned back on the spear, tossing the writhing beastrider over the edge of the ascending stairs and into the black abyss.

The masterless beast snarled and charged directly toward the nimble monk, its head held low in attempt to drive Zyr into the chasm below. Two other beastriders appeared and flanked behind the charging beast.

Zyr moved swiftly upward, pushing as many villagers aside as possible, until the last moment. He somersaulted backward and struck downward with great force, stunning the creature. In its momentum and disorientation, it spilled over the precipice, to follow its master.

Zyr landed just in front of the next two enemies and dodged through several slashes and thrusts from their spears and vicious blade-like maws. The monk slammed his hands into the black stone beneath his feet and ripped large jagged boulders from their resting places. Roaring in echo of the power that swelled and nearly exploded from his frame, he hurled the large chunks of basalt toward each rider. One rock completely separated a beastrider from his legs locked firmly in the stirrups, which twitched nervously, driving the unknowing beast into the rock face. The other foe attempted to block the projectile with a shield, and though successful, felt charged fingers slice through his armour and body, as the young warrior swept past.

Landing deftly, the monk's mind worked quickly. He determined that the great hammering mechanism was the key to the whole corrupted and cursed operation, and in the massive, circular-hewn expanse there was only one visible way to get to it. The stair of stone was jammed full of dazed people, but the young weaver was already engaging his next move. Zyr launched his body upward onto the sheer rock surface and began to scale it quickly. Driving hand over hand into the stone surface he ascended as an ant upon a tree trunk, skittering white across the dark surface toward the opening in the ceiling. The Alacritor crawl, as he often referred to it, was a careful burst of power through the fingers to penetrate the foreign surface. The timing was incredibly finite so that when releasing the power, his hands did not slice through the rock when he sought for leverage.

Great heat was belching from the machine below, nearly scorching the young man's exposed skin.

Zyr pulled himself over the edge and rolled quickly as a large spike whizzed through the space he had occupied. Thrusting to his feet, the monk looked upon a terror his young mind could not have imagined.

Hissing and swaying high above, a great serpent-like creature glowered down at him. Its body was serpentine, yet the torso was strangely humanoid. Thin wiry arms wielded a large ornate spear deftly, and slowly the creature's tail slid across the floor, twitching in anticipation. Zyr remained still as the monstrous thing hissed sharply. It waited for any sense of motion from the monk.

Zyr noticed something beyond the strange creature, a tall robed figure standing in the shadows atop a protrusion carved from the far wall. Next to the figure were hewn tables of stone upon which a dark object was placed quickly. The hands of the shadowed figure began to move in gestures and the mouth shaped words which were drowned out by the incessant pounding. The young man's eyes opened wide in surprise as the rocks beneath suddenly enveloped his feet and ankles, gripping them like a smithy vice. The snake-creature shot toward him in a heartbeat, it jaws spread wide, as black venom streaked from its long teeth. Zyr had a moment to react and bent his body backward until his head brushed the floor. Despite the evasion, the serpent head brushed over him, the venom splashing across his face. Crying out, Zyr felt the sticky substance sink into his skin, indeed into his very soul. It scraped and clawed upon his spirit, seeking to corrupt his very essence. The sea of bright blue emanating from Zyr began to dim, its brightness beginning to shift toward blackness. Zyr straightened himself and gasped as his body and spirit recoiled in shock. He blinked as his vision began to blur slightly.

The large serpent stood poised to strike again, menacing its weapon.

"Your effrontery is returned upon you one hundred-fold, foolish one," a deep voice called out through the crashing booms of the machine. The voice was strangely amplified. It came from the man in the shadows, high above on the plateau. The figure had stopped and seemed to take in a long deep breath. "Ah ... Zyr, so much potential ... a fettered blade that only requires the proper hand to draw it forth." Zyr slumped down as the cursed poison sapped his will and strength. He prepared his soul for a fate which would envy a simple quick death. Somewhere in the recesses of his consciousness he wondered how he was known to his enemy. He wondered about the strange feeling of familiarity flowing in those words.

A bellow shattered the deafening cadence of the foul machine. Zyr glanced to his right to see Tey'ur charging over the stairs, his massive two-handed sword whistling high above his head. Two arrow shafts protruded slightly from his torso, the ends jagged from being broken for increased mobility. The roar filled Zyr's soul, momentarily staying the poisonous effect, and reviving his will.

The creature appeared to be stunned and wavered upon its tall body, the large spear faltering in its hands. Tey'ur barked an order which Zyr could not discern as the pounding drowned all other sounds. Though his vision was blurred and his body weak, Zyr attempted to smash away at the rock which had formed in cool prisons around his feet. Suddenly the air was filled with electrical charge and static. Zyr felt a familiar sensation and dully gazed to the stair to see Tehsa rounding the last stair, arms outstretched in Categor form. Zyr wanted to shout at her, and rebuke her stubbornness. Yet even if his voice could be heard over the incessant gonging, he felt gratitude for Tehsa and the potent Master of Arms being there for him.

Tey'ur was truly awe-inspiring to watch as he literally overwhelmed the massive creature. His mastery of a very difficult and dangerous weapon hushed even the most hardened veteran. The blade flowed through the air like the relentless wind through the banners of the Hall. It was an intricate dance, each step built upon the previous. The sheer battle ferocity of the master caused a large lump to develop in the monk's throat. He sheepishly continued to work away at his bonds, disgusted at his youth-like astonishment.

Lights began to light every crevice and crack, and suddenly the air was filled with sharp jagged bolts which streaked toward the cloaked enemy which had imprisoned Zyr. With a wave of the shadowed figure's hand, the electricity arced to the ground and fizzled to nothing. Tehsa emitted an oath of frustration for all to hear. She continued to weave more threads of power but Zyr could sense a feeling of despair coming from her. Her most potent attack dispelled with a simple gesture. It was a rare feat. Yet, his faithful Jyril continued to press onward, managing at least to drive their foe to the defensive.

The massive serpent screamed in great pain as Tey'ur's massive weapon sliced through its undersides. Despite all of its innate agility, the Serpentine could not counter the tall burly opponent below. It reeled as time and time again the warrior's large tooth bit through its scales. Tey'ur was summoning all his strength and agility, driven to bodily limits and beyond through adrenal bursts. The tide was shifting on the floor, but the clash of magical energy was still pitched and uncertain.

Tehsa screamed out in pain as she dropped to her knees. Her hands were smoking as if burned and she held the scarred flesh to her bosom, wincing. The man above had an amused look upon his face as he considered the girl. Zyr watched as the man stretched a hand slowly toward her. "I mark you mine."

'No!' he thought and feverishly chipped away at the resilient stone. Normally, his skills would permit him to free himself easily. However, the young man's mind was dulled by poison and desperation and any sense had been cast to the wind. Blackish strands of energy streaked from the weaver's fingertips, twisting and curling through the air, licking the air hungrily as they sought their target. The monk watched helplessly as Tehsa raised her head for a moment, and watched her green eyes dilate in horror. The strands wrapped around her body and began to worm their way through her flesh. She screamed violently again and again, thrashing upon the ground. It appeared to him, as he watched helplessly, that her body was near translucent. Energies were beginning to be drawn from her body, collected and snatched by the swirling black strands of power.

Then Zyr knew what had caused the agonizing sounds from earlier and the true horror of the mountain mystery dawned in his mind. The machine boomed in tandem with the harsh cries of his Jiryl. He understood it clearly. The energy of so many souls, collected for some dark purpose. He drew in his breath sharply, and smote the rocks at his feet, shattering the fetters. In his mind he knew what was required.

As Tehsa's body thrashed upon the ground, he dashed past Tey'ur while pulling in his last energies. The snake made to stab at Zyr, for which Tey'ur relieved the creature of its weapon and limb in one fell swoop. Zyr ran on unperturbed; for the young man it would be one final act, which would incapacitate him, but it was worth the cost. He might even save her.

Zyr brought all of his force down upon the bellows frame, which cracked and splintered under his blow. The torment of Tehsa stopped immediately and, in an instant, Zyr's body convulsed and sunk to the floor from a viscous attack from energy most vile.

The shadowed Ashori was now scowling, his outstretched fingers trembling as if in great exertion. Indeed, Zyr could feel his heart being pressed, squeezed as his blood ran suddenly fast. The enemy was a Defiler and had corrupted the use of Mother's power to stop his heart; already it beat painfully fast under the strain. Rising from the ground, Zyr brought his hands up again. Great stabbing pains wracked across his chest, causing the young man to gasp and falter.

With a prevailing thought of his Jiryl, his Tehsa, he summoned his resolve and brought his pulsing white hands down upon the weakened frame. It groaned and bent under the strain as new grinding noises screeched through the air, as gears were pressed upon and bent out of shape. A thousand daggers pieced through his heart, and Zyr felt his conscious slip like a shadow upon the wall. In one last surge he beat upon the great thundering machine and brought the structure crashing down to the ground and upon himself.

The young monk's mind began to drift as the black streams of venom and lingering energy coursed heavily through his veins. He imagined he heard a terrible sound, so overpowering it froze his weakened body. It echoed everywhere and became everything. In his dazed state, locked down to the floor, the monk felt like a reed tossed about by waves on the lakeshore. Great flashes of power and intense feelings of fear washed over and consumed him. His eyes were closed now; the world was fading, and his soul edging over the lip of the black abyss. Then his mind slipped away from the physical world.

*   *   *

"Zyr?" the voice was soft, drawing him from the darkness. "Zyr ... there are things I need to say, and the master says that you can hear me."

The monk felt his body drifting, floating weightless as the words passed through his mind. "I wish I could have told you everything that I was feeling, that moment on the mountain. I'm not sure where to begin, and I don't know if you'll remember ... but maybe ... you know already. I love you. Why is it so wrong to say that? I cannot believe how much my feelings have grown for you."

Silence.

"I wish you could show me some sign that you hear me. I don't even know if you care the same ... It frightens me that you might not. I felt something in your gaze upon those slopes, warm and inviting, but those things are so foreign to me. All you have ever cared about is yourself and you have pushed me aside for so long. I hated you so much back then, and in some ways I still do. It's funny. Though you cannot speak, all I want is to tell you everything I feel, and hear your voice telling me what I want to hear. Yet, somewhere deep within, I am glad you are here, listening. I can finally share everything with you, without everything else getting in the way."

As the young man's mind caught hold of the voice, he felt himself slowly being pulled from the mists. "I want to leave the Order … with you … and … and start a new life together. You know, no more Mihyl or Jiryl. I could take care of everything! You won't have to work if you don't want to … you don't have to train anymore. I'll make sure everything is perfect for you … and maybe … you can love me enough to … just think how happy we will be! Oh Zyr, it will be so wonderful, away from here. I hate these halls; I only stay to be with you! My worst fear is that you will leave me here … alone. Or grow apart from me. Something happened in that horrid mountain. I was frightened; I still am. That strange power wasn't destroying me, it was like it was seeking to know me … to discover something. I wish I could explain … wait ... no, why now …?"

A sound of metal sliding across metal came to the monk's ears. Then footsteps coming close to where he lay.

"How is he faring, young Seeker?"

"Humble Servant, I … he seems the same as always. I just wanted to be near him."

"That's perfectly understandable, young lady, as you two have never been apart. The Tetsu is a delicate balance and to lose one half is to lose the whole."

"I wish I could help. He just lies there, for days now. Are you sure that he can hear me?"

"A mind-sleep is a difficult state to assess and yet we can assume certain things. His body is healing itself and we must be patient. He used up every last thread of power in his body, which is no small recovery. The venom had spread through his entire system. Also, breaking the curse of his enemy took a substantial amount of energy, and such powerful weaving may bring unfortunate side effects. He may not retain every memory from the recent past. Thankfully, his body will be fine and it is simply recovering from the shock of the curse breaking.

"And how have you been faring? I understand you had quite a duel of power. You say you are in fine health and need no aid. How can this be? Tey' ur cannot explain as he was dealing with the Serpentine whelp. How is this possible, Seeker?"

"It was simple, I was able to counter his abilities, and he departed from us after Zyr broke the cursed machine."

"Hmmm. As you say, we have no other witnesses or story to rely upon, and Zyr will probably forget these past days, even weeks. Still, I'm confident you will have your Mihyl back soon."

"Thank you, humble Servant, for doing this. I know it wasn't easy for you ..."

"That is the way of the Servant, young one. I serve all from the least to the greatest. I accept no payment or acclaim. To serve others is to be beneath all others. It is the path I have chosen. Now, come. You have not eaten in quite some time."

"Perhaps I'll stay a little longer ... my voice may comfort him."

"The time for words is past. Please tend to yourself before you are as weak as he."

"Yes, humble Servant."

The voices leave. All is silent now and I am clearing the mists, lightness is so near ... so close to touch ... like her voice ... like her.

*   *   *

The breeze swelled within the body of the resting monk, and passed. Yet the memory, unlocked from its long slumber within the mind, remained. As the weary monk lay strapped within the tarp, a smile caressed his lips and a tear collected outside his eye. It welled over, sliding silently down his cheek, and then it was gone.

A Question of Loyalty

 C6-51, 3rd Darkwood, New Moon, Celi

I wish I knew where to start. I thought that life was so simple until recently. I felt everything was settling into a certain sense of order. Now I cannot escape the chaos which has distorted

*everything I see about me. Why do I care? She is all but a stranger
to me, mysterious and deadly. She is all that I despise.*

Then why do I still care?

*I cannot believe that she is the same person I knew. I
should leave and try to figure out what is happening to me, and
stop associating with those who would bring my death. And am I
any better? I have destroyed so much life! I am a murderer of the
coldest kind. What terrible power has coursed through my veins,
and scraped like a razor all that was green and lush from the land.
My deeds are as black as her skin at midnight. I tremble to think I
had feelings. Why do I still care for her?*

*I do not care one whit for these people - not one whit! I am
a survivor and always alone. Soon it must be so again. I must be
patient and wait for the proper time. I cannot live with beasts and
demons. Why ...*

*   *   *

The camp was bustling with motion, as the White
Guard unpacked shelters and supplies. The hunting party
required many provisions and goods to assist in the long
tours. The men moved cautiously around the center of camp,
casting quick glances toward the visitors and moving along
swiftly. Large elms loomed overhead, as the forest became
an effective living wall to the south. After picking up the
unknown guests (Tey'ur had taken them personally into his
own tarped waggon) they had moved swiftly south and

pitched camp at the Veiled Forest. The trees and undergrowth stretched along the base of the Tamers Reach for miles. Why Tey'ur had chosen to pause here was a mystery. The men would never question an order from their Lord, but still, the degree of secrecy surrounding the new guests was unnerving. As dusk approached, the men shuffled about their chores hoping to glean some gossip to help answer the many questions which floated through the air.

"You are very kind, Tey'ur, but I can manage from here," Firah replied as she adjusted the tent poles and bindings. She had erected her shelter personally, turning aside repeated attempts from others to assist. She now wielded a small hammer in an almost menacing way, to clear off any more male assistance.

"I must say," Tey'ur chuckled, "you are a remarkably resourceful young woman." He stood back, his large frame silhouetted against the sky. Firah began to hammer in the last support peg. Her locks of ebony flowed through the air with every hammer stroke. She grunted with the last blow, stood slowly and snapped the tarp absently for tensile strength.

"I've lived alone for all my life, well except for Tohm, of course ... while he's a dear friend, he's not a father." She wiped the sweat across her brow, her pale arms glistening in the dying sun. She stretched her small wiry form and placed the hammer down next to the tent. "I suppose I had to learn to do everything myself." She cast her ruby gaze upon the large soldier. He simply looked upon the girl with a slight tilt to his head. She was not sure what to make of his unusual sense of chivalry, but she intended to learn more of the modest soldier. "So, where does the White Guard reside?" she inquired while tying her hair back into a manageable pony tail.

"Our guild hall lies to the north-west. It's modest in some respects, but we call it home. I have rarely seen visitors to our plains, aside from the enemies of Mehnin. Your appearance is unexpected if not somewhat strange. What caused you to leave the southern trails and take a route across that charred wasteland?" He had moved closer to her, his large armoured body towering over her. Firah appeared to be unperturbed.

"That would be our business, Lord." She turned and moved into the tent, releasing the ropes which bound the entrance flap. His expressionless face slid from view as the tarp fell across the entrance. Firah slumped to her knees and clutched her chest, her breath coming fast. Lord Tey'ur frightened her, with his constant prying into her life. Slowly, he had uncovered aspects of their journey in their talks and she feared that the longer they stayed the worse it would be. The worst part was that she had no idea where they were to go next. She looked across the tent to see Zyr resting peacefully. When would he rise? She desperately needed his wisdom! Tohm was somewhere in the camp, at least so she thought. Since stopping near the forest, Shien had disappeared. 'The ignorant mutton-head!' she cursed silently 'I'll be happy if he becomes some forest-stalker's lunch!' She couldn't understand his cold and callous behavior to her recently, especially since she thought they were …

Angrily, she cast her jacket from her shoulders and rose to her feet. There was a wash basin and a crude mirror set upon a small table, which she moved to slowly. She untied the leather strap, and grimacing, watched her brown hair fall about her shoulders. It was hopeless. She would be a wreck, an utter hag with this tangled mess until she could find a decent stream to wash in. She moved close to the mirror and checked her complexion. She looked into her own green eyes and mused to herself 'Maybe that's why he's acting so odd. Hmmm … if I could …' She tossed her hair and patted her cheeks till they tinged a rosy color. Humming to herself, the girl pursed her lips in the mirror and then smiled. After a moment, she sighed and turned the looking glass down to the table surface. 'I need to stop this!' she chided herself.

A low whistle came from outside the flap. 'Not again' she thought. "Who is it?" she asked a little more sternly than she intended.

"The guild healer, m'lady," a voice called out, muffled by the tarp across the entrance. "I'm here to check on your companion." Firah glowered with disgust. This was a common ploy of the guild, to ensure their stay. The monk would come in, make a nuisance of himself, and after several minutes of bustling, would say something like "No change."

It aggravated her, as it was a constant link to their hospitality, and the more they remained with this troop, the more indebted she felt. The ride to the forest was the only reason that she stayed with them. The healer had done nothing for Zyr, and that was the most frustrating part of all. She had begrudgingly accepted Shien's logic about an alternate purpose for the White Guards help. It stung her ego like a swarm of thirsty Menil-bees.

"Come in," she blurted out, with exasperation. The healer pushed the tent flap aside and walked in slowly completely indifferent to her obvious flustered state. He nodded to Firah and brushed past her, his robes billowing with his stride. As he passed she felt that same tingling sensation, she felt every time he came to see Zyr. As the monk reached her motionless friend, the feeling left. The guild healer spent the next short while checking and adjusting things, essentially doing nothing in Firah's opinion. Finally, he stood and opened his mouth to speak.

"No change?" She interjected in an apparent sarcastic tone.

The monk closed his mouth and stared at her. His mouth was set slightly downward; she knew she had jangled a nerve. "Indeed," he replied curtly and stepped out of the tent without a further word. Firah waited until the flap was fully closed before leaning toward the doorway and casting her ugliest face in the passionless healer's direction. She smiled with satisfaction and slid into the wooden chair near Zyr's resting place. She touched the brooch she wore, which brought her a strange sense of comfort. She sighed heavily and watched her humble friend's chest rise and fall below the blanket which warmed his body. The smile was fading fast under the tide countless worries.

"Oh, Zyr. Please come back to us soon. I don't know where to go anymore. Just show us what to do, please." The room fell silent as the tarp tossed and floated, resisting the cooling breath of nature.

Ⅱ   "She is a feisty one," the monk submitted to his Lord. Tey'ur smiled slightly, and clasped a hand upon the healer's shoulder.

"Bear with this task a little longer, Menhol. It is not entirely her companion that I am truly concerned about. What of her condition?"

"It is progressing." The monk rubbed his bare scalp in thought. "I feel something will happen tonight, but it is hard to gauge such things. I am not a master of demonic lore." Menhol cast a look to Tey'ur.

"Nor I. Yet any fool can clearly see the signs of change upon her. They always show the same. How I wish that her companion was awake. I would have certain words for him. You say it will be any day now?" His grip clenched the monk's shoulder, to which the healer's eyes raised in question. Tey'ur removed his hand and turned himself towards the near fire which blazed bright upon his armour.

"Any day. Might I inquire …?" The healer began.

"You may not." Tey'ur snapped, his voice a harsh growl. Menhol politely bowed his head and moved away from the troubled leader. Tey'ur's grey eyes followed him, like a wolf's glare. Quietly, Tey'ur placed a trembling hand over his face. How long had it been since he had lost control like that? His eyes strayed to the girl's tent where the coward lay.

What was it about that self-righteous traitor that unnerved him? It was strangely predictable that where trouble brewed, that ingrate would follow. How he wanted to punish him, and then cast him into the fire and purge the traitor's stain from his mind. But he could not act yet; he would keep them here and he would have his answers when the time came. He would not let the traitor or the girl escape his grasp. Inside his throat, a small growl emitted. He found it impossible to rest while the past, and all of its blood, cried for vengeance. Judgment was screaming in its terrible wrath, issuing forth from the remains of the Broken Halls. Unspeakable betrayal warranted a suitable punishment. At this thought he shook his head wearily ... nothing could bring back the dead after they had walked the Unknown Path. While the Defilers had their way with the corpses, the spirit or soul was long departed upon its journey back to Llian. No, the hand of justice would fall to him, one last duty for the Order.

*　　*　　*

⩔   Tohm lay low to the ground and waited. The wind was shifting and soon the time would come. The master had warned him days earlier; if he ever came to harm or had to leave, Tohm was to tend to the girl. The burly man grimaced, his brow furrowed. It was deep into night and the men and women were settled down for the night. He had felt overwhelmed by the masses of newcomers and attempted to stay away from the cluttered and busy camp. As a result, he had spent the day roaming the forest, letting his senses feast upon the diverse odours which prevailed in the air. Now he sensed the change. Something was about to happen. He lay crouched between two knolls just outside the camp perimeter. He would have to be quick and silent. The rational side of his mind was not resisting this time. Rather, his splintered mind was oddly unified in one purpose, that the girl must be protected from what lay within her body. Suddenly, Tohm lifted his face into the chilling stench upon the wind. It had begun!

Moving like lightning, Tohm crossed the perimeter into the camp. His dark eyes flashed in the torchlight as he threaded his way quickly and undetected through the darkness. He ran upon all four limbs and dodged from shadow to shadow. Her shelter lay ahead, and Tohm could smell the black demon stench flowing from within the tent-folds. He dodged from the shadows in a direct course toward the tent.

Just as he neared the small shelter, he sensed movement. "Hold!" Two soldiers stepped quickly from the shadows next to the tent. One held a large broadsword out toward Tohm, who continued his rampant strides toward them. Perceiving Tohm's noncompliance they prepared to hew the large man down. Tohm's rational mind retreated deep within. It would not interfere. The released animal leapt high as one soldier swung a wide arc across its path. The fevered beast felt the sting as the sword bit across his thigh, but ignored the feeling and stretched a long muscled arm out and wrapped it about one soldier's neck. He twisted the head around quickly and firmly until he heard the satisfying crack. The other had reacted, but the bestial man was already whirling about and smashed a fist into his victim's throat. Tohm had reached the flap by the time the second one had fallen to the earth gargling froth and spit spraying from his mouth.

Growling within himself, Tohm recalled in fury how the demon had caught him off his guard the previous night, when all was in chaos. It had not killed him, and for whatever purpose the frenzied warrior cared not. It would prove to be the undoing of the forsaken specter.

Tohm ripped through the tent flap and moved swiftly to where a large billowing cloud was forming. He ignored the master lying quietly upon the ground as he charged past. The beast would need its predatory sense to "see" this night. He thundered into the growing blackness, which swallowed him up wholly. The large man sensed the black creature within the cloud, in front of him clutching a dark blade. Reaching out, he contested the hold of the blade. His hand covered the creature's grip. At once the demon began to thrash about; however, the beast resisted its struggling, as the demon had yet to achieve its full form. Tohm had since learned that every death would make it stronger. 'Appease the dagger with living blood' the master had said. Quickly, Tohm shifted his grip above the hilt. As the creature writhed in fury, the blade slid across the flesh inside Tohm's clenched hand. He felt his hot blood flowing like a river of magma down his arm.

"Leave!" he cried out gruffly to the demon. The dark demon screeched loudly in response and Tohm felt it clawing with its free hand and feet, his skin burning from the scathing black claws. "Leave!" He bellowed again more forcefully and then in one swift motion, reared back and laid a blow full into the form that he was struggling with. Firah's body flew across the tent space before colliding against the tarp and collapsing to the ground. The dagger lay a few feet from her hand. She was completely unconscious. The black cloud dissipated with echoes of tortured screams that faded into the night air. Tohm howled with satisfaction and then heard the sound of turmoil outside. Quickly, he dashed out the other end of the tent and sped away into the night. He had done what the master asked. Now he was through with people. The forest called.

*   *   *

⚔   The approaching militia had emerged from the night and descended swiftly upon the unsuspecting White Guard camp. The sentries must have been removed skillfully without a whisper of warning. Shien determined the strength of the enemy from his high vantage point. They more than doubled the White Guard company who numbered a hundred strong. Most of the enemy were adorned in many different types of armour, with no coherent colouring. Mercs, he thought to himself dolefully. Shifting his gaze he noted that the White Guard's forward defence was in disarray from the ambush, and would be cut down soon. He watched as warrior met warrior, axes and hammers swinging viciously in attempt to beat down the opponent. A warning horn had just sounded loud and long throwing the camp in chaos. But it had come late. Many struggled to put on a semblance of armour, while some simply grasped their weapons and moved to the east side of camp where the battle was ensuing. Shien closed his eyes slowly. Death had followed him for so long, and again this

night many more would die. He wrapped his cloak tightly
around his body, as the wind chilled his bones. Agonizing
screams of men filled his ears. He knew that it was time to
leave, and yet he hesitated a moment. He adjusted the pack
on his shoulders; he could feel Kuros and Isil throbbing with
his own pulse. It was if they had become attuned to his soul.
He grit his teeth and turned his face southward. A three day
trek to the southern pass across Tamers Reach and he was
free! Free to live off the land once again. Yet, his feet would
not move, and he cursed his lack of resolve.

"Forget her! Just forget her! Leave while you can!" an
inner voice demanded. More sounds of metal upon metal
rang out as he heard a deep voice calling to arms, directing
orders. Something within that voice was inspiring and
powerful. He took a long breath in and descended the hill
toward his future.

*　　*　　*

Ⅲ　　"Form forward ranks!" Tey'ur boomed out above the
noise of war. The attack had been swift and well designed.
His attempts to counter and regroup had met with failure.
The attacking force was fairly commanded and had utilized
the element of surprise to their advantage. A soldier next to
him gasped in horror and then fell to the ground dead.
Tey'ur took a moment to glance at the arrow that punctured

through the white painted plate mail. The feathers told the story he knew too well … Grey Wilders.

"Upper echelon, left advance! Form right guard!" He bellowed out harshly. The soldiers moved upon his command, drawing upon the discipline he had drilled them with so many times. "Dammit!" the old warrior cursed as more arrows cut through the air. He felt the wind upon his face as one passed deathly near. "Corbin!" Tey'ur called out gruffly; in a moment the hooded figure was by his side. The Lord of the White Guard did not even look, he knew the man would be there. "The Grey are killing our forward guard! Put some fire on that upper ridge, now!" he said indicating a far rise that ran high into the south forest.

"As you command, Lord." Corbin spoke quietly. He darted away swiftly, moving into position, tracing his hands through the air in preparation. Tey'ur knew he needed only a few seconds, but he dared not risk losing his Ignitor.

"Archers! Counter flank! Pin them down!" He felt the surge of arrows, all ablaze and packed with incendiary potions as they passed overhead. Large fiery explosions rocked the far flank and the opposing troops scattered, some aflame. That was all the time Corbin needed. Streaming trails of hot energy threaded through the air and lighted upon the far ridge where the forsaken Greys had set up. He listened to cries of surprise and anger as flame struck men and ground alike. This battle was far from over, for both sides. Tey'ur had the feeling that the enemy was simply testing the waters before pressing their advantage. The weathered face of the White Guard commander glowered in anger. What was the purpose of the attack? Having no answer was maddening.

*   *   *

θ   Firah's unconscious body lay across the ground and had not stirred since Tohm's attack. The breeze billowed at the entrance of the tent. The ripped fabric where the large stalking man had dashed away fluttered in the night breeze. From outside, tumultuous noises of battle drowned out the once calm night. The flap of the tent tossed and flipped about, suddenly enshrouding a tall slender figure. It moved silently from the entrance toward the girl. The torchlight was out and shadows moved across a billowed black cloak as it trailed behind the figure. Stooping down, a pale, gloved hand stretched out and took up the slender blade which lay near the girl. For a moment, the cloaked form stood silent and still, regarding the blade and then the girl. "Incompatible," the visitor whispered harshly.

Then slowly, the hood shifted downward to its left. The gaze of the silent thief rested upon the motionless monk upon the ground. Slowly, the figure's feet moved, swaying the cloak as it moved through the room. Clutching the dagger, the thief's voice dripped with acid in hushed and steady tones.

"Look at you. You have not changed a bit. Always catering to your selfish interests. Well, now your feeble attempts have led you to this end. To think that I have finally surpassed you. How pathetic it feels, when I think of how much I feared you and wanted you - and in the end it was you who could not see beyond your precious code. That will always be your weakness." The wind rustled the tarp gently. The black cloak shifted as the stranger's feet turned toward the entrance. As a foot left the cold hard ground, the wind fluttered. A blanket drifted upon the air. The stranger fell to the ground, lying now atop the body of the fully alert monk.

"I may be stubborn, but your overconfidence always complicated things," the monk whispered quietly as he clasped his own hand about the trembling clenched fingers which grasped the dagger haft, the black blade a mere fraction from the skin of the stranger's neck. The now silent intruder did not stir nor struggle; one slip and the dagger's thirst would steal life. As his words echoed in the air, the monk's free hand came up slowly and gently, drawing back the hood from the newcomer's head. He removed long thin spines one by one from her bundled hair and tossed them away. Dark locks of ebony spilled over his face while red eyes glowered in deep fiery anger as the veil was slowly drawn away. The woman's face was clenched in fury, mere inches from the icy blue gaze of the monk. "Isn't that so ... Tehsa?"

*   *   *

Gaeth's smile twisted in morbid satisfaction. All was going according to plan, and soon the mistress would return with the blade. He glanced toward Ebyn who shouted commands to the Grey Wilders and spat upon the ground. 'That useless mage' Gaeth swore within. 'Look at how he gives out orders! He thinks he will rule the guild someday?' The Cerephor-Defiler turned his gaze away. It would not do to continually struggle over the present situation. He could deal with Ebyn in the near future, but for now it would be suicide to move against his guild rival. He turned to look below at the different squads of mercenaries under their command. From the high ridge all was visible. The mercenaries formed a staggered southward front down to the forest wall. The battle was going well for the Blade of Ahtol. Many of the mercenaries which had fallen were reanimated by him and Ebyn, supplying a near endless flow of reinforcements. Granted, they weren't as able as their once live host, but they served to impede the White Guard offensive. Suddenly, fire erupted high overhead and impacted near to where the Grey had set up their strategic point on the ridge. At that moment the southern White Guard flank made a push. With great roars of noble justice they pressed upon the mercenaries. Against newfound courage, the Ahtol front began to buckle.

Gaeth moved swiftly into range. He would need but a few moments to crush the offensive. This was the art of the Cerephor, swift retribution upon the weak-minded. As he neared the edge of the forest, the master of mind lore lashed out upon the enemy's front lines. Men of valor screamed and snatched their helmets off of their burning minds. They dropped to the ground, contorting in agony. The Ahtol line was reforming, and as they did Gaeth struck out again and again. Sometimes the foe would simply stop fighting, their heads bowed under burdens of guilt. Other times crying out for death. They soon became easy prey for the mercenaries who were given strict orders to kill or be killed. He laughed cruelly; it was always pleasurable to watch their behaviour. Every nightmare and incapacitating thought that poured over them gave Gaeth a sense of sweet satisfaction. "You are all insects below my feet!" he screamed as he thrust his arms forward, catching some of the mercenaries in the wave of power bursting from his body. Gaeth's twisted grin echoed his thoughts; within every slash of power across some fool's mind he envisioned others who stood before his ambition. Fellow guild servants, Ebyn, even Lady Nuril would scream in agony before him. The front was almost won, the White Guard reeling in despair. Almost won.

Gaeth had but a fraction of time to turn his eyes to the crashing sound to his left. A large form burst from the trees, loping along the ground with impossible speed.

"Defiler!" The form called mightily as it thundered into the smaller caster. Gaeth twisted and tried to free up his belt knife, but it was everlastingly too late. His assailant was upon him. He felt his head grasped by massive hands and he was lifted off the ground. He kicked out violently upon the assailant, but he might as well have struck out at the tree trunks around him. He felt his face drawn to his attacker's and in a flash of light from a nearby swirling inferno, he met the gaze of his executioner.

"You!" Gaeth grunted as he felt his skull compressing slowly. The hands were like great vices which mercilessly began to seal his fate. "Wai ... wait ..." He whimpered. The blazing brown eyes were tight and aflame as Gaeth squirmed, throing near to death. His brain frantically sent signals to his body, as it thrashed about in the dead lock of his enemy.

"This beast," his attacker spoke into the blackening mist forming in Gaeth's vision. "You uncaged." The brown eyes blazed with fury. All went dark.

Gaeth of Ahtol fell crumpled and lifeless to the ground.

Ⅱ   The battle was not faring well. Tey'ur placed his foot upon the body hunched over his massive blade. He withdrew the blade roughly while thrusting the body away. The battle had ebbed and flowed, and so many had fallen.

The enemy, aided by their forsaken arts, were animating the bodies of the mercenaries which had fallen in battle. The White Guard were outnumbered on every turn by the living and dead. There was the smell of death and fire all around him. He wiped his scorched face quickly to remove the sweat from his brow, smearing black streaks. He needed a report on the battle conditions. He espied Mehnol, his trusted Alacritor dashing to a fallen comrade, chanting the Rite of Return. He moved toward the monk, and as he reached the weary holy mender, the fallen Guard member rose swiftly, despite being pierced with many arrows.

"I heard your call, Mehnol. You called me from the Path." The burly warrior spoke, his voice was filled with both anguish and wonder.

"Then heed my command!" The monk barked. "Move to the line, hold the front! The ward will not stay your pain for long!" The warrior nodded and growling burst forth in a fiery hot rage. He charged the wall of combat and felled an enemy with one sweep of his axe.

"Numb warriors serve me little, Mehnol!" Tey'ur spat as he rounded on the monk. "He'll soon fall to those wounds when the ward fails!"

"What would you have me do, Tey'ur, forsake my Ashori oath and embrace the way of the Defiler?" the monk retorted angrily above the tumult of battle. Tey'ur had rarely witnessed the calm man lose his resolve, a telling sign of their plight. His trusted healer raged on. "The strain of healing is too great! I have no time or energy for such things!

At least this way, they can throw their whole selves into the battle. Besides, the near-death have nothing to fear, nothing to lose. We are going to lose this conflict if we don't act now!"

They watched the warded-warrior hew down a foe in relentless frenzy. Then as if the hand of fate was looming over the battle, the soldier began to falter as the ward gave way. "Llian's wrath! We don't have time to … uk." The monk stopped mid-sentence as the arrow shaft slid clean through his robes and torso. A clean and decisive shot. Tey'ur caught the monk as he fell toward the earth.

"No!" The grizzled warrior roared. He looked around furiously. The lines were failing and now his last thread of hope slid gently down his chain skirt to the ground. The lines of age were hard and drawn thin around his mouth and grey eyes. 'The final battle … somehow I never imagined it would be like this,' he thought harshly. The days of youth and all its rashness were gone. He would offer no petty remarks to swell his heart into action. No, he would sell his life to his enemy with cold and bitter payments in blood. The tired and aged warrior stood erect and brandished his terrifying weapon. He kissed the blade one last time and brought it high over his shoulder. The enemy broke forth from the remnants of the White Guard front. Savage mercenaries charged the waiting Lord, the battle almost won in their mind.

The wave of combatants crashed upon the lone warrior. Weapons sung through the air and then collided with tremendous force. Soon, the younger warriors were brought to begrudging respect for the tower of a figure before them. As each massive stroke of the two-handed blade descended, life spilt upon the bloodied ground. Tey'ur merely grunted as sword strikes found the gaps in his defence, as hammer blows dented upon his armor. The enemy continued to fall, and yet they still came. The old warrior's face was strangely set. It showed neither pain nor anger. Neither was it bold and firm. It was somewhat whimsical and aloof. His motions seemed to come from a different place. For all who could see, the battered warrior's mind was already in another realm.

Still they came.

*   *   *

"What would you do with me?" Nuril spat. Zyr merely continued to gaze into her red eyes, saying nothing. "Be done with this mockery!" she screamed in fear-tinged anger. His lips twitched and rose slightly into a small grin. The Lady Nuril was nearly past reason. As she breathed in to rain another verbal barrage upon him, she felt the knife blade prick lightly the skin upon her neck and she held her breath.

"Have you finished?" he asked quietly. She nodded slowly, her long hair caressing his face. She looked strangely into his eyes. Nuril was unsure of what was to come, the prospect of death was maddening, and yet somehow she clung to a thin thread of hope. He had not slain her. "I have waited long for this, to finally gain answers to questions many years old." His brow furrowed slightly and he paused for a moment.

"Why did you leave?" he said quietly.

Nuril regarded him harshly. "What in Aeredia are you talking about?" Her ruby eyes flashed. "If you are asking why I pursued you, then you are a great fool." She waited for him to speak, mystified in her rancor.

"Oh, enough. Your clever facade is broken as was your table. Do not think that our years apart have weakened the bond we shared as Tetsu. Now, why did you leave the Order, Tehsa?" he repeated calmly and slowly, his eyes fixed upon hers.

"I ... I don't have to answer to the likes of you ..." she fumbled. Memories from the past came racing upon her mind. The grey clouds that hid past events were parting, like the sun illuminating the dark recesses of her mind. "You left me ..." she whispered almost imperceptibly.

"I left because of you. I saved you once and swore an oath of fealty for payment. I left to save my soul, as I surely would have forsaken it to be with you had I stayed." His voice was almost soundless. His eyes dropped from hers. He felt her chest swell sharply as she took in his words.

"Don't you say that! Don't you dare place this blame upon me! I loved you and you left, chasing your honour through that field and out of my life!" Tears fell down upon his face. She seemed unaware of the dagger at her neck. Her eyes were aflame, deep and sorrowful, years of anguish spilling over the brim. "I would have gone with you ... I hated you for leaving! I always cursed you, and do still for every moment of my sick existence! You stole my life!" The woman was holding nothing back from him, though her body remained still. Her hand was growing warm and slick under his grip.

⸸ "Don't act with such innocence! I returned and the Halls were destroyed. I secretly came for you. Hard it was, to find you and everyone else gone, nothing but ruins. Yet, to learn in time that you allied with this forsaken and ill-fated guild; impossible, I thought. Tehsa would never have consigned herself like this!" His eyes were now a chilling blue which burned cold. "That night in the tower confirmed what my heart would not accept! You betrayed the Order, allying with these fools, these world-renders!"

"Be silent! You have no idea what I ..." Her eyes were shut, but tears flowed in great streams upon his face. Her body shook in wracked sobs. "I hope you suffered! I hope that you hurt every night for what could have been yours!" Her body shifted on his, and he pressed the blade closer. Nuril screamed in fury and frustration. "End it! End it, Zyr! What life remained after you left, ended when she died!" She made to thrust herself upon the black blade. The monk's mind flashed both in alarm and shock and he flung her from him. Wrapping his hand about his robe he stooped and snatched up the fallen dagger. Nuril had collapsed upon the ground and did not move, the sobs gently subsiding.

"What did you say … who … is she?" he asked, his voice coming shakily. She did not respond. Zyr opened his body to the swirling pool of power and sent a portion of it through her. She did not move as it passed through and returned swiftly.

"You have been with child," he said slowly, disbelievingly. The monk slumped down to his knees, barely taking the woman in. His mind was reeling from the information the Alacritor energy had extracted. She had given birth many years prior if the signs were correct in her system. "Who?"

"I wanted a life … outside the Order," she said quietly, behind dark fountains of shining hair. The one soft lantern cast a low light around the tent. All other noises were unheard by the once unified Tetsu. "Since you were unwilling to be the one to give this gift to me … I found another, while on a mission. He was a back-countryman, a good man." She shifted herself upon her knees and looked upon her former Mihyl. "I made plans to leave and escaped the Halls, to be with him. He became my husband, and a father …"

The monk said nothing but continued to listen. He drank in the words as if water from a desert oasis. An aged desert of unanswered questions.

"Life was good, and he tried to give me all that I desired. I placed my training aside, to be the mother for this wonderful baby. Still, in my heart I longed for you. I really never found true peace. At least I was far from those wretched Halls." Her face paled and she took short, quick breaths. "Then one day, they came from the mountain, Racur, where we had once infiltrated. It was another raid. He died trying to save me. The fool. He never learned who truly held power in our home. Yet, in my desire for a simple life I never told him … there was nothing to be done against their numbers. Had you been in his place … everything would be different. I watched in vain as he was torn to pieces. They found me and I did not want the baby to suffer pain and death at their hands. I determined to kill her - quickly, but they wrenched me away before I could … she fell from my arms …" Zyr stood upon his feet as Nuril slowly rose. "I was taken, Zyr. I was taken and used for a terrible ritual. It changed me. They would have killed me, except that they sensed the power within. I was permitted to live. So I trained again with new masters, but this time I relished it. With time I would surpass all their feeble arts. I am who you see now, not your precious Tehsa." She smiled with a strange manner.

"That is strange irony, isn't it? The frozen climbs where I first found love would house the means for a much deeper longing. Power is my only priority, and commanding those who once abused me."

Nuril moved toward him, the fear and pain all but gone from her face. Standing, he watched her carefully as she came in front of him. There was no hostility there, but a return to the ice cold malice. She took his robed hand which gripped the dagger and placed it next to her throat, her hands were cold as a mountain stream. Her red eyes locked with his, steady and bright. "I believe we were here, before you dragged the past unnecessarily into this deliberation. Please do not do so again." She waited for him to speak. He took a moment and then broke the silence between them.

"Do you pursue her still?" the Alacritor asked quietly.

She studied the girl for a moment and then responded. "No. She is useless to us now as a Compatible. She has been too long unchecked with the blade. We will have to search elsewhere. Oh dear, have you been having trouble sleeping with the demon?" Her question carried a slight mocking tone but also a strange understanding. Zyr ignored her quip and continued.

"We both know the dagger cannot stay here with the girl. She has progressed too far. The signs are upon her. Keeping it only endangers her from a different enemy. It comes to an impasse of strife. With either choice comes difficulty." He closed his eyes, his brow furrowed in thought. Nuril made a motion, but stopped immediately. It did not escape his notice. To Zyr it was almost as if she was reaching up to the pressure point like she always did when he labouring under stress of an assignment. Her touch would always assuage the turmoil. Her face was expressionless and flushed ever so slightly from the broken gesture.

"What will you do?" she asked with a guarded air, her grip upon his wrist steady.

"I propose a solution," he said tersely.

"I am always open to civil negotiation," she replied while releasing Zyr's hand. He brought it to rest by his side.

"It is clear that you have a similar attunement to the weapon as she does. I will permit you to take it, seeing as you would easily locate it if I hid it away. Also if I could entrust it to someone, they would soon become the hunted. It does not concern me where you go, as long as it is away from the girl." He looked into her eyes with firm resolution.

"I see that your protective instinct has deepened. Such a troublesome one you have been given charge over." Her eyes shifted to the Firah's still form upon the ground. "The Dark Lady has long been silent and of no help to those in need. All that remains for that girl now is a life of running and hiding from ignorant fools and the Hunters. I would have spared you from a meaningless pursuit by killing her earlier, but that would have drawn the White Guard Alacritor here. What a tragedy for Mother if the girl died; if only someone could hear Her weep," she responded with a sarcastic cutting tone.

His eyes narrowed slightly. "Don't be so quick to pass judgment on Aerluin. You have forgotten that she is only silent to those who have chosen to stop their ears to her gentle pleas. Mother has preserved this girl despite all your attempts to corrupt her gifts and take her life."

Nuril's brow raised in rebuttal. "Don't be a fool. Her erratic evasions were nothing more than chance, a fortunate twist of fate. Nothing more."

Zyr wearied of his former Jyril's obstinate will. She was a masterful word-crafter. He had felt the advantage slip to her favour. However, there was one more move she would not expect. All sense and reason cried out against it, and yet there was little of their past that relied upon the safeguards of reason. He took hold of her fiery crimson gaze and allowed the words to flow.

"Regardless of your cynical views, Firah still has a purpose. Know this; I will always know where you are, for, like you, she will feel drawn to the dagger continually. When the time comes, she will return prepared to do what Mother requires, as will I." He held the blade out in front of him. She placed her gloved hand upon the hilt but as she grasped it he seized her wrist and pulled her to him. "I swear by Aerluin, I will come." Zyr slid his free hand through her flowing locks and pulled her to him until their lips caught in a passionate embrace. She resisted only for a moment, but then brought her hand up behind his neck and gripped it roughly, pressing forward until the dagger hung dangerously between them. For both, the moments passed as millennia and neither sought release. All at once they were standing in the golden fields of memory. Then, silently as if from an unspoken cue, they parted softly and gently.

She stood there a moment before him and then silently slid the dagger through her belt. She tied her hair back with one motion, collected her veil, turned from him and was gone with the fluttering wind. Zyr simply stared upon the space she had previously occupied.

After a time, he turned to look at the girl, resting silently upon the floor. "The chosen high road lies ahead … may Mother guide us … for the end of the path will soon show itself." He turned and walked from the tent into the darkness beyond.

* * *

Tey'ur's body trembled, the adrenaline pumping through his veins as he spun the blade rapidly in a circular arc. Three opponents drew back, retreating from the masterful slash as the veteran set his stance. Fear was betrayed in their faces from the near torchlight. Within a heartbeat he charged and sliced rapidly at them, his movements with the two handed weapon nearly impossible, and yet he hewed them down to the bloodied earth.

"Tens of hundreds I have slain … you are eager and ripe for reaping." He spat as he set to riposte their attacks. The mercenaries were completely nonplussed. They truly had never encountered a foe of this caliber before. Though they clearly surrounded and outnumbered their resilient enemy, he continued to hold them at bay. Strangely, he had never cried out, neither in pain nor strength. It was unnerving, the stoic cool effrontery he threw in their faces. They had begun to lose heart, and many were warily guarding instead of pressing a foolhardy and fatal offensive. All around the battle had raged, a long and deadly course to which the Blade of Ahtol had suffered the most. In the old Master's ears he could faintly discern the sounds of other skirmishes just above the thumping drum of his heart. Blood seemed to drip carelessly from Tey'ur's legs as it gathered from the various wounds he had suffered. He had been struck countless times, bruised and bloodied and yet not one fighter had been able to land a critical blow. It had taken some time, but the more adept of their ranks realized the strategy. They sensed that their foe had no intention of foolishly committing himself to a battle of powerful life-ending blows. He was purposely evading the heaviest strikes and finishing those individuals as they threw themselves off balance. The smaller nicks, near misses and feints he took upon his body without a thought. They realized that he would send as many to the Mother as possible before his own demise. It appeared that the battle was following some unseen plan, a terribly morbid strategy, with the pieces moving constantly. Their old grizzled opponent seemed to sense the plan as it developed, it was drawn upon every line in his face. His presence of mind in the battle was uncanny; he would detect the strongest assaults and deal with them with lethal efficiency. Truly their opponent was as the warriors from legend, from the old stories.

Tey'ur noticed something that told his mind the battle was over. The enemies were edging back, almost surreptitiously. No other warrior would have noticed, not the common variety anyway. He chuckled to himself. They had solved his strategy and now it was over.

A grey and black fletched arrow slammed full into the shoulder of the lone defender. Another shot came fast, which Tey'ur swiftly countered by hoisting a nearby body as a shield that served to absorb the devastating attack. He felt a tingling where the first shaft had entered. So it was poison, 'and why not' he mused to himself. It was a sound strategy considering the problems he had caused the enemy. He was surprised that they had taken this long to move to this obvious logical maneuver. He looked into the faces of his warrior opponents and divined the answer. Warrior pride; a great source of strength but also a weakness not easily dispensed. Those before him knew Tey'ur had won the day, and the shame in their hearts would sting longer and deeper than the arrow. It would be a matter of time now. It would be slow and gradual. The poison would work its way through the body as the blood loss would drain his strength. Then his defence would falter. The end had come to countless others at his hands, and now fate dictated that his turn had come. He was strangely accepting of the inevitable end. He was not some foolish lad to fight on clinging to a sense of false hope. He had one raging regret that he wished he could have resolved. It would haunt his final moments, until his heart thumped its last beat.

Tey'ur tossed the body to the ground and stood slowly. He extended his good arm in invitation while the other rested upon the hilt of the sword which stood propped into the ground. They clenched the hafts of their weapons tightly. Scowls and grimaces adorned their faces. Tey'ur released one hearty laugh which caused the warriors to pause. "Come, let us end this day." With silent affirmation they began to slowly move upon the old Lord of the White Guard. He was loath to relinquish his rest upon the large sword as he drew in deep, shuddering, ragged breaths. Indeed, the end was near - the poison was running its course.

Suddenly, a cry went up from the high ridge. Some warriors glanced to see commotion and conflict upon the embankment. The Grey Wilders had set up position upon that ridge. Something was happening, and yet they could not divert their eyes long. The old warrior had stepped into a battle stance, seemingly unaware of the disruption. Two warriors were sent to help, leaving ten to deal the final blow upon their persistent enemy. They raised their weapons in readiness and waited. The tension was palpable.

After many agonizing moments, one warrior fell prey to the seductive call of battle, despite his companion's cries of cursing and warning. He raised his hammer high and screamed a dirge to his own funeral. Tey'ur smiled sadly and obliged the foolish one. It was ended swiftly, a single slash devised from the blade master, Tuloth. Executed with clean and convincing accuracy, the warrior dropped to the ground, his mouth wide in the shock of the dead. As if from a cue, the others rushed.

Tey'ur could feel his old muscles dragging; yet, still he managed a capable defence waiting patiently for his life to end. Someone would land the blow soon. As he raised his weapon high overhead, he felt the reassuring bite of a blade penetrate through his chest cavity. He slumped to the ground, coughing spit and then blood. A lung puncture most likely, the Lord mused quietly. The sword was now a waste of time and energy. He withdrew a small dagger and switched the grip with a flick of his hand. As the swordsman stepped in, he received the dagger through the ball of the neck, which caused him to tumble to his knees next to his opponent, gasping. In one swift motion Tey'ur reached out, grabbing the struggling warrior's head and then snapped it around to end the man's suffering. He raised himself up, upon his knees and watched as the others prepared to strike. "Mother, may I come to ..."

"Hold your weapons, men at arms!" A voice interjected from without the circle. The eight turned swiftly to see a man standing apart from them, through the dust and smoke upon the field. He carried no weapons; he simply stood there with an arm outstretched. His voice was powerful and profound, snatching the battle-weary souls from their trance. "Men of war, I implore you now - leave this field of battle! Your leaders have fled or been destroyed.

Stop the needless shedding of blood!" The men were
stunned at the man's force of speech. They remained
motionless and regarded each other. Quick glances were cast
upward to the ridge. There was no sign of the command, or
their rear guard. The mercenaries appeared uncertain, many
looked upon their weapons of war in question. The heat of
battle was cooling in the breeze. The young man's voice
called out again.

"Look around you! You have been paid for your
service, but the cost of this meaningless battle has tainted
that payment. Why would you fight for those who have
taken up the bodies of your fellows as puppets and deprived
them an honourable death? Do you have nothing left to live
for?" The young man's voice seemed to swell, growing more
steady and sure with every word. "This is an empty fight!
There is no more honour here, only shame. Now, you will
leave the dead to their end, and depart this place in peace."
The remaining warriors stood in shock. Then slowly, a
weary fighter came up from the ring of combatants to stand
before the bold interceder. He regarded the young face and
then, bowing his head, wiped the stains from his weapon
and sheathed the sword. His head remained bowed as he
departed slowly from the scene.

One by one, they all lowered or sheathed their
weapons and departed the body-strewn ground, without a
backward glance.

Tey'ur lifted his head wearily to where the young
man stood. 'Why is it' he thought to himself 'he reminds me

of someone … the likeness of great leaders past … clearly, he has the gift.' He closed his eyes and breathed in shakily. The end was near, he could feel the Council urging him onward, to meet with them in the great realm of the dead. There was a moment of clarity and reassuring peace which calmed his racing heart. The end of the Symian race had come.

"Are you ready to die?" A familiar voice spoke in his ear. Tey'ur knelt upon the ground in silence, but his heart leapt inside. One last burning regret … his hand slipped to the secret dagger inside his vambrace.

"Have you come to see the last of us fall?" the warrior responded.

"That would depend on whom you consider the last," the voice returned.

His foe was close, and he could do it. He must do it to honour the memory of the Council, the whole Order. It was a question of loyalty to the past. He slipped the dagger from the armour.

"It ends now!" Tey'ur screamed with rage as he moved with the last of his might, the dagger blow to fall true.

All was quiet. The wind blew through the near trees, through the long strands of graying hair which fell upon the old warrior's shoulders. The dagger was quivering in the hand of the guild Lord, the blade wet in blood. The Lord of the White Guard looked into the eyes of his once-dead guild healer in utter disbelief. The dagger was imbedded in Mehnol's hand, who knelt next to his Lord. Zyr stood just behind the solemn healer, his eyes cast toward the evening stars.

"Enough, my Lord, enough." Mehnol whispered.

ϴ   *The Sapling had thrived. Though the violent weather had nearly uprooted the young tree at times, it remained firm. The roots of the tree ran deep and received strength from the roots, of other foliage, that ran through the earth. The Sapling would not fall easily, unknowingly supported by the others. Even the corrupting weed could not disrupt the support of the young tree. And so it was that its roots ran deep ...*

OLD SCARS

THE WIND blew softly the pungent smells of war across the wastes of southern Mehnin. It carried and listed amongst the fallen, through the nostrils of the living. It blew eerily through the strange uncomfortable silence in the remnants of the White Guard camp. The clamour of war had ceased and the sun rose anew in the east sky. Tey'ur watched as the two monks went about assisting those fallen in battle. They reverently covered those who had long departed on the Path. His gaze slid coldly over the younger monk, the upstart who had somehow acquired knowledge in the healing arts. The veiled gestures of mercy infuriated the old warrior. He knew the man's true heart, his true nature. Zyr was anything but merciful or giving, which he had demonstrated in every lesson he had ever taken from the Master of War. Memories of utter selfishness and defiance swam through the void of thought, yet one vibrant remembrance struck deeper and more painful than them all. Traitor. He had used the Order for training and resources and removed himself on the very eve of his calling to the Council of Masters. Tey'ur hands clenched in frustration. As his muscles contracted, his body reminded him with painful jabs that the healing was not complete. He put his hand to his brow, seeking to remove the blasted memories from his mind. Would he never find peace?

"He's something, isn't he?" A voice commented beside him. Tey'ur glanced toward the sound. His curiosity had been piqued since he witnessed this young man's actions to bring an end to the conflict.

"He certainly has demonstrated skill in the healing arts …" Tey'ur spoke, suppressing pain and hurt; he would need time to bolster his resolve, to determine a course of action. The young man, Shien his name was, stood looking out over the tangled mess of bodies and war's attrition. He carried a pack on one shoulder, with a hand clasped firmly around the support strap. His hand caressed the material, subconsciously.

"He is much more than a healer. A pity you never saw him in battle." Shien commented as he watched the monk move to another of the White Guard soldiers.

"Indeed." Tey'ur murmured as he looked on grimly, choosing to conceal the bitter truth. Zyr would confront his past at a time of Tey'ur's choosing and not a moment sooner. They watched the scene for a moment before the old veteran broke the silence. "What you did last night was very foolish, despite its apparent success. One slip in your little speech and you would have had a place amongst the dead, with all of them." Tey'ur indicated toward the great masses of the slain.

"You're welcome, my Lord," Shien replied with a nod and small grin. He looked back to the scene of carnage. Tey'ur's brow dropped slightly, creases forming across his face. This man reminded him of Zyr, which was little compliment. Why was it that his instincts spoke differently? There was something extraordinary and vibrant behind the crass and ego. The young man had great potential, and yet he would never find it in the company of the morally weak. The old Lord looked back upon the scene and his eyes sprung wide in astonishment. Shien simply put a hand to his head and made a small sound of disbelief.

Zyr had made his way to the fallen lines of the Ahtol front. He was just then lifting one warrior to his feet. The warrior looked perplexed and disorientated which was a common trait among the near-dead who had begun their journey along the Path. They watched as Zyr placed a hand upon the bloodied shoulder of the warrior, his mouth was moving in some dialogue with the Ahtol mercenary. After a few moments, the warrior's head bowed and others watched as the near-dead man clasped the arm of the monk in an embrace of friendship, openly weeping. Zyr drew the man into his bosom and clasped the other arm over the warrior's sturdy back. The moment was tender and brief. The warrior released the grip, picked his weapon from among the quagmire and turned from the field of battle. His form disappeared behind the low hills and was gone.

'My eyes must be …' Tey'ur mused to himself. Shien was scratching his head in similar bafflement. Something within Tey'ur sensed the sincerity of that simple act, and he watched in begrudging respect as Zyr tended to friend and foe alike. Each time, the reaction was the same, an outpouring of compassion to the enemy, to a stranger. Tey'ur was not sure how to deal with the situation before him. His feelings of hate were being slowly doused with every prayer the monk offered in behalf of the fallen.

"It's amazing, isn't it?" Shien reported suddenly. "The man has little regard for himself. He always puts others first. I couldn't believe my eyes when he raised those Gnarel, the other night, especially after using so much energy to put down that horrid demon. It left him completely drained, to the point of death. Yet, there he goes … unbelievable. I wonder what drives him to do it?"

Tey'ur took the information in without a response. So the Gnarel mystery was solved in a fashion that would never have entered his lucid mind. The answer would have eluded him for a millennia, if he lived that long. The cursed upstart … Zyr, the agitator, who merited punishment at the edge of his blade (never mind the hand) so many times; and always escaping. And yet, what was transpiring was undeniable and validated the young man's musings.

"Lord Tey'ur." A female voice called out behind the two men. Shien had turned to see the young girl walking closer.

Firah had appeared over the low rise and walked with a small limp, her arm was held across her shoulder as if in pain. Her eyes were fixed on the guild lord while Tey'ur looked on in curiosity. The girl barely registered the young man next to him. She limped slowly closer until stopping in front of the tired warrior.

"We'll be moving on this morning. We thank you for your hospitality." She spoke, her face set firm with a certain annoyance. He chuckled inside and regarded the sky whimsically. She reminded him of Morellyn. The girl was equally as headstrong as his now departed Mihyl. She would need to be. He looked at her with a guarded air of curiosity. The old Lord had wondered what had transpired the previous night, when the battle was long and at it fiercest. It seemed he would never know as he could detain the group no longer. Honour dictated such things. Still, there was unfinished business.

He stood slowly, muscles aching and sore. He looked down into her determined visage. "Please, be our guests for a short time longer." He watched as her face fell and she took in a deep breath. He caught her with an upraised hand before she could unstop a hurricane of wrath. "Hold. I know your feelings. I do not intend to delay you any longer. My business is with your monk friend." He pointed vaguely in Zyr's direction. "He has been busy since third watch. When he is ready, I will only need a few minutes." Firah's expression softened and she turned to look at the monk as he worked in the distance.

"Alright, I guess," she replied curtly. She turned slightly with a cool gaze toward the waiting young man. The wind blew blonde locks across his face, his grey eyes meeting her fiery gaze. "You turned your back on us … and now you are changing your mind?" she queried chillingly. He took a moment before responding. Tey'ur turned and began walking through the host of the dead. He heard the response before the wind carried the words into nothingness.

"I'm here, aren't I?"

⊥   Zyr watched the tall and rigid old warrior approaching. The monk sat upon the ground with weary, blood stained arms resting in his lap. The timing was strange. Zyr never dreamed that he would encounter the old Master, not in this setting. It was strange because of their

346

proximity to the Halls. He knew Tey'ur's feelings well, dark thoughts full of hate and disgust. More importantly, Zyr felt every last baleful thought was deserved. What he had done in the past was in the past; yet he could not escape the consequences of his actions. That was part of his life now, reaping the seeds sown in youth.

His reminiscing brought her image searing across his mind like a burning brand. Memory recalled the softness of her lips; the sensation was still lingering like the hidden coal amongst the ashes of a diminished fire. He wanted to pull himself from the fresh memory, but he could not. He would deny his feelings no longer, the time for secrets was past. Zyr opened his hands and stared down upon the course skin. He had lived inside a lie for so long, pretending to be someone else, training his very soul to encase his heart within a cold chest.

He looked upward to see the old warrior draw closer; Tey'ur's lined face was set in grim determination. Whatever the cost, Zyr would not run from his past or his heart anymore. He dropped his gaze to his hands once again, they were scored and flecked with dry blood, the marks of the Alacritor's duty.

He felt the power emanating from the presence before him, standing there in quiet rage. It was many minutes before either moved or spoke.

"Why did you revive the Gnarel?" the deep voice whispered low.

"They are under Mother's watch as much as you or I. There is nothing so evil in them that cannot corrupt common people as well," the younger replied. Silence carried along the cool wind which caressed the robes and tabards of the still figures.

"I assume you feel the mercenaries deserved the same?" Zyr nodded his head without looking up. He could see the clenched fists in his peripheral vision. The war still raged within, decades old. Slowly, Tey'ur raised a hand and rubbed his right temple softly in silence. After a moment, the Blade Master of the broken Order spoke.

"I cannot easily disregard the past. You know how deep old scars run. I cannot easily change a heart that has burned in hatred for so long … yet my soul would burn ever brighter in Llian's gaze if I were to strike you down now. Sadly, it seems that I have receded over the years while you have grown. I will say but one thing to you. I understand what the Council affirmed. Yes … I believe now, after all these years, their wisdom and judgment shines the truth through a clouded mind." Zyr's brow dripped sweat casually upon the ground. He had been ready to fall; he would never have dared guard himself. It was the duty owed to the past. The prospect of death was something he had come to terms with, and it was necessary to accept his weakness to find the peace he sought for. In the past he had scoffed and loathed the old warrior; now as a mender and restorer of life he saw things differently. It was Mother below who had instilled such a dynamic change in his heart and mind. It had taken many years, but the youthful ideals had slid away, the layers of pride and ego stripped away with every healing and moment of servitude.

"We are in your debt," Zyr replied solemnly. It was a double meaning which he was sure was received. Tey'ur waved a gauntleted hand absently.

"That won't be necessary. What of this woman, Nuril? Does she intend to rejoin the conflict?"

"No. She acquired what she came for," Zyr chose his words carefully. By sharing too much he would risk revealing the nature of his work. The oaths he had sworn in Mother's service were guarded meticulously, and punished with severity. "It appears that their goal was to recover a cursed blade in Firah's possession. Her unguided attunement to the dagger thwarted her use to them. I suspect any further hostility would only deter their plans, until they are ready to move again. It seems my actions in Khyvla have not ended their schemes, only delayed them." Tey'ur's eyes narrowed slightly at the monk's words.

"Indeed. Though as usual you mask the full truth. The matter of this demon, Ahtol, cannot be countered by mere force of arms. I can see you have a reason to return home. Perhaps this is the wisdom finally affirming the choice of the Council?" His mouth shifted to a slight smile for the briefest moment. Then he made a quick nod toward the Halls. "Mind yourselves in there - it is likely more a forum for the fallen spirits than our treasured home."

349

Tey'ur turned to face the south and the sentinel phalanx of trees. He said nothing for many moments but maintained his gaze upon the dense forest wall. At last he spoke without turning, almost as if addressing another beyond their sight. "I had pushed you from my mind and swore to never return. I thought you were dead to me, and yet you draw me near again for a hidden purpose." The warrior's head bowed as he placed the mailed glove gently to his brow. His steps fell soft upon the torn soil.

As he watched the last Blade Master of the Order's Council walk away under the new bright dawn, Zyr pondered his last words. It was another mystery to solve. The past was weighed down in unanswered questions, and when he gained one answer two questions would follow. The Council … what was chosen?

Through all the clamour of his thoughts came a sudden clear and discernible impression that caught his breath. It was brilliant and profound and lifted the heaviness from his heart. His mind deciphered the feeling.

Your enemies have not guessed the Sapling's true purpose. I entrust her to your care. Bring her home.

The monk's head slipped down while his fingertips touched together lightly, his mind slowly coalescing thoughts into unity. The sun rose slowly higher in the heavens.

GLOSSARY

Aeredia: The commonly accepted name for the world.

Aerluin: A feminine being of immense power. She originated from outside of the world in the heavens and is now bound within the world. She is considered benevolent but not omniscient. She communicates in a variety of ways at times to people in Aeredia. Her power emanates from her indiscriminately and interacts with substances and creatures within the world in unique ways. Known also as the Dark Lady, Mother.

Ahtol: A being of immense power that exists within the core of Aeredia. Considered to be evil and malign and seeking to be free from the prison of the world. Ahtol's physical form consists of viscous shadows that meld and flow like water.

Ashori and Ashori-tar: (Also known as Weavers) A living soul in Aeredia who has established a knowledge of and connection to Aerluin's power. Each of these souls can access a portion of this power. This portion or refraction typically has a certain flavour, such as the power to understand or heal living patterns or the power to manipulate one of the four elements. The soul rarely accesses more than a single refraction of power in his or her lifetime. (See Root for specific detail.)

The ability to refine and shape the raw power is a life-long pursuit for an Ashori. Governments and Cadres use Ashori in various roles. These individuals are not common and are generally feared and respected throughout the land.

Ashori-tar are those who are untrained but have the capacity to interact with the Root in lesser degrees. They often adopt titles such as magi, sorcerer, alchemist, necromancer or witch if they actively utilize their limited potential.

Cadre: A group of people who bond together to form a political and military block. They have similar professions, talents, abilities, skills and ideologies. They can compete for the One Seat in each province of Kenhar. Apart from vying for political power, under Kenhar law they are expected to keep the peace and promote local laws that will bring order and stability to their region.

Character Symbology and Pronunciation:
θ = World
𝕏 = Firah [Fē-rŭh]
⊥ = Zyr [Zēr]
𝕎 = Tohm [Tōm]
𝕏 = Shien [Shē-ĕn]
𝕎 = Nuril [Nū-rĭl]
𝕀 = Tey'ur [Tãr]

Chota: Martial garment worn during practice and combat. It provides some protection and padding in vital areas while allowing for freedom of movement in flex areas around the shoulders and groin.

Deepstone (Bloodstone): Any rock, stone or precious element that has been altered through specific conditions and contact with the Root. Deepstone formations are rare. A connection between a Root sensitive and the Deepstone occurs when blood is transferred. Blood sharing is a form of attunement and can cause a specific effect to occur based upon the unique properties of the stone.

Dorgyn Circles: A gladiatorial game organized at Terlan in Jandor Province. This competition serves many purposes: a test of skills, sport for gambling, resolving political disputes, serving debts owed and others. The challenge is centered on an elaborate Darkwood structure which is comprised of several spinning rings at various elevations. Hazards and fatalities are commonplace in the competition.

Dryke: A migratory creature that is reptilian in nature. Migration patterns take the creatures through parts of Kenhar before leaving the country for many moon cycles. Drykes are generally considered to be non-sentient. One province in Kenhar is named after this creature for their constant presence and nesting grounds located there.

For-: Previous week, always accompanied by a day of the week. Example: *For-Mena*

Ge': A combative weapon comprised of heavy weighted spheres of stone or metal. Each is linked by bands or straps of various material ranging from crude rope to metal links. The Ge' is thrown in such a way as to grapple a target at the legs, neck or other parts. Its full length can vary as well as the style of throw.

Gnarel: A bestial nomadic race that moves through the lands of Kenhar. The Gnarel are honour driven and respect strength. They bear heavy hides with long manes. They walk as bipeds and can use simple technologies. The males bear horns (skull bone protrusions) of impressive size and variety. Gnarel tend to plunder as need dictates, but not for sport.

Jazyn: A non-sentient creature which is sensitive to the flows from Aerluin. Any manipulation of the Root can be detected like a scent which can dissipate over time. The Jazyn are rarely seen and guarded carefully due to their small population and slow reproduction. Most citizens have never seen one but are aware of them.

Jyril: Junior member of a Tetsu.

Kenhar: A country found in Aeredia. It is ruled by a king who shares power with ruling cadres who vie for power among their peers. The country is broken down into provinces where a local council represents the King's authority in enforcing accepted laws. Local laws can be modified to suit the ruling cadre's needs but cannot supersede basic laws enacted by the ruling king.

   The capital province of Kenhar is Syrion. Other provinces include: Jandor, Mehnin, Leil, Dryke, Rhylos, Khayl, and Sym.

Khyvla: The capital and largest city in the province of Mehnin.

Kota: Protective martial gear worn on the hands.

Llian: A being of immense power that exists outside Aeredia, sometimes called the Heavenly One. She was charged with the care of the world along with her younger sister Aerluin. Together they kept a protective weave of power moving about the world, promoting its movement and stability. She grew careless and longed for other places and neglected her song of binding. The chaotic powers within Aeredia lashed out and pulled Aerluin into the world. Llian now dwells beyond the moon which circles Aeredia. Due to separation from the world, she can do little to impact the affairs and elements.

Lliankor: A curse first used to reference Llian's wayward lapse and the accompanying frustration of the user.

Lunar Calendar: The measure of time is based upon an ancient Lunar calendar which is attuned to the seasons.

A cycle has 100 years. (Designated by 'C')

Each year has 4 seasons (Designated by Blackrill (Spring), Bloodstone (Summer), Darkwood (Autumn), Shadowveil (Winter))

Each season has 3 moons cycles (Designated by 1st, 2nd, 3rd)

Each moon cycle has 4 phases (Designated by New, Waxing, Full, Waning)

Each moon phase has 7 days(Luin, Teli, Tera, Celi, Mena, Solari, Llian)

An additional moon cycle between Blackrill and Bloodstone is called the Festive Moon Cycle.

The moon phases within the Festive Moon Cycle are Festive Moon Phases. Each is dedicated to the four enhanced elements:

Bloodstone Festival, Darkwood Festival, Blackrill Festival, Shadowveil Festival

This equates to a 364 day year. One day is added to the end of the Festive Cycle to moderate the seasonal discrepancy. This is usually designated a sacred and peaceful holiday through all the land. It is known as The Day of Unity. Aeredian scholars have noted that the moon does not fall out of phase from the extra day and attribute this to the Omnipotents who created the world.

Cycles are recorded and usually connected directly to the ruling monarchs and the dynasty that follows. The passage of time under each dynasty is recorded and kept for purpose of time passed upon the land; however, every new ruling dynasty resets the Cycle to '1'.

An example of a recorded date goes as such:
C6-51, 3rd Shadowveil waxing Moon, Llian.

Hence C6-51 refers to the 51st year of the sixth century of the present dynasty's rule. Shadowveil (as with all the seasons) is broken into three moon cycles. The cycle is the complete change from a new moon waxing to full and waning back to new. In this example, the third Shadowveil cycle moon is nearly full as Llian is the last day of the week. On the next day, it would be full and in the middle of moon cycle.

Mehnin: A province located in the Southern lands of Kenhar. The capital of Mehnin is Khyvla.

Menil-Bees: A particular breed of bee known for its unusual aggressiveness and protective instincts.

Mihyl: Senior member of a Tetsu

The Order of the Open Hand: The organization formed to train those attuned to Aerluin's Root. The Order was comprised of strict rules of governance and discipline. The Order was broken and only ruins remain along with a handful of Ashori who survived the massacre.
Ranks within the Order: Servant-Initiate-Seeker-Convert-Master.

Pattern: The combination of all Aerluin's threads throughout the world. The formation of the pattern is always changing and never static.

Racur: A fortress-mountain located in the southern-most region of Mehnin. It is self-sufficient and exists outside the rule of law in Kenhar. Invasions from Racur upon the lands of Kenhar and countries to the south are a common occurrence.

Reykal: An insult of extreme offense uttered by the lower classes. Intended as a much stronger and deeper form of 'idiot'. Wars have been known to have begun over improper (or untimely) use of the word.

Root: The actual bands of power that twist and vibrate through the lands of Aeredia. The Root generally exists within the land with a few exceptions in parts of the world. The Root exists as a pure energy form that spreads outward from Aerluin as bands or threads. Aerluin cannot control the direction or potency of this effect; it simply exists. No one can guess the number of threads that pulse through the land at any time. These bands are constantly in motion and rarely remain in fixed places. In certain conditions the Root can manipulate the substances it comes into contact with. This can include people, animals, plants, rocks, wood and water. When two bands happen to cross they tend to latch into a focal point and amplify their effects upon nearby substances. If the hold is strong the weaves will wind upon themselves and form a rift. The rift can only form in certain conditions, and if those are not present, the threads will typically unwind and resume their solitary journeys.

    For the trained hand and mind, the bands can be accessed for use. This can be done in a variety of ways, but it is generally implied that any who access or manipulate the Root are called Ashori (see Ashori for specific detail).

    The Root also grants to anyone certain gifts of insight and inspiration as way of enhancing creative thought. Those who dwell near focal points or rifts for prolonged periods will experience changes in physiology and intelligence. Some lower species have been changed to forms of sentience and naturally enlightened races have found superior ability and vitality.

Serpentor: A large reptilian species that can grow to great size. The variety of colour and identifying features exists within the species.

Servant: The lowest rank in the Order of the Open Hand. There is only one Servant at a time in the Order. The Servant is chosen carefully by the council from among their peers to fill this specific role. The choice is coupled with the matter of compatibility with the Root and of the character of the candidate. The Servant must exhibit an attitude of humility and is often assigned menial tasks as a part of everyday duties. This is to alleviate or prevent the risk of corruption in such a vital task.

The Servant is the most disciplined and studied member of the Order. The same can be said of the Masters who govern the affairs of the Order, however it is very rare for a Master to be chosen as Servant.

The Servant wields the Scepter of Power which is a potent artifact to manipulate the weaves of the Root. As such, the Servant must have the knowledge and ability to manipulate various portions of the Root at once. The Servant is guardian of the seals which protect the boundaries of the Order of the Open Hand.

Spear: A unit of measurement. 1 Spear = 5 yards or 15 feet.

Tamers Reach: The southernmost mountain range in Kenhar. It adjoins to other branching ranges: Serpentor March to the north and into countries to the south. Tamers Reach is a natural boundary between Kenhar to the West and the Wasteland to the East.

Tetsu: A combative pair of Ashori teamed together for the purpose of instruction, training and combat effectiveness. A tetsu can consist of male or female members. There are no age limitations, as Ashori tend to come into power and knowledge in various stages of life. Typically, a junior member will be younger, but this is not always the case.

Vyn-Shi: A country located to the far east beyond the Wastelands.

Wilder: A member of a mysterious order who operate outside of the known laws and capacities of the Root. It is said the Wilder's connection to Aerluin is much more visceral, primal and deep. As such, Wilder's live in close connection to the Dark Lady's whisperings. Many serve Her directly and seek to further her cause.

In addition, they use a variety of tools and weapons in conjunction with their affinity to the Root. Their stealth, accuracy and potency make them deadly opponents. Wilder's are the most misunderstood and mistrusted of all beings who claim any connection to the Root. Due to their reclusive nature, the exact number of Wilder's who exist are unknown, but it is understood to be limited.

They have been known to accept employment when it suits them but they hold no allegiance to any but Aerluin herself. As such they have been known to disappear suddenly in the thick of war, much to the consternation of their employers. This only lends credence to the feeling of mistrust swirling about this secluded group.

MAP OF KENHAR

AEREDIAN CALENDAR

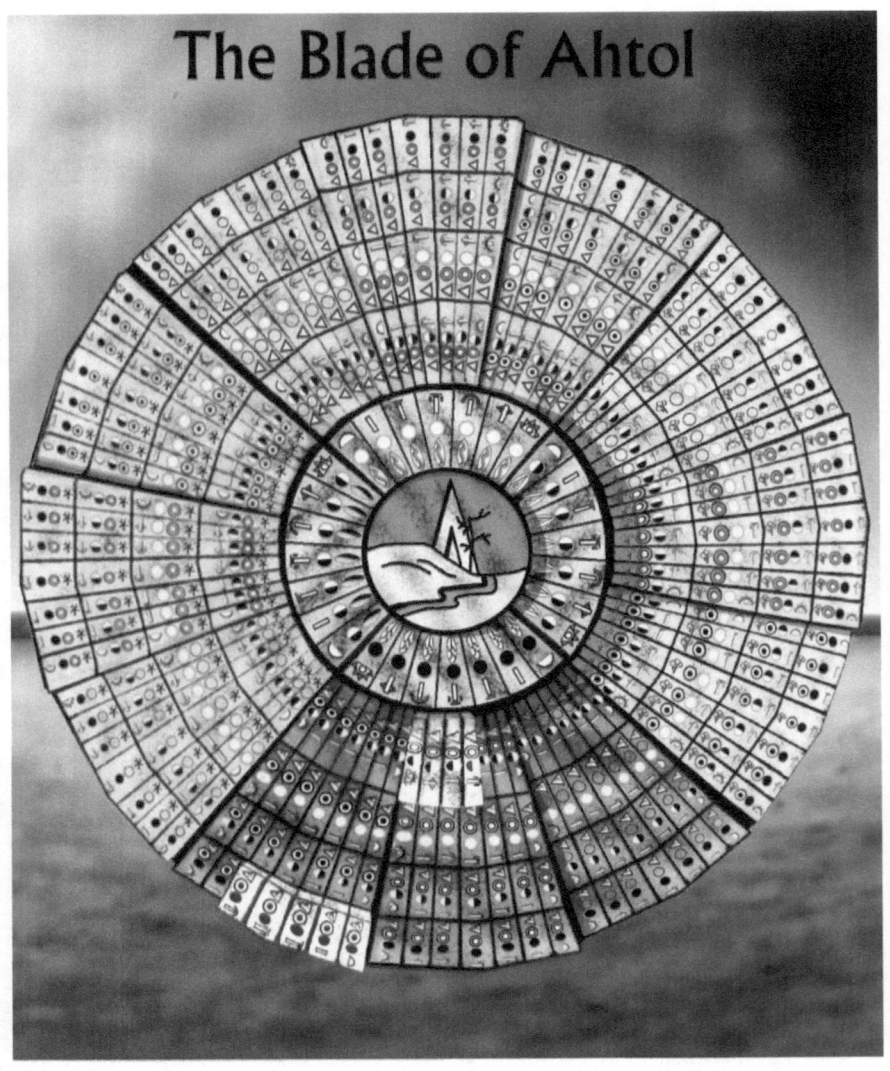

An Excerpt from the sequel to *The Blade of Ahtol*

Sapling: The Broken Halls

GREY ENCOUNTERS

STEFAN crouched low grasping the reassuring stone, the only firm assurance he could cling to. The wind howled about his ears and gusted wildly in ever-changing vectors. The highest spire in Syrion wound ever upward until all stone fell away, leaving naught but a narrow stair (no wider than a quarter-spear) jutting into the heavens. He dared not look down into the vast expanse all around them. He stared in utter amazement at the king, who stood upon the highest step boldly and upright, casually gazing out over the land which lay many hundreds of feet below. It would be dawn soon, and the young king made to satisfy his desire to see the definitive moment, when Tamers Reach would release the captive sun to the land. There were no words to describe the beauty and majesty of the occurrence.

Stefan was terrified. His Lord had always done this, and the overwhelming feeling of terror beat harshly inside his chest. One slip, or a strong gust and he or the King would fall ... down and down ... it would take an eternity to reach the ground, as the tower height surpassed any other structure in Kenhar, perhaps Aeredia herself. A burly draft nearly drove his light frame over the stair as he desperately grasped the stone steps, struggling to regain balance. His knuckles were white from exertion.

The voice of the king rang out in clear tones, his face still turned toward the east.

"It is not that I do not appreciate your company, Stefan but not all are accustomed to the open tower," Toryn remarked as he waited upon the red orb. "What exactly brought you up here this morning, before most of the world has yet to awaken?" Stefan breathed in slowly while regarding the back of the king; the royal cloak and light brown hair tousled about in the wind.

"I was thinking about the Defilers." Stefan replied as he adjusted his body so as to address the young monarch as directly as possible without rising from his precarious perch. He strained his voice over the incessant howling of the wind. "Perhaps if we sent another envoy to strike a negotiation?" As he finished his sentence the king turned toward his chancellor, his grey eyes set deep with emotion and futility.

"The time for deliberations is past, Stefan. The servants of Ahtol have made their move …" The young king's frame lifted and then drooped under a long exhaled breath. "Only four left … four, Stefan … Dryke, Mehnin and Syrion … and Sym. The rest have all fallen into shadow." Toryn's hand came up from his side, now clenched and shaking slightly. "Not a prayer for any of them … and what have I done? I was charged to protect them all … and now we all wait for the end. Hope is foolishness, Stefan … one day our sun will fail to rise." He fell silent and turned himself about, regarding the light which was near to peaking over the far mountains. "How careless and obtuse we have been … the leaders of this country. We opened our doors to this evil, gave them refuge." Toryn's head bowed low. Stefan could read the pain and frustration in that simple act.

"L - lord … surely, you are not giving up?" Stefan had to ignore his fear, as far greater matters consumed his mind. He had never seen the young king in such a state of mind, defeated and demoralized. The chancellor had accompanied him on many campaigns and had seen Toryn in many battles. This behaviour was so unlike him - unnatural and alarming.

"When have I ever shirked my duty, Stefan?" the voice of the monarch carried a sharp rebuke. Toryn sighed and paused before speaking again. "I cannot cling to hope any longer; my heart is drawing faint. I would prefer to reside up here, in my solitude, and wait for the end than lead a country through false hope. That would be more deceptive than the darkest acts of the Ahtol cadres." The young man turned, the years as The Standard of Kenhar seemed to weigh his shoulders down to the cold stone.

"My liege!" Stefan called out vigorously, "I cannot bear to hear these things! Forgive me but your words are what the enemy would rejoice to hear! Come to your senses!" Stefan swallowed uncomfortably. Those words could easily land him in the stocks or time in the cells. Yet, he could not refrain, his face was flushed in anger and sorrow. The young king did not flinch upon the outburst but remained still for a moment.

"Peace, my friend … I understand your sentiment and I would react the same had our places been reversed. I …" As the king made to step down to his chancellor, a powerful wind crashed over the high precipice, and Stefan looked on in horror as it caught his Lord in its potent lashings. It all passed as brief moments in time. The king was swept to the edge of the stone, his body all but carried over into the air. Toryn's eyes were set strange; so calm and accepting. His large frame seemed to linger there upon the edge. The wind, as if acting as the cruel hand of fate, was judging the monarch. Then simply and unnervingly the howling ceased and all was calm and silent. Toryn slumped to the stair, one leg thrusting down over the edge. Catching himself upon the edge, the King of Kenhar looked about in wonder. He looked to the east.

The fiery orb had begun its escape from the jagged teeth of the captive mountains. The sky was thrown into vibrant luminous colours and the streams of light pierced the top of the tower. Colours, bright and fervent, spread like streams of holy power across the heavens. Toryn sat in a daze, the new day light brushing his face and glistening in his grey eyes. A tender tear fell across his cheek as he paused motionless upon the brink.

"So beautiful …" he whispered.

"My liege! … Toryn …" Stefan called out and despite his fear he scrambled up to his king and helped him to the safety of the stair. "Please … let us go down …"

"Yes. The moment has passed." The king rose under his chancellor's arm and took a few steps down the stair. Then Toryn stopped and turned his head slightly. "Can you feel that Stefan? There is change in the air … it is like a strand of the sun's power breaking the shadows. It feels … like something has moved in the land. In Aerluin's mercy the heavens shine down upon the faithful." He stood for a moment and basked in the warmth that shed from the rising sun. The shadows began to flee like a drawn veil across the land. "Thank you, Mother."

The king of Kenhar turned his face from the sun and slowly the two men descended the long open stair.

*   *   *

The ground around Firah was scorched black in areas, as were the trees which had blazed unchecked until they were consumed - black and lifeless. Mother and her skin were abused. The whole needless scene angered her. Though considered immature at sixteen years, she picked up all the particulars of the skirmish as she walked through the torn camp. Mournful whispers from the survivors who thought to subdue their talk from her ears. It was in more than just words. All the surrounding area cried out in anguish. Now standing atop the ridge she could see the scene in a grander scale. Grey Rangers had positioned above the camp while mercenary forces pressed upon the defenders below.

Firah could hardly blame the White Guard for anything they had done, for survival and victory were powerful forces. They had not been the aggressors in this event. Rather her ire was directed against the senseless actions of their enemy. She could hardly fathom the folly of the leaders of the company that had ambushed the White Guard. What was to gain? Was there any purpose to their raid?

Suddenly, her eyes caught hold upon something moving in a copse of trees ahead of her.

Thinking it was some sort of animal or a fawn, the girl decided to investigate. She focused all her thoughts and energy around her, as she had done so many times before.

Gradually, she slowed her breath to long deep passes. After a few moments she reached out and touched the bark of a nearby tree. It pained her to mimic the tortured blackened skin of the tree. At once her skin took on the hue and texture of the surface she touched upon. The young thief strode swiftly and silently upon the ground. Her breathing was slow and deliberate and her heart thumped away with its hammer inside her veins. Each time she reached out and contacted a new surface she would change with it.

Firah proceeded further into the wood. The ground gave way to endless twisted and tangled roots which jutted out everywhere. Her every step was measured and placed with the utmost care. Firah loved to watch the wild creatures; however they would never permit an intruder into their private world. As a result, she had to rely upon her ability to sneak about; not only in the towns but also in the wild. Animals had such highly developed senses, she was often detected even while concentrating with all her ability. As she pressed on, her whole body was tingling with energy, her form constantly shifting with the surrounding wood.

Firah drew silently under the thin tree canopy. Her eyes drew to what had originally caught her gaze and she was surprised to spot three cloaked forms. Large and splendid bows and partially filled quarrels were strapped to their sturdy backs which were hunched slightly as they conversed in low tones. They were all large in stature and shifted occasionally in their stances with cat-like motions. They were dressed to match the colours and environment around them, though she noticed that they all also wore grey in some fashion.

Firah was unsure what to do. She did not recall seeing these people in the camp. Their colours did not match that of the White Guard. While the Guard scouts dulled down the white significantly (it would prove difficult to prowl in glaring white), it did not match the grey apparel of the strangers before her. She presumed that they could be spies of some sort. Her heart beat hard inside her chest. Should she chance it? Not that she owed anything to Lord Tey'ur but payback for a few days of misery and frustration. Rather, she was inherently curious, to a fault. She wanted to know what they were talking about; afterward, she would decide what to do with the information. Gathering her courage, she began to slide ever closer to the small cloaked group.

As the forms grew larger and more detailed with every step, she began to hear some muttering. She still could not discern words, only quiet rumbling. She stepped gingerly around a large root, taking care not to break the underbrush or shift the fallen leaves. She silently cursed the Darkwood season. Moving was slow due to the numerous fragile and crispy leaves which lay as a coloured blanket across the wood's floor. Firah steeled herself, bringing her body into complete harmony with the environment. She edged ever nearer, until finally she stood poised behind a tree mere feet from the huddled party. Perking her ears, she strained to listen.

"… is inevitable. The Guard will be unable to recover."
One spoke quietly.

"That may be true; however …" another voice rose and
fell in volume while Firah gripped the tree nervously. She
could only catch bits and pieces, like morsels of information
falling from the wind. "… so it must be so. There is no other
option." The silent observer was turned away from the
group and could not discern any movement. She suppressed
her breathing as best she could, yet her heart raced like a
chased roe through the woods.

"I propose that we act …" the voice trailed off for a few
moments. "… will be ours. Victory is assured." Firah's throat
constricted tightly. They were planning some sort of counter
attack, but where and when?

"We will alert the guild. You will remain to observe their
progress. Swift the shaft brings …" A brief pause and then
two voices rung low in response.

"… Grey death." Firah heard nothing more and waited
for a few moments before daring to breathe outward. It was
an eerie calm that prevailed. She waited an eternity it
seemed. Her mind was swaying in anxious excitement.
Despite her dislike of the cadre Lord, Tey'ur should know
what she knew, as limited as the knowledge was. Yet, she
needed to escape first from the situation. She still heard
nothing, no evidence of any movement or voices. Finally,
she decided to chance a look.

Firah moved her head gradually around until her vision
just cleared the trunk, attempting to keep the thick tree

between herself and the group. To her surprise, only one form came to her sight, resting quietly upon the ground cross-legged. 'Where are the others?' she thought frantically. The silent figure was motionless and turned away from her; she took a second glance. They had left as silently as she had arrived. Her heart sank in contemplation of the mortal danger she had put herself in. These people were extremely skilled in the same art as she. How many others could there be in the area? 'How careless!' she chided herself. She knew that she must get away and quickly. Firah lifted a foot slowly to begin her slow escape.

"I was wondering when you would move, little mouse. Your Root is good enough for amateurs, though hardly a test for me." A deep voice rang from the sitting figure. Firah jumped and emitted a small noise of fright. The man had caught her completely off guard and frightened her unexpectedly. Her mind raced in fear, what should she do? "You may try to run if you wish, little one, but you will not leave this wood. Your life is mine."

Firah had heard enough. She dashed with all her might toward the camp. Leaves crunched harshly and twigs snapped. She did not care; she did not want to die. She heard no sound of pursuit, which unnerved her, but she saw the exit to the wood and charged onward. 'So close' she chided.

The air around Firah burst into a grey cloud which swirled violently. Dust particles plumed and churned around the girl's body. Firah swiftly covered her eyes, but the stinging sensation told her it was too late. Her eyes now burned intensely and when she attempted to open them for a moment, her body forced them shut again. She cried out in pain and brought her hands instinctively to her face. When she rubbed her eyes, the stinging grew much worse. In her stumbling about she came into contact with a tree, her face striking hard against the bark. She fell to the ground, blind and helpless, tasting her blood.

As her terror heightened her mind struggled to maintain a semblance of sanity. The thief was dragged back to the fields of carnage she had walked through that morning. Although Firah knew it was not real, she could not stop the strange memory unfolding with alarming corporeality. She could not escape the nightmarish web of past events.

The girl walked unsteadily amongst the rows of bodies. She still ached from a bruise that covered her entire right side. Something had happened last night, in her sleep. Something terrible … her gaze fell over the mangled remnants of the dark battle. Truly, the two monks had given miraculous service, yet not all could be saved. War disturbed her greatly, to see the expressionless grey faces of so many fallen men and women. It all seemed so senseless and futile. All of them, thinking and breathing human beings but hours ago - now lifeless husks rotting upon the earth, waiting in vain for a nameless grave. Most were now a shadow of their former selves; some had been reanimated into grotesque twisted shapes, others fated to be hewn down again and again. In her young life she could not have believed such a thing possible, and yet what she had been told was terribly evident in her gaze. She turned away from their faces.

As Firah limped her way past the endless rows of cold sentinels, her heart trembled within her breast and her breath came short. She was deathly frightened of the dead. Somehow, deep within she felt something had fled from her. She had lost a reassurance, a steady bulwark that had always been there. Now she felt empty as a void, stumbling about in dark uncertainty. The sky seemed darker, the dull greyness weighing down her every step. She looked toward the heavens while drifting through the rows of tangled bodies. The sun was shrouded in a thick grey veil. Her steps faltered upon a slope, yet she barely noticed the change in elevation. Everywhere she looked was grisly death, pale eyes casting their jealous gaze upon her. The trembling girl wrapped her slender arms about her body. The cold autumn wind picked up and tossed her ebony hair about as she ascended the rise. After a few steps, she stumbled over an outstretched leg and fell to the earth. She reeled, caught in frantic terror. She twisted around to see the body of a mercenary which she had tripped over. It lay crumpled and bent inward, almost in the act of consuming itself. In a heartbeat she saw the head move slightly. Firah checked her gaze and was unable to detect any sign of movement from the collapsed husk. Yet, she could feel things shifting about her, twitching.

She emitted a small cry when she felt something brush the back of her arm. Her breath came rapidly as her crimson eyes, wild with fear, flicked about the area. Still nothing was moving ... in her direct sight. Subconsciously, her hand drifted to her belt for that reassuring comfort ... and found it bare. Firah jerked her head

down in panic. The blade was gone! She patted her belt all around;
her mind reasoned frantically 'Perhaps it could have fallen when I
tripped.' She felt all around the area and madly searched in vain
for her prized possession. She heard the sound of distant moaning.

The sounds were closing and bodies were shifting all around
her. One body caught her attention, a great gaping wound revealed
the flesh and sinew within. A gargled retch emitted from her
mouth, as her body nearly vomited from sheer terror. Slowly, her
face turned to see one of the distant bodies, an armoured mercenary
rising upward silently. The face was ghastly, the neck turned to
one side from a vicious and lethal hammer blow. She watched
speechlessly as the warrior slowly turned as if gliding upon the air,
its eyes slowly settling upon her. A droning filled her ears, which
seemed to come from all around.

Firah moved herself backward slowly, out of instinct. 'I must
get away!' she thought. Again her hand went to her belt and found
it bare. Impossible, it couldn't be gone! She kicked her legs to
propel her backward until she bumped up against a tree. She
turned to grasp the trunk only to find the side of a White Guard
slumped over upon a spear that had impaled the warrior through.
Screaming hoarsely, she shot upward and ran up the slope swiftly.
The sky had darkened considerably and clouds billowed black
overhead. Without glancing, she could sense the hammer-stricken
was overtaking her, as it appeared unencumbered by the terrain,
simply gliding over all the fallen dead, toward her. The wind was
howling and whipping her about violently, delaying her escape.
The monstrosity drifted ever closer.

"Get away! Leave me be!" She screamed in futility as she ran
into the forceful wind. She had ascended the rise and now moved

across the scorched ground with all haste. Twitching her gaze, her heart froze as the monster was almost on top of her. Its hand was stretching outward toward her small body. Firah froze where she stood, her fear all but consuming her soul. She waited for the cold fingers to squeeze the life from her body - just as they had nearly done before that night in Khyvla. She slumped to her knees and closed her eyes tightly. Every sensation tingled along her skin as she waited for the end. Something touched her shoulder and Firah shrieked in despair.

"Such a foolish little one," a voice whispered in her ear, "you should not have come here." Firah felt reality stab through her dark delusions. She struggled in vain to detect the voice, swinging her arm around her head. The voice sounded like it was right next to her. It was cold and impassionate. Remorseless.

"Stay away from me!" She shouted through puffed lips. Her eyes were still darkened from the dust attack and she flailed her arms again in vain toward the sound of the voice. The assailant stopped her struggling with a solid kick to her abdomen which drove the breath from her even as it escaped her lips. She gagged and retched for breath that would not come. She was so disorientated, her body screaming so many signals that she felt completely useless. She could hardly form a conscious thought. Suddenly, she felt herself being shoved onto her back and something heavy pressing uncomfortably down on her chest. "Wait, I promise I won't ..."

"Lies have no place here," The voice spoke coldly. She felt a hand moving over her body, not in lust but searching for something. She heard the man muse softly, "What are you doing with something like this?" She could not imagine what he meant and she could hardly breathe so she chose not to answer. She felt a tug against her leather vest near her shoulder and realized that he was taking her brooch. Despite the pressure on her chest and the pain she was experiencing, Firah spoke.

"Please, don't take that!" she gasped out in desperation. Struggling to open her eyes she found everything a blur. Her eyes were slowly washing away the painful dust but it was still impossible to see clearly. She felt the brooch snap from her tunic.

"Why are you worried about it?" he commented quietly, "you will be dead soon."

Firah could stand no more. She lashed out at the weight that held her down, finding it to be a sturdy leg belonging to her captor. Not only was the attempt futile but the man shoved down hard upon her chest. She heard a popping sound and tried to scream with all her might, in intense pain and frustration. All her breath had left her. She clenched her fists tightly and shook her head weakly from side to side. "Heh. You don't like this? You should have reconsidered when you entered the wood. You thought you were skilled, but you're now hardly a concern for anyone. That is why we finished our business before dealing with you." She felt the boot slide upward toward her throat.

'No ...' she thought. 'Never again. I won't be beaten like this!' Her body shook in terrible anger. Her vision was blurred and red. All she felt was wrath toward this man and every other who had beaten her down. She felt the power within well up. Something was coursing through her veins and slipping out of her body like streams of blood. She had felt this once before.

"What in Aeredia ...?" She heard her enemy speak suddenly. Firah desperately channeled all her aggression, her hatred, toward the man. "Girl, this is your doing! Stop this now! You ..." Firah felt the terrible pressure leave her chest and she rose up slowly. She could barely make out a blurred motion in her eyes. Screams and cries of terror echoed through the wood. Firah's hand stretched outward subconsciously. She could feel the channeling of the bands of energy, glowing red hot in her mind's eye. She imagined the scene in her mind, even as she took in the man's vocal protests to the harrowing energy. She imagined the red cocoon enveloping him, over every inch of his body. She heard the screams become more terrified.

Suddenly it was over.

There were no sounds but those of the wood; yet the wind, small creatures, all living things had become subdued by the explosion of energy. After a minute, Firah could make out details of the area. She grimaced in pain, something was wrong with her ribs. She could hardly breathe. She looked to the ground and saw her attacker's cloak, the bow and quiver, all the clothes, and her brooch resting quietly upon the cloth. There was no evidence of the assailant, his body had disappeared completely. There were strange new developments as well. All was unnaturally still around her and fresh vibrant growth had sprung up around where the man had been. Its lush green colour stood out from the faded Darkwood hues. The new trees gave way to the ridge just a few feet away, and she watched as Zyr, Mehnol and others ascending the small ledge swiftly. She had less than a minute to decide what to do. Her mind suddenly determined a course of action which was so clear and direct that she launched into action. She plucked up the brooch and reattached it to her tunic. Pushing aside the discomfort in her chest she bundled up all the articles into the cloak and moved into the wood as quickly as her aching body would allow. She found a small opening under a large fallen tree and stuffed the articles there. She quickly memorized the spot and tossed many leaves upon the cache. It was meant to be this way: survival of the fittest. It had been this way her whole life and these things belonged to her now. There was no time to examine the items or explain it to the others, not yet. She would return later for what was hers.

Firah moved away from the spot and tried her best to cover her trail. She had seconds now. She limped toward the edge of the wood as quickly as she could, purposely skirting away from the strange growth deeper within. Zyr came running into the wood with concern and alarm creasing every line of his face. She recognized Mehnol and also Corbin, who she learned was an elementalist for the White

Guard. Lord Tey'ur was not present. Shien brought up the rear, looking perplexed as usual. He had no sense in the mystic arts; therefore, he could not have felt the power she had unleashed. At best, he was following the crowd. In perceiving the small group she simply sat down amongst the leaves and waited. Despite her efforts, Corbin was a blood hound on the scent, as he tracked to the very spot where she had fought the man in grey. She truly had no voice to call out, so she waited. In time they came to her and she began to tell a story - most of it true - but she altered it a little for herself. 'Always pay yourself first' she mused as she croaked out the events to the anxious group. She thought she saw Zyr look at her with skeptical discernment but then the moment was gone. She was carefully led back down the ridge toward camp. Firah smiled within herself all the way. She could still take care of herself.

✗ "Are you sure you want to be alone? I can stay longer if you like ..." Shien spoke quietly. After their return to the camp, Firah repeated her testimony of what had happened. Zyr had mercifully healed her swollen face and eyes. All Shien could manage to help was a suggestion to the others to give her some space. When she asked him to join her, his empathic senses buzzed with illumination. She was feeling uncertainty and desire.

They found a secluded spot away from the battle. It was strange to find a quiet and reflective spot so close to the remains of war. The fields drifted lazily in the cool Darkwood wind as the sun masked itself in the white robes of the heavens. The moments had slid by like longing eddies cast aside by the steady stream. Time had been misplaced in their quiet retreat.

Shien remained still and watched her, standing as a reed in the wind. Her dark hair coursed about her features. In this light ... despite the changes upon her ... she was truly beautiful. She looked at him with a knowing glance and then turned back to the peaceful scene. He waited as she pondered for words.

"Shien, I only have one thing to say. Yet, I don't want you to answer now ... I only want you to listen." She paused and gathered her breath as her brow furrowed. He waited patiently upon her. "Things have happened. I don't understand what it all means. What is certain is that *we need you*; after helping with so much, perhaps you can understand. Now, I know I cannot understand your life, your past. Please, I want you to be with us."

She looked away, unable to meet his gaze. "As I said, you don't need to answer. I will know your decision when we depart the camp. Please consider my request. For now, I need some time by myself."

He watched her carefully. She seemed to have recovered from the fit that had taken her. Her mind seemed lucid. He considered her request. If he stayed, he would stay until

Aeredia's end. He could sense the fates depicting the patterns along both roads. He had arrived at the fork, the paths jutting away into different directions. It would mean trading one life for another: one life of ease and freedom, where he was free to choose his own destiny, for another which was darker and constricted, a difficult path with little freedom.

"I will leave you then … I'll be with the others if you need me."

She nodded as he walked back toward the torn fields. Why were the decisions so hard, so difficult? His mind and heart were divided. 'Logic' Shien mused 'has little use in matters of the heart.' He moved down toward the camp. A watch was placed along the perimeter of the remaining tents and shelters. Shien nodded to one respectfully, as he entered the area.

Would he have the courage to give his life over to her?

*   *   *

"Thank you, Firah." The Guild Lord was truly humble and sincere in his gratitude. "The White Guard stands always indebted to you." He knelt to one knee before her and took her hand gently. Firah blushed and cast a quick glance around to the others assembled. All who had survived were there, heads bowed in respect. Tey'ur pressed a small gilded token into her palm, which was bound to a slender gold chain. He closed her hand upon it and kissed her fingers gently. Firah blushed and shifted awkwardly at the act. Rising, the Lord's voice boomed for all around. "Firah of Lenhir will always be welcome in the halls of the White Guard!" He pressed a hand to his chest and shouted aloud "So is it spoken!"

"So shall it be done!" the remnant of the guard exclaimed in one vigorous cry. Firah was taken aback by the simple yet moving ceremony. She bowed slightly to Tey'ur and then retreated back to where Zyr and Shien awaited. A cart was supplied providing all their needs for ten days in the way of provisions, packs, blankets and an assortment of things the Guard could spare. Following the customary inspection of the campsite, all were ready to depart. Tey'ur signaled Zyr to approach. Moving ahead, the monk bowed deeply and simply to his old master. Firah watched as the old Lord placed a hand upon the shoulder of her friend and a small smile fell across his lips. They simply looked at one another with no words being spoken. After a moment, Zyr nodded and stepped back next to Firah. Next, Shien was called forward. Tey'ur presented him with a letter, sealed by the crest of the White Guard and bade him to read it when he had less pressing concerns. Shien took the letter and stepped backward. The Lord of the White Guard raised a hand in farewell and spoke the traditional parting words of Kenhar.

"May the grace of our Mother be upon all of you. May your journey be swift upon Her song and sheltered from Her wrath." The three companions bowed a final time and the White Guard moved slowly away, treading the path back to the White Halls to await the inevitable siege. Firah felt a small degree of remorse, despite the difficulty of the past days. She had come to understand these men and their duty to the land. Silently, she said a prayer to the Mother for their safety.

"Are you sure Tohm will not return?" she asked Zyr quietly, while turning to face the monk. He seemed lost in thought, his face staring off into the horizon, his eyes far away. He slowly turned and looked down into her waiting face.

"Not until he is able to gain control of himself. He feels that he is a danger to the group and despite my efforts, he has chosen solitude for the time being. Do not worry, Firah, of all able men and beasts, he can find us if he chooses. That I know. I believe it is for the best." Zyr sighed deeply and turned back to the horizon. "Somehow, I feel we shall see our loved ones again." Firah stared up at the monk's face. That was her friend, always full of mystery. She shifted her gaze to Shien, who looked back at her. He smiled slightly and she made a funny face back. He laughed softly and Zyr turned to look at them both. "It will be a short journey now to where we must go. I want you both to trust me this last time." He placed his healing hands upon their shoulders and carefully looked into their eyes. "We are seeking answers to questions. I believe that we can find them in a place that has long remained hidden from the world. We go to the Broken Halls." The group stood in silent repose at the mention of the name.

SAPLING

The Broken Halls, the shrine of death and hope.

θ   *The black weed had been stripped from the tender plant leaving scars within its small branches. The evil was gone, yet the memory had marked itself upon the tender plant. All that remained was a longing - searching in vain for the memory*

ABOUT THE AUTHOR

Dan Gillis resides in Alberta, Canada. Creativity runs rampant in his family of six and at any given time someone is singing, writing, drawing, or creating.

Dan has enjoyed many years as an educator in the public system. Humanities and the Arts are his passion and joy.

He credits University for being the catalyst for his successful career, but also for the stress that sparked his writing outlet.

www.ingramcontent.com/pod-product-compliance
Lightning Source LLC
Chambersburg PA
CBHW020508260626
47156CB00006B/1920